Darling Duke

SCARLETT SCOTT

Darling Duke
Heart's Temptation Book 6

All rights reserved.
Copyright © 2018 by Scarlett Scott
ISBN: 978-1721728404
Paperback Edition
Edited by Grace Bradley
Formatting by Dallas Hodge, Everything But The Book
Cover Design by Wicked Smart Designs

This book or any portion thereof may not be reproduced or used in any manner whatsoever without the express written permission of the publisher except for the use of brief quotations in a book review.

The unauthorized reproduction or distribution of this copyrighted work is illegal. No part of this book may be scanned, uploaded, or distributed via the Internet or any other means, electronic or print, without the publisher's permission. Criminal copyright infringement, including infringement without monetary gain, is punishable by law.

This book is a work of fiction and any resemblance to persons, living or dead, or places, events, or locales, is purely coincidental. The characters are productions of the author's imagination and used fictitiously.

For more information, contact author Scarlett Scott.
www.scarsco.com

Dedication

For my sister, Heather. Thanks for being so understanding about the time I emptied an entire perfume bottle all over your closet when we were growing up. And the time I bit your big toe, and the morning I sprinkled salt and pepper on your face while you slept…and for introducing me to romance novels, for the road trip to Atlanta, *The Man in the Brown Suit*, deadline week mojitos, raising awesome boys, and so much more.

Acknowledgments

Special thanks to an exceptional team who effortlessly rolls with my crazy schedule and deadlines: my editor, who has been with me from the beginning of this adventure, and who is truly a joy to work with, to my formatter for making my books look better than I imagined, and to my cover artist, whose vision is impeccable. Thank you, as always, to the readers! Thank you for your support and for making it possible for me to live my dream. And thank you to my family for being understanding and encouraging, and always cheering me on to the finish, even if it means putting up with a grumpy writer on deadline.

Contents

Chapter One	1
Chapter Two	13
Chapter Three	21
Chapter Four	27
Chapter Five	35
Chapter Six	42
Chapter Seven	54
Chapter Eight	70
Chapter Nine	80
Chapter Ten	90
Chapter Eleven	103
Chapter Twelve	113
Chapter Thirteen	123
Chapter Fourteen	143
Chapter Fifteen	153
Chapter Sixteen	168
Chapter Seventeen	184
Chapter Eighteen	201
Chapter Nineteen	211
Chapter Twenty	224
Chapter Twenty-One	239
Chapter Twenty-Two	253
Chapter Twenty-Three	265
Chapter Twenty-Four	278
Epilogue	293
Preview of *Her Deceptive Duke*	297
About the Author	302
Other Books by Scarlett Scott	303

Chapter One

You are the prickly pear
You are the sudden violent storm
~Lorine Niedecker, *"Wilderness"*

Oxfordshire, 1884

OF ALL THE CHITS IN ENGLAND his nonsensical brother could have gone lovesick over, Lady Boadicea Harrington was, indisputably, the most unsuitable. Spencer had never been more certain of it than the moment he caught her in his library with a bawdy book in her hand.

Oh, she'd disguised the tripe in a pretty, embroidered cover. The ordinary observer would never guess the contents of the small book she'd held nestled in her elegant, fine-boned hands. But she'd dropped it when he startled her from her rapt reading.

Naturally, he'd played the gentleman despite his acute dislike of her. He'd known without a doubt she was trouble. Everything about her—from her bold auburn hair to her vivid blue eyes and her beauty so singular that the first time he'd seen her at close proximity, a jolt had gone straight through him—yes, *everything* about her was in bad taste.

She flirted with each able man in her vicinity. She smiled too much. She laughed too loudly. She was gauche and opinionated. Even her dress, a dark-scarlet satin trimmed with velvet rosettes, was far too attention-seizing and daring for an unmarried lady. Fresh from Paris unless he missed his guess, the gown hugged her body as though fashioned to bedevil any poor sod who gazed upon her in it.

But he wouldn't think of the gown now. Nor her perfectly shaped mouth with the tiny beauty mark offset to the right like a planet in orbit around a blazing sun. And he most certainly would not contemplate the sudden snug fit of his trousers as the scent of her, jasmine and lily of the valley, hit him with the force of a blow to the gut.

Dear God. He could not possibly be aroused by such a creature. No. He was not.

Spencer forced himself to read another sentence in the small volume he held in his hands, just to be certain he hadn't misjudged.

I was well-pleased at the tumescence of the shaft I held in my hand.

Jesus Christ. He snapped the book closed and pinned Lady Boadicea with the most cutting glare he could manage. "Lady Boadicea, you are trespassing in my personal library."

A charming flush traced her cheeks. Her wide eyes attempted, it seemed, to judge how much of the obscene drivel he'd read. "Your Grace, please forgive me. I do have a tendency to wander, and I'm afraid the beckoning sight of books and these lovely windows were too much of a temptation to resist. I hadn't realized, of course, that it was your private library."

Damn it, that flush on her skin went down her throat and disappeared beneath her décolletage, making him wonder if her lush breasts were tinged pink as well. Bloody hell, this wouldn't do.

His brows snapped together as he pinned her with the frown he saved for the truly recalcitrant. "See that you do not come here alone again, my lady. Not only is it most improper, but I treasure my solitude."

"I have heard, Your Grace." She held out her hand impolitely. "Once again, I do offer my sincerest apologies. If you'll just return my book to me, I'll be on my way."

She had *heard*. He stiffened, wondering what else she'd heard. The whispers about him seemed to always abound, regardless of how much he tried to remain above reproach.

"You heard?" He could not keep the displeasure from his voice.

He despised being the target of others' conjecture above all else. Too many years of his life had been steeped in ruinous gossip. Though he'd become adroit at numbing himself and the rumors about him no longer stung, he guarded his privacy with an intensity that even he had to admit bordered on fanatical.

Lady Boadicea blinked at him, a tentative smile curving that beautiful mouth of hers. "Why yes, from Lord Harry of course. Don't worry. I shan't tell a soul that we crossed paths here."

Bloody hell. He didn't need her promises. And he damn well didn't need her smile. "Forgive me if your assertion is far from reassuring, my lady." His tone was deliberately frigid and forbidding.

He'd feared her unacceptability from the moment Harry had requested he extend an invitation to their annual Boswell Manor house party for Lady Boadicea and her sister and brother-in-law, the Marchioness and Marquis of Thornton. But Thornton was a potential political ally for Harry, and Spencer had relented on that account alone.

Look what good his equanimity had done him.

"Make of it what you will," the chit dared to snap at him in dismissive tones now, her hand still stretched out in anticipation of the lecherous volume he had no intention of returning to her. "My book, if you please, Your Grace?"

He tucked the slim volume inside his jacket. "No. I don't think I'll be relinquishing it."

Her smile was gone, and some ridiculous part of him—a part he'd thought long buried—felt the loss like a physical ache in his chest. She considered him, lips pursed, her expression shifting to one of irritation. Her hand remained open, waiting. Rude, damn it all. Even if some far more ludicrous part of him contemplated running a finger over her palm just to see if the circle was as soft as it looked. To trace the lines bisecting it with his lips and tongue.

"I'm afraid I don't see why you're so unwilling to return my property to me, Your Grace." She cast a sweeping glance around her. "Surely you have a more than ample supply of reading material at your fingertips?"

The baggage had more temerity than he'd imagined. "Indeed, though perhaps nothing quite so…edifying. I wonder what Lord and Lady Thornton would make of your reading proclivities, my lady."

Her eyes flared. "Are you threatening me, Your Grace?"

"Perhaps." It occurred to him that he could use this discovery to his advantage. "Here is what I propose, Lady Boadicea. I'll hold on to your little book and keep it our secret. In return, you stay the hell away from Harry."

At last, she withdrew her waiting hand, bringing it to her waist as she struck a defensive pose. "You mean to bribe me?"

Had he thought she possessed temerity? That wasn't the proper word for the impudence emanating from the lush beauty before him. First, she'd dared to trespass upon his private library. Not to mention he'd caught the hoyden reading the sort of filth that should make any proper, unmarried female faint from horror. Instead of being duly chastised, she dared to challenge him. She stood, as fierce and defiant as the warrior queen who was her namesake.

No question of it.

The wench was as troublesome as she was comely. And he had neither time nor inclination for beauty or trouble in his existence. All the more reason to send her on her way. He needed to keep her far, far away from his nauseatingly romantic brother. Leave it to Harry to have his head turned by a luscious mouth, a beautiful face, and a prettily nipped waist.

He gritted his teeth. "Bribery is rather an ugly word, is it not? I prefer to think of it as bargaining to achieve our mutual ends. Keep away from my brother, and I'll give your lecherous book back to you at the conclusion of the house party. No one ever need be made aware of your depraved nature, and Harry won't find himself shackled to a wanton tart masquerading as a lady."

The alluring pink that had clung to her skin vanished as she paled at his viciousness. He ought to be ashamed, he knew, to speak with such savage indifference to a lady, albeit one with unseemly tendencies and a vulgar reading habit. Had Millicent destroyed all the good in him so that there was nothing left save cruelty and ice? Or, a more troubling question prodded him, was there something about Lady Boadicea that unleashed the beast within him?

Lady Boadicea didn't remain silent or pale for long. In a heartbeat, twin flags of angry red rose on her patrician cheekbones. "Did it ever occur to you that it's Lord Harry's prerogative who he decides to marry?" She paused. "Or, for that matter, that perhaps a wanton tart wouldn't want to marry into a family with the reputation of yours?"

The arrow of her insult found its intended target with deadly accuracy. He stalked toward her, closing the distance between them before he could think better of it, and stared down into her upturned face. But she didn't look at him, as some in polite society did, with fear or suspicion. Every bit of her, from the irritatingly lustrous auburn locks that had been woven into an intricate series of braids, to the firm set of her sensual mouth, oozed defiance.

"The family is one of the wealthiest and most well-known in England, madam," he growled as another note of her airy scent swept over him. Tuberose.

She raised a brow, challenging him still, seemingly unmoved by his proximity. "Is it? I confess, I hadn't realized."

Without warning the words he'd read returned to him. *I was well-pleased at the tumescence of the shaft I held in my hand.* Bloody, bloody hell. The vulgar words and her scent entwined, inciting a fire in his veins that pulsed through him and shot straight to his groin. For a moment, he imagined that fine-boned, slender hand of hers—the one that had awaited her book's return—on his cock. Stroking.

What the hell was the matter with him? His brother was wearing his heart on his sleeve for the vixen. Yet here he stood, the Duke of Bainbridge, a man who had not wanted any woman in three goddamn years, fantasizing about *her*. A minx who was unacceptable in every way, who read obscene books in his bloody library and dared to defy him, whose name was as ridiculous and fierce and lovely as the rest of her. Hadn't the last few years taught him anything?

The familiar coil of resentment and bitterness tightened within him as memories of Millicent returned to him again, chasing lust back into the dark recesses of his soul like Cerberus. He could control himself. His time of penance had cured him of the need to fulfill his desire.

He sneered down at her. "Hundreds of ladies would do anything to marry Lord Harry, and any one of them would be far more deserving of being his bride than you."

But she refused to stand down like any rational, well-bred miss in her place would. Instead, her eyes flashed up at him. Her chin upturned with stubborn firmness. "Then perhaps he ought to ask for one of their hands, for the last thing I should like to do is marry a man with such an insufferable nodcock for a brother. Kindly return my book to me and go browbeat someone else with the misfortune of being beneath your roof."

He didn't bloody believe her. She still wanted the book. Still believed she could best him. Still tried him at every turn, as though she were in the right and he was the interloper here on his own turf.

"No," he snapped. "Now get the hell out of my library and consider yourself lucky I don't take this book and your behavior both to Lord and Lady Thornton."

"Very well," she said grimly.

But if he'd thought she had at long last chosen to show him deference and humbly go on her way, he was wrong. For in the next instant, she closed the final step between them. Her face was so near he detected a smattering of bewitching freckles over the bridge of her nose. Her full skirts swished against his trousers, and his cock went stiff again.

"My lady," he warned tightly.

"Oh do shut up," she said, and then she locked her arms around his neck and pulled his mouth down to hers.

Kissing the Duke of Bainbridge was a necessity, Bo told herself as she pressed her lips to his. She didn't *want* to kiss the arrogant oaf. No, indeed. It was the most expedient way of killing two birds with one proverbial stone. Kissing him would distract him enough that she could fish her book from his jacket and it would silence his infuriating mouth at the same time.

A wanton tart masquerading as a lady.

His frigid words, so censorious and judgmental, mocked as his scent enveloped her. Who would have guessed that the Duke of Bainbridge smelled so irritatingly good, like pine and musk with a hint of masculine soap? She wasn't meant to notice the way he smelled, drat it all.

Nor was she meant to be attracted to such a man, a hypocrite who dared look down his nose at her when his past was far more tarnished than her reputation could ever be. A man who would bribe her to keep her away from his brother, as though she wasn't good enough to marry a duke's second son.

But the strangest thing had happened the moment she'd looked up when he'd barged into the library with that commanding air and equally commanding stride. Some foreign, misguided sensation inside her had blossomed. Their gazes had locked, his forbidding green burning into hers. There had been—however unwanted—a searing connection in that moment. Until she'd dropped her book and he'd picked it up, read a few sentences, and deemed her unworthy of his brother's attention.

Ah, yes, her whirling mind prodded. The book. She really did need to get it back. And he hadn't pushed her away, had he? His hands had, in fact, gone to her waist. She felt the possession of his touch, those large hands, like brands straight through all the layers of her dress and undergarments. He held her tightly, as if anchoring her to him.

The duke was a large man, for he had a good two inches on her, and she was tall herself by a lady's standards. The resulting fit of their bodies seemed too natural, as if they had been made for each other's arms, and the knowledge rattled her. Once, she had possessed a romantic heart, and she would have been swayed by such a thing. But now she was older, wiser, made of sterner stuff. This man was no match for her.

Even if his lips were firm and well-sculpted.

She drank in his breath, and it was sweet, with a hint of port. She couldn't deny the unwelcome heat sliding through her and settling low in her belly. Undeniable, and thoroughly foolish. She was attracted to the Duke of Bainbridge.

The brother of her suitor.

A man she privately referred to as the Duke of Disdain.

The man who had just called her a wanton tart.

Before she could think better of it, she settled her upper lip into the seam of his, catching his full lower lip between her teeth. She nipped him. The breath hissed from between his parted lips, hot decadence to her senses.

A shock jolted through her like a current of electricity, sudden and dangerous. What was she thinking, biting the Duke of Bainbridge, regardless of how supple and sulky that lower lip of his was? Little wonder her mother and father despaired she'd ever make a decent match. But there was something about his arrogance that made her long to ruffle his feathers. He was so perfect. So dispassionate. So icy and rigid in his bearing and manner.

Before a further, coherent thought could form, his mouth moved, insistent, demanding. He kissed her as she'd never been kissed. As if he meant to consume her. As if he couldn't get enough of her, his lips firming and claiming hers.

A growl tore from his throat. The hands on her waist tightened, and he yanked her into his chest so that her skirts crushed between them. The hard wall of his chest pressed against her breasts. His palm slid to her lower back as if it belonged there, forcing her closer. Another low sound of desire sounded between them, masculine and dark.

His tongue swept past her lips, smooth as wet velvet. This too seemed at once familiar and right. As though there was no act more natural than for her to stand in an Oxfordshire library and have her world as she knew it forever altered by his masterful kiss and knowing touch.

Her fingers slipped into his hair, those thick strands rich as chocolate and softer than any man's ought to be. She raked her nails over his scalp, learning the curve of his head, relishing the intimacy and freedom. What was it about him that made her yearn to mark him as hers?

It didn't matter. The kiss deepened. Her tongue touched his. He tasted as sweet and forbidden as she'd imagined he would. She sighed into his mouth, opened for him as he fed her kisses, owned her with his lips and tongue. Worshipped her. His hand splayed open, sweeping up her back, skimming the boning and laces of her corset, following her spine all the way to her bare neck. Here, he stopped.

The pads of his fingers brushed against her, drawing lazy, delicious circles that tantalized before tunneling into the elegant twists of braids her lady's maid had fashioned earlier. Pins rained to the carpet. Plaits fell from her crown. More pins scattered. Bo didn't care. Her every good intention fled, taking with it her common sense, intuition, and all her defenses.

She forgot about her book.

Forgot that she didn't like this supercilious ice block of a man.

And she certainly forgot all about her promises to her sister Cleo that she'd endeavor to behave for the duration of the house party.

How could she think of anything but him? It seemed suddenly as if fate had led her to this moment. To this merciless onslaught of unexpected passion from Bainbridge. To his complete and utter dismantling of everything she'd thought she'd known. For she had never been properly kissed by any man before him, and she knew it now. This was no mere joining of mouths.

This was…

It was…

Transcendent.

Yes, that was the word her whirling mind wanted, a name for this wild burst of desire unfurling through her veins like honey on a summer's day. Scorching, sweet, languorous. Her breath came in shallow bursts, and she was acutely aware of the kittenish noises emerging from her throat, of his scent and the way his chest rose and fell against hers, the way he hummed before tearing his lips from hers to drag them down her neck. The way he breathed her in, his fierce and hungry mouth on her skin as though he couldn't possibly fill himself with enough of her.

"Witch," he muttered as he found his way to the hollow behind her ear and licked.

Oh.

No one had ever done such a thing to her before, and now she wondered why. It made a frisson of something warm and potent shoot through her, settling between her thighs. She'd read enough illicit literature to know what it meant. She wanted the Duke of Bainbridge.

And the rigid length of him, prodding her stomach through his trousers and the layers of her corset and gown combined, told her that he wanted her too. Thanks to the book he'd thieved from her, she had a name for that particular marvel.

Tumescence.

He licked her again, drawing a moan from her. She wasn't meant to be enjoying herself. She'd intended to distract him, fish her book from his jacket, and flee. That wicked tongue of his robbed her of thought. And the way he kissed. Lord in heaven, she never wanted to be kissed in any other fashion ever again.

But she ought to protest. Surely. After all, he had maligned her. Attempted to bribe her. He still held her book firmly inside his coat.

"Nodcock," she whispered for good measure as he dragged his sinful mouth back down her throat. She couldn't resist rubbing her cheek against his, relishing the scrape of his neatly trimmed beard. She inhaled deeply of his scent. How could one man, particularly a man as surly as the Duke of Bainbridge, smell so bloody good?

How unfair.

He didn't seem to mind her insult. Quite the opposite, in fact, as he pressed into her with his tall, strong form. His hardness seemed more pronounced. *Good. Heavens.* Bo tried to squelch the fresh rush of desire her discovery created. She tried to recall the book she wanted to retrieve. He kissed along her décolletage, pausing at the swell of her left breast. This was madness, her conscience reminded her.

The book.

Ah, yes.

She extracted her right hand from his hair, touched his shoulder. Dear Lord, his tongue flicked against her skin. Her nipples tightened, and she pictured him dragging her gown down, exposing her, sucking a rosy peak into his mouth as the wicked groom in her book had done to Lady Letitia.

And then, her fingers—meant to glide over his jacket to better discover the little lump of her book and rescue it at last—went straight past his jacket. Curiosity had ever been the greatest weakness of Lady Boadicea Harrington. That, and handsome men, good wine, and depraved literature.

What would be the harm in touching him? Investigating the part of him that currently intrigued her as much as his proficient lips and tongue? Her wanton hand went between her skirts and his body, and opened. Suddenly, there he was, warm and firm and large, burning into her palm.

Oh.

Chapter Two

*D*AMN IT ALL TO HELL. Her hand was on his cock. Never mind that no lady should ever imagine such a violation of propriety, let alone commit it. Never mind that she was an anathema to him. He didn't like her. She was too bold, too brash, too beautiful. Her family was an assorted portmanteau of scandal and ruin. His brother was salivating over her, for the love of all that was holy, attempting to court the minx.

Somehow, none of that mattered.

Something primitive and unpolished, deep inside him, knew that the fiery woman in his arms was not meant for Harry. She wasn't meant for anyone else. She was meant for him. Her body, her scent, her sweet lips, curved waist, the secret place behind her ear that drove her to distraction, the swell of her breasts, the pounding of her heart…it was all his.

Surely.

Or was this madness?

He rocked against her again. So good. So bloody good.

Yes, madness.

The breath hissed from his lungs. His hips jerked. Three years without a woman. He had not wanted. Had not lusted. He had controlled himself. He had bloody well learned to tame the beast within. He could govern anything. No impulse could rule him ever again. Control and solitude were all he needed. All he craved.

Or so he'd thought.

Because Lady Boadicea Harrington was cupping his straining length as if it were a baby bird—gentle and tentative—and his ballocks were tightening as though in preparation to spend.

Fuck.

His face was buried in her luscious bosom, a place that smelled and looked like heaven on earth, and he was about to spend in his trousers from nothing more than an untutored touch. Her fingers tightened then, clutching him.

He snapped. Spencer Marlow, unimpeachable Duke of Bainbridge, wrangled the woman his brother was courting about the waist, lifted her from the floor, and carried her halfway across the haven of his library, hell-bent on debauching her. She was in his arms, her voluminous skirts billowing about them, and he didn't give a damn. In six steps, he had her on a divan. In under three seconds, he caught her skirts in his fists, rucking them to her waist.

She watched him, her vivid forget-me-not eyes taking him in with an intensity that gave him pause. His conscience pierced him, reminding him that his brother, who was beloved to him, fancied himself in love with her. And then his customary jadedness returned full-force, replacing all else.

For a woman who was being courted by another man, she was awfully responsive. Not a hint of protest had fallen from her facile tongue. Perhaps she was the wanton tart he'd accused her of being. But what did that make him? Far, far worse. For what manner of man would take such daring liberties with the woman his brother wanted as his own? No gentleman, certainly.

But then again, no gentleman would be responsible for his wife's death.

The reminder dampened his ardor. Millicent had died because of him. He couldn't forget. Wouldn't forget. Penitence. That was how he lived day by day, in the attempt to forgive himself. By denial, by sinking himself into the abyss of the duchy and his myriad duties. And by feeling nothing, neither passion nor gratification, and never this shameless, unsettled yearning that threatened to upend his carefully crafted life.

He willed his arousal to abate, reminding himself that he didn't deserve the pleasures of the flesh. That Lady Boadicea Harrington was unsuitable and fast. That he had made a vow over Millicent's cold, ashen form. Years could not dim the hells he'd endured.

Time provided distance but not a panacea.

Nothing could heal what ailed him.

Why then, did his hands span Lady Boadicea's waist? Her legs, clad in silk stockings and adorned in tempting scarlet garters, claimed his attention. Trim ankles, shapely calves, feminine thighs hidden beneath her frilled and embroidered drawers. By God, he swore he could smell her musk, fragrant and heady, sweet and alluring as all the rest of her. His eyes settled on the vee of her limbs, her hidden center, and his mouth went dry.

Right or wrong, he longed to have this woman.

He would give his bloody soul over to slide home inside her now.

Would she be wet for him? Slick and hot? His body thrummed with pent-up need. Three years of living a monastic life had taken its toll. He felt like a drunkard who'd just been given his first dram of whisky after giving his life over to the temperance movement for a decade. He shouldn't want her. Everything about her was wrong. He'd never forgive himself.

He sank to his knees, body wrangling control of his mind. He'd lost all ability to resist. Their gazes met, level to level, and she framed his face in her small, fine-boned hands, and she closed the scant distance between them. Her mouth, lush and full, landed on his, demanding, open.

Madness. Stupidity.

Wrong.

So bloody good. He palmed her hip as they kissed with the sort of hunger he'd never experienced with another woman. His hand traveled higher, skimming to her inner thigh. He found the slit of her drawers. *Ah, yes.* His fingers swiped down her seam and then back up. Smooth, wet skin, warm and divine, greeted him.

Wetter than he'd imagined.

Better than he'd dared hope.

She whimpered into his kiss, and he hummed his approval. He found her pearl next, dancing his index and middle finger over the sensitive bundle. Her hips worked against him, lifting from the cushion of the divan, demanding more.

He would give her more.

In that moment, he would bloody well give her everything and anything she required of him: a fleet of ships, a railroad, the dowager's jewels, *anything*. She'd brought him to life for the first time in years, and he was seizing the aberration. The bud of her sex fascinated him. She seemed almost more sensitive than other women as she bucked, whimpered into his mouth, sucked his tongue. She was made for this. Made for him.

And he...

Twin gasps pierced the surreal fog of lust mucking up his brain.

A familiar voice rang into the sudden silence of the library, making him tear his lips from Lady Boadicea's enthusiastic kiss.

"Bainbridge? Sweet heavens above."

His bloody mother.

A grim sense of propriety overtook him, and he moved without even being aware of what actions he took, withdrawing his hand, flipping down her skirts.

Another, much less cherished voice followed the first. "This is an abomination, Eloise. I thought you said he'd *changed*."

The contemptuous voice belonged to the Duchess of Cartwright, his mother's bosom bow and society's most notorious stickler for propriety.

"Fuck." The word escaped him, low and feral, torn from the deepest recesses of his conscience. He said it softly enough that the interlopers at his back wouldn't hear, but Lady Boadicea did, for her perfectly formed auburn brows went aloft. Her pink cheeks shouldn't enamor him. Nor should her swollen mouth or that bewitching beauty mark. He had shocked her, but he didn't give a damn. He had, in fact, shocked them both.

With the crazed choke of lust abruptly banished from his body, he stood and turned to face his mother and the Duchess of Cartwright. They hovered at the threshold of the library, hands pressed to their hearts. His mother's mouth was drawn, her skin tinged with an unhealthy pallor. He had failed her again.

Dismay settled on his chest like a weight, along with disgust and self-loathing. What the hell had he done? He swallowed down the bile that threatened to choke him and gave the two stunned, august ladies before him an abbreviated bow. "Your Graces, pray forgive me for the familiarity with Lady Boadicea. I'm afraid that she overturned her ankle, and I was attempting to assess how badly she'd injured herself."

It was a lie, a blatant one, and he knew it didn't fool either sharp-minded duchess before him. He had undone Lady Boadicea's hair, had been on his knees. But what could he say? *Forgive me for almost fucking Lady Boadicea on the library divan? Forgive me for sliding my fingers along her wet, delicious seam, and intending to lick her until she spent before I slid my cock inside her so deep and so hard that neither of us would be able to move afterwards?*

Good God. Undoubtedly, that was the influence of the god-awful book. His trousers were once again uncomfortably snug.

"Bainbridge," his mother bit out, her high cheekbones flushing a mottled, angry red. "This is a disgrace."

Yes. It was. Most importantly, *he* was.

He schooled his features into an icy mask. "I regret that Lady Boadicea's injury necessitated a lapse of propriety, and I will make amends as expediently as possible."

The Duchess of Cartwright's lined visage brightened, her hawk's eyes pouncing on him with unerring efficiency. "I daresay your amends shall be of the most formal variety, Your Grace?"

There was only one way to rectify his stupidity.

Only one option if he meant to save his mother from further embarrassment, to spare his family name from additional scandal and whispers. Lord knew they'd all borne more than enough in the last few years, and he had been culpable for that as well. He could not ask his proud, aging mother or his brother to endure another moment of shame because of his sins.

He swallowed hard, forcing the knot in his throat to sink all the way to his stomach like a brick. "Lady Boadicea and I will be married as soon as can be arranged."

"Married!" His mother looked positively bilious. "To a Harrington girl? Bainbridge, I cannot countenance such a misbegotten misalliance, particularly after…"

Particularly after the debacle of his last marriage. Her words went unspoken, but he knew as well as she what she'd been about to utter. It weighed the air of their godforsaken vignette with loaded stillness.

Spencer's ears hummed, and the familiar heft of blame curdled in his stomach. His jaw tightened, his fists clenching at his sides. By God, his mother ought to know better than to allude to Millicent. No one had dared breathe her name to him after the last shovel of dirt had been laid on her grave.

And this day was not the one to begin resurrecting old ghosts. Indeed, there was never a day on which he cared to revisit that particular brand of perdition.

"Madam," he warned, biting out the word as though it tasted as bitter as poison.

The sound of shifting silk reached his ears, and his entire body went on edge. How odd that he should be attuned to Lady Boadicea after one ill-conceived folly in his library. But he was. Some perverse part of him imagined he could sense the tenor of her thoughts as well.

She appeared at his elbow, dipping into a formal curtsy, playing her role to the hilt. He didn't look at her, for fear that her beauty would once again undo him. She was a siren. An unwanted complication in his life after he had only just rediscovered a notion of purpose.

"Your Graces," she soothed in that dulcet voice of hers, smooth as freshly whipped cream and just as sweet, "please do not fault the duke for my appalling lack of balance. I'm afraid my eagerness to reach the library resulted in my injury. His Grace was only too kind to assist."

Wise girl for avoiding the insult his mother had delivered. He shot her a cautious look. If they played this properly, perhaps they wouldn't be required to marry after all. Say the words, feign an apology, meet the hypocritical and sanctimonious demands of two elderly duchesses, and no one need spread this gossip any further.

He hoped.

"His Grace's singular *kindness* aside," the Duchess of Cartwright said in tones to rival Wenham Lake ice, "I'm afraid the damage has been done. He should have had a care for propriety, regardless of your…*injury*, Lady Boadicea."

Bloody hell. It would seem that not even her old friendship with his mother would be sufficient reason for her to turn a blind eye to what she'd witnessed.

His mother's face had lost all color. She had always been a handsome woman, but the last few years of unrest had aged her. Her stern gaze snapped into his, and she straightened her spine, a grim cast to her thin mouth. "Bainbridge, I'm afraid you must marry as expediently as possible. It is the only recourse for what we have seen."

Admittedly, the sight that the two duchesses had intruded upon had to have been damning. He'd been pleasuring Lady Boadicea, his hand between her glorious thighs, not remotely in the same region of her anatomy as her ankle.

His cheekbones went hot. He did not like this realization: the depths of his own depravity. "You are correct as always, Duchess, which is why I will marry Lady Boadicea as expediently as possible."

Lady Boadicea's bright eyes swung to his, the alarm in her expression more than evident. "You cannot mean to marry me," she whispered.

He ignored her. The dye was cast, and his own inability to resist temptation was the cause. It had been some time since he'd last felt this low and abominable. He would have to wed Lady Boadicea Harrington, regardless of how distasteful he found the prospect. The answer was plain and clear on the Duchess of Cartwright's face. She would not overlook his egregious conduct. Mauling an innocent lady—Harrington or no—beneath one's own roof just wasn't done.

And his mother couldn't withstand any more scandal. He couldn't ask it of her. Nor could Harry's fledgling career as an MP survive the bitter knowledge that his brother had abused and tossed aside the woman he'd once longed to make his bride.

No, he would marry the Harrington chit.

Even if it killed him.

"It would be my greatest honor to make Lady Boadicea my duchess," he lied.

Chapter Three

BO BLINKED, HER GAZE SWIVELING from the duke to his outraged mother and the red-faced Duchess of Cartwright as his bald pronouncement hovered in the silence of the library. He had offered to marry her. She'd allowed him to kiss her senseless, to lead her to a piece of furniture, lift her skirts. Good heavens, she'd allowed his touch on her most intimate place, where she'd never let another man take such shocking liberties. Worse, she'd enjoyed it.

What had she done?

She'd fallen down the rabbit hole, just like Alice, that's what. Perhaps next, a mouse would appear and begin to explain William the Conqueror to her. It seemed every bit as likely as marrying the haughty man at her side.

Yes, that was the explanation for her inability to steel herself against the persuasive kisses of a man who had derided her as a tart masquerading as a lady. A man who thought she wasn't good enough to marry his brother.

Her skin went numb as realization assailed her. She hadn't been worthy of the matrimonial prize of his brother, but he'd had no compunction about touching her himself.

Because he imagined her the sort of lady he could trifle with. He thought her fast. He thought he could offer her a furtive coupling in his private library—after mocking her—with no repercussions.

And she had proven him correct.

She would not marry such an oaf, a man who believed himself her better because he'd been born the heir of a duchy and she hailed from a family laden with scandal and eccentricities. She would be her husband's equal, or she would have no marriage at all.

Not to mention the matter of Lord Harry, who was a dear friend. She was aware that he imagined he harbored tender feelings for her, even as what she felt for him was platonic. Still, she wouldn't hurt him for the world by suddenly marrying his brother.

"No," she said to the room at large. Three sets of eyes swung her way. So she said it louder, this time with more force, holding her head high with a dignity she didn't feel. "I must decline any such offer."

Bainbridge was first to react, his lip curling in what was either amusement or a sneer—she couldn't be certain. "You must decline."

She inclined her head. "Regrettably." And then she smiled, her brightest and most entrancing smile, because the part of her that waved the flag of her tattered pride wanted him to know that she didn't feel a single dram of regret at turning him down.

"Such cheek," interrupted the dowager duchess, her voice as cold and cutting as a dagger buried in a winter's snow bank. "How dare you insult the Duke of Bainbridge by refusing him?"

Bo couldn't wrest her gaze from Bainbridge, whose emerald eyes glittered with something she couldn't define. His jaw, however, was firmed into a harsh, unforgiving angle. "Don't be a fool," he said for her ears alone.

Presumptuous.

"I'd rather be ruined," she whispered, fury making her hands shake as she clasped fistfuls of her silken skirts to hide them.

And it was true, anyway. She would far prefer to seclude herself in the countryside, or perhaps travel abroad. Why, she could venture to America. Her best friend Clara, the Countess of Ravenscroft, currently traveled there on her honeymoon, and her letters contained such rhapsodies of the land that Bo had longed to visit one day and take in the sights for herself.

Freedom could be within her grasp. Perhaps the Duke of Disdain had done her a favor.

"Lord and Lady Thornton will need to be informed," the Duchess of Cartwright announced next.

Ah, yes. Her brother-in-law and sister served as her chaperones for this farce. How helpful of the duchess to suggest an audience with them. "I'll inform them myself forthwith," she returned, tearing her eyes away from Bainbridge's disconcerting, intent regard. She met the duchess's gaze without blinking. If the august lady thought to make her cower, she would have to think again. "I'm certain that when I offer my explanation, they shall understand that the duke was assisting me. Nothing untoward occurred."

The elder woman's gaze narrowed, her lips puckering into a displeased moue. "Your appearance at our arrival suggested otherwise, Lady Boadicea. However did your hair become so dislodged in your fall?"

"I cannot tolerate another scandal, Bainbridge," snapped the dowager duchess to her son. "It will be the death of me, and then you'll have the deaths of two duchesses on your conscience. Do what must be done."

Another scandal. The deaths of two duchesses.

For some reason she could not fathom, Bo's eyes returned to Bainbridge, noting the almost imperceptible way he tensed at his mother's veiled insinuation that he had been responsible for his wife's death. His mouth, so sensual and full, tightened into a grim line, strain furrowing his brow. Despite herself, she knew a pang of sympathy for him. While every effort had been made to quiet gossip following the duchess's death, whispers followed Bainbridge everywhere. All the *ton* knew the former duchess had killed herself.

She'd shot herself in the head, as rumor had it. In the duke's own presence. The Marlow family had done its part to attempt to keep the matter silent, but a scandal so paramount could not be contained.

Without doubt, he must know what was said about him behind closed doors, and his mother's callousness could not help but smart. For all that he was arrogant and cool, he possessed an undeniable intelligence. He was not vapid as some peers were. Of course he knew. His reaction to her earlier words had more than confirmed that.

Bo had not even been presented at court yet when the duchess's death had occurred, but she knew the tale as well as anyone. Lord Harry had never once spoken of the departed duchess, only of his brother. She would never have asked, knowing the common fame. Gossip was an ugly beast best left in hibernation. When riled, it could inflict all manner of havoc.

"These young people," sniffed the Duchess of Cartwright, lip curled, "a generation going straight to the dogs, I say. What have we? What defines us from animal, if we have no standards, no proprieties, no proper course of order? This is an affront to every guest beneath your roof, Eloise."

Bainbridge remained still, features hardened as if they were honed marble. The blood had drained from his face, and he'd gone alarmingly pale. Then she noted his breathing, shallow and rapid. The unflappable duke was falling apart before her, like a poorly sewn frock.

She shouldn't take pity on him. He had been rude and callous. He had deemed her unworthy, and yet he would have taken her on the divan. She had no doubt that if the door hadn't opened, if the duchesses hadn't come upon them, he would have compromised her in the truest sense.

She would have let him. She would have enjoyed it.

Bainbridge wasn't the sort of man she liked. He was not droll. He was not open and giving as Lord Harry was. Aside from his talent at kissing—unparalleled, in her estimation—and his fine face and form, he had nothing to recommend him, unless one was the sort of lady who was keen for a ducal coronet. Which she most definitely wasn't.

Why, then, should she care when he appeared unable to speak or move? Why should she notice his upset? Why should she be so aware of a man who only deserved her contempt?

It didn't matter. Her mind was settled. She was empathetic to a fault. Dear Lord, Cleo would have her hide for this. As would the rest of her sisters, should word reach them. Bo barely contained a wince as she made her next play.

"Very well. I accept the honor, Your Grace." For the moment, she added silently, if only as a way to rescue the both of them from this untenable situation.

His eyes connected with hers, but he said nothing. He appeared neither relieved nor appreciative. And certainly not pleased. This man didn't want her as his wife any more than she wanted to take him as her husband. The realization shouldn't affect her, but somehow it nettled all the same.

To hell with him. She was doing him a favor, and he could sort the rest on his own.

She stalked across the chamber next, taking care to affect a limp in accordance with their nonsensical story. She stopped before the duchesses and pinned them with her most uncompromising stare.

She addressed the Duchess of Cartwright first. "Bainbridge was being gentlemanly and gallant, and he is undeserving of your scorn." She looked then to his mother, who had blanched. One couldn't determine whether it was from Bo's sudden acceptance of Bainbridge's suit or from

Bo's crass method of confrontation. "A mother ought to speak better to her son. I only hope that when next we meet, it will be under more favorable circumstances."

The dowager stared, mouth open as if she meant to form a setdown, but none was forthcoming. Bo sailed forth, between the duchesses, over the threshold, and down the hall, feigning a halt in her gait as she went.

She had a great deal of explaining to do to her dear sister. And she also had a battle plan to form, for there was no way she would actually allow herself to be married off to the Duke of Bainbridge. No way indeed.

Chapter Four

*L*ADY BOADICEA HARRINGTON had championed him.

And it was bloody mortifying.

Not just because he was the Duke of Bainbridge, hailing from one of England's most esteemed families, and he should have been capable of defending himself to a pair of silver-haired biddies. But because she had seen him, truly seen him, at his weakest.

Three years later, and thoughts of Millicent's death still broke him. Still rendered him immobilized and numb, powerless.

Because death was a common enough word, meant to cloak and shield, to insulate polite society from the ugly, disgusting truth. The truth was covered in blood and brain matter. The truth was a single shot firing into his wife's head, the splatter of scarlet on his wallpaper, the warm spray of blood on his face.

She had done it before him, raised the gun, pulled the trigger. And she had done it in his private space, his study, so that he would never again cross the threshold without recalling what had happened within its walls, without hearing the reverberation of the shot, the sickening sound of entry, the suddenness of it all. The sight of her eyes, open and stunned. Her body falling to the carpet in one swift thump. And the blood, seeping, seeping.

In the aftermath, he had attempted to oversee the redecorating of his study, finding solace and distraction in useful tasks, and he had found a curious little thing beneath the sole of his shoe. Further examination had proven it a shard of Millicent's skull. He had fallen to his knees, shaking, retching, and he'd never again returned to that chamber. All further attempts at salvaging the carpet and removing the blood stain had been abandoned.

He had instead employed an architect to redesign a series of small chambers into his private library, the room in which he now sat, staring into whisky in his hand. Perhaps it was fitting that his sole haven in Boswell Manor should also be the setting for his ruination.

A sturdy knock sounded at the door, breaking into the grim silence of the moment, and he knew who it was at the other end. He tossed back the remnants of his whisky and poured himself another. He didn't often imbibe, as it sometimes served to enhance his disquiet, but the interview ahead of him seemed to merit nothing less than a thorough foxing.

He was still reeling from the spell he'd had earlier, and now he had to face the one person he had sworn to never betray. Spencer's skin went cold. More whisky went down his throat, singeing with its mercurial strength.

Another knock rang.

He swallowed. "Enter."

The door opened, and his brother Harry strode through with the boisterous confidence of a young man who had never known a day of hardship. As the portal banged behind him, Spencer winced. Harry was golden to his darkness, charming and giving to a fault. His expression was open and inquisitive as he crossed the thick woolen rugs, his footfalls muted, hands clasped behind his back.

Spencer wished for the floor to open up and swallow him.

Sadly, the boards beneath him were not accommodating.

And so he stood, whisky in hand for himself, another for his brother. "Brother," he acknowledged. Good God, how was one meant to tell one's sibling that he'd ruined the woman who was the object of his affections? That fate and circumstance and his own bloody lack of control had rendered it necessary for him to wed Lady Boadicea?

"Spencer," his brother greeted, raising a quizzical brow as he accepted the whisky. "Tippling in the afternoon with the house party just underway? Is there some cause for celebration of which I'm unaware?"

Harry's soft jibe found its mark. He regretted that his relationship with his brother was not what it should be. They were opposites in every fashion, from appearance to temperament, but he had always cared about his sibling. Had always wanted only the absolute best for him. Still, there had been a distance between them over the last seven years—from the moment Millicent's troubles had begun until now—that he wished he could breach.

Such a thing would be impossible after the unfortunate news he had to impart. This was the first of two dreaded audiences, but this one would affect him the most. The other was perfunctory. He was already a prisoner trapped in a cell, no need to flinch at the slammed door and the turned lock.

"No celebration, Harry." He raised his glass to his lips, took another long, bracing drag. The trouble with liquor was that it never got him soused enough to forget. No matter how much he consumed, the memories returned. So too the nightmares. "Drink."

His brother stared at him, hesitating to imbibe. "Does this sudden, funereal air have ought to do with my intention of supporting Lady Boadicea with her Lady's Suffrage Society?"

Hell. He'd *known* she was trouble. "Suffrage Society?"

Harry smiled, resembling nothing so much as a well-pleased puppy in his exuberance for life. Oh, to be so untouched. So unjaded. Spencer downed the dregs of his glass, envious of his brother all the more.

"Yes," Harry said. "She and the Countess of Ravenscroft have begun a gathering of likeminded ladies. They mean to gain the attention of parliament. They could have a chance to be taken seriously, don't you think?"

"No," he pronounced baldly, not because it was true that women's suffrage wasn't a cause that should be taken seriously but because he knew it was a cause that would take many years and a great deal of campaigning before anyone could accomplish change. He knew Parliament all too well, and he'd lived long enough and hard enough to no longer claim the blind hope he'd possessed in his youth.

It had been stripped from his marrow.

Spencer turned to pour himself a third whisky. Two bloody well wasn't enough.

"You don't think the cause worthy?" Harry frowned. "Cannot you see the rightness of it, Spencer?"

"Seeing the rightness of a course of action and knowing the difficulties of passing it through Parliament are two disparate things. Others have tried and failed before them. More still will fail long after." Another sip of whisky. Still not soused enough, damn it. "But that is neither here nor there. You haven't touched your whisky."

Somber now, his brother studied him with a penetrating stare. "What has you rattled, Spencer? I haven't seen you like this since…"

Although Harry allowed his words to trail off, they both knew what remained unspoken. *Millicent.* The astute observation made him flinch, fingers tightening on his glass. For a moment he wondered absurdly whether he could crush crystal with a grip. He envisioned it, the glass shattering, raining shards to the floor, jagged edges impaling his hand. He deserved such a punishment, and worse.

Once, in the darkest days following his wife's death, he had made himself bleed.

Something was wrong with him. Clearly. He possessed some inherent form of cruelty that caused him to inflict suffering upon those closest to him. First, he had driven Millicent to her violent death before him, and now he was about to watch the light flee his brother's eyes. What blackness lived inside him? Three years outrunning his demons had not been long enough.

For now, here he stood, numb with a combined distillation of grief and spirits, on the precipice of hurting the brother he cared for more than another soul in the world. His vision darkened, a rushing sound roaring in his ears like the current of a flooded river. The glass dropped from his hand, landing at his feet.

He looked down. At least it had been empty. The soft carpet had cushioned its fall. Nothing was broken or ruined, except for Spencer himself.

"Damn it, Spencer, are you ill?" Harry rushed forward, entering his line of vision, expression drawn taut with concern. "Tell me what ails you, for God's sake."

He forced himself to speak. "I compromised Lady Boadicea Harrington this afternoon."

There. He'd done it.

Harry froze. "Lady Bo?"

Ah, so his brother was familiar enough with her already to condense her name. For some reason, that revelation irked him, sending something needling through the haze blanketing his mind. He refused to believe it was jealousy. But he couldn't help but wonder whether Harry's tongue had ever been in her mouth. The notion made him ill.

He cleared his throat, meeting Harry's gaze. "The same."

Harry's jaw clenched. "How can that be possible? She was going to take a rest in her chamber, read a book. Yesterday's journey here left her in need of settling."

Damnation. Spencer closed his eyes for a moment. His brother imagined Lady Boadicea had been reading an innocent tome in her chamber when in fact she'd been closeted inside his library, devouring filth. The book was still in his jacket, seeming to burn a hole straight into his skin. Mocking him.

"I'm afraid she did not seek out her chamber," he managed with as much gentleness as he could muster.

Harry seized his jacket, shaking him with surprising strength given his leaner form. "Don't dare to suggest she went looking for you. She doesn't even like you."

That rather stung. She had seemed to like him well enough when his hand had been up her skirts, but he refrained from offering that particular gem of wisdom.

"She mistakenly came here. We were alone. Mother and the Duchess of Cartwright happened upon us, and I…she is ruined, Harry. I will rectify matters, but I wanted to grant you the dignity of informing you before I speak with the Marquis of Thornton to ask for her hand."

A frown furrowed his brother's brow, but his grip on Spencer's jacket hadn't relented. "You were alone with her. I don't see the concern. With our mother pressing her, I daresay the Duchess of Cartwright won't breathe a word of this to anyone. Crisis averted. There's no need for you to approach Lord Thornton or for you to marry Lady Bo at all."

Harry's insistence upon calling her Lady Bo grated on him in a way that it should not. After all, he had been courting her, squiring her about, spending time in her presence. Spencer didn't know anything else about her save that she read bawdy books and smelled like a lush bloom and her mouth was made to be ravaged by kisses.

His kisses.

No. He mustn't think such thoughts. It was not where his addled mind was meant to head. First, it appeared he would have to explain his follies in enough depth to compel Harry that his courtship of Lady Boadicea was indeed at an end.

He wished he had another whisky, but his glass remained on the floor, and his brother continued to hold him with the grip of a man caught between rage and denial.

"Harry," he said again, "there is need."

"What are you saying, damn you?" Harry growled, giving him another shake.

He allowed it, accepted his brother's rage, for it was well-deserved, and it was the least he could do. He would let Harry imagine anything he chose of him, if it could lessen the sting of what he'd done.

"Her skirts were raised," he elaborated with a cool, detached air he little felt. "The Duchess of Cartwright was correct in her outrage."

"You bastard." Harry released his jacket, face going white. "Did you force yourself on her?"

Good God. Even his own flesh and blood believed him a monster. He stared, unblinking. "Believe what you will. The salient fact is that I must meet with Thornton in half an hour's time, and I will be asking him for Lady Boadicea's hand in her father's absence."

"No." His brother shook his head, his fists clenching at his sides. "You won't. I will. I don't care what's happened. I'll marry Lady Bo before I see her shackled to you."

Shackled to him. As if he were some sort of beast rather than one of the wealthiest men in England, bearing a title almost as old and as noble as the Queen's. "I doubt she'll find it a persecution. She will be a duchess."

"Your duchess," Harry spat, bitterness underscoring his angry tone. "Have you forgotten what became of the last one?"

The barb hit him with the precision of an assassin's blade. He supposed he deserved that as well, but the reminder of Millicent's death coupled with the tumult of the day undid him. The rushing in his ears returned with a vengeance. His gut compressed, a fresh wave of nausea assailing him.

But he couldn't allow the darkness to overcome him. Not now. He had to see this through first.

"I have not forgotten." He forced the words to emerge.

"I'll marry her." Harry's face twisted. "I'm in love with her, damn it."

Perhaps his brother did believe himself in love with Lady Boadicea Harrington. But a lady did not love a man when she kissed another as she had Spencer. She had burned in his arms, blooming for him. Perhaps she was inconstant, perhaps fickle, or worse, an unfeeling flirt. He didn't know her well enough to determine the source of her overwhelming reaction to him, but he did know that he was equally afflicted, and he could not allow Harry to marry her in his stead.

"No," he said. "I ruined her. I'll marry her."

Harry's lip curled into a sneer, and for a beat, he swore his brother would raise his fist against him. But he did not. "I understand why Millicent was so desperate to escape you, Spencer. You're bloody heartless."

Yes, he was. That sentimental organ had been torn from his chest long ago. It had no place in his life. Nor did emotion, though he knew a twinge of something foreign as he stared at his sibling. Remorse? Sympathy? Self-loathing?

It little mattered.

He inclined his head in acknowledgment. "I'm sorry, brother."

Harry recoiled as though he'd been struck. "Go to hell."

He didn't respond as he watched his brother leave the library, slamming the door with so much force that the paintings on the walls shuddered. It was a matter of course that hell was a place he'd gotten to know quite well over the last few years.

Spencer retrieved his glass and stalked to the sideboard.

More whisky was in order.

Chapter Five

A RECKONING.

That was what this was, Bo thought.

"The Duchess of Cartwright was quite firm in her assertions," Alex, the Marquis of Thornton, doting husband to her sister Cleo, informed her. His expression was grim. He pinched the bridge of his nose.

He wasn't the first person she'd ever given a headache in her life, and she was reasonably certain he wouldn't be the last. She got into scrapes. She got herself out of them. Surely this wasn't any worse than the time she'd flung a forkful of aspic into the coiffure of the detestable Lady Thistledowne.

"Her Grace was mistaken." Bo kept her voice calm and unshakeable. The Duke had kindly granted them the use of the green salon for this unwanted and unnecessary meeting, presided over by her brother-in-law and sister.

She loved the pair of them dearly, but everything about this was wrong.

"Bo," Cleo interrupted in her older-sister voice, "the duke was clear as well when he had his interview with Alex. Whatever happened in the library, the Duchess of

Cartwright has no intention of keeping this secret unless you wed Bainbridge."

"Why should the Duchess of Cartwright care that the duke assisted me with an overturned ankle?" she asked, incensed at the woman's self-righteous meddling.

"Dearest, you haven't been limping," Cleo pointed out.

Oh.

Perhaps she'd forgotten to continue her act, given the flurry of nonsense that had assailed her from the moment she'd left the library. This was why she detested country house parties and sanctimonious prudes both. Not to mention the Duke of Bainbridge.

Yes, this had all begun because the arrogant lummox had *stolen* her book.

"I have a hearty constitution," she argued. "I heal remarkably fast, you know. Why must my good fortune be suspect?"

"Bo." Cleo frowned at her. "This isn't the time to be glib."

Fine. Bo sent her a frown of her own. "Well, it certainly isn't the time to cow before the whims of the Duchess of Cartwright or the arrogant stupidity of the Duke of Bainbridge either. I'll not be made a sacrifice for the sake of someone's misguided sense of propriety."

Never mind that the duchess had not been wrong about what she'd witnessed. Bo still wasn't about to marry Bainbridge. She had agreed earlier as he stood there, stricken by thoughts of his dead wife, because she felt compassion for him. But compassion was not enough to warrant the loss of her freedom forever to a man she didn't like.

To a man like Bainbridge.

Even if he kissed better than any other man who had ever set his mouth to hers.

"I'm afraid these aren't whims, Bo," her brother-in-law said next, interrupting the inappropriate bent of her thoughts at the right time. "You will be ruined. And as your sister's husband, I cannot countenance such a thing happening while you're beneath my protection."

When she'd paced in her bedchamber earlier, parceling out what she would say and how she would avoid having to marry the insufferable duke, she hadn't thought about how her actions could affect those around her.

How dreadfully selfish of her. Cleo and Alex's love was old and true, but they had been torn apart in their youth and reunited while Cleo had been married to her scurrilous husband. Only upon the blackguard's death had Cleo and Alex been free to marry, and they'd weathered a great deal of scandal to maintain good standing in the *ton* and Parliament both. Alex was a vaunted politician, and if he were deemed responsible for her lapse in judgment, she would never forgive herself.

She sighed, and the knot in her stomach that had begun as small as a thimble tangled and grew within her. The chamber seemed suddenly robbed of air. Her cheeks went hot. Her corset was laced too tight. Even her silk stockings itched. She wanted to be free of every encumbrance, free of this room, free of propriety and duty and the repercussions of her own foolishness.

"But you aren't responsible," she told Alex needlessly. "I am my own woman, capable of making my own decisions, regardless of however stupid they may prove."

His expression remained impassive as Cleo chimed back in. "Whilst we're speaking of decisions, perhaps you'd care to explain how you found yourself in the duke's private library when you pleaded a headache and asked to return to your chamber for a rest."

Bo's brows snapped together and she gave her sister a did-you-truly-just-dare look. Cleo had once been notorious for pleading megrims at fashionable gatherings. Now that she was the Marchioness of Thornton, with Alex's political connections and responsibilities, she could no longer employ her clever subterfuge. But that didn't mean Bo couldn't. "Where do you think I learned such a strategy, dear sister?"

Cleo flushed. "You lied to me, you little scamp?"

She grinned, the heaviness of the situation dispelled for a moment. "I prefer to think of it as offering a creative suggestion."

"God save me from Harrington women," Alex gritted. "Boadicea, may I remind you that you swore to me that you'd behave for the duration of the week? And yet here we are, not a full day into our stay at Boswell Manor, and the Duke of Bainbridge has been witnessed compromising you in his bloody library?"

She winced, her levity fading in the face of her brother-in-law's thunderous scowl. "I had every intention of behaving. My sole goal was to convince Lord Harry to aid me with the Lady's Suffrage Society."

"By allowing his brother to compromise you?" Cleo asked slyly.

She supposed she deserved that.

Alex scrubbed a palm over his face. "Hell."

Cleo leaned forward, lips compressed in disapproval. "What happened, Bo? If we are to extricate you from this mess, you must be honest with us. No more prevaricating or evasion."

Another sigh escaped her. She didn't like being told what she must do, and she never had. Nor did she particularly care for rules. She was a perverse creature, she knew, but if she was told a lady ought not to do something, she wanted to do it. If someone said to walk, she decided to run. If she was told to stay, she strayed. Her mother had wanted a wardrobe for her made of ruffles and pastel, and she'd chosen the boldest colors she could find instead. It was her nature.

But this was different. Rules were made to be ignored unless doing so would hurt someone she loved. And she loved her sister and Alex.

"I intended to read," she said at last into their expectant silence. "I wandered a bit—Boswell Manor is so frightfully large that I'd wager one could get lost in it for three solid days. And at last, I came upon a library with no one about. It seemed the perfect place to spend a few hours alone, until the duke interrupted my solitude."

"You overturned your ankle while reading a book in Bainbridge's library?" Alex's eyes narrowed.

Her cheeks went hot. "I didn't overturn my ankle." She paused, wondering how to phrase what had happened after the duke's unannounced arrival. "He took exception to my choice of literature, and stole my book from me. When he refused to return it, I…I kissed him."

Cleo and Alex stared at her, apparently united in their loss for words, before sharing a telling look. They were the sort of husband and wife who required no words to communicate. Bo found it both adorable and nauseating.

When they glanced back to her, she was sure she was red as a beet from the tips of her ears to her toes. "He still has my book, the arrogant oaf," she said, for she wasn't about to elaborate on what had occurred in the wake of her ill-advised kiss.

No, there was honesty and then there was futility. She was sure Cleo and Alex—whom she had once witnessed emerging from a carriage all flushed and misbuttoned—could surmise as much without her confession.

"You kissed him," Cleo echoed at last, her voice weak as she shared yet another troubled glance with her husband. "Oh dear. This is worse than I feared."

"Did Bainbridge take liberties?" Alex demanded, sounding like a protective older brother.

Yes, of course he had. But she had encouraged them. Had allowed them. Heavens above, she'd started the entire string of unfortunate events by kissing him. And liking it.

She considered her response with care. "He still has my book in his possession, and I'd like it back."

"Oh dear Lord, Bo." Her sister's gaze was knowing, disapproving. "Please tell me it wasn't one of *those* books."

Drat. Why did her sisters—every sainted one of them—always know her so well? It was a blessing and curse all at once. Cleo had caught her reading one of the bawdy books she'd pilfered from their brother Bingley's stash and had forced her to turn it over like spoils of war. Her elder sister hadn't known, of course, that Bo had about ten more volumes, all surreptitiously removed from their brother's chamber over time, to which she could turn for further edification.

But she was no fool when it came to the protection of her cache of lewd, outlawed books, and she wasn't about to reveal that she had more to a sister who wouldn't be above scouring her chamber and confiscating the rest. Not to mention informing their parents. Bo was curious. She had much yet to learn.

She blinked. "Poetry, do you mean? Truly, Cleo, marriage has turned you into a dreadful prude. What can be the harm in Lord Byron?"

Alex took in the exchange between the two of them.

Cleo glowered. "Boadicea Harrington. You know what I refer to."

Bo pursed her lips. "It was the Bible, if you must know, and it's most vexing because I'd only reached halfway through Genesis when he thieved it from me. I am clamoring to know what happens next."

Her sister made a sound low in her throat. "Bo."

Well, and what did Cleo expect? That she would own to reading a journal whose printing had landed the publisher in jail? That she would admit she'd been reading about the lord of the house's swelling member in the presence of his sister's comely governess? That she'd eagerly learned new, wicked words like slit and pearl and tumescence? That she would never again think of walks in the woods in the same manner ever again?

Or libraries, for that matter.

A frisson of something unwanted and curious simmered through her and settled between her thighs, rather like the aches she'd read about. She banished it.

"I won't marry the Duke of Disdain," she insisted. "He is cold and arrogant and unfeeling. I have no intention of marrying any man, let alone one who would insult me, look down his nose at me, and then kowtow to the sense of propriety of a vicious old biddy."

"I'm afraid you may have no choice," Alex interrupted gently, his tone stern but his eyes flashing with sympathy. "Bo, what you've described to me, taken in consideration with the duchess's words and those of Bainbridge himself, convinces me that this was no innocent tableau. It must be rectified."

Rectified.

The blood leached from her face. "You intend to force me to marry Bainbridge? Alex, how could you?"

"I'll not force you into anything." Caution steeped his voice. "But marrying him may be the only way to squelch the impending scandal before it's unleashed. You are not the only one who will be affected, Boadicea. Keep that in mind."

"And there is the matter of your Lady's Suffrage Society to consider," Cleo pressed, always knowing what to say. "If you are ruined and must withdraw from society, all your efforts will be for naught. How are you going to give voice to your cause if you allow yourself to be silenced?"

Blast. Her sister was right on that count, but marriage still seemed like every bit as much of a mistake as allowing herself to be become a pariah. "You do not think marrying Bainbridge will silence me just as well?"

"No, dearest sister." Cleo's voice softened. "Far better to be a duchess than an outcast, for your sake just as much as for your cause."

Bo swallowed, and the knot inside her grew until she couldn't bear one moment more of this interminable interview. Shooting to her feet, she excused herself and fled from the chamber before she embarrassed herself by bursting into tears as the full effect of her own recklessness collapsed upon her.

Chapter Six

SPENCER COOLED HIS HEELS in his mother's favored salon for intimate familial gatherings. Decorated in shades of green—from the damask and the sylvan oil paintings on the walls to the silken drapes and thick carpets—it resembled nothing so much as a depressing venture into an old thicket. But it was private, ensconced deep in the north wing, its floor-to-ceiling windows overlooking the lake and gardens that gave Boswell House part of its distinction.

The day had dawned unusually bright and rainless, the sun glinting through those windows now with a brilliant cheer that seemed to mock him. He'd woken before dawn, torn from the old nightmares he'd hoped he'd shaken forever. Shuddering, covered in a fine sheen of sweat, he'd been certain his dead wife had called his name in those moments as wakefulness and sleep melded into something indistinct and hazy.

But it had been the dreams again, where he relived watching Millicent raise the pistol to her temple. Where he could see the cloud of smoke, the spatter of blood, the final expression on her face. Where he tried to reach out and was immobile, attempted to speak but could not force his tongue into action.

He paced across the salon, hands clasped behind his back to stave off their trembling, awaiting the last woman he wished to see. At most recent glance of his pocket watch, she'd been thirty-eight minutes and twenty seconds late. He had requested she meet him at eight o'clock. In private, so that they could discuss a plan of action.

But Lady Boadicea Harrington, devotee of lascivious books, didn't appear to have any inclination of meeting him. She had not replied to his note. He had gone anyway, thinking her lack of response down to her stubborn nature.

It would appear, however, that he was wrong.

That in a matter of less than half an hour, he had undone his every careful attempt to distance himself from scandal, weakness, women, and the madness that threatened to close in on him ever since Millicent's death. That he had compromised a lady who had no compunction about reading smut in his library or cupping his cock through his trousers—tentative though her touch may have been—and that said lady was wearing his madcap brother's heart like a battle victory on her bosom, and yet didn't even feel a hint of compassion for what she had done, for what she would yet do, if she refused his suit, if she—

The door to the salon opened, and in swept Lady Boadicea Harrington in a seductive whisper of silken skirts and soft footfalls. Her auburn hair was coiled into a series of braids, a fashionable fringe on her forehead, and the luscious beauty of it struck him, fiery and glinting in the sun.

She wore a vibrant morning frock of purple velvet, silk, and taffeta shot with cream that should have rendered her gaudy against the green confines of the chamber. Instead, it had the opposite effect, complimenting her, showing her to advantage. She put everything else in the room—hell, she put every woman he'd ever seen—to shame.

The door closed behind her. She stilled, elegant and regal and ineffably lovely. All the resentment festering inside him since he'd seen her last reminded him that she was the reason he was once again battling to maintain a tentative grip on his sanity.

If she hadn't kissed him…

If he hadn't kissed her…

If he hadn't raised her skirts and touched her hot, silken quim…

Damnation, he couldn't do this. She'd stretched him to the edge of madness.

"Lady Boadicea," he greeted curtly.

She stiffened, whether at his tone or his presence he couldn't tell. Her blue gaze, cutting and intense, clashed with his. "Your Grace."

She didn't curtsy. Nor did he bow. He supposed this meant they were dispensing with the formalities. And anyway, what did it matter after he'd thrown her skirts up to her waist and slipped his hand inside the slit of her drawers? Ruffled, white, silk, they'd been embroidered with roses. He shouldn't think of them now. Nor should he think of the prize they'd shielded. She'd been so wet for him.

He swallowed, battling back his unwanted attraction to her. "If you'd arrived but half a minute later, you would have found yourself utterly alone."

She pursed her lips, considering him in a way he didn't like, as though she could see straight to the marrow of him and still found him lacking. "I've been alone for twenty years, Your Grace. A moment without your company would be neither here nor there."

Her cutting words found their mark. He strode toward her before he could check himself, as though he needed to be nearer to her. To smell her delicate scent. To inhale her as if she were as necessary to him as the air he breathed.

What in God's name?

He stopped, four paces away, forcing himself to keep his distance and his cool both. "Twenty years? I daresay you've scarcely more than one-and-twenty years altogether."

"You would be correct." She pursed her lips, taking inventory of him once again as if he were something that caused her a great deal of displeasure. "What is the purpose of this audience, Your Grace? Do you mean to return my book?"

Her book. That bloody bit of nonsense she'd been so keen on devouring when he came upon her in his library. The leather-bound home for licentious drivel that shocked even his sensibilities. He'd read the first chapter of the volume in question in the midst of the night after his nightmares had rendered sleep impossible. He hadn't believed his bloody eyes. And damn him if the knowledge that her bright-blue eyes and rapier wit had taken in the same wickedness hadn't left him inflamed.

The daring of the woman. He wasn't sure if he ought to be horrified and repelled or if he ought to take her up in his arms and never let her go. As it was, he wanted her so damn much that his entire groin ached and pulsed with a ferocity he'd never even known possible.

He stalked closer. Closer. Until his trouser-clad legs pressed into her heavy skirts, making them bell out behind her. She inhaled sharply, tensing even more, leaning away as he caught her around the waist and hauled her against him. Her head tipped back, leaving her ripe, supple lips a scant distance from his, open and ready, awaiting his claiming.

Temptation was the devil.

"I've no intention of returning your book," he informed her coolly.

"Oh?" Her eyebrows hiked up her flawless ivory forehead, making the slightest crinkle that he found somehow riveting. "Well, it would seem we are well-matched in determination if nothing else, for I've no intention of marrying you."

He couldn't tell if she was bold or if she was foolish, or both. "How much of it have you read?" he demanded in spite of himself. He shouldn't want to know. Curiosity ought not to burn inside him like a hearth fire upon which someone had thrown a bucket of lamp oil. But it did.

Her full lips quirked, tipping up at the corners as though she attempted to repress her humor and couldn't quite manage it. "You read my book, didn't you?"

Something alarming and unprecedented happened to him in that moment, as he held her against him and accepted the knowledge that this minx could somehow see through him in a manner no one else before her had.

His ears burned. "Of course not," he lied.

She shook her head slowly, and he noted how the light glinted from the hidden undertones of red in her luxurious hair. Her hands went to his shoulders in a familiar gesture that aroused him even more. What the hell was it about her?

Lady Boadicea leaned nearer. Jasmine wafted to him. Her gaze lowered to his mouth for a moment before burning into his once more. "Tell me, Your Grace, did you enjoy the chapter about Lady Letitia and her groom?"

She was beyond any woman he'd ever known in his life. Was she mad? It was a possibility. Having lived with a mad wife, it only stood to reason that he would be drawn to more of the same.

"You're the most forward female I've ever met." He wasn't sure if he issued the observation as praise or as condemnation.

A complete smile blossomed on her luscious lips then, and if he'd thought her beautiful before, he'd been wrong. She was stunning. A goddess. A witch. Surely the Lord himself had fashioned her with the sole purpose of one day punishing him for his sins.

Her brow arched. "You didn't answer my question, Your Grace. I can surmise from the flush on your cheekbones that you were curious enough to read a few pages at least."

"It's filth." He disliked that she could read him, know him, see through to the bloody heart of him, with such dispassionate ease. It rankled. It shook him. It goddamn grated. "I wouldn't lower myself to allow such rot to fall beneath my eye. Hardly surprising that you did, given your unseemly nature. Of course, when you are my wife, you'll abstain from all such imprudent leanings toward the prurient."

"When I am your wife," she repeated, the sentence punctuated on a low and delicious laugh that he felt down his spine. "You still insist on believing this fiction that you and I will marry? How amusing."

"Do you know what was amusing, Lady Boadicea? Watching that little book of yours burn in the grate of my library." Also a falsehood, but he longed to steal the smirk from her kissable mouth. She made him want to be more of a beast than he already was.

That beauty mark of hers taunted him as her words did. The urge to set his lips there, flirting with the corner of hers, beset him. As he watched, the amusement fled from her lively eyes and expressive features. Watching her brilliance fade was rather akin to a cloud passing before the sun on a summer's day. That he was the source of the sudden darkness wasn't lost on him, and his momentary victory was hollow for it.

She surprised him by a touch, butterfly-light and fleeting, on his jaw. Just a flutter of her fingers and then gone. But bloody hell, he felt it like a brand. This girl made too free with his person. He hadn't felt a woman's soft caress against his skin like this—a lover's touch—in as long as he could remember. He wasn't meant to feel this way now, as if something inside him might shatter and the bitterness he'd fought so hard to control would break free at last.

Her intent gaze searched his. "You're lying. I'd be willing to wager that even now you've got it hidden away somewhere with every intention of reading about Lady Letitia if you haven't already. I cannot blame you, Your Grace. It *is* a particularly enlightening tale."

"Unfortunately, I'll never know." He kept his tone mild, but inside, he felt oddly discombobulated, as if he'd somehow woke from a long slumber, uncertain of where he was and how he'd managed to find himself there.

She was the most vexing woman he'd ever met. He ought to allow Harry to take his place as he wanted, make her his bride. He ought to be disgusted by her flagrant disregard for propriety, the way she flaunted her smutty books without shame. By no means should he be drawn to her, entranced by her, or want to kiss her bloody well senseless. But even as he had all those thoughts, intended to reassure his common sense that he had worked too diligently to escape his former hell to descend into another, he tugged her nearer to him.

"You *want* to know, don't you?" she whispered, and there was her touch once more, two fingers, pressing to his lips in a mimicry of a kiss.

And yes, he did want to know. Thus far, he'd only managed to read the letter from Lady Pokingham to her niece, detailing the birch treatments she'd received from her governess, along with a description of her clandestine walk in a garden with Lord Longwood. Naturally, the walk had turned into a frenzied burst of kisses, Lord Longwood flipping up the lady's skirts, and sampling her *honey pot* first with his tongue and then with his tumescent member.

Sweet Jesus.

Lady Boadicea Harrington was a menace. That much was plain as the shoes on his feet. Her insistence on toying with him fueled his ire. He was too damn old and too damn world-weary for games.

He caught her wrist in his grip, breaking the contact between the pads of her fingers and his mouth. "You will cease this nonsense at once, Lady Boadicea. I didn't invite you here so that you could insult my offer while acting the brazen hussy. I invited you here to sort out the details of how we shall proceed with our arrangement."

She stiffened at the cold lash of his words. "I'm sorry for whatever happened to you to make you conduct yourself with such frigid condescension, but I have no wish to marry you. Can you not convince your mother and the Duchess of Cartwright that nothing so extreme is necessary?"

Whatever happened to you, she'd said, in a lightly veiled reference to Millicent. The knowledge that Lady Boadicea Harrington was aware his wife had killed herself before him filled him with rage. How dare she flirt with him, touch him, make light of him? He thought then of how she had feigned acceptance of his suit before his mother and the Duchess of Cartwright, how she had even defended him to them.

He saw it all for what it was now: pity.

Something violent and ugly twisted free inside him. He wouldn't be pitied by this forward chit or anyone else. He set her from him, ignoring the loss of her on his mouth, the unanswered desire to take her lips. Spencer embraced his anger, let it spring free of its cage.

"Do you know what it looks like when someone holds a pistol to their temple and pulls the trigger, Lady Boadicea?" The words were torn from him, a question he had never dared pose to another living soul for fear that it would break him. For fear they'd think him every bit as mad as his wife had been. The truth of it was that sometimes he wondered if the madness had infected him.

Lady Boadicea's creamy skin went pale as she gave her head a slight shake. "N-no, Your Grace."

Ah, a stutter. Perhaps he had disarmed her at last. He raised his hands, palms facing the ceiling, embracing the viciousness coursing through him. He wanted to punish her. To make her look at him with anything other than sympathy. "What, no barbs, my lady? No shameless remarks about the tripe you've smuggled into my home? Why, I do believe that for once you may be robbed of speech. A rarity for you, surely. Shall I describe the aftereffects of the bullet's violence to you? Is that what you long to hear?"

"Your Grace." She pressed the same fingers that had touched his lips over her mouth now, looking as if she may be ill.

But he wasn't done with her yet. He stalked toward her once more, and not even the sweet scent of her was enough to dispel his wrath. How dare she look upon him with pity?

How dare she refuse his hand as though he offered her nothing more than a waltz at a country ball? As though he, Spencer Marlow, the Duke of Bainbridge, was beneath the scandal-courting youngest daughter of the eccentric Earl of Northcote?

By God, he had devoted himself, these last three years, to living an unimpeachable life. He adhered to propriety. He never lost his temper. He repented for his sins. He worked hard to make his estates profitable, to be a good steward of the land and people assigned him. In short, he did everything he could to make amends for what had happened.

"Do you know," he continued, "what it's like to watch someone you care for lose their mind, Lady Boadicea? No? I do. What I've seen would gut you, my dear, and you'd never again have time for filthy journals or turning up in the library of the brother of the man who's been courting you and ruining yourself."

She threw back her shoulders, assuming what he could only imagine was her battle stance. "I've no doubt you suffered, Your Grace, and greatly. I'm sorry for that." She stepped forward, her skirts crashing into him, her finger catching him in the chest. "But none of that gives you the right to be an overbearing brute. And forgive me for my impertinence, but I do recall that I had assistance in ruining myself, as you so blithely refer to your mauling of my person before your mother and her simpleminded bosom bow."

Something smarted on his chest. Once, twice, thrice, four times. He looked down to find that the termagant was poking him. And hard. He trapped her wrist again in one hand while the other sank into the voluptuous fall of her skirts. He didn't stop until he found a handful of the lush bum hiding beneath all her fripperies.

The mauling of her person, indeed.

He released her wrist and tunneled his fingers into the silken hair at her nape, angling her head before his mouth took hers. The tense lines of her body softened. She melted against him, falling into his body, her mouth opening. He recognized her surrender, and he took it like an invading army, plundering, owning, making her his. She tasted like sugared tea. Her tongue moved against his, tentative at first, and then with meaning.

He groaned, driving the soft curves of her body into his hard angles as he cupped her arse, holding her to him. His cock pressed into her belly, when where he wanted it most was deep inside her channel. He kissed her hard, open-mouthed, hungry. He kissed her as he'd never kissed another woman before her, told her with his lips and licks and body that she was his.

He staked his claim.

Spencer tore his mouth from hers, his breathing labored. Lady Boadicea was gratifyingly dazed, her lips swollen and berry-red from his kisses. "Did I maul you just now, my lady?"

She blinked. "Your Grace?"

He didn't answer but kissed her again, taking his time. When had putting his lips to a woman ever been this divine, this intoxicating? He could lose himself inside her. Little wonder Harry had fallen beneath her spell.

Harry.

Damn it all. The reminder of his brother was enough to make him withdraw his lips from hers once more. Guilt settled heavily in his gut. How could he have forgotten that Harry had fallen for her, that she was too bold and unsuitable, that the last thing Spencer wanted, having narrowly survived his first marriage, was to undertake another?

Nothing made sense, not his reaction to her, not this burning desire within to make her his, not the way she could make him feel more than he'd felt in the last three years in just a moment of being within her presence. He wanted her, yet he didn't, he longed to push her away, and yet to hold her forever to him. Regardless of the tumult within, he knew what he must do.

He stared at her, bemused but determined. "You'll be my duchess." It was a pronouncement rather than a question. Like it or not, she would wed him. He wouldn't put his family through any further scandal.

She exhaled slowly, her hot breath colliding with his lips. "No."

Spencer kept her where she was, in his arms, ripe body tucked to his. He touched their foreheads together. He didn't understand this any more than she did, but life was an endless parade of false autonomy. Christ knew he'd never had a choice or a chance to live the life he'd once imagined for himself. Why stop now?

"Yes," he insisted. "My honor demands it."

"Your honor." She frowned, attempting to shrug from his grasp.

He wouldn't allow it, holding her fast. "Yours as well. Think of your sister. She and Thornton are not long off a scandal themselves, and he can ill afford even a breath of impropriety."

He sensed her mind working, could read some of it in her flashing eyes. Her mouth went pensive, twin lines forming at either corner. Her beauty mark moved along with the frown. He watched, considered flicking his tongue against it in some nonsensical fantasy that he could lick it up and make it his.

Lady Boadicea unleashed an aggrieved sigh. "You are correct in one matter, if nothing else, Duke. The last thing I would wish is to cause harm to my dear sister and her husband. I love them both frightfully."

A pang of jealousy beat to life within him. How embarrassing that he should know envy that the flighty creature before him loved her sister and her sister's husband. It was only his baser nature at work. For love was an invention of man designed to allow him to believe himself better than a rude animal in the wild. It didn't exist. It was a fancy, a chimera, nothing more.

In this instance, however, he could use that outlandish emotion to his benefit. "If you love them, then you know what must be done. Just as I care for my family and know the only course left to me. We must marry, Lady Boadicea. We owe it to those we could taint most by our indiscretion, if nothing else."

Her rebellious and bold nature aside, he had no doubt that this argument appealed to her in a way that nothing else would. He looked upon her, drinking in her beauty. How odd that just yesterday, he had scorned her when in this moment, he couldn't imagine her as any other man's wife save his.

And then, before he did something inordinately foolish, like kiss her or take her up in his arms and carry her off to his chamber, he set her from him. He offered a hasty, mocking bow, and then he left her alone with her thoughts and the decision she must make.

Chapter Seven

A FUNEREAL PALL SEEMED TO DESCEND upon the entire assemblage at Boswell Manor. The gentlemen had come to enjoy the shoot, but a miserable, driving rain that afternoon rendered any such pursuits impossible. Instead, they settled for isolating themselves from their female counterparts and engaging in "indoor sport," which Bo was sure was a euphemism for getting soused and fleecing each other at cards.

She and Cleo sat on the fringes of a massive drawing room decorated in gilt and an alarming amount of daffodil-yellow. Truly, it was akin to sitting within the sun itself, but it was where the ladies of the house party had assembled for nonsensical parlor games, and she had little choice but to suffer its brashness.

Cleo disagreed about the fleecing and the sousing, *sotto voce*. "Alex said they'd be playing at billiards or some such. A tournament, I believe he said."

"Involving wagers and the consumption of an inordinate amount of whisky, one can be sure," Bo grumbled back to her sister, for she was vexed and in a deleterious mood, and she had no patience for men and their double standards.

Why couldn't they be forced to witness Lady Abigail Featherhead pretending to be a chimpanzee during charades? It was hardly fair.

The last place she wanted to be at the moment was here, trapped amidst a throng of ladies who she could count more as foe than friend. The Marlow family, even after the scandal of Bainbridge's duchess, was nearly royalty itself. Only a select group of *ton* families were invited to join them for their annual house party, and none of those families included anyone Bo cared to know.

Chief among them, the Duchess of Cartwright, who had been eying her as if she were a smear of excrement befouling her hem all bloody day. The woman's sour face was enough to make Bo quite cantankerous. But if she were honest, it was her meeting with the duke that had unsettled her the most. Her morning interview with Bainbridge had left her more confused and aggrieved than ever.

He had kissed her again. Aside from galloping through the countryside on her favorite mare, nothing else had ever given her such a rush of exhilaration. She'd left the salon feeling the same quivering in her stomach and leap in her pulse that she'd experienced the time she'd taken a dangerous jump with Deity that almost unseated her: dazed, yet also somehow euphoric.

This wouldn't do. She had to put an end to the kissing. The man knew how to do it all too well.

"How would you know what gentlemen do when left to their own devices?" her sister asked then with a smug smile, interrupting her whirling thoughts.

"Whatever it is, I'm sure it's a great deal more entertaining than watching Abigail Featherhead make a cake of herself. And if Lady Lydia Trollop extols the virtues of Bainbridge one more time, I'm going to tear that silk rose cluster from her gown and stuff it in her mouth."

Cleo compressed her lips together to stifle a smile, but then arranged her expression into one of proper, older-sister condescension. "You mustn't poke fun at them so loudly.

What shall you do if someone overhears you referring to the Duke of Buxton's daughter as a trollop? You know very well that their surname is Trulle."

"Near enough." Bo sniffed, shifting in her uncomfortable chair. The Duchess of Bainbridge—whichever one had been responsible for this monstrosity masquerading as a drawing room—had deplorable taste.

The Duchess of Bainbridge.

How odd to think it was a mantle she could soon wear herself. Odder still to think that she'd arrived a mere three days past, eager to gain Harry's support for her Lady's Suffrage Society, never having been formally introduced to the duke himself, an oversight down to his recent abstention from polite society and her relatively new entrance. Bainbridge had greeted her with icy arrogance on that day, and she'd felt rather like a tradesman who'd shown up unwittingly to the wrong door.

But now, she felt...oh, she didn't know...as if her corset was laced too tight. As if her heart was about to leap from her chest and gallop away. As if she was firmly down Alice's rabbit hole, with no chance of ever returning to reality.

How was it that she was even contemplating marriage to the man? She, who had prided herself on the ambition of remaining a spinster wedded to her cause rather than accepting the life society apportioned for her? Cleo, she told herself, and Alex. It was for their sake alone.

"The duchess spoke with me earlier today," Cleo said, her tone sympathetic.

Bo stiffened. "Not of Cartwright, I hope?"

The ladies tittered and clapped as the Countess of Carnes apparently stumped the entire congregation with her attempt to invoke a vicar.

Her sister shot her a telling glance. "Of course not. The Duchess of Bainbridge. She expects an announcement, though I must warn you that she is not pleased."

What perversity. The duchess and her sour-faced friend had witnessed a lapse of propriety. They could have chosen to ignore it, but they were the sort of ladies who imagined their principles would save them. The reaction of Bainbridge's mother alone had told Bo that the woman deplored her. And yet she would force her son to marry a dreaded Harrington, all to avoid another scandal.

Her heart ached as she recalled Bainbridge's bitter words from that morning. She couldn't help but feel that she'd gotten her first, real glimpse of the true man hiding behind his cold façade. *What I've seen would gut you.* She had no doubt that it would.

"An announcement," she repeated, the phrase enough to curl her lip. For she didn't want to marry the Duke of Bainbridge.

Oh, she was drawn to him, that much was undeniable. She could be honest with herself, at least, and own that the Duke of Bainbridge was a breathtakingly handsome man. His features were assembled in the sort of masculine beauty she'd never seen—lips too sensuous and full for a man, a long blade of a nose, high cheekbones, and a strong chin. With his dark hair, emerald eyes, and towering height, he was enough to rob the breath from any female, even herself.

She liked his looks well enough. She even enjoyed his exceptionally skilled kisses. But the man was a cipher she'd never be able to unlock. His past had wounded and changed him. He was hardened. The man she'd seen this morning, in spite of the heat in his touch, had been deadened.

It was as if his duchess had taken him with her.

Whatever part of him remained, she didn't wish to bind herself to it for the rest of her life. But everything and everyone at this blasted house party seemed to be conspiring against her with one common goal: to force her into a marriage with the Duke of Disdain.

"Tonight," Cleo added. "At the Welcoming Ball. As you know, Thornton has granted his approval on behalf of Father."

Their father, forever occupied with pursuits of greater interest to him than his children, would be well pleased if his youngest daughter snared a duke. One less wild Harrington for him to fret over, she reasoned, etcetera.

Her freedom was down to hours. Dread commingled with the already tightening knot of trepidation in her stomach. Of all the times she'd defied propriety—and they were legion—she'd never been caught. The breadth of her foolishness shamed her now.

"And if I refuse?" she dared to ask.

Cleo frowned, her delicately arched raven brows snapping together into a sad frown. "The Duchess of Cartwright will not bend, I'm afraid, though her friendship with the dowager tolerated this brief delay to allow for an announcement that would not embarrass any of the parties."

By *any of the parties*, the officious woman of course meant the Marlow family. The Duchess of Cartwright didn't give a damn if she shamed Lady Boadicea Harrington. Or if she forced her into a match with a man known for driving his wife to kill herself before him.

Bo had to admit the gossip she'd heard about Bainbridge gave her pause. He had been cool and rigid, yes, but he also clearly possessed the capacity to turn his ice into molten flame. *Do you know what it's like to watch someone you care for lose their mind, Lady Boadicea?* Had the duchess gone mad as he'd suggested? There had to be more to the sad, sordid tale than the gossips knew.

She needed to cling to that hope if she was indeed to be forced into cleaving herself to the man. Bo wished the Duchess of Cartwright to perdition.

"She will ruin me," Bo simplified, keeping her voice hushed so that none of the eager ears surrounding them could become engaged.

Cleo patted her hand, her lovely face wreathed in sympathy. "Yes."

Bo wouldn't have cared so much for herself. She prided herself on her enterprising nature. Her parents had made every effort to stifle the rebelliousness from her and had failed as soundly as the Spanish Armada. But she loved her sisters—all of them—fiercely. She loved Clara and their Lady's Suffrage Society. She believed in their cause, of giving the women being governed the fair chance they deserved to have a voice. And for all those reasons, she would not act in selfishness.

For the first time in her life, she would wave the flag of surrender.

"That woman is a hedgehog." But though she decried, she knew what she must do. "I'll do it, Cleo. For your sake, and for Alex, and to keep the Lady's Suffrage Society I'll do it. But I will not like it."

"I will not allow you to sacrifice yourself for me." Cleo's lips compressed as she searched Bo's gaze. "You are at fault for your actions, but I want more than anything else for you to be happy, dear sister."

"I'm the architect of my own happiness." She turned her palm over in her lap and gave her sister's hand a reassuring squeeze. "I shall own the consequences and forge my independence by whatever means necessary."

"Bo," her sister protested.

"It is done."

"Lady Boadicea, you've been selected next," announced Lady Hyacinth Beaufort.

Bo had never met a female with a flower as her namesake that she'd liked. Lady Hyacinth was no exception, simpering and perfectly coifed, narrow of waist, melodic of voice, honeyed in her every manor, and dressed at all times as though she were a confection.

"Bo," Cleo said again, her voice stern. "I meant what I said."

She stood, shaking out her skirts, and forced a feigned smile to her lips. "It would be my great delight," she lied to the chamber at large. She cast a glance back at her sister. "I did as well, Cleo. The announcement will be made, and that is that."

And then she made her way to the forefront of the festivities, feeling like nothing so much as a doomed prisoner en route to the gallows. In more ways than one.

Bo slipped into the Duke of Bainbridge's private library for the second time in two days. But today, she was more than aware that she trespassed and whom it was that she trespassed against. She didn't give a damn.

Charades ended, and Bo had somehow managed to throw enough feeling into her representation of Anne Boleyn to be declared the unofficial—and unenthusiastic—champion of the entertainment. It seemed bleakly appropriate, if a bit silly for someone who made no secret of her distaste for trifles like insipid amusements.

While the ladies had thankfully dispersed, she hadn't been able to return to her chamber for a quiet nap before dressing for the first of the Duchess of Bainbridge's two balls that week. No, indeed. Her mind was far too preoccupied.

The door closed at her back, enveloping her in silence and the beloved scent of books blending with leather and another scent that her body recognized as the duke's, although he was nowhere within the library's charming confines. She rather liked this room, even if she didn't belong here, and in spite of her inauspicious initiation to it.

"Hello?" she called out as she strode across the luxurious carpet, just to be certain that he was still otherwise engaged with the gentlemen of the gathering.

No one answered.

Alone, then.

"Good," she murmured to herself, going to the wall of spines nearest to her in search of something that piqued her interest. She didn't wish to have another clash with the duke. But she did require some distraction, and what better method than reading? Bainbridge had to possess something here, some volume, worthy of a read. He had stolen the only book she'd brought along with her.

"Latin," she grumbled as she studied the spines before her, finger skating over them one by one.

"You don't know the language?"

The voice, deep and low just over her shoulder and so delicious that it could have been velvet itself drawn over her bare skin, made her finger go still. Where had he been hiding? Of course, that explained the reason why she had smelled him.

She stiffened but refused to turn for fear of his nearness and his capacity to disarm her. "I know it well enough."

"Ah. These works are not prurient enough for your voluptuary tastes, I take it, Lady Boadicea?" His delicious baritone raised gooseflesh on her arms. Was it just her imagination, or had he drawn nearer? Was that the heat of his breath that she felt upon her neck, just below her right ear? And why did the word "voluptuary" uttered in his sinful voice incite tingles in her belly?

"Not nearly enough," she quipped with a frivolity she little felt, wishing that the tomes before her hadn't become a jumbled sea of nothingness. How he unnerved her. The knowledge that she would become betrothed to him tonight did not aid in the matter.

"*Quid tu hic?*" he asked. *Why are you here?* The question, bold and without a hint of artifice, somehow had the opposite effect upon her of what it should have had.

Instead of warning her, chilling her, reminding her that she had once again ventured where she didn't belong, she was riveted to the spot. Intrigued. Keeping her back to him was somehow thrilling. How could his cool arrogance make the heat rise within her? It defied explanation, and yet her response to him was undeniable.

"Why are *you* here?" she returned. "I thought the gentlemen of the assembly were all otherwise engaged. Should you not be off somewhere drinking yourself to oblivion in the name of sport?"

"Undoubtedly yes, and yet here I am, once more discovering an intruder in my library." He paused, and she glared at the stamped spine of the book nearest to her, trying to ignore the unsettling effect of his deep voice. "You didn't answer my question."

"You stole my book from me," she told the wall of books.

"And you thought to find it alongside Ovid?" He sounded amused.

That did it. She spun about to face him, startled to discover that he was nearer than she had even imagined. Her gaze collided with vibrant green. Why did he have to possess such beautiful eyes, the lush, verdant hue of new grass in spring? All she needed to do was lean forward a scant inch, and her mouth would brush against his throat. For some reason, that realization wasn't at all alarming. Indeed, she couldn't help but wonder if he would smell every bit as divine there, in that sensitive and private place where his jaw met his neck.

No, Boadicea. You must not harbor such thoughts.

What had he said? Oh, yes. *The book.*

"I thought you'd burned it," she reminded him, her lips curving with a knowing smile.

His confiscation of her book still nettled her, and she couldn't resist the urge to needle him in turn. Of course he hadn't burned it. Indeed, she'd wager he was reading it just as she'd accused. His flush had said enough.

The flippancy fled from his expression, and he was once more his customary self, all angles and irreproachable lines. He glowered. "Of course I did, but that doesn't mean I don't suspect you of infiltrating my library again with the hopes of proving me wrong."

She pursed her lips, noting that his gaze lowered and clung to her mouth for a beat before raising once more. "Do you think me a fool, Your Grace?"

He appeared to consider her words. "I think you impulsive, obstinate, and improper. But not a fool, I don't believe."

"How gratifying." Her eyes narrowed. Irksome man. "Why should I imagine you would hide my stolen book in plain sight? Or are you truly that lacking in imagination? One does wonder."

His brows snapped together in an eloquent illustration of hauteur. "What else would explain your presence here when you've already been informed you are most unwelcome?"

"Was I meant to think myself unwelcome?" She favored him with her most winsome smile. "I confess, your conduct yesterday left me with a distinctly different impression, Your Grace."

His expression remained impassive. Cold and superior. The vulnerability he'd shown her that morning was nowhere to be found. "You're the most forward bit of baggage I've ever met."

She raised a brow. "Touché, for you're the most insufferable lout I have ever met."

"Indeed." Somehow, he could infuse even a mere word with condescending scorn.

Truly, it made no sense that a man so unyielding could also be capable of kissing her senseless. That a man imbued with such ice was also filled with fire. She found herself staring at his mouth, recalling how those sensual, defined lips had melded perfectly to hers, coaxing and possessing all at once.

She shouldn't wish to kiss him now, particularly when he was being such a beast. Particularly when every scrap of common sense told her to flee from a marriage with him and from Boswell Manor altogether. But somehow, when she imagined kissing him, absconding was the last thing on her mind.

How could she be so drawn to a man she also wanted to clout over the head?

Her fingers busied themselves, twisting in her silken skirts to cool her agitation. Unfortunately, the distraction did little for her peace of mind. "My sister spoke with Her Grace," she said at last, addressing the subject they'd managed to dance around thus far.

"I am aware." His jaw clenched as he clasped his hands behind his back, almost as if he didn't dare trust where they would land if free.

She knew the feeling, and it left her disgruntled. Rather as she imagined a bear might feel upon being rudely stirred from her hibernation. "And?" Her limited store of patience for him ran thin. "Do stop being so loquacious, Your Grace. My ears cannot possibly stand it."

He stared, his gaze as flinty as his tone. "Have you any manners at all, my lady?"

She refused to flinch. "I do have comportment enough to keep me from filching other people's reading material, regardless of whether or not I agree with the subject matter."

"There is disagreeing and there is obscenity, Lady Boadicea." His curt tone mocked her. "You are aware of the laws in place against such filth, surely."

Of course she was. The publisher of the book he'd taken from her had already been sent to gaol for his efforts. But she remained undeterred. Bo was not like other ladies her age, and she never had been. Once upon a time, she had wished she'd been a Lydia Trulle, all golden and lovely, simpering and petite.

Lydia Trulles were always surrounded by admirers. They were perennially thought of as pleasant and lovely. They never dumped ink on the heads of their enemies at finishing school or read wicked books or dared to consider that the world into which they'd been born was meant to be defied and questioned.

But she was no longer a naïf in short skirts, and she'd learned some time ago that being clever was of far more use than being perfect.

It was that reassurance that guided her now as she tilted her head back and considered the handsome, surly duke before her. "Do you mean to see me thrown into the nearest dank prison cell for daring to read the word 'cockstand'?"

The breath hissed from his lungs, and suddenly, his hands clamped on her waist as he thrust her back against the bookshelves. She released her skirts to grip his upper arms, finding purchase after his sudden movement lest she tip to either side and upend herself before him. The knot of braids at her crown met with the resistance of half a dozen leather-bound books.

"Do you have no shame?" he demanded.

Perhaps she had pushed him too far. But if anyone needed pushing, it was the Duke of Bainbridge. "None," she said blithely, gifting him with a serene smile that was all bravado, full stop.

His nostrils flared. Those vibrant, emerald eyes glittered with repressed emotion. "What are you to my brother?"

His question took her by surprise, and landed somewhere in the region of her heart with enough force to rekindle the niggling sense of guilt that had not left her since she'd lost her head with Bainbridge yesterday. She liked Lord Harry. He was handsome in a boyish manner, and quick to laugh but slow to anger. Even in appearance, he was the opposite of the duke, all golden-haired and blue-eyed in contrast to Bainbridge's dark hair, exotic eyes, and beautiful yet severe face.

"Lord Harry is my friend," she said, struggling to explain, for she'd suspected his feelings toward her ran in a deeper, far different vein than hers to him. But she'd been too caught up in wanting someone—anyone—to aid her and Clara with their Lady's Suffrage Society that she hadn't thought to discourage him.

The duke's eyes settled on her mouth. "Have you kissed him?"

The notion filled her with unease. An awkward, unintentional laugh escaped, proof of how discomfited the duke rendered her. "That is hardly any business of yours."

Bainbridge's mouth tightened. "As your future husband, I would disagree."

Future husband.

The words seemed to suspend between them.

Something foreign and warm slid through her, straight to her core where it pulsed like an ache. Only it wasn't an ache, not precisely. Rather, it was a strange feeling. Overwhelming.

She exhaled slowly, rallying her wayward thoughts back into battle formation. "I have yet to agree to marry you, Your Grace."

One of his hands left her waist to slide into the hair at her nape as though finding its home. "Answer the bloody question."

She'd wrung a curse from his perfect lips, and that small victory left her gratified. "No. I have not kissed Lord Harry."

Her answer made him roll his lips together for a moment before he sighed and tilted his head, considering her in that manner of his that was simultaneously thrilling and terrifying. She couldn't tell if he liked what he saw or if he inventoried her like a chemist taking stock of his wares, finding her lacking.

"He fancies himself in love with you," Bainbridge said with cool, calm precision.

As though his tall, lean body wasn't crowding against her. As if his mouth weren't near enough to kiss. As though they discussed a banality such as the new electrical marvels in London rather than their combined futures.

She swallowed. "I am sorry if he feels an emotion which I cannot return. You may think what you like of me, Your Grace, but my sole intention in coming here to Boswell Manor was to win a champion for my cause. Your brother is progressive enough in his views, and his desire to ally himself politically with Thornton seemed the perfect foil."

He stiffened. "You used your wiles upon him, then, intending to manipulate him into doing as you saw fit?"

This was a different sort of *tête-à-tête*. She wasn't certain if he was angry, irate, jealous, or protective. Perhaps all of them at once? Bo blinked. "I daresay no one has ever before accused me of using wiles. It sounds inherently nefarious, almost as if I am some sort of villainess who beguiled your poor brother into spending time in my company. Tell me, is my conversation that boring, my mind so banal, that I could only cozen a man into speaking to me by using *wiles* upon him?"

"Damn you, is there nothing you take seriously?" he snapped, his fingers tunneling deeper into her hair, caressing over her skull with a gentleness that belied his tone and demeanor both.

"I take marriage seriously," she said then, sobering. His warm breath teased over her lips in the precursor to a kiss that her body wanted more than her mind did. She forced herself to focus, to remain impervious. "What manner of husband will you be, Duke?"

He had already been a husband once, and the knowledge settled between them like a boulder, unwanted and hard. Dangerous, even. She didn't like to think of his past, of whatever had happened between him and his dead wife. Had he been responsible? Were the gossips and his mother both right? Another emotion—sharp and stinging—cut into her when she thought of how her predecessor had seemed to break him.

She could recognize it for what it was: jealousy.

How foolish. How selfish. She resented a ghost.

A mocking smile flitted over his sensual mouth before disappearing. Lines grooved the skin bracketing his lips as they firmed into a forbidding frown. "I'm no bloody good at being a husband, Lady Boadicea. Just as I suspect you will be no bloody good at being a wife. All I ask is that you not embarrass me. I'll not be made a cuckold."

Her cheeks heated. Of course he would think her fast, given her freedom of speech and her propensity toward the improper, not to mention his cavalier treatment of her and her shameless inability to resist him. She would not be made to feel ashamed of who she was, however. The Lady Lydia Trulles and Duchess of Cartwrights of the world could still go hang for all she cared. But she rather found herself wishing that the Duke of Bainbridge hadn't judged her. He was too intelligent, she was certain, not to realize that not everyone needed to endorse the same mores.

That different wasn't necessarily a threat. That the act of judging others did not render one better than those being judged, but rather the opposite instead.

"I thank you for your confidence in my ability," she said airily to veil her wounded pride. "If you are to be believed, we can both rest comfortably tonight in the knowledge that neither of us will make a decent helpmate to the other and that we will rue the day we married. I am certain we shall be gloriously happy in our shared misery. Tell me, Your Grace, have you a mistress?"

"That is none of your concern."

"It is if you wish me to marry you." On this, she would draw her battle lines. Lady Boadicea Harrington did not accept hypocrisy in any of its varied forms.

"No," he bit out.

"That would explain a great deal," she muttered, hoping that his reaction to her was not solely borne of his lack of bed chamber romping. After all, she had read a great deal of her brother's naughty books. She liked to think she knew at least a bit about the complicated dealings between man and woman.

"Jesus Christ." He closed his eyes for a moment before opening them once more. "Are you always this way?"

But as he asked the question, his voice so patently irritated, those adroit fingers of his teased her with long, slow strokes through her coif.

"This way?" She leaned into his touch, in spite of herself.

"You're an aberration," he accused, but without bite. "You are the most inappropriate, bold, insulting, insinuating lady I know."

"I will accept your compliment," she told him gravely. "As for the announcement this evening…I have not acquiesced."

He made a sound of impatience deep within his throat. "This, at least, is a road we've traveled before. Do you wish to ruin Thornton and his marchioness?"

He had her there. She searched his handsome face, wishing she could read him, but he remained impenetrable as ever. At last, she gave in. "You know that I do not."

He inclined his head. "Just as I do not wish to expose my family to further ruinous gossip after they've already been forced to endure so much. We are in agreement, then. For the sake of our families, it is in our best interest to announce our betrothal this evening during the course of the ball. We will dance together, act the part of a couple in love, and wait until the thing is well underway and everyone half in their cups before doing so."

"I'm sure it isn't in our best interest." She forced herself to move. Three steps to the right, and she was removed from his touch and the charmed sphere of his heat. She could breathe again. No kisses had occurred. Her sanity, she fervently hoped, was restored. "But I will accept your offer of marriage just the same."

Chapter Eight

SPENCER'S HAND SHOOK AS HE LIFTED a champagne flute to his lips and downed the entire contents of the glass in one swig. He detested balls. He deplored announcements. He bloody well loathed the institution of marriage. He no more wanted to entrap himself within its strangling confines again than to leap from the roof of Boswell Manor. His brother couldn't stand to speak to him. His proper mother was horrified at what he'd done, so much so that she'd burst into tears when he'd sought her out yesterday evening. The unshakable dowager had been inconsolable.

He couldn't blame her. Good God, everything about the events of the last two days left him reeling and ashamed.

And in a perpetual state of arousal. There was the crux of it. He wanted Lady Boadicea in a way that defied logic, for he abhorred her cavalier manner, her insouciance, the bloody bold way she walked into a room crowded with a hundred other guests and drowned out the sight of anyone else.

His eyes lit on her, and he couldn't tear them away. Drinking in her beauty made a strange, heavy sensation settle in his gut. His future wife had dressed for his mother's Welcoming Ball as though she'd gone into mourning, and perhaps indeed she had. Her entire gown was fashioned of silk and lace the same hue as a raven's wing. Its exacting style—emphasizing her narrow waist, clinging to her luscious bosom, and glittering with a lace and jet bead overskirt—would have rendered any other woman wan and severe.

Not Lady Boadicea.

Rather, the black magnified her beauty, providing the perfect contrast to her creamy skin and fiery locks, which had been piled high atop her head in loops, showing her elegant throat to advantage. Three-quarter length sleeves capped her delicately rounded shoulders, leaving her supple upper arms bare. She was vibrant enough not to require any ornamentation at all, whether it be color or gem.

A fringe of small curls kissed the sides of her face, forcing his gaze inevitably to her berry-red lips and that taunting beauty mark hovering at the corner. She was ten paces away and he could still make it out, though whether from memory or acute vision, he couldn't be sure.

He should have kissed her earlier that afternoon in his library, should have taken that soft mouth and owned it until she fed him the honey-sweet sighs that had been driving him mad since he'd first heard them the day before. But he had not, and now here he stood, empty champagne glass in hand, mouth dry, cock straining against his trousers as the most vaunted families of the peerage tittered and conversed around him.

Before he could move across the crush to her, the familiar, lanky form of his brother appeared at her side, standing too near. Harry took her hand, raised it to his lips for a kiss that lingered.

Something within him that he hadn't known existed clanged shut, like a trap manacling an unsuspecting animal's paw. Spencer was dimly aware of a passing servant accepting his flute before he stalked forward. A sea of bustles and trains parted for him. Several pairs of eyes looked at him askance as he jostled his way to Lady Boadicea. He ignored them all. He didn't want this farce of a union any more than she did, but he would not, damn it all, allow his brother to flirt with her just prior to the announcement of their betrothal.

He reached the cozy pair, stopping only when he was shoulder to shoulder with Harry. Her exotic fragrance hit him, and before he could stop himself, he inhaled deeply. Lady Boadicea's forehead crinkled with a pensive frown as her brilliant eyes swept from Harry to Spencer, and then back to Harry again.

Spencer didn't like that order. Not one bloody bit. "Lady Boadicea," he greeted her with a formal bow that would put anyone else's to shame. Halfway mad and hunted by demons that kept him from sleep he may be, but he was the Duke of Bainbridge. Proper form had been beaten into him from the time he was a lad in leading strings. His inner beast was firmly under control tonight.

She extended her hand with flawless formality. "Your Grace."

He accepted it. Was it his imagination, or did her tone contain a hint of censure? He favored her frown with a matching one of his own, unable to resist baiting her even if that made him an unmitigated bastard. "You are looking exceptionally saturnine this evening, my lady."

She stiffened, her grip tightening on his as he raised her fingers to his lips at last for a slow kiss. "I've dressed in proper mourning attire for the loss of my freedom."

"Bloody hell," Harry gritted with such violence that Spencer would not have recognized his voice had not he been standing at his side. The resentment emanating from him was undeniable. "Marry me, Bo. It isn't too late. I don't give a damn about a scandal."

Spencer went stiff, his body feeling as if it were drawn on a rack that would pull from every angle until he'd be torn asunder at last. Deep conflict, even after three years, still had the power to completely unravel him. It was why he had withdrawn from his seat in the House of Lords, why he never went to London, why he no longer spoke to any of his old friends. He had changed, forever. He hadn't died that day with Millicent, but in some ways, he may as well have.

"I cannot, Lord Harry," Lady Boadicea said into the silence he couldn't seem to puncture with words. "I'm so sorry."

Spencer's tongue felt heavy. His pulse pounded. His emotions remained a confused jumble, ricocheting off his chest. And yet, he couldn't speak.

"I'll never forgive you for this, Spencer," Harry growled in his ear.

He wanted to face his brother, but he couldn't.

Lady Boadicea's blue gaze burned into his. He fell into it, needing to focus his mind and stave off the clamor within. She seemed to sense his wildly fluctuating thoughts, for she gave his fingers a reassuring squeeze. "Bainbridge, you look as if you're about to cast up your accounts."

Her grim—though likely apt—pronouncement wrung a startled laugh from him. He released her hand, dispelling the clouds from his mind. How had she known what to say? It seemed almost impossible that this fierce, improper female before him should have only been a part of his life for the span of a day.

He forced himself to look at his brother, who stood ready, like a knight of old, to defend his lady love. "Harry," he said calmly. "Stand down."

Harry sneered at him. "I'm attempting to save the lady from folly."

"It is decided." His tone was flat but firm.

"I'm sorry, Lord Harry." Lady Boadicea's voice was strong and clear, the throaty rasp sending a fresh arrow of lust directly to Spencer's groin against his will. "You are a treasured friend whom I should not like to lose."

Treasured friend. That rather had a dampening effect on

his ardor. His eyes narrowed. The soft expression on her face for Harry nettled him. A sharp, unfamiliar stab of emotion wrenched through his gut. Envy. Bloody hell, what ailed him?

"You're making a scene," he growled at his brother, taking out his vexation on him "For the final time, stand down and let the lady do what she must or risk making this night even worse for her."

Harry gritted his jaw, clearly wishing to argue, but in the end, his common sense won the inner war and he bowed. "My offer stands, Lady Bo. Good evening." With a parting glare at Spencer, he took his leave.

He took note of at least half a dozen guests eying the exchange with curious gazes, and he knew that his brother's ire would have been readily spotted. He could only hope that wagging tongues would put it down to two brothers fighting to win the hand of the same lady rather than what it truly was.

A horrible muck.

Not so far removed from the rest of his thirty-three years.

An ominous sense of foreboding rising in him, he turned to the woman he would marry. How odd that two days ago, she had been nothing more than a lovely menace in danger of luring his brother into an ill-advised alliance. Odder still that the thought of making her his duchess didn't disturb him as much as it ought.

It must be the shock mingling with the suddenness of his downfall. Perhaps the champagne could be added to the blame as well. Regardless, he had but one task this evening, and it wasn't to argue with his brother. Staying the course and making everyone believe he'd lost his head for Lady Boadicea Harrington was.

Where was a servant with more goddamn champagne when he needed it? A surreptitious glance proved nowhere near, and the orchestra was readying a set.

"Dance with me," he demanded of her before she could say anything that would further ruin his mood.

"Duke," she protested, as though he'd asked her to leap a horse over a wall of flames. "I do not care to dance at the moment. Can you not see I am distressed?"

"Bainbridge," he corrected as he slid her arm through his and led her into the throng. They needed to maintain appearances for the evening to unfold with aplomb. "Or Spencer, as you prefer. And I do not give a damn if you don't wish to dance, Lady Boadicea. You will dance and smile at me and call me anything but Duke."

She remained quiet as they took up their positions, her full lips firming into a line of displeasure. Her eyes sparked up at him. "I prefer Duke. Or Your Insufferable Arrogance. The last rather has an agreeable sound to it, does it not? Quite pleasing to the ear."

One of his hands anchored her waist as her hand settled on his lower back, their palms pressed together. Every part of him was keenly aware of the places where their bodies made contact. He looked down at her, trying to make sense of the way she undid him, and caught a heady whiff of jasmine.

Damn her.

"If you wish anyone to believe our charade, you must call me either Bainbridge or Spencer." He refused to take her bait.

The defiant minx raised a brow. "Are you always this way?"

It wasn't lost on him that she'd thrown his earlier words back at him. He clenched his jaw. For some reason, he wanted to hear his Christian name in her throaty voice, needed for her to acknowledge that their circumstances had changed, and not just for the sake of fooling the revelers around them.

He waited as the music began, but she maintained her silence.

Very well. He could play her game. "This way?" he asked in an echo of her.

His future duchess was only too happy to elaborate. "Demanding and pompous."

"Only when in the presence of maddening ladies who trespass in my library with a filthy book and then kiss me in a misguided effort to regain said book." He was careful to keep his voice low, lest anyone else hear, but she had pushed him too far.

Her cheeks flushed. "I daresay it was a horridly flawed plan. You are correct, Duke."

Yes, it had been. But his reaction had been even worse. "If I could take back the incident yesterday, I gladly would. But I cannot. Now smile, my lady, for half the ballroom watches us."

She stiffened beneath his touch, but the smile she gave him dazzled even as he knew it was false. "We must give the ballroom their show, then, must we not?"

His lips stretched with a smile that was equally feigned, for the sight of so many inquisitive stares accompanied by the inevitable whispers affected him. In truth, it affected him far more than it should have, but he realized in that moment that this was the first time since Millicent's death that he'd ever ventured into a dance at a ball. And everyone had noticed while he had not until that precise moment as the orchestra struck up their tune.

He didn't even have time to wallow in the familiar old hell that reminders of his dead wife inevitably produced. The music had begun. He could either freeze and give in to his demons or move. The woman in his arms was vibrant and warm and lovely and infuriating all at once. But she was here, and she would be his.

He moved. He forced the ugliness from his mind. Here, beneath the heat of the old gas lights and crush of guests, with Lady Boadicea, he felt shockingly, brazenly *alive*. Millicent's death and three years of isolation from London had robbed him of the ability to feel. But now, his heart thumped wildly in his chest.

They whirled into a waltz, and he pulled her a bit nearer to his body than was necessary. He'd been half afraid that he wouldn't recall the steps, but with Lady Boadicea in his arms, her beautiful face tilted upward, her sweet scent enveloping him, he did not even falter. One, two, three, one, two, three, and away they went, gliding over the polished floor with such synchronicity that it took his breath.

She was an accomplished dancer. He supposed he should not have been surprised by this discovery—after all, she was the daughter of an earl, even if the Harrington family name was plagued by scandal and eccentricities. She moved with a lissome grace that he couldn't help but admire.

By the time the set almost reached its completion, his smile was no longer forced. He pulled her a scant inch closer on another twirl, setting his mouth near her ear. From this proximity, he discovered that her hair possessed not just glorious hues of red but shots of sun-kissed gold as well. It was utterly transfixing, and he could say in all honesty that he had never even noticed the precise color of any other lady's hair before.

"You are an exceptionally gifted dancer, Lady Boadicea," he said, his voice rough. It was the sort of compliment he may have paid years before, when he'd been innocent and unjaded and had never learned the bitter, abject despairs of failure, guilt, and loss. Something about the evening and the lady and the champagne buzzing through his veins made him want to believe in the fiction they would present tonight.

Indeed, he could almost forget, with the glitter of the lights and the whirling colors, the alluring melody of music. A primitive and foreign urge made him want to snatch her up in his arms and carry her far away from the din of the ballroom where they could be alone and he could press his lips to that delicate patch of silken skin where her jaw met her throat.

"You are a fine dancer as well, Duke," she murmured at last, determined as ever to needle him by refusing to do as he'd asked and call him either by his Christian name or his title.

Her tenacity should have vanquished the rogue feelings simmering within him. He must be in his cups. Had he consumed more champagne than he'd realized? Two flutes, he could recall. That hardly seemed enough to lay a man of his size low or render him witless enough to be charmed by a lady with a dogged need to oppose him at every turn.

The set concluded. He found the Marchioness of Thornton waiting on the periphery and steered them in her direction. "One more dance," he warned Lady Boadicea. "And then the announcement."

Her fingers tensed on the crook of his arm in the only betrayal of emotion she gave, for her profile remained serene and her step didn't falter. "How grim you sound."

"Accepting," he corrected with a smile he little felt. "I want this forced union no more than you do, my lady."

"Of course not," she muttered. "Why should a vaunted Marlow wish to marry an unacceptable Harrington who reads filth? I wonder, do you hate me, Your Grace?"

They were almost within earshot of the lady's sister, so he slowed his steps, as much from shock at her question as from a desire to keep their words private. "The same could be asked of you, Lady Boadicea. Do you hate *me*?"

She stopped, midstride, and faced him, her vibrant blue gaze seeking his. "I hate having no choice."

He thought it must have been the truest statement he'd heard from her yet. "You are not alone in that sentiment. But I've lived more years than you, and I can assure you that life is a deception. None of us, regardless of rank or birth, will ever have a choice in anything."

Her lips compressed. "That is where we differ, Duke. You accept that you have no choice."

Spencer didn't know what the hell to say to that, so he tugged her along toward her sister. "Allow me to return you to the marchioness. Save another dance for me, my lady."

"Yes, Duke."

Her submissive response grated, as he knew it was disingenuous, and it sounded wrong. For all her wayward notions, he found that he actually preferred the way Lady Boadicea spoke to him, like an equal.

"Spencer," he corrected her as they reached the marchioness, whose wide smile didn't reach her eyes.

"Duke," Lady Boadicea said.

He gritted his teeth as he greeted Lady Thornton, who was lovely and kind and an older, gentler version of Lady Boadicea sans the glorious hair. "Lady Thornton."

"Duke," said his betrothed's sister in greeting, her voice and tone so similar to Lady Boadicea's that he would have almost mistaken it.

The sisters exchanged a telling glance. Well, hell. At least he knew where he stood.

Chapter Nine

THE COLD DAWN WIND BATTERED BO'S CHEEKS as the sleek Arabian mare beneath her thundered across a field. The sun—orange and fiery this morning—peeked over the distant horizon, and she and Damask Rose were fast proving kindred spirits. Both a bit on the wild side, with a love of freedom and the need to go as fast as they could possibly go, yes indeed, they were a matched pair.

She had been warned away from Damask Rose by the duke's head groom the day of her arrival when she'd attempted a much-needed ride. And that was why, when she'd been unable to sleep after the wretched ball and even more wretched marriage announcement of last evening, she'd snuck away to the stables, saddled Miss Damask Rose herself, and galloped away.

No one knew she'd gone, and she had no one to answer to. Not the guests with their shocked expressions and curious glances following the betrothal announcement, not the supercilious Duchess of Cartwright or the dowager, and definitely not the icy Duke of Bainbridge himself.

They had danced twice. The second time had been notably more staid than the first, though perhaps it was down to the set itself rather than the duke. She couldn't be certain. But what she did know was that beyond feigning a smile and standing at her side for the obligatory half hour following the Announcement of Doom, the duke had promptly disappeared from the gathering.

Naturally, there had been whispers aplenty. Speculation abounded. Ladies offered her their contrived felicitations before no doubt retreating to the shadows and tittering amongst themselves about the hasty nature of the betrothal.

It had been the most lowering four hours of her entire life, though she refused to admit it to anyone. His withdrawal should not have affected her. She didn't wish to be his duchess any more than he wanted to take on a wife he'd deemed too unsuitable for his brother, let alone his august self. They didn't suit. They'd make each other miserable. She resented him already. Masterful kisses were well and good, but they didn't merit saddling herself to an icy, judgmental husband for the rest of her days.

She had made a grievous mistake, first in going to the duke's private library and then in kissing him and allowing him to take such shocking—if delightful—liberties. She was to blame for her current predicament, and she knew it. Lady Lydia, who had set her cap for Bainbridge if her ceaseless prattle and moon eyes were any indication, was particularly snide in her congratulations.

By grim morning light, Bo wasn't certain how she'd managed to suffer it all. Back in the privacy of her chamber, she'd toed off her painful heels, let down her hair, and allowed herself a thorough session of self-pity after her lady's maid had let out her tight lacing and gone to bed.

The only way she could work out her frustrations now was by soaring over the earth with the magnificent mount beneath her. If nothing else, the Duke of Bainbridge was an excellent connoisseur of horseflesh. He had a stable of pure Arabian stallions and mares that put any other she'd seen before to shame. Not even her father, who was a dedicated lover of horseflesh, possessed such impressive bloodlines. Perhaps after her marriage to the Duke of Disdain, she could at least find solace in the stables at Boswell Manor.

Dear God. Before long, she would be the mistress of this vast, palatial estate. She urged Damask Rose into a faster pace, needing more speed, more wind, more space between her and the duke and his insufferable mother and his equally insufferable guests…

Oh, blast.

Her heart pounded as she raced her mount straight into certain peril. Caught up as she'd been in the tumult of her thoughts, she'd failed to notice that the field dipped into a valley. At the bottom of the valley, a crumbling stone wall bisected the field. But she was galloping too fast, and the wall was too near for her to adjust. Her mind raced in the scant seconds before disaster. If she slowed Damask Rose, she chanced not clearing the wall. If she continued at this pace and jumped her mount, she risked being thrown.

She could not put the beautiful, trusting horse in danger because she'd been too selfish and reckless to mind that she was riding on unfamiliar terrain. Bo had no choice, really. Time was running out anyway.

"Three, two, one," she whispered.

Damask Rose leapt into the air with muscled grace, clearing the wall with ease. Bo knew a moment of pure, unadulterated joy as the height and speed of the jump rushed through her. And then, something happened that had never happened to her before.

She lost control.

Her horse landed. Bo's momentum continued. She lost her seat on the saddle, the violence of the jump jostling her free of the stirrups. At the last moment, she released the reins before she went soaring through the air. Lord in heaven. Everything seemed to move slower for a moment as she twisted her body away from the horse to avoid being trampled.

The landing took her by surprise, hard and bone-jarring. Her teeth gnashed together, her rump taking the brunt of her fall. Pain, sharp and angry, split through her from her bottom upward. She gasped for air, stars swirling in her vision.

"Lady Boadicea!"

Perhaps she had hit her head as well. That was the reason why, in this moment of anguish as she lay on the hard, cool ground, unable to catch her breath, she heard the voice of the Duke of Bainbridge, accompanied by hooves pounding on the earth.

Or she had gone to her reward, which was clearly not heaven as one would have hoped. She'd landed in one of Dante's circles of hell, where she was to be tortured by a contemptuous duke for all eternity. Was it the second circle or was it the eighth? Each seemed likely. She coughed out a groan as her lungs seemed to work at last, once more taking in air.

Hands touched her shoulders. A dark shadow fell over her. A voice again. His. And that familiar, decadent scent of pine and musk and soap.

"Lady Boadicea, speak to me."

She blinked, and he was there, his handsome face hovering over hers. His jaw was rigid, his expression severe. Unless she was addled, she detected concern in his emerald eyes and the frown lines bracketing his sullen mouth. Was it just a puzzling side effect of the fall she'd taken, or was he even more lovely to behold out of doors than he was within them?

If she hadn't gotten there already, the second circle, she decided, was where she was bound. How could she be capable of feeling such wicked warmth deep inside her at his proximity even when she could scarcely breathe? Why did she feel so drawn to a man who was as cold as ice?

He isn't always cold, a depraved voice inside her reminded. No, he was not. And that most decidedly was the trouble, wasn't it?

"Lady Boadicea." He gave her a shake. "Are you hurt?"

Of course she was hurt. Every bone in her body seemed to ache. Her breath was coming in fast, uneven gulps. She didn't think she could manage a coherent word. She stared at him, mute, wondering at the misfortune that should have led him of all people upon her in this moment of supreme ignominy.

His grip on her upper arms tightened, and she realized belatedly that he was on his knees before her. If she hadn't just suffered the horse fall of the century, she would have taken great pleasure in the sight, which seemed to have become a habit of sorts for him. Yes indeed, some perverse part of her rather rallied to the notion of the Duke of Bainbridge as her loyal vassal, even shaken and sore as she was.

The duke, however, was not struck by the same sense of whimsy clouding her fogged mind. His frown was severe enough for a funeral. "Damn it, say something. What in the hell were you doing, riding Damask Rose hell for leather on your own? She's a hellion. You could have been killed, you bloody fool."

"Damask Rose," she forced through a mouth that had gone dry. "Was she injured?"

It was the first lucid thing she could think of to say. Truly, she would hate for her actions to have caused such a beautiful mare to be hurt.

The duke glowered at her. There was no other word for it. "She is fine, cantering in the field ahead, no thanks to your foolishness."

"Go to her," she urged, as much because she wanted the mare to be secured as she wanted to be free of his presence. In her vulnerable state, bruised and shaken, she could not control her emotions, and above all, she did not wish to be weak before this man. "I am fine."

"You are most certainly *not* fine," he gritted, running his hands all over her person in inspection. Across her jaw, the back of her head, down her arms, lower still, riffling through her skirts, and sliding beneath them to find her ankles. "What in the hell were you thinking?"

His fingers probed beneath her boots, sliding against her stockings, seeking the knobby protrusion of her bones. She would have shooed him away, swept her skirts back down, but there was something about the Duke of Bainbridge's touch on her ankles that made her heart leap in a different fashion than being unseated from her horse had.

"I was thinking I longed for an escape." She strove for honesty. "Also, I was not thinking. I did not wish to endanger Damask Rose. She is a beautiful horse, Duke. I greatly admire her."

"You would," he muttered, continuing his inspection of her person. His touch skimmed her calves, searing her through the barrier keeping him from her skin. "She is wild. I instructed the grooms not to allow guests to ride her."

Was it her imagination, or did he linger overly long on his inquiry into the state of her calves? His fingers were long and strong, enveloping the muscled curve of her lower limb, stroking in a way that made her feel flushed despite the cool chill of the early morning.

She met his gaze, doing her best to pretend indifference, for she would not allow him to see that she liked this search. No, indeed. "I prefer wild, Duke. And I never ask for permission. I do as I wish. Life is much better lived in such fashion. Perhaps you should try it."

He made a dismissive sound deep in his throat. He found her knees and lingered. His thumbs traced circles in the sensitive hollows beneath. "Fools do as they wish and suffer the consequences."

Perhaps he had a point there, but she refused to acknowledge it. His examination moved on, beyond her knees to her thighs. What was wrong with her that she longed to open wide, feel him glide his fingers even higher?

She forced herself to think. "You are wrongheaded in that statement, Duke. In truth, fools suffer the consequences for not doing as they wish."

"On this, as in many other matters, we are in disagreement, Lady Boadicea." He worked over her inner thighs. She gasped when his touch grazed the slit of her drawers. "Are you injured?"

No. She was not. Her cheekbones went hot. She fell into his gaze. "Yes," she lied, hoping it would make him remove his touch.

He stilled, his mouth tensing even more. "Where?"

"My pride," she said tartly. "Is that located inside my drawers, Your Grace? I'm sure you would know better than I. You seem to be quite familiar with them."

"Fuck," he ground out, withdrawing his touch and flipping her skirts back down and into place. The delicious rumble of his voice sent a frisson of something unwanted and yet pleasant through her. "Where do you find your impudence, Lady Boadicea?"

She should have been shocked by his curse even though it was the second time in as many days that she'd heard him utter it. She ought to have been offended as a proper lady would be. Definitely she should have recoiled. But Bo had never been the sort of lady who did was she was supposed to do.

"Where do you find yours, Duke?" she asked instead.

He rose to his full, commanding height and held out his hand for her. His expression was tight. "If attempting to ascertain whether or not you'd suffered harm to your person is impudence, I stand guilty as charged."

She ignored his hand and hauled herself to her feet on her own strength. A twinge of pain scored her lower back, but aside from that, it would appear she was none the worse for wear. She wondered then at the odds of him happening across her path when Boswell Manor encompassed thousands of acres.

Suspicion blossomed. "You were following me, weren't you?"

He raised a haughty brow, and she was sure he was the only man in all the world who could smolder with arrogance. "I found myself unable to sleep, and I decided to go for a head-clearing ride. Imagine my surprise when I discovered a Lady Boadicea-shaped figure making off with my prized broodmare."

She shot him a look of disbelief. "You expect me to believe you could discern my identity by my shape alone?"

The thorough glance he swept over her body made heat rise to her cheeks anew. "Yes." He paused, his lips twisting into a half-smile, as though he didn't dare allow himself to find humor in the moment. "There was also the certain knowledge that no other lady present would have the effrontery to steal one of my horses from the stable at dawn."

Her bottom ached, her pride stung, and she felt oddly weak after her fall, and she was still quite put out with him after yesterday's ball. Yet she could not quell the smile that curved her mouth in return. "Touché. One thief recognizes another, I suppose."

He clenched his jaw. "Are you certain you didn't hit your head? It would explain a great deal."

She pinned him with a glare. "Very amusing, Your Insufferable Arrogance, particularly for a man of little humor. I'm so heartened you find entertainment in my brush with death."

The moment the word left her lips, she wished she could call it back. *Death.* It fell between them with the harsh severity of a dropped guillotine. His façade changed, the hint of amusement flirting with his mouth firming instantly into a frown. His handsome countenance hardened back into its customary mask of icy disdain, those vibrant green orbs of his going flat and cold.

He stepped closer to her, gripping her upper arms once more, and lowered his face to sneer into hers. "That was not a brush with death, my lady. That was a fall from a horse caused by your own idiocy. Consider yourself fortunate you did no serious harm to either yourself or the mare."

His derision pricked through her defenses. He was right, of course, but that wasn't her greatest trouble just then. The odd weakness that had held her in its thrall ever since her fall assailed her then with renewed force, and she swayed and lost her balance, falling into his chest.

"I am sorry," she whispered into his coat, for she was, as much for her foolish lack of care in riding Damask Rose as in the thoughtless way she'd forced his mind to return to the demons that still haunted him.

"Bloody hell," he muttered, gathering her up in his arms in the next instant as if she weighed no more than a mewling babe.

She made a sound of protest, clutching his lapels for purchase. "Duke! Put me down at once."

But he was already striding for his mount. "You need to be seen by a physician after that fall. It's possible that you struck your head and you're none the wiser. I wasn't yet over the rise when you were thrown, so I didn't see it for myself."

"My legs are in working order," she protested, "as are my faculties. I insist you release me."

But even as she said the obligatory words, she had to admit that there was something lovely about being suspended in the duke's strong arms. Something alarmingly delightful about being cradled against his broad chest. She turned her nose into the fabric of his coat and gave a discreet sniff.

Ah, there was his rich scent, masculine and earthy. At this proximity, she could discern the shadows of his whiskers stippling his wide jaw. What would it feel like to press her lips there, feel the rasp against her mouth and tongue? Would he taste like a woodland god?

"You'll ride with me back to Boswell Manor, and that is final," he ruined her rampant thoughts by issuing a ducal decree.

She jerked back to look up at him, abandoning her lascivious enjoyment of his strong throat and the oddly alluring ridge of his well-defined Adam's apple. "I'm capable of walking and riding on my own, Duke. I insist that you cease this nonsense."

"Lady Boadicea, you are to be my wife," he snapped, finality in his baritone. "You will ride with me, and upon our return to Boswell Manor you will be seen by my personal physician."

His wife.

Yes, she would be that, and heaven help them both. Mustering up her common sense, she chased away any lingering, foolish fire such a reminder lit in her belly. It was her baser nature that attracted her to him, and she'd read about as much in Bingley's naughty books. Perfectly natural. It couldn't be helped. The best she could hope for was that he would wish to live separate lives once they were wed, which would suit her fine. She could pursue her cause and he could continue to haunt the halls of Boswell Manor, thinking everyone else beneath him.

"I am not yet your wife," she was compelled to argue. "Therefore, you have no jurisdiction over me. I demand that you stop this barbaric treatment of me and put me down forthwith."

A muscle ticked in his jaw, but he continued to stalk through the grass to his mount, eyes fixed to the horizon. "Do shut up, Lady Boadicea."

Well, he certainly did like to use her words against her, didn't he? The fight seemed to drain from her then, dispersed by the shock still coursing through her system and her rapidly pounding pulse, which had yet to slow to its normal pace. What was the harm in letting him win one of their battles, she reasoned as she stole another discreet sniff of his person.

Just the one, for there would most assuredly be many more awaiting them.

Chapter Ten

THERE MUST BE SOMETHING WRONG WITH HIM.
 He was pacing a hole through the carpet of the sitting room outside the duchess's bedchamber as his mother and Lord and Lady Thornton looked on. He didn't give enough of a damn to stop, regardless of how many dark looks of admonishment his mother sent his way and in spite of the quizzical glances Thornton and his marchioness directed toward him.

Dr. Martindale had been within the chamber with Lady Boadicea for—a consult of his pocket watch revealed—thirty-one minutes and forty-nine seconds. Too bloody long by his estimation. Perhaps the frustrating chit had actually done herself grave injury. If she had, he shouldn't care more than the natural human inclination to not wish ill upon another.

Why, then, did his chest feel as if it had been seized in the grip of a giant? Why did his heart pound and his palms go damp? Why could he not stop trekking up one end of the chamber and down the other like a bloody lunatic?

He didn't know. It didn't make sense. He shouldn't be worried about her. He shouldn't care so much that he couldn't think of anything but her, and what the damn doctor would reveal when he at last came through the door.

Lord knew she'd brought upon her fall with her own rash behavior, and she was the sort of female who had never been checked. He could see that she must have been a handful for her parents, who had likely pawned her off on her sister and Thornton to relieve themselves of the Sisyphean task of getting her to behave. She was all brash, unapologetic energy, going about her life like a gale of wind.

And while everything about her drove him to distraction—the inherent wrongness of her, the blatant disrespect for propriety, the vulgar books, the bright dresses, the tongue that couldn't be tamed, the lush figure she didn't bother to hide—yes, while everything about her drove him mad, he had been consumed with fear when he'd cleared the ridge and seen Damask Rose galloping away, rider-less.

That fear had lodged into his chest with the force of an ax blade, and all he'd been able to think about was getting to her. Finding her. Making certain she wasn't dead. In the frenzied moments of his race across the field to where he'd spotted her fallen form, he had wondered what he would do if he found her dead, neck broken. The sudden anguish within him had been choking.

But she wasn't dead. Wasn't even injured, if she was to be believed. Certainly, her rapier wit had not been damaged in the fall. She had flayed him alive with her tongue for the hundredth time in their incredibly abbreviated acquaintance.

"Will you not sit, Bainbridge?" his mother asked yet again in her signature tone that was half disapproval and half rebuke at all times. "You must not overset yourself. Dr. Martindale is seeing to the Harrington chit's wellbeing."

"Her title is Lady Boadicea Harrington," the Marchioness of Thornton said with soft warning. Her flashing blue eyes were not unlike Bo's, though he couldn't think them half as lively.

He turned to stalk back across the sitting room, which had been stripped following Millicent's death and had been redecorated at the sole discretion of his mother. This meant that it was a godawful combination of the gaudy and the severe. There was far too much gilding about, though he took comfort in the fact that the chamber had undergone a complete change. The furniture was old and heavy and looked as if it fit more in the last century than in the current one. His mother's fondness for mid-century oil pastorals was evidenced on every wall, as was her love of stripes.

"Yes, forgive me as I am quite overset by the recent turn of events and my constitution was not a fortified one to begin with," his mother said with obvious insincerity. "Bainbridge, do stop pacing. You're making me seasick."

He ignored her, pacing to the other end of the chamber. It was either move his legs or give in to the demons trying to claw him apart. Something about seeing Lady Boadicea laid low, something about the turbulence of fear within him, had brought everything down upon him. He longed for a drink, but he would not have one.

Not until he knew she was healthy. And perhaps not even then.

"You should not have brought her here to the duchess's apartments," the dowager continued, apparently unimpressed by his refusal to do her bidding. "It is vulgar and improper, Bainbridge. What will our guests think? She is not yet your duchess, and she has no place here."

"For the final time," he gritted, "I carried Lady Boadicea in from the servant's stair so as to attract the least amount of attention. It was either bring her here or carry her the entire way to the west wing where anyone could have seen her and made us both further fodder for gossip."

And in truth, he hadn't truly thought. He had been an automaton, bringing her to where she would be safest. To the place where she would ultimately belong in just a few short weeks' time. If it was odd that he had unerringly carried her to the chambers adjoining his, he didn't wish to dwell on that just now.

"This will bring gossip," his mother predicted with a pinched expression before muttering beneath her breath, "and a *Harrington* girl, of all things. How could you have been so reckless, Bainbridge? After all that this family has endured?"

Dear God. His mother was incapable of comprehending the concept of *sotto voce*. He knew that she didn't just speak of his impetuousness in bringing Lady Boadicea to the duchess' suite but in touching her that first day. And it was simple: he had no explanation. None. Lady Boadicea Harrington wreaked havoc upon his body, mind, and soul.

Lady Thornton, of course, heard every word his mother spoke. She stiffened, her expression hardening with disapproval. "Your Grace, I am a Harrington girl as well, and proud to be so. Your choice of words insults me and my sister both, and I'll not stand for it as she lies in the adjacent chamber, perhaps grievously injured from her fall."

His mother raised a brow. "Indeed. We must all be proud of something, must we not? Even the lowest among us must find something with which to be satisfied. I daresay even the scullery maid can. There cannot be insult in truth, can there? And as for Lady Boadicea's injuries, from what I understand, she brought them on herself by behaving the hoyden."

He gritted his teeth. Where the hell was Martindale? He feared he would need to intervene to keep the Marchioness of Thornton from delivering his mother the slap she so richly deserved.

Who to defend, his mother or his betrothed? Both were in the wrong. One had birthed him. One he didn't know what the devil to do with. Here in this stuffy chamber—interminably small, abominably decorated—he felt as if his clothing had all grown too tight. Particularly his neck cloth. Discord and confrontation tended to affect him that way, making his temples pound, his head swim, and his heart thump, ever since Millicent's death.

But he could not, would not, think of that now. Not in this moment, with worry for Lady Boadicea eating him alive and three sets of eyes watching him as though he may be a candidate for the nearest lunatic asylum. He made his choice in the next instant.

"Mother," he said with care, "you pay Lady Boadicea a grave disservice. Apologize at once for the insult."

His mother stared, brows flying to her hairline, forehead creasing with a series of deep grooves wrought by age and judgmental living. "Your Grace?"

And well she should gawp at him, for he could not honestly recall the last time he had ever opposed her. Perhaps, he thought, he should have been more firm with her. He certainly ought to have made her aware of her place as the dowager. He was the duke, a man grown. She did not rule him. Rather, her future rested in his hands. Why had he never realized as much before this moment?

He met her gaze, hands clasped behind his back, and stopped his pacing so that she could receive the full brunt of his censure. "You will apologize for calling Lady Boadicea a hoyden," he elaborated, even if a part of him could agree with her blistering assessment.

His betrothed was wild and improper, a true hellion, and he little knew how to cope with such inhibition. But cope with it he must, for she was *his* hellion now, and for some odd reason, the thought of her laid low, possibly hurt far worse than her stubborn nature allowed her to realize, left his chest with a searing ache and his gut with a hard knot of worry.

"Bainbridge," his mother exclaimed then, as if he had wounded her.

He drew no quarter, for his mother had overstepped her bounds. While his betrothal to Lady Boadicea had been sudden and forced, and while she was as manageable as a wildfire, she was still the future Duchess of Bainbridge. His wife. *His*, full stop. And for the first time, that knowledge sank into him, imbuing him with a new sense of possessiveness. No one could insult Lady Boadicea now. Not even his mother. "You will apologize, madam."

His mother's nostrils flared, the only sign of her pique. "Forgive me, Duke, Lord Thornton, Lady Thornton. I did not intend to insult Bainbridge's bride."

As apologies went, it was tepid at best. Insincere at worst. But the dowager was saved when the door to the duchess's chamber opened, revealing the bespectacled Dr. Martindale with his shock of fiery red hair, carrying his physician's satchel.

Spencer forgot about his mother's apology. Forgot about everything that wasn't Lady Boadicea. "How is she, Doctor?"

The doctor blinked, but if he was taken aback by the vehemence of a man who was not yet wed to the patient he'd just seen, Dr. Martindale didn't dare reveal it. "Lady Boadicea is fortunate. The fall appears to have rattled her, but will leave her with no permanent damage. Naturally, a fall from a horse at that speed could have resulted in grievous injuries. However, all she requires is some rest, and I daresay she will be right as rain in a few days' time."

Relief hit him like a fist to the gut. He almost doubled over, so tremendous was the force of it. "Thank you, Dr. Martindale."

"Rest is paramount, however, to recovery," the doctor cautioned. "Lady Boadicea ought not to overtax herself, whether by merriment or other means. I understand that you have a great deal of festivities planned, and I urge caution in her participation."

The doctor's vagaries didn't do enough to satisfy Spencer's worries. "Did she strike her head, Doctor?"

Dr. Martindale shook his head. "I was unable to find any evidence, Your Grace. Likewise, her ladyship advised that she did not recall such an impact. In my opinion, Lady Boadicea will recover nicely if forced to indulge my strict orders."

Strict orders. Nothing in the English language sounded less suited to Lady Boadicea Harrington. Spencer grimaced. "Your orders being?"

"Rest above all else." A cautious smile flitted over Dr. Martindale's countenance. "When is the house party at an end?"

"Four days hence," he clipped.

"Ah, yes." The physician stabbed at his spectacles with his index finger, shoving them over the bridge of his nose. "I recommend that her ladyship disengage from the remainder of the house party. Several days of rest will be just the thing for a full recovery. Fortunately, you have the rest of your lives ahead of you, and this temporary withdrawal will be a trifling matter in the grand scheme of all your days."

Days of Lady Boadicea cooped up in her chamber. Or, to be precise, cooped up in the duchess's chamber, the chamber adjoined to his. For he daren't move her now. She was an invalid. Wasn't that true? How could it be anything but proper to place her where she belonged? Spencer's mouth went dry. Dear God. He would secure himself another chamber. At once.

"Thank you, Dr. Martindale." He took a deep inhalation in an attempt to corral his thoughts. "Your expertise is most appreciated."

The doctor took his bow and left.

Spencer looked to his mother, his mind already made. He was sick to death of all attempts to make merry. He wanted quiet. Fewer eyes and ears that did not belong within the walls of Boswell Manor. "We will cancel the remainder of the house party. See that the guests are notified and transportation arranged wherever necessary. Lord and Lady Thornton, naturally, will remain on with Lady Boadicea."

Twin flags of outrage appeared on his mother's faded cheeks. "We will do no such thing. The Marlow family has never failed to host this house party. Not in decades, Bainbridge. I refuse to countenance such an outrage, and all because some silly miss went off in flagrant disregard of your authority and had herself thrown from a horse."

In that moment, he rather wished it had been the dowager who had been tossed from Damask Rose instead of Lady Boadicea. He compressed his mouth into a flat, uncompromising line. "You go too far, madam," he warned her.

"How dare you?" In her dudgeon, she didn't bother to hide her affront for the benefit of their audience. "Have you not already done enough to hurt this family? You are a disgrace to the Marlow line."

Yes, he was, wasn't he? For thirty-three years, he'd attempted to do everything right. He had married the young lady of his father's choosing in an effort to beget the perfect heir. He had lived a life of staid propriety. He had learned the business of making an estate as large and lavish as Boswell Manor profitable. He had buried himself in the price of wheat and the planting of fields and the dairying of cows. He had devoted his life to being the best Duke of Bainbridge he could be.

And what had his efforts gained him? A mad wife who'd killed herself before him, a son in the grave, the resentment of his mother and brother both, and a betrothed who was most certainly everything he did *not* seek in a bride.

"I've heard enough," he snapped at his mother, drawing the line at allowing her to emasculate him before the Marquis and Marchioness of Bloody Thornton. "You will leave this chamber and you will do as I say, or I shall have you removed to Marchmont Hall."

His mother blanched. Marchmont Hall—a crumbling affair from the Plantagenet era—was drafty, dank, overrun by mice, and it smelled like nothing so much as a sheep farmer's worn old boot, manure and all. "You would not be so cruel."

Spencer didn't say anything, merely returned her stare.

She straightened her spine. "I will do as you wish, Duke." With a departing, insincere pleasantry for Lord and

Lady Thornton and an agitated twitch of her skirts, she was gone from the chamber.

He turned to the marquis and his wife, who had watched the ugly exchange with his mother unfold with guarded expressions. "I apologize on the duchess's behalf. I fear her…agitation has left her overwrought."

"A kind way of saying she's as subtle as a bear," Thornton said with a commiserating nod. "My own mother suffers from a similar affliction. I can empathize, Bainbridge."

Lady Thornton gave him a tight smile of sympathy but said nothing. If she was anything at all like her sister, she was likely biting her tongue to keep from airing her opinion. Lady Boadicea, however, would not have even bothered to keep a bloody word to herself.

Thoughts of that particular flame-haired siren had him pacing toward the closed chamber door keeping her from him, intent. He didn't give two goddamns whether it was proper for him to enter the duchess's chamber while she was within. He needed to see her. And he didn't wish to examine why his need was such a pressing concern. It simply was.

"Your Grace, I do not think a personal audience with my sister a wise course of action just now," Lady Thornton called to him.

He stilled, his hand on the knob, and looked back at her. "Nothing that I've done in the last three days has been wise, my lady. I dare not break form by acting with reason now. But by all means, feel free to accompany me within."

"Leave the door ajar," she relented, frowning. "We will allow the two of you a moment of privacy."

He nodded, and in the next breath, he crossed the threshold into a chamber he had not entered in years. It should have taken his breath, filled him with the soul-clenching anxiety he had come to know whenever he was reminded of his wife's death. Instead, his gaze lit on the still form on the bed, and all he could think about was *her*.

Lady Boadicea Harrington, who was rather too still and too small-looking and far too pale in the big, canopied high tester for his liking. He crossed the rug, grateful for his mother's managing nature, which had led her to strip every last remnant of Millicent from the room. The wallcoverings, the paintings, the drapes, even the bed itself, were different. It smelled different too, like a room that needed to be aired out more often, and sweet, like jasmine and lily of the valley.

"Duke," she greeted him at the same time as her scent.

"How are you, Lady Boadicea?" A gruffness he could not like had entered his voice. His pulse leapt as he awaited her answer, and the ever-growing dread in his gut made itself especially known.

"Rather as if I've fallen from a horse at breakneck speed." Her wit, at least, continued to remain intact. She attempted a smile, but winced as she shifted herself in the bed.

"Let me assist you." His hands went to her arms without thought as he tried to help her achieve a more comfortable position.

It was a grave miscalculation on his part, for she'd changed into a loose nightdress to aid in the doctor's examination, which meant that only a fine layer of fabric separated her skin from his. The heat of her, the supple curves of her arms, burned into his palms. Devil take it, he grew more depraved by the day, finding the mere grasping of a lady's limbs arousing whilst she was in her sickbed.

"You need not aid me," she protested. "I am fully capable of tending to myself. And you ought not to have brought me here. I'm sure it will be remarked upon and present even further fodder for gossipmongers. I would like to return to my chamber at once."

She was right about that. He should have had a care before bringing her to the duchess's chamber. But he'd been half out of his mind with worry, and the only place he could conceive of bringing her was the place that was nearest in proximity to himself. That was a rather sobering realization to make as he stood there with his hands still upon the betrothed he didn't want, breathing in her sweet fragrance as though it was as essential to him as air. Odder still was the fact that in that moment, he could swear that it was.

There was nowhere else he would rather be. No one else he would rather touch. No other lady could so vex him and yet so render him incapable of resisting her. She was wrong. And right.

Astounding.

He blinked. Nothing made sense, but the coil of fear inside him unwound itself and dissipated beneath her bright-blue regard. He counted at least a dozen freckles charming the bridge of her nose. Where else did she have them? When she was his, he would strip her bare and investigate every lush curve of creamy flesh with his lips and tongue, seeking to find each golden fleck.

Perhaps he was the one who had suffered a fall. Or at the least a sharp blow to the head. That was the only explanation for such absurdity.

"Bainbridge, are you well? You've gone pale all of a sudden." Lady Boadicea's voice lacked its customary sting. She sounded almost…concerned. For him.

Even more astounding.

"You are remaining in this chamber," he ordered, still unable to remove his hands from her person. Instead, he moved them in a slow, upward caress, over her rounded shoulders. "Dr. Martindale insists you are to have rest, and rest you shall have."

A vee furrowed her smooth brow, but did nothing to detract from the lovely picture she presented in her white nightdress, her hair loosened and trailing down her back in arresting contrast. "I can rest in my assigned chamber, Duke. If you will only see that my lady's maid is sent to me, I will change and be on my way. I shouldn't prefer to wander about the halls in my nighttime attire."

"No." His thumbs traveled the enticing ridge of her collarbone, and he wished it was her soft skin he touched rather than uninspiring cloth. He could not ever recall being so entranced by a lady's clavicle. And why did her uttering of the phrase *nighttime attire* make his mouth go dry again? "You will remain here, where you belong."

As he said it, he realized the truth of the statement. Soon, she would be his wife. This chamber would be hers. If it would satisfy propriety, he would marry her tomorrow and have done with it. There was nowhere else he wished her to be.

Except perhaps in his bed. Beneath him. Or astride him. His cock went painfully hard, which was the devil of a thing to occur when Lady Boadicea was a bloody invalid and they had yet to wed.

"I do not belong here," she argued, "in the chamber that belonged to your wife. I am sure there must be painful memories—"

"There are none," he interrupted, irritated by the undertone of sympathy in her voice. "The room has been furnished anew, according to my mother's tastes."

Lady Boadicea wrinkled her nose. "She appears to have an unmerited affinity for all shades of yellow."

He was grateful that she had not mentioned Millicent further. He had no wish to speak about her with anyone, and least of all his new betrothed.

His lips twitched at her insouciance, and he almost allowed himself to laugh before stifling it and removing his hands from her lest he grow any more deranged. Perhaps she was making him mad via osmosis. "It is a cheerful color. Like the sun."

"If you stare at it, you shall go blind," she said. "Also like the sun. Truly, Duke, we must have a dialogue about your drawing room. There is the matter of that salon as well. It's rather akin to a venture into an old thicket, quite depressing."

He gazed at her, thinking how odd it was that she had repeated his own thoughts, nearly verbatim. One long curl had fallen free from her loosely gathered hair, trailing over her cheek. He fought and lost the urge to tuck it behind her ear. His fingers lingered there on the silken shell, and a strange sensation seized him.

He withdrew his hand and straightened to his full height. Good God, what was the matter with him? "I am glad that your rapier wit has not been diminished by the fall you suffered. Have your rest, now."

An expression of displeasure flitted across her fine features, but despite her fiery nature, he could see signs that the incident had rattled her. She remained pale, her vibrant sky-blue gaze seemingly tired, those lush lips drawn into a thin line. "I do not like rest, Duke."

"Of that I have little doubt, princess."

Chapter Eleven

BO TOOK DINNER IN HER CHAMBER. Well, to be precise, she took it in the *duchess's* chamber, which was not currently hers but which—by actions rooted in her own foolishness—would be soon enough. Staring at it now from her perch on a horridly uncomfortable hard-backed chair, she couldn't help but feel dazed by the realization that this unfamiliar room with its hodgepodge of excessive color and gilding would be where she slept whenever in residence at Boswell Manor.

That thought in particular gave her singular pause, for suddenly, ensconced in the duchess's chamber, the ramifications of the last few days seemed real for the first time. She was marrying the Duke of Bainbridge, a stranger with a dark past she couldn't begin to fathom, who looked down his haughty nose at her and yet touched her with such tender care that it took her breath.

What manner of man was he? Moreover, what sort of husband would he make? If Bo were to judge from his past, reason told her she ought to be worried indeed. Perhaps, she ought to even be overseeing the packing of her cases and her removal to the opposite end of the hemisphere.

A knock sounded at the door then. "Bo? It's Cleo. May I come in?"

"Of course," she called out.

She'd mustered the energy to battle the pain savaging her entire skeleton long enough to move from the bed to an escritoire from the last century. She was still wearing a *robe de chambre* belted over a nightdress, but one hardly stood on ceremony with one's beloved eldest sister. Cleo had checked on her after the duke's visit, and again three times thereafter, clucking over her in concerned, mother hen fashion.

Cleo swept into the chamber, regal and elegant, her raven hair plaited in braided coils with a few wispy curls framing her face. She wore an evening gown of navy and aubergine silk, and she was lovely as ever, even with concern pinching her expression.

She swished across the carpet, arms outstretched. "Darling, you're out of bed. What can you be thinking? The doctor said you must rest."

"I could not remain in that bed for another moment more." She tried to suppress the frown tightening her lips and failed.

Though Bainbridge had suggested his mother had been responsible for stripping the chamber of all remnants of his mad duchess, she still wondered whether or not that thorough redecorating included the bed itself. Exhausted, she had fallen asleep for most of the afternoon, but when she'd finally risen from the cocoon of slumber, she'd been plagued by the notion that Bainbridge had lain in that bed with his dead wife.

It had rattled her. An unworthy surge of jealousy had accompanied the unwanted thoughts, until she'd had no choice but to leave the bed behind in favor of the godawful chair.

"But dearest, how can you be comfortable in such an old-fashioned, ungainly beast of a chair?" Cleo demanded, taking Bo's hands up and giving them a loving squeeze. "Why, you look positively miserable. What can you be thinking, torturing yourself so?"

Bo inhaled, pressed her lips together, looked at the bed with its garish drapery of yellow satin and golden tassels. "I dislike the bed."

Her sister's eyebrows rose. "Oh," she said with feeling.

Bo scowled. "Do not look at me in that manner."

"In what manner?" Cleo blinked and pursed her lips, keeping her expression carefully bland.

"As if you pity me." Her head, previously calmed of its day-long thumping, took up the megrims with renewed persistence. Yet another fault she could lay at Bainbridge's door. "I cannot bear another drop of pity, Cleopatra. I've endured enough of it to make me have a headache even greater than all the abominable shades of yellow in this chamber and a fall from a horse combined."

"Why should I pity you, other than that you've obviously done yourself harm in your ill-advised race on Bainbridge's prized mount?" Cleo's tone was tart. "If it seems as if you're developing tender feelings for the duke, I would never dare to comment upon it."

"Tender feelings," she all but spat, as though the phrase left a bitter taste in her mouth. As if it was the last thing she would be induced to feel for the Duke of Bainbridge. Because it was, of course. She didn't even like the man. Why, he had mockingly referred to her as *princess* before quitting the chamber earlier, and she hadn't forgotten, even if the husky quality of his voice had settled somewhere in the vicinity of her core. "I am not developing anything for the Duke of Bainbridge, save for a hearty amount of dislike. The man is arrogant and haughty and overbearing, and if I hadn't kissed him in the name of restoring my book to me, I should never even have noticed his existence."

That was a horrid lie, of course. How could anyone fail to notice a man of his stature, so tall and lean and brooding and handsome? The Duke of Bainbridge didn't grace a room with his presence. He owned it with his dark, smoldering elegance. She could not look upon him without wanting to throw her arms around his neck and yank his sinfully knowing mouth down upon hers.

No. That was her addled mind playing tricks upon her. For there was no earthly way she was so drawn to the Duke of Disdain after three days, a few kisses, and a disproportionate quantity of insults.

"Of course not." Her sister's placating tone was not lost upon her. Cleo gave her a knowing look as she released Bo's hands after one final, tender squeeze. "I am so grateful you didn't break your foolish neck on that horse this morning. Promise me you will not be so reckless in the future, if for no other reason than that I cannot bear to face our family if anything ill befalls you whilst you're in my charge."

It was Bo's turn to raise a brow. "Anything worse than being trapped into marrying the Duke of Bainbridge, do you mean?"

"Surely there are worse fates." Cleo studied her in that searching way she had, seeing far more than Bo wanted her to see, no doubt, as sisters did. "For all that he is a cold man with a troubled past, he remains a duke, from one of the finest families. And while he did compromise you, his every action since has been one of honor. He offered for you immediately, and following your fall this morning he brought you to the chamber that would provide you greatest comfort."

Bo rolled her eyes heavenward. "A virtual paragon. I'm sure Lady Lydia Trollop continued to slaver all over him at dinner tonight, in spite of the betrothal announcement. I would also wager that he did not discourage her. He has been inordinately kind to her, smiling and listening to her nonsensical chatter. Everyone knows she hasn't the brain God gave a chicken, but to hear Bainbridge, you would suppose her the next Socrates."

Cleo frowned. "Oh dear, did I not tell you?"

"Tell me what?" Bo's mind whirled. If that insipid chit had thrown herself at Bainbridge, she would hunt her down this hour and let her know the lay of the land. Like it or not, want it or not, the Duke of Disdain was hers. No one else's. And in the words she'd learned in one of the bawdy books she'd pilfered from her brother, Lady Lydia could sod off.

"Lady Lydia is gone, Bo," her sister said, dispersing Bo's unkind thoughts. "Bainbridge sent everyone home today. He was determined that you would get the rest the doctor said you require for your recovery."

Cleo's words sank into her mind slowly, almost as if they had been spoken in a language she didn't know. "He sent everyone home? On my account?"

"Yes." Her sister paused, seemingly weighing what she wanted to say next before sighing. "I know you are not pleased at this match, Bo, but Bainbridge seemed concerned for your welfare this morning. He quite put the dowager in her place, and that was no easy feat. He has even moved from his ducal apartments to another wing of the house to preserve your reputation."

He had given up his bed.

For her.

Comprehension stole into her mind then. She had taken his prized broodmare without his consent, ridden her hell for leather across his lands, putting the mount at risk of injury or worse. Yet when Bo had been thrown thanks to her own foolishness, he had gathered her up in his arms and carried her as if she were fashioned of the most precious Sèvres. He had taken her back to Boswell Manor, called for his doctor, brought her to the best chamber in the entire edifice. He had inquired after her welfare, had been alarmingly unlike her impression of himself—concerned and almost warm. And he had dispersed his house party and taken new rooms, all on her account.

But he had also called her princess, and he had bowed when he'd left, and his face had been wrought from the same impassible lines as always. Had he made these moves for the sake of propriety, in an effort to salvage his already tottering respectability? Or did he actually…care?

She didn't know. What she did know about anything, anyway? Precious little, it seemed.

"I cannot remain in this chamber, Cleo," she announced then. And she meant it, wholeheartedly. "I cannot abide by it. I refuse to spend the night here."

Cleo made a sound of exasperation. "It is the best-appointed chamber in all Boswell Manor. I should consider myself fortunate to stay here."

"You are staying in a lovely, sunlit bedroom that overlooks the beautiful gardens, with the man you love at your side," Bo pointed out. "Forgive me if I think that trumps being assigned to the chamber of a dead woman, with said chamber being rife with the stylings of a lady who was born before our queen took the throne. A lady, who I might add, holds me in contempt and wishes she had never allowed my unwanted presence to grace the hallowed halls of her home."

"Thornton's mother continues to disapprove of me on a daily basis." Her sister's smile commiserated. "Neither time, nor love, nor heirs have seemed to disabuse her of the notion that I did not deserve to marry her darling son. Sometimes, the mothers of the men we marry are beasts, and sometimes they are angels."

How fortunate for Bo's sake that the dowager Duchess of Bainbridge fell into the former category rather than the latter. "It stands to reason that only a beast could have spawned the beast I am about to marry."

"He did not seem so beastly today," Cleo chided.

"That is because you are madly in love with Thornton and it has addled your mind," Bo grumbled. "As your sister, I insist you must take up the cudgel for me. You are not, under any circumstances, to consider the Duke of Disdain anything less than Beelzebub himself."

"Pray keep your heart open, sister darling." Cleo's gaze probed hers. "I know that this match is not what you hoped for—"

"I did not hope for a match at all," she interrupted, indignant. "Do not dare to condescend to me, Cleopatra, or you may leave. Don't let the door hit you in the bum on your way out."

"Always so prickly, little sister. Why, one wonders?" A clever smile curved Cleo's mouth upward. "What was it Shakespeare said? 'The lady doth protest too much, methinks'."

Such a wit, the Marchioness of Thornton.

Bo pinned Cleo with her frostiest look. "You are wrong. It was Queen Gertrude who said it, not Shakespeare himself. And if you insist on bedeviling me, you may proceed to your own chamber and leave me to my misery."

"Very well." Cleo leaned forward and bussed her cheeks with airy kisses, and her perfume, as ethereal as the rest of her, enveloped Bo in a cloud. "I daresay I am relieved that you are once more back to your prickly self. You were so pale and listless when Bainbridge first brought you back. I took one look at you, all limp and white in his arms, and swore for a moment that you were dead. If you ever indulge in such recklessness again, I shall be forced to box your ears."

Her sister was not jesting about such a threat. Bo took one look at Cleo's hardened jaw and knew that she'd meant every word. It would not be the first time one of her sisters had boxed her ears. Once, she had slathered treacle beneath her sister Tia's pillow. When Tia had rushed from her chamber, she'd been met with a cup of ice water over the head that Bo had carefully rigged to drop at just the right moment.

She grinned at the memory. "My ears have already been soundly boxed on numerous occasions. You do not alarm me with such coercions."

Cleo sighed and straightened. Even in her irritation, she was lovely, in the manner of all Harrington girls except Bo herself. Bo wished that she could hold a candle to her sisters, but she did not dare fool herself. Next to them, she had always felt as if she were an old sack being compared to a Worth evening gown.

Her sisters were light or dark, golden or raven-haired, and only Bo had been cursed with her full mane of curly auburn hair that never wanted to be coaxed into the proper styles. Not to mention her freckles. And her height was another matter.

"I want you to be happy, Boadicea," Cleo said then, interrupting her grim musings. "You deserve to be so, and now that you have chosen your course, you must give the duke a chance. The man I glimpsed today is not as cold or as insufferable as you think."

She did not want to hear her sister's words, which the rational portion of her brain acknowledged could be true. For she did not like to think of the Duke of Disdain as a man who was kind or compassionate or concerned for her wellbeing. She preferred to think of him as an icy, pompous statue of a man. She didn't like to think of the glimpses she'd seen of a man in torment, struggling with a dark past he couldn't reconcile with his present.

No.

Because if she thought of the way he had kissed her with enough fiery passion to turn her body into flame, or the way he had taken her into his arms so effortlessly that morning, or even the stark pain in his expression when he'd spoken of his wife's death, her guarded heart would weaken for him. If she imagined his woodsy scent, thought about him leaving his bed and sending a hundred merrymakers home so that she could rest, if she recalled the way he had touched her, running his long fingers over her collarbone in worship, she would melt.

Princess.

The mere recollection of his deep, velvety voice calling her what should have been an insult but what somehow, in retrospect, seemed to almost be a term of endearment, derailed her. She should have been insulted. Should have corrected him, reprimanded him for his cheek. It mattered not that he was a duke. He was high-handed and superculious, and so handsome that whenever she looked upon him, an ache blossomed deep within her, radiating through her body like a lover's caress.

You will remain here, where you belong, he had ordered her. And she had remained, as if obeying him. What had she been thinking? Why were the walls of the chamber so dratted yellow? Her head began to pound once more beneath the pressure of her whirling contemplations.

Dear heavens, the fall had rattled her mind. Cleo's nonsensical belief in tender emotions—a symptom of her fierce love match with Thornton—was infecting her, making her weak.

"I will be happy when I am allowed the vote," she announced, cutting through the fog of nonsense invading her brain. Yet another sin to cast upon the Duke of Disdain. Her distraction was his fault. Indeed, he was also likely the reason she'd lost her mount and currently felt as if the devil's own blacksmith had hammered upon her spine. "I do not seek happiness in a forced marriage brought about by one regretful instant of lost inhibition. I know that you love Thornton, but do not fool yourself that the union between myself and Bainbridge will be anything like yours. I don't like him, and he doesn't like me."

Cleo pursed her lips. "You liked each other well enough."

Bo's cheeks went hot. Curse her pale skin and fiery hair. She could not fend off a blush to save her life. "He excels at kissing. I won't lie. And he is so handsome it irks me. But by and large, when he opens his mouth, I long to close it again by force."

By force of her lips upon his.

Oh dear. From where had that errant thought emerged? Never mind—she dispelled it as if it were a troublesome fly. *Shoo. Be gone.* No more thoughts of kissing the Duke of Disdain. Even if she did suddenly remember how hard and hot and large he had been, beneath his trousers, against her palm. Bo's mouth went dry.

Sweet God.

"Hmm." Her sister seemed unconvinced. "We shall see. For the nonce, I recommend you get yourself back to bed. The doctor was firm on his orders, and you took a great fall. You cannot afford to be stubborn about the bed in which you find yourself. For one reason or another, you are here. Make the best of it."

Bo's brow furrowed. She had the distinct impression her elder sister was not just speaking of the duchess's chamber or even the bed. But about something larger, and far more important. Something she did not wish to contemplate.

She flashed Cleo a brief smile. "Yes, some rest will do me in good stead, I think. You as well. Thank you for checking in on me, Cleo."

"Of course." Her sister leaned down, pressing a kiss to the crown of Bo's head. "I love you, you know. Even if you are a rapscallion in skirts."

Bo shot up in her seat. "Who called me that?"

Cleo bit her lip. "Oh dear. I do believe it may have been our sister, Helen. Good night, my love."

And then she was gone.

Chapter Twelve

OF COURSE, HE COULDN'T BLOODY WELL SLEEP.

Spencer paced down the hall of the east wing, skulking through the dark without benefit of light. He didn't require illumination. He knew where he was and where he was going, but the quiet calm of the darkness mollified him, if only slightly. He liked being alone. Preferred it actually. It was the only time he could be himself.

Ironically, it was also the only time he could forget who and what he was.

Well, that and whenever he had Lady Boadicea Harrington's lips crushed beneath his. But he did not wish to think of her now, in this moment of blissful solitude. And so he drove all meditations on fiery curls, freckles, beauty marks, feisty ladies who didn't listen to reason, and the scent of jasmine and lily of the valley from his mind.

For the first time in years, he had taken a chamber other than the duke's apartments at Boswell Manor. The chamber wasn't at fault for his restlessness. The bed was firm, bedclothes laundered and soft. The room itself—known as the emerald bedchamber—was done in shades of green, which he did not find quite as offensive as the salon. Though perhaps Lady Boadicea did have a point about his mother's penchant for ostentatious color. It seemed at odds with her ordered, repressive personality.

He had never thought his mother's stylings at Boswell Manor garish or *de trop*. But now, he did. Lady Boadicea could change wall and window coverings as she pleased when she became the Duchess of Bainbridge, and he wouldn't mind.

The notion of her as his duchess seemed at once foreign and not as alarming as it should be. An odd sensation skittered through him, as though the warmth of the sun blazed into his skin. He felt alive and rejuvenated and yet also…peaceful.

This would not do.

The woman was invading his mind, ruining his pleasant seclusion, making him feel things he had no longer believed himself capable of feeling. Unless—yes, that had to be it. *Lust* was the true cause of it all, not Lady Boadicea herself. Clearly, he had been wrong in his belief that he could abstain from congress with a woman and not suffer for it. The use of his hand alone was not sufficient to make him impervious to temptation. Or to losing his bloody mind.

Naturally, he silenced the stubborn voice that rose in his head to remind him that no other lady before or since Millicent had ever had such a profound effect on him. Quite. He told it to go straight to the devil and never come back.

The alluring scent of jasmine hit him three seconds before she ran smack into his chest. He caught her to him, absorbing the impact of the collision without even taking a step back.

"Please tell me that isn't you, Duke." The husky voice that never failed to settle as an ache in his groin interrupted the stillness.

His hands spanned her waist, feeling for the first time nothing but soft, rounded woman beneath his touch rather than the staid line of a corset. The ache grew in size and magnitude until his cock twitched. Damn. He lowered his head before he could stop himself and ran his cheek over the silken cascade of her hair.

Lady Boadicea Harrington was sleek, yielding, and warm. Everywhere. He took a discreet inhalation, savoring that sweet, floral musk once more. He would never again, for as long as he lived a day on God's earth, be able to smell lilies of the valley without getting a cockstand.

One of her filthy little words had invaded his brain.

What was it she had said? *Do you mean to see me thrown into the nearest dank prison cell for daring to read the word "cockstand"?* Such smut. The woman was a menace. She had trespassed in his library, kissed him, defied him at every turn, stolen his horse and almost broken her foolish neck, and now she was sulking about in darkened hallways in search of Christ knew what.

"What the devil are you doing about at this time of night?" he demanded, irritated by her lack of common sense yet again. It rather seemed to be an ongoing affair.

Did she not have a care for herself? She had taken a bad fall, and the doctor had prescribed rest. Sitting still. Slumber. Remaining abed. Spencer had given her the best goddamn chamber in the manor, and yet here she was, clad in only a *robe de chambre* with nothing more substantial than a nightdress beneath, smelling so sweet that he wanted to lick her from that saucy beauty mark down to her dainty toes.

"I could not sleep." Her hands, which had fluttered to his chest in their crash, moved slowly, as if she put a great deal of effort into studying the firmness of his flesh, the delineation of each honed muscle. She stilled as he took another deep breath of her scent. "Are you sniffing me, Duke?"

He winced at her incredulity and straightened to his superior height. Thank God for the darkness. His cheekbones went hot. "Of course not, Lady Boadicea. Why would I do such a ridiculous thing?"

Her caresses resumed, leisurely. Torturous. He wanted to push her out of reach and send her back to her chamber, yet he never wanted her to stop touching him.

"I pondered the selfsame question." Her physical inquisition continued, traveling down his abdomen, her clever fingers undoing him. "And yet you inhaled, just as one might if a particularly aromatic dish had been laid before him. The sort of dish one could not wait to consume."

Bloody fucking hell. Those low, wicked words sent a fresh bolt of heat to his cock. His dressing gown rendered it deuced difficult to hide the effect she had upon him. He was erect, pressing into her belly, and it was too late to push her away.

Anger swirled within him then, and he welcomed it, needing to banish this dangerous careen of desire. "Do you think to goad me with more of your bawdy references, princess? Or perhaps you really do want me to consume you, like an aromatic dish. Is that it?" He led her backward, not stopping until he had pinned her against the wall with his much larger body. "Should I consume you here? Now? What did you read in your book that stirs you most? Do you want my tongue on you? In you? Say it, Lady Boadicea."

"I did not intentionally collide with you in this hall, for it is dark and I've an abysmal sense of direction." She leaned into him, and she had to have rocked on her toes, for her hot breath stole over his mouth in a maddening impression of a kiss. "But how you do intrigue, Duke. Continue. Where were you? Ah, yes. Your tongue, I believe."

Did her wickedness know no bounds? Did she have no shame? He didn't know whether to kiss her or throw her over his shoulder and deliver her back to the duchess's chamber where he'd last left her. He had intended to shock her with his vulgarity, but instead she sidestepped him and leveraged his words against him. For hearing her refer to his tongue made him want to wield it. To take her mouth, lick into the satin depths, to do far more wicked things elsewhere.

"You are impertinent." He steeled himself against the lush enticement of her form and innuendos. For an innocent, she possessed a shocking imagination and vocabulary.

Of course, there was the possibility that she wasn't, in fact, an innocent at all. It would explain a great deal. However, he felt certain that her boldness had its roots in her personality and not in her depth of experience. Either way, he supposed he would discover the truth soon enough when they were man and wife.

"You are large," she pronounced.

He sucked in a breath at her shocking statement. His shaft was pressed against her. Of course she would have felt it. But remarking upon it…

"Tall," she added, sounding smug. "An insufferable oaf. Do you mean to keep me trapped against this wall all evening, Duke, or will you take pity and let me free?"

Spencer blinked. The minx was forever three steps ahead of him. It vexed him that she could have taken a severe tumble from a horse and yet turn up in the midst of the night with her sauciness and still make him want her. "That depends."

"Upon?" Her hands were somehow once more upon him, studying him, sweeping over his abdomen and lower still.

"Jesus," the sibilant whisper tore from him. Those small, elegant fingers—suited to playing over the keys of a piano— were a scant inch from his engorged prick. He caught her wrist in a firm grip, keeping her from the sort of foolishness that could only end with her nightdress around her waist and him deep inside her. It had been far too long for him, and she was far too tempting. If she touched his cock a second time, he did not trust what he would do. "Return to your chamber, princess."

"I was attempting to do so," she informed him, her tone lofty, "when you accosted me."

"You threw yourself into my chest," he corrected, but he somehow could not find it within him to release her wrist and step away from her. Her heat seeped into him, welcome and intoxicating. How perfectly her body fit to his, the supple curves melding to his hardness. There were a hundred other occupations he could be about at the moment—sleeping, reading, poring over the newspapers or his estate ledgers and correspondence, even drinking whisky—and yet he could not think of anything he longed to do more. He wished to remain where he was, memorizing the feeling of Lady Boadicea Harrington in the dark while she said wicked things and her scent settled about him like an opium cloud, sweet and intoxicating.

He could not recall when he had last felt so deliriously invigorated. So bloody alive.

"Surely if one of the two of us knows his way about in this sprawling manor, in the darkest pitch of night, it would be you, Duke," she still found the temerity to argue.

Amazing. Nothing would knock it out of her, not even a fall from Damask Rose that would have made able-bodied men cry like babes newly born. She had not shed a tear, though she'd been undeniably shocked, the wind stolen from her. The fall had rattled her but it had not undone her. Lady Boadicea Harrington was a force of nature, as subtle as a hurricane, and he rather found himself admiring her pluck.

Clearly, the lateness of the hour had addled his mind.

"Of course I know my way," he forced out. "But not when spirited minxes are skulking about in my path when they ought to be abed, resting as the well-trained physician who attended them recommended."

"I am attempting to rest," she muttered. "I cannot do it in that chamber. I was seeking the chamber originally assigned me. It would seem I am hopelessly lost, however, and the gentleman I came upon would rather seduce me than offer his assistance."

"Seduce you?" He could not contain the mocking laugh that escaped him then. If she thought his nearness and slight touch were seduction, then she was indeed a true innocent. "Is that what you think this is?"

As he posed the question, he loosened his grip on her wrist, stroking the soft skin where her pulse pounded with his thumb. And then he canted his hips, pressing into her more fully, until he knew there was no doubt that she felt every inch of him. Her swift inhalation cut into the night.

"Duke," she whispered, but her tone was not one of protest. Rather, it was akin to a sigh. An affirmation.

Yes, his body said. *Take her. Haul her into your arms, carry her to the emerald chamber, and make her yours.* He longed to. Wanted with a fierce desperation to lose himself so deep and hard inside her that nothing else could dare intervene. But reality intruded in the form of a creaking door and footsteps down the hall, along with the reminder that she had indeed suffered a fall from a horse that morning. She needed the rest that Dr. Martindale prescribed. She needed to recover. And he most certainly did not need to fuck her against the wall as if she were a lowly whore he would tup for the night and never see again. She would be his wife. His duchess.

He released her and stepped away, though the loss of her scalding heat and delicious curves reverberated through him. "Someone is here," he whispered. "Do not say a word. Whilst I offer distraction, remove yourself to the duchess's chamber, which is straight down this hall in the opposite direction and then two turns to your right. It is for your own good."

Hoping she would for once in her life forego her inner hoyden and listen to caution, he stalked toward the sound of the interloper, which could only be his brother. In the absence of their guests, he and Harry alone had chambers in the east wing for the moment.

His eyes had already adjusted to the darkness, and as he reached the end of the hall, he finally recognized a tall, lean shadow. "Harry," he said quietly, feeling awkward, for he had not spoken with his brother since the last interminable quarrel at the ball, and he felt guilty as hell for wanting the same woman his idealistic sibling imagined himself in love with.

Love was a fiction invented by fools, for fools. But Harry had yet to discover that the impractical dreams of one's youth never translated into a reality. Life was bitter and bleak and ugly and rife with disappointment, hurt, and pain. The sooner Harry resigned himself to that excruciating truth, the better, for his sake.

"Bainbridge," came his brother's terse acknowledgment.

"What are you doing, lurking about at this bleak time of night?"

His attempt to infuse lightness into his tone fell flat even to his own ears, but he did not know how to speak to his brother. Didn't know how to cut through his anger. Or even how to make sense of the events of the past few days. If he could explain how the lady he disapproved of as a wife for his impressionable younger brother would soon become his duchess, he would have. But he could not. Weakness? Stupidity? Lust?

Something else that was far more disturbing, with far greater implications?

He refused to contemplate it any further.

"I should ask the same question of you." Suspicion colored Harry's tone. "I could have sworn I heard a female voice."

He stiffened. "I was going to the library for a whisky and a book. I neither saw nor heard anyone else."

"I know she was here," his brother said. "I can smell her perfume. By God, Bainbridge, you better not have further compromised Bo. Have you not done enough damage already by taking my bride for yourself?"

He winced, Harry's taunt finding its mark. For the first time, a strange, unwanted thought occurred to him. What if Lady Boadicea had ventured into this wing with the intention of finding Harry? What if the two of them had somehow arranged an assignation?

Rage, raw and molten as lava spewed from a volcano, erupted over him at the prospect. Millicent had not been faithful to him for the entire duration of their marriage, though he had never strayed. She had made certain he'd known. He had caught her, several weeks before her death, in *flagrante delicto*, with a stable hand. He still didn't know which offense was worse, the fact that she had allowed the man to fuck her with full knowledge that Spencer would see the act, or the fact that she had gifted the rogue servant with coin and precious family heirlooms, enabling him to disappear forever.

His hands clenched into fists at his sides. "It would behoove you to think of Lady Boadicea as your sister from this moment on, for that is all she will ever be to you."

"If I were made of ice as you are, that would be a simple feat," Harry growled. "But I am nothing like you, thank God, and I cannot forget the way I feel for her."

Something snapped within him, and he grasped through the darkness, gripping fistfuls of Harry's dressing robe. "She is mine, and if you touch her, I will thrash you to within an inch of your life. Do you understand me?"

His brother released a laugh that was equal parts bitter and cocky. "She will never be yours, brother. Never."

Barely checking his rage, Spencer forced himself to release Harry's robe and take a step back. "I bid you good night," he said curtly, before turning and stalking away.

More laughter chased him down the hall.

And the devil of it was that he knew Harry was right. He didn't understand why the knowledge filled his gut with the heavy weight of dread, or why his entire body was coiled tighter than a spring, or why in God's name he should give a damn about a wife he did not want and could not even abide one half of the time.

But he did.

As he stalked back to his chamber, he swore he could still smell her scent lingering in the air. But like all his demons, she had vanished back into the dark night from which she'd emerged.

Chapter Thirteen

BY THE THIRD DAY OF HER FORCED REST AND ISOLATION, Bo was beginning to think she was a prisoner. Her body's aches and pains had lessened, but now a different sort of malaise descended upon her: restlessness. If there was one thing she loathed, it was being confined. She couldn't abide by restrictions and definitely not by a rigidly enforced mandate of rest.

She paced the limits of the duchess's chamber for what must have been the fiftieth time that morning. Breakfast had been delivered. Cleo had yet to make her obligatory appearance. And Bo was tired of being trapped in Purgatory, lingering where she did not yet belong but would soon be indisputably tethered, rather like a dog upon a chain.

She had not seen Bainbridge since their unexpected collision in the hall, and this omission nettled her in a way it ought not. The morning after that turbulent night, she had awoken to find a guard at her door. Oh, her lady's maid claimed the man was a footman, but the fellow was quite firm in that he would not allow Bo to step over the threshold.

"His Grace's orders," the oaf had said by way of apology, blocking the doorway and refusing to allow her egress.

The adjoining door between her chamber and the duke's chamber was locked from the opposite side, also ruining her escape via that medium. Subsequent attempts to pick the lock with her hairpins had met with failure. As had an ill-fated effort to shimmy out the window and climb to the ground—her skirts had caught upon the ledge, almost sending her tumbling to her death, and she had deemed it wise to forego all such inquiries into her freedom.

Bainbridge had sent polite notes to her chamber questioning after her wellbeing, as though they were strangers and his hand had not been inside her drawers, and as though he did not still hold her book hostage, likely reading it each night whilst he lay abed. She did not like the distance or the pretense any more than she liked the torturous notion of him reading her book, lying in bed all alone. Something had shifted between them in the hallway, and yet he still seemed determined to pretend as though he was the block of ice he would have the world believe.

Bo wanted to melt his ice. She wanted to go back to that night in the hall and rattle him. Kiss him. Make him do something, anything, other than walk away and then go about the business of pretending she was a simple guest—strike that, *prisoner*—in his home rather than the woman he had compromised.

Her reaction to him didn't make sense. Part of her wanted to punish him, and part of her wanted to lure him closer. Perhaps it was all down to her being trapped in her chamber. And nearly going mad for it. Was that what he had done to his wife before her? One began to wonder, and when Bo's mind wandered, trouble inevitably followed.

"Bloody hell," she muttered, stalking back about the chamber again. Her back remained sore, but the rest of her was fine. Her mind was in the most trouble, for Lady Boadicea Harrington did not appreciate rules of any sort.

She was firmly of the mind that if a rule had been made, it had been necessarily made to be broken. By her.

And so she was thoroughly having enough of Dr. Martinriver's orders, or whatever his surname had been. To hell with Bainbridge's high-handedness as well. He had not even deigned to see her in person in three days' time, so he could not have any inkling as to her wellbeing.

She was perfectly well. The fall had not done her any permanent damage. One more pace around the perimeter of the chamber. She glared at the door. And finally decided she'd had enough.

One steps, two, three, four, and her hand was upon the knob. She turned it without impediment. The door opened soundlessly, and by sheer miracle, the corridor outside was empty. Not a guard or other soul to be seen. She looked to the left, then to the right to confirm before stepping out into the carpeted hall.

Ah, freedom.

The chamber door closed behind her with a quiet snick. For a moment, she stood in the hall, basking in her liberty. Her hesitation proved a dire mistake, however, for the lummox who guarded her chamber appeared at the far end of the hall just then.

"My lady!" he called, his strident voice echoing off the wood-paneled halls.

She turned and beat a hasty path in the opposite direction, pretending as though she hadn't heard him. His harried footfalls, muffled by the thick carpets, sounded at her back. She increased her pace, tossing a glance over her shoulder to find him gaining upon her.

No.

Bo could not bear one more day of forced imprisonment. She could own that the initial rest had benefitted her, but she was not the sort of person who relished lying about. She was filled with energy and purpose. Being imprisoned in a chamber—whether in the name of her own health or not—did not suit her in the slightest.

"Halt, my lady! You are under His Grace's orders to rest," he called.

"His Grace can go hang for all I care," she muttered before increasing her speed from rapid walk to outright run.

Bo had mastered the art of sprinting—having a bevy of mischievous sisters and brothers necessitated such an ability. But her jailer's heavy footsteps seemed to ring ever closer, and this called for more devious means. She headed in the same direction she had taken the night she had wound up colliding with Bainbridge.

Of course, as she attempted to make good on her escape, it occurred to her that traveling in the same path that had led her to the duke was unwise at best and stupid at worst. But the jackanapes charged with confining her to her prison was gaining on her, his feet pounding down the hall behind her as though he competed in a footrace. And above all, she did not wish to be caught. Though she hadn't been chased by anyone since she'd been in short skirts—not literally, at least—and her robe's long hem proved something of an impediment, she was still quite quick. And quite determined.

She turned a corner and decided that the best course of action would be to find a chamber and hide herself within until the wretch stomped past. Choosing the first door she came upon, she threw it open and swept inside, closing it as soundlessly and quickly at her back as possible. She leaned against it, catching her breath and holding still as the sound of footfalls pounded in the hall.

Continue on, she urged him inwardly.

All she needed to do was find Cleo and convince her that they must leave this madhouse at once. Perhaps she could even persuade her mother and father to send her to the Continent. Yes, that would be far preferable to consigning herself the fate of being the next Duchess of Bainbridge. The last one had fared none too well. She could lead the Lady's Suffrage Society from Paris and Clara would do an admirable job of the London post.

The footsteps went past her.

The breath she'd been holding escaped, and she inhaled deeply, as if she had been starved for air. That was when she realized something was amiss. For she smelled *him* and his delectable concoction of pine, soap, and musk. Pressing a palm to her pounding heart, she scanned the chamber.

Aside from the color theme—the window dressings, wall coverings, and even rug were all varying shades of green—it seemed innocuous enough. She did not spot any signs of him. Yet why did his scent linger in the air? It made no sense, unless she had gone so mad being trapped for three days that she now suffered from delusions.

What were the odds that she had happened into the chamber to which he had moved? That evening she had run into him, the halls had been dark, and with the tumult of their run-in coupled with Harry's unexpected presence and her need to hastily disappear, she had not been certain where he'd emerged from or even where they had met in the corridor.

Another thought occurred to her then. If this was indeed the chamber he had taken, then it stood to reason that her book was here. And Bainbridge was not. Elation surging through her, she hastened across the chamber, thinking that his mother ought to be banned from ever again decorating anything.

The deeper she ventured into the chamber, the stronger his scent grew. She was quite certain that he had taken this room, a suspicion that was confirmed when she caught sight of her book lying on a bedside table, still in its neat embroidered cover to keep the true nature of its contents from judgmental eyes.

"There you are," she said with a gleeful chuckle, snatching it up. "*Watching that little book of yours burn in the grate of my library.* What balderdash."

She had known his words for the prevarication they were when he had spoken them. But finding her book at last, laid out at his bedside as though he had been reading it each night, filled her with vindication. She clutched it to her still madly beating heart. Dear Lord, it also filled her with something else. Heat, slow and licking and taunting, spread through her entire body.

Here was the bed he slept in, her book within arm's reach. Had he read the wicked words and become aroused? She wanted to know so much that she ached with it, and she ground her teeth. This would not do. She would take her book and leave and never look back. On to Paris. The Duke of Bainbridge could melt his own ice. He could…

The chamber door swung open to reveal the object of her frustrated musings. He was dressed as if he had just come from riding. His green gaze crashed into hers, his sensual mouth going tight, his jaw instantly rock-solid. "What in the bloody hell?"

He stepped over the threshold, slamming the door at his back.

She could have asked the same of question of him. His brooding good looks were on full display this morning, and the way his riding boots hugged his muscular calves made her mouth go dry. Was it possible that he was taller, stronger, broader than she had recalled?

"Why are you here?" she demanded, holding the book to her bosom in a protective grip.

He raised an imperious, ducal brow. "Lady Boadicea, you are in *my* chamber."

She tipped up her chin, defiance taking charge as her displeasure for his high-handedness replaced her momentary stupor over his unexpected appearance. "I am in the first chamber I could spy after rounding the corner thanks to the jailer you planted at my door for the last few days. Had I known it was yours, I would have taken the risk of managing a few extra steps and landing myself in the next one."

He stalked toward her, making her resist the urge to retreat to the far end of the chamber. She would not show him her weakness. *No.* She would be strong. Unyielding. Above all she would not allow him to weaken her resolve or once again take possession of her book. Now that she had it back, she was not giving it up any more than she was flying to the moon.

Bainbridge stopped only when he was so near that his riding boots brushed her hem. She knew she should wonder if he was transferring mud to her silk, but she couldn't be bothered to look away from his arresting face.

"You took a great fall," he said slowly, his tone cool. "Being the stubborn, wrongheaded wench that you are, you seemed to have no concern for your wellbeing and recovery. Therefore I, being possessed of sound reasoning, endeavored to make certain that you would rest."

"I am not yours to order about," she argued, trying not to notice the strong cords of his neck or the breadth of his chest. Allowing her weakness for him to get the better of her just would not do. "Nor am I a wench, wrongheaded or otherwise. I am a woman fully grown, and if I require rest I shall take it. If I do not, I will not. What I most assuredly do not need, Duke, is a man who thinks he knows better than I making my decisions for me."

There. Let him stew upon that.

"I care for your wellbeing," he said quietly. "You are stubborn to a fault, and I did not wish to worry about you wandering the halls at midnight or stealing my horses."

He'd rather ruined the first bit of what he'd said with the second. She frowned at him. "You are the most vexing man I have ever met. Your unfortunate personality aside, I never stole your horse."

His expression remained impervious as ever, revealing nothing. "I will not argue semantics with you, my lady. You are, as seems to be your singular talent, once again trespassing where you are not welcome. I need to change. Leave the bawdy book and go."

Ah, so he had noticed. "This is my book, and I want it back."

"It is filth." His lip curled.

"Such filth that you threw it into the fire?" If her tone was arch, it couldn't be helped. Something about the man before her irked her in ways she could not fully comprehend. He was cold and reserved and forbidding, and yet he also made her melt.

He tilted his head, considering her in an intense manner that left her feeling flushed and exposed. "Perhaps I wished to know what to expect from my future wife, having already been cursed with one unfaithful duchess. Tell me, Lady Boadicea, what manner of bride will I bring to my bed?"

Something inside Bo froze. His wife had cuckolded him. It should not come as a surprise, she supposed, for marriages in which husband and wife sought comfort in the arms of lovers was commonplace in their set. And so it would seem he intended to paint her with the same brush.

The gauntlet had been thrown. She stepped forward, straight into his large, unyielding body, and she didn't care. "What do you mean to ask, Duke? You have only to ask, and I will answer."

"Why do you read such smut?" His hands settled upon her waist.

Smut. She did not like that word. But she studied him, unable to resist the smug grin that curved her lips. She could see right through his pretense. "Because I like it. And so, I would wager, do you, else it would not have been so readily available alongside your bed. It would seem that you did not burn it in the library grate after all."

"As you can see, the thing is still in fine fettle." He was solemn. "In spite of my strong inclination to destroy it."

"And it is mine." Her grip upon it tightened. She didn't know why it should matter to maintain possession of a small, unassuming volume of erotic literature. Though she hadn't yet read it halfway through, she knew some of the stories it contained were frankly profane, some silly, and others still quite intriguing. Bainbridge clearly shared her opinion, or he would not have kept it at his bedside. There were layers to him, hidden depths, which appealed to her.

And yet, she could not be certain if she was better off leaving him intact or attempting to find the pulsing heart of him.

Did he have a heart?

The icy Duke of Disdain—the man she'd thought him—would have her believe he did not. But she had glimpsed more than the façade he showed the world. More, even than the façade he had initially showed her. He possessed passion and fire. He was not an immovable iceberg at all. Rather, he was an enigma, a man who had known pain and hurt, who had perhaps loved a wife who had betrayed him and taken other lovers to her bed. The more she knew about him, the more she suspected that her opinion of him was wrong.

"Take it, then." His voice was a low, decadent rumble to her senses. His eyes had dipped to her mouth, and she felt that gaze like a kiss. Her lips tingled.

For a moment, she had forgotten he spoke about the book in her hands, the shallow prize she had at last wrested from him. She blamed it upon his eyes, so vibrant and green that she swore she had never seen a shade as beautiful. And the angular lines of his handsome face, that ruggedly masculine stubble clinging to his jaw that made him seem somehow powerful and seductive all at once. Not to mention his sensual lips, that defined upper bow she longed to kiss.

"Take it and go, Lady Boadicea," he repeated, though he had not released his grip upon her waist. "The longer you linger here, the more likely you are to end up on your back in that bed, and we will have to hasten our nuptials even more than already necessary."

On your back in that bed.

The words were meant to shock her. Instead, they sent a rush of molten desire straight through her body to the sensitive flesh between her legs. The book in her hands had given her a word for that forbidden place: cunny.

Yes. She liked those words. That threat. When the Duke of Bainbridge issued it, there was no threat at all, only promise. It had the opposite effect, for instead of making her hasten out of the chamber door, leaving the emerald of his eyes and the matching décor behind her, it only made her want to stay. To rise on her tiptoes. To link her arms around his neck. Press her breasts shamelessly to his wide, unforgiving chest.

So she did, dropping the book to the carpet, heedless of where it went. It was no longer the prize she sought. Instead, she luxuriated in the searing heat of him sinking into her being, burning and delicious. Shifting from side to side, she rubbed against him like a feline as her pebbled nipples dragged against him. He stepped into her, one of his sinewy thighs parting her legs. She grew moist between her thighs. Ached. For him, for the forbidden. For all of him or any part of him—however trifling—he dared to give.

God, how he undid her, and she ought to be frightened by the knowledge. Yet somehow, it only served to heighten her arousal. Desire charged the air. She arched her back, seeking more, yearning for contact with his body everywhere she could manage.

"Spencer," she whispered his name for the first time, trying it on her tongue, a slow hiss. It suited him, that name. It was cool, austere, and yet beneath it hid a seductive current. She wanted to say it again. "Spencer."

He was handsome, so handsome at such proximity, and she couldn't stop the tumult roaring through her, dangerous though she knew it was. They had already crossed far more boundaries than she had ever imagined possible. Here she was, in his chamber, in his arms, and though it should not, nothing had ever felt more right.

"Hellfire." He swallowed, but his large hands swept up from her waist, over the small of her back, tracing her spine, leisurely painting circles with his traveling palms. "Princess, grant us both this favor. You must leave. I cannot…you are wearing naught but a dressing gown and chemise, and I cannot stop touching you. Damn it."

The visceral swear made her flinch, the urgency and feeling of it, as though he hated himself for his weakness yet remained powerless to step away from her and put a safe distance between them. She held herself still, locked in his gaze.

"I do not wish you to stop," she confessed before she could stay the revelation.

The air rushed from his lungs, heated and moist over her lips, as his jaw hardened into stone. "*Fuck.*"

It was not the first time she had heard him use the crude epithet, but it was the first time that the mere utterance of it, delivered from his beautifully sculpted lips, made a sharp ache pulse through her. She knew what the word meant. Had read it in many a naughty book.

Perhaps she was shameless. This was not the manner in which she had been raised. Finishing school had not taught her to act with such flagrant disregard for propriety, nor to offer herself so freely and without compunction. She was meant to be a lady, treasure her comportment, never be alone with a gentleman, never invite him to sin with her. But she was Boadicea Harrington, and she had never found a single rule she hadn't longed to smash to bits.

"Do you feel it?" she asked in a whisper. Her eyes searched his. "Tell me, Spencer. Do you feel whatever this is between us?"

"Damn you," he gritted, his expression tense. One of his large hands swept lower, cupping her bottom, driving her body into him so that she rode his thigh. "You are madder than a March hare, I swear it on my life, and yet…"

"And yet," Bo prompted when he allowed his words to trail away, as though loath to speak them aloud.

He did not need to say it, for she could read his thoughts. They mirrored her own.

And yet, he could not resist this. Could not avoid the burning desire, the need to become one, that sparked like live electricity wires in the air. Nor did she want him to, for she felt the pull every bit as much as he did. He was nothing she had ever wanted, the last man in the world she should desire, and yet she could not think of any other man she had ever wanted more. He transcended everything—person, place, time. In the heat of his stare, beneath the magic of his touch, all else faded.

All that remained was him. Spencer. Bainbridge. The Duke of Disdain. They were all varying versions of the same beautiful, complicated man. And she wanted them. Every last one of them. All of them.

All of *him*.

"And yet," she prompted again, unable to squelch the restless desire to hear the rest of what he would have spoken though she knew it already.

He did not respond, merely scorched her with his relentless stare that seemed to see to the heart of her, to unlock all the secrets she kept within. And then, in the next instant, his mouth was upon hers. Fierce. Hungry. Devouring.

She opened to him, feeding on his kiss, sucking his tongue into her mouth. He was all she wanted without ever having known it. He was vital. Air. Water. Succor. He was everything, and it was as if his kiss could sustain her even if she was lost in the deepest, darkest wilds of the world. He kissed her as if she were someone he longed to consume and someone who was precious to him all at once. His hands were gentle. His mouth was firm, hard, demanding.

A moan tore from her throat, her fingers delving into his thick hair. His scent enveloped her, filling her, overtaking her. She welcomed it. Welcomed him. His questing touch smoothed over her waist, finding the belt of her robe, made short work of undoing the knot.

He groaned, tongue playing against hers, gliding with deep, languorous sweeps as though he had all the time in the world to discover her. To pleasure her. But Bo did not feel nearly so generous. She wanted everything she had read about, and she wanted it now. She wanted him to strip her of the layers keeping her skin from his, wanted him to lick and suck and nip her everywhere and anywhere he chose, wanted him between her thighs and deep inside her body.

The knot opened. Her *robe de chambre* slipped down her shoulders, puddling to the floor in a whisper of fabric. Only a chemise, thin and transparent, kept her body from his traveling hands. Knowing, traveling hands, and everywhere he touched her, her traitorous body seemed to sing.

His thumbs found her nipples, circling, plucking. He pinched them between his fingers, rolled them, pulled, made her moan into his mouth with his tender yet skilled ministrations. Her breasts were so sensitive, heavy and full, desperate for his touch. She arched her back, licked her tongue against his, fisted her hands in his hair.

Nothing had ever made her feel more depraved or alive than this forbidden moment with the Duke of Bainbridge in her arms, his hands on her body, his mouth playing with wicked abandon over hers. He set her aflame as no other man before him ever had, and as she was beginning to suspect no man after him ever could.

How had she ever thought him icy?

For he was not. Not cold. Not cool. Not rigid or frigid.

Rather, he was on fire, singeing her with his kisses and his caresses, the sweep of his hands over her back and lower still. And she wanted that fire more than anything. Wanted to get burned. It would be an inferno, claiming everything in its path. But it would be worth it.

He cupped her bottom with both hands, kneading and squeezing before angling her to his body more fully. She felt him against her belly, erect and uncompromising and so tempting. The books she had read made it impossible for her to remain ignorant of what he would do with that part of himself or what it meant. He wanted her. Despite their differences, in spite of all that had happened since her arrival at Boswell Manor, the Duke of Bainbridge *wanted* her.

And she wanted him. More than she had ever wanted anything or anyone. So much that it frightened her. So much that she stood in nothing more than a chemise, in his chamber, tossing the last remnants of her reputation into the proverbial flame. No good would come of her presence in his chamber.

No good would come of his hands meandering over her body or the restless desire within her to feel his bare skin pressed to hers. No good would come of anything that was happening now, in this moment, in the emerald chamber without the ghosts of his past and the fears of their future curtailing them.

For the moment, it was as if they were suspended from reality. No one knew she was within his chamber. No one knew she had gone from hers with the exception of the servant posted at her door, and she suspected that he would not wish to alert his retainers of his failure now that he had lost her. Indeed, no one, then, would suspect at all. No one would ever know what she had risked, what he had taken, or what she had given. It was as if time ceased to exist, and they were the only two souls in the world, both on fire for each other, both needy and desperate for something they did not comprehend.

She trailed her hand down his strong arms to his hip.

Not many days before, she had touched his cock, cupping and stroking. While she had not known what to do then—and still did not—the heaviness in her veins, the heat settling in her belly, and the wetness between her thighs urged her onward now. She arched, making certain that her breasts burned into his chest and his arousal connected with her mound's soft flesh.

Yes. This was where she wanted him. Where she needed him. Nothing else mattered, not consequences or propriety, nor the fact that they were sharing a roof with their respective family members. Any part of her that would have objected to the depravity threatening to consume them both was hastily squelched, firmly shoved to the far recesses of her mind. Here, in this moment, there was no room for rules. No room for decorum. No room for anything other than pure, animal want.

She wanted Bainbridge. He wanted her.

Simple. She sucked his tongue, ran hers against it, bit his lower lip until he grunted, and then she kissed and licked away the sting. He had done this to her. Had turned her into a raw, unadulterated wanton. The final remnants of the girl she had once been—the girl who had tried to please her parents, who had made an effort to conform, the girl who had dutifully attended finishing school—dissipated. That girl was gone, and in her place stood a woman in her chemise, who knew what she wanted.

Rules and everyone and everything else be damned.

A groan tore from Bainbridge's throat then, and he dragged his lips from her mouth, down her neck, open, hot, wet, hungry. She threw back her head to grant him better access. He licked the tense cord of her throat, sucked her skin, gently bit the taut corner of flesh where her neck and shoulder met. His hands were everywhere, kneading, caressing, making her untutored flesh come to life.

Someone moaned into the silence, and she supposed it must have been her. The longing inside her continued to tighten and build, a delicious pang of want echoing between her thighs. She had read about such primitive feelings, but she had previously imagined them embellishments perpetrated by the authors with the intent to titillate.

It wasn't so.

Those feelings—the wicked, the prurient, the wrong, the desperate—all of them, were as real as the breath leaving her lungs on an exhale of pure desire. He dragged a path of kisses over the bare décolletage above her chemise. Then lower still, his hand cupping a breast, his mouth closing over her nipple through the thin linen.

"Bainbridge," she gasped, arching. Nothing could have prepared her for the decadence of his hot, wet mouth on her. Suckling her. Suddenly, she longed for the last barriers between them to be gone. "Please."

He nipped her then, not with enough force for pain. Pleasure, clear and strong, shot through her. And then he raised his head, his gaze meeting hers. "You need to get out of this chamber, Lady Boadicea. At once."

But as he issued the authoritative command, his hands molded her waist, swept lower, back to the swell of her bottom, and he angled her against him. His hips thrust against her, the stroke of his cock over the sensitized bundle of flesh at her core inciting an answering twitch of her hips.

"I do not wish to leave," she told him then on a half gasp as he pumped against her. The friction was delicious, her undoing. She could not get enough of it, of him, and yet she still wanted more.

More of him. More of his tongue, his mouth, his hard body, his demanding cock. More of everything. He brought her to life, and she couldn't help but wonder if, at least in some small measure, she didn't bring him back to life as well.

Thoughts such as these were abruptly disbanded when he caught her chemise in his hands and rent it in two. "I want your skin. I want your body. Damn you, Lady Boadicea Harrington. I cannot think or move for wanting you."

Her ruined chemise fell away, down to the floor, and she was naked before him. She knew not a moment of embarrassment, so overcome was she with the newness of the sensations ricocheting through her.

Nothing she had ever felt could compare to this—to him. He had swept into her life with the unexpected turbulence of a summer thunderstorm, changing the landscape indelibly. It did not matter that they had not known each other long, that in truth, they still scarcely knew each other at all. Apart from the way they could not seem to stop their mutual desire despite their best efforts to the contrary, they had little in common. Nothing mattered but want, need, and longing. Mouths and hands and bodies and skin, his hardness to her softness, his ice to her fire.

She would melt him, she thought again as she moved against him, answering his every thrust with an arch. She was hyperaware of each stroke of him against her pearl, that part of her that was most receptive to touch and stimulation.

His hands found her breasts, kneading and cupping, his thumbs swirling over her nipples. Once. Again. And again, each stroke pure bliss. He caught the hard buds between his fingers, rolling and pulling. She moaned. Decided it was not fair that he remained fully dressed in his riding garb while she was naked and vulnerable and horribly wanting, standing before him. With a palm to his chest, she shoved him back by a few inches. He allowed her to overpower him, watching her with his heavy, half-lidded stare.

God, how she wanted him.

"We are well matched then, Duke." Even bared before him, his hands on her body, his cock rubbing against her most intimate flesh, she could not shake the feeling that this moment would be the moment she would one day realize had changed everything. "I want all of you as well."

Bo took her turn in touching him, longing to have him free of his clothes. Feverishly, her fingers worked over his jacket, removing the layers separating him from her. Fabric dropped to the floor. She found the buttons of his shirt, freeing them from their moorings. Bare chest, defined and strong and breathtaking, met her fevered fingertips.

"Damn you, Boadicea Harrington," he swore, but his hands were upon her with equal fervor, coasting over her waist, her hips, cupping her bottom. "Damn you."

"You do not like the effect I have upon you," she observed wryly, leaning forward to brazenly run her tongue over one of his hard nipples. The breath hissed from his lungs. She took that as encouragement and bestowed the same attention to the opposite flat disc, feeling unaccountably bold. Perhaps it was the moment, the wildness of it, perhaps it was standing before a man she barely knew without a stitch to protect her modesty. "Admit it, Duke. You cannot resist me."

"I have resisted far greater temptations than you," he said coolly.

"Hmm." She did not believe his attempt to keep her at bay. He could play the ice king all he liked, but she knew that there was more to him hiding beneath the surface, waiting for her to discover. Her hands traveled lower, relishing the solid planes of his abdomen, rippled with muscle she would not have expected from a gentleman like him, to the trail of hair below his navel.

He tensed beneath her touch, his skin at once firm and hot and yet soft as velvet. Such a dichotomy. She wanted to run her hands over his bare skin forever, and it would still not be long enough. Provided that he was forced to keep his supercilious mouth shut, that was.

He caught her wrist in his grasp. "Hmm? What does that mean?"

Irking him was a pleasant diversion all its own, heightening the bold desire surging through her. She smiled, extricating herself from his grip with ease. "It means that I do not believe you, Your Grace. Or that I do believe you, and I do not care. You may take your pick."

His handsome face hardened, jaw going tense, eyes darkening. "Do you want to be fucked, Lady Boadicea? Is that the purpose of your bawdy books and your presence in my chamber? Your wandering hands and your crude insinuations?"

He was a beast. But as much as she wanted to punish him, she rather enjoyed hearing his frigid, clipped voice uttering such wicked obscenities in conjunction with his cold accusations. It made her want him more, truth be told. Yes, he was a beast, and she was an aberrant creature. Perhaps they were a match after all, for while they seemed forever at odds, they nevertheless could not keep their distance from each other.

"Would that make it more convenient, Duke?" she asked boldly. "Would your need for me be somehow more palatable if you imagined I was the sole instigator, that I am a wanton tart masquerading as a lady?"

She used his words against him like a weapon. Of course she did, for she still found offense in them, and he was such an obstinate sapskull that she wanted to make him suffer, just a bit. Her fingers continued their investigation, finding the fastening of his riding breeches. She made short work of it, opening them, her fingers drifting lower still. She kissed his chest, inhaling the scent of him, male and potent and delicious.

He jerked. "Bloody hell. What do you think you are doing, my lady?"

"This." Her hand slipped inside his breeches and his smalls.

Oh.

She found him, hard and thick and hot and smooth. Instinctively, her fingers curled around his shaft, squeezing with gentle pressure. His hips twitched, but he did not withdraw from her touch. How strong he was, holding himself as tense as a marble bust, as though he dare not move or breathe for fear he would reveal himself to her. Realization hit her then, sudden and invigorating. She was seducing him. And he would allow it.

Wanted it, she would daresay. But for reasons all his own, he was attempting to resist with all his might. Control was important to him. Perhaps it was the way he made sense of things after the tragedy he had suffered. All she knew for certain was that she wanted to rattle him. She wanted him to admit that he burned for her the same way she did for him.

The abrupt shift of power between them emboldened her, sending an insistent, aching pulse between her thighs. For some reason, he was attempting to resist her. But he fought a losing battle. And she enjoyed pushing him. Taunting him. Provoking him. Stroking his cock as she had only read about in her books. She did it now, once, twice. Tentative at first and then with firmer pressure, taking cues from him, learning what made him weak.

A deep growl sounded in his throat.

Her heart thumped madly. Her breasts felt heavy and full. She hungered for him in a way she had never known, deep within her core, as though only he could fulfill her. She stroked and stroked, and she wanted that part of him where it belonged. Where the books told her it went.

Inside her.

"You cannot resist me," she said again, determined to make him admit it.

Chapter Fourteen

Good God.

Boadicea was stroking his naked cock, her touch like a brand. He had allowed things to progress too far, and now every inch of her creamy skin was on display for him, and he was so hard that he feared he was about to spend in her hand. He should push her away, wrap her in her flimsy dressing gown, leave her virginity and his honor intact, send her out the door. He should wait until they were wed to own her body the way he longed to, and yet the infernal woman was right.

He could not resist her. But he would be damned if he would deliver her victory on a silver platter by admitting it aloud. She thought she could seduce him with her boldness, make him bend to her every whim. The beast he had attempted to restrain flared to life, ready to conquer.

His fingers sank into the silken hair at her nape then, fisting, dragging her head back so that he could kiss and lick her throat. He dragged his teeth over the sensitive skin as she continued to grip his shaft, working it up and down. He jerked his hips, groaning. The cords of her throat fascinated him, such strength encased in softness. She tasted sweet, like musk and jasmine and every tart he had pilfered from the kitchens as a lad, only better.

He lost himself in that moment, his control shattering. Nothing else mattered except the warm, perfectly curved, utterly divine minx in his arms and his need to bury himself inside her. With his free hand, he caught her wrist, withdrawing her from his breeches.

When she made a needy sound of protest, his cock throbbed. He gently nipped the side of her throat, working back to the hollow beneath her ear before pressing an open-mouthed kiss there. "Get on the bed." She hesitated, and he took her earlobe between his teeth, biting into the tender flesh. "Now."

Wordlessly, she obeyed, lying on the bed, her riotous auburn locks unbound and fanned around her in contrast to her pale skin. He shucked his boots, breeches, and smalls, never tearing his eyes from her, for he could not look away. Her breasts were full and round, tipped with hard peach nipples that he longed to suck. The curve of her waist, the hollow of her belly, her long, luscious legs… God, he could not wait another moment to put his mouth on her.

He sank on the bed, beginning at her ankles, so trim and fine-boned that his hands dwarfed them. She was so bloody beautiful, a taunting goddess, an outspoken vixen, everything that appalled him and yet everything he could not get enough of. Lowering his head, he kissed the arch of each dainty foot. Even here, the workhorse of her body, she was soft and bewitching. Her feet were as lovely as the rest of her.

"Bainbridge," she protested, her voice breathless. "What are you doing?"

He slanted a glance up over her glorious body, swept his palms up her calves, kissing as he went. Reached her inner knee and licked. "Tasting you." He found her thighs next, parted them and fully exposed her to his hungry gaze at last. Pink and slick with desire, perfect and his. He kissed the soft flesh of her inner thighs, the scent of her, musky and intoxicating, luring him on to his ultimate goal.

She jerked beneath him, attempted to close her legs but he stayed her. "You cannot mean to…*oh.*"

He licked her slit, running his tongue over her in slow, teasing swipes up, down, up down. He avoided her channel and her pearl, the two places he knew she longed for him most. She gasped and writhed beneath him, her fingers sinking into his hair. Her breathy sighs spurred him on, and he felt each one in his tightening ballocks. He licked and laved, drawing no quarter with his torture. Here, she tasted sweetest of all, and he rewarded her by running his tongue over the demanding jewel at the center of her folds at last before working his teeth over it. She stiffened beneath him, and he knew she was close. He alternated between sucking, licks, and nips, adding pressure, burying his face so deep between her legs that she was all he could taste and breathe.

She came apart for him, arching off the bed and crying out as tremors of release shook her body. He cupped her luscious bottom, holding her to him, lapping the sweet spendings of her release like it was manna from heaven. He would have happily remained there all morning, pleasing her with his mouth again and again, but the need to be inside her surged through him then with such force that his teeth ached.

He dropped another kiss on her mound and worked his way up the rest of her body, worshipping her belly, the fullness of her breasts, suckling her hard nipples until she moaned and he was about to come on her thigh like a green lad. He kissed her neck, tongued the hollow behind her ear, rolled his hips against her so that she could feel his cock straining to be inside her.

"Is this what you want?" he asked into her ear.

Her hands swept up his back, urging him on. "Spencer," she whispered, bringing him to the edge with one word. His name on her lips. That was all it took.

Fuck, he was desperate. Primal possession roared through him. He had to be inside her. Now. He reached between their bodies, dragging his cock over her slick flesh. "Tell me what you want," he gritted, his cock poised at her entrance now. Her heat beckoned, and it took every ounce of self-restraint he owned to keep from slamming home. He wanted the filthy words on her luscious lips. For her to say it.

"I want you inside me," she said, shifting so that the tip of his cock sank into her.

On a groan, he pressed slowly forward, not wishing to cause her pain yet dying to have her. He kissed her on the mouth then, forcing her lips open, letting her taste herself on his tongue, and she moaned, writhing beneath him. He sank deeper, giving her shallow thrusts to allow her body to stretch and accommodate the new invasion. And then, he could not wait a moment more. One more deep thrust, and he was fully sheathed inside her.

She stiffened, and he stilled, his fingers finding her clitoris, stimulating her to take away any pain she may have felt. Everything in him longed to thrust hard and fast, again and again, empty himself inside her. But he reigned himself in, kissing her, pleasuring her, waiting until she relaxed and her hips bucked against him, taking him deeper.

Damn. She was so tight, so hot, and being inside her felt better than he had even imagined it would. He lost himself. Perhaps it was that it had been so long since he'd had a woman. Perhaps it was just *this* woman. He didn't know. Spencer's strokes grew faster, harder, taking him deeper. He could not be deep enough. Could not have enough of her. She clenched on him as she came again, sudden and hard, and he was close, so close to following. The slick sounds of her desire, the mewling cries she made in her throat, the scent of her, her tongue in his mouth. It was too much, and he was delirious with it, with raw, unadulterated pleasure.

She was his, and he sank home inside her once more, deep and true, before recalling himself at the last moment and withdrawing, gripping his cock as he spent all over the coverlet in thick, white streams. He collapsed against her, kissing her one last time before breaking away.

He had just debauched his bride-to-be in the emerald room in the midst of the morning, and while his body didn't regret a moment of the explosive passion they'd shared, his conscience chose that moment to reappear. What the hell had he done? If his mother caught wind of his recklessness, she would roast his heart on a spit.

"We will get married as soon as possible," he announced grimly. "I will procure a license tomorrow."

She muttered something that sounded suspiciously like *arrogant oaf*. Surely not?

He raised his head, frowning down at her. "What did you say, madam?"

She blinked, and he could not help but notice with pride how her cheeks were flushed from pleasure and her lips swollen from his kisses. *Mine*, he thought again with an instinctive surge of possessiveness.

"I said you're an arrogant oaf," she repeated sweetly. "And do not call me madam, Bainbridge."

Bloody hell, the woman was a menace. His cock stirred to life once more. This would not do. Her effect upon him was equal parts maddening and absurd.

He removed himself from the bed since he did not trust himself. She lay, beautiful and unashamed and bold, naked on the coverlets, her eyes dancing with defiant fire. She looked thoroughly fucked, and it made him long to fuck her again. To come on her porcelain skin this time, mark her with his seed. Christ, he was an animal.

"Spencer," he rasped. "We are beyond the point of titles now, princess. Put on your robe and return to your chamber before…"

She raised a brow, and her knowing look had him ready to pounce upon her again. "Before what, Spencer?"

He made a choked sound. In the span of all but a week, she had gone from being an abstract irritant to being the woman he deflowered in the emerald chamber. The woman he could not seem to resist, regardless of how hard his rational mind worked to force him to realize she was wrong for him in every way.

She was too bold, too lovely, too sensual, too rebellious, far too outspoken. If he had to describe her in a simple phrase, it would be this: *too much*. And yet, the crux of it was that he could never have enough of her. She was opium and he was the addict, always chasing her, ready to lose himself in her. She had damn well beguiled him.

"Spencer?" Those big, vibrant eyes sparked with laughter. Her full lips, lush and deep-red with kisses, tipped into a smile that took his breath. "You did not seem to finish your command, and I do so wish to heed it."

Her insincerity was transparent. The witch. He would not admit it. "Have you no shame? Cover yourself," he growled, for his cock was painfully hard already, and he had to avert himself from her gaze in an effort to maintain the last remaining shred of his dignity.

With the grace of a feline, she rolled from the bed and stood facing him, raising her arms high over her head to stretch. His besotted gaze tracked the movement of her breasts rising and falling. Her nipples remained pebbled and hungry, pointing to him as if in invitation. He rather thought he would accept the devil's invitation to hell in that moment if it meant he could suck those sweet, peach buds one more time.

"Since we are to be husband and wife," she said, dragging his eyes back to hers at last, "there is one fact with which you ought to acquaint yourself. I do not—nor have I ever—possessed the capacity for shame. I am me, and I like me."

She liked herself. What a strange creature she was. Here she stood, naked, ruined, debauched, and she remained as bold and unrepentant as ever. She wore nothing but the evidence of their lovemaking, and she made no effort to cover herself. She cried no maidenly tears at having lost her innocence.

The first time he had taken Millicent—the only other virgin he had ever bedded—she had sobbed uncontrollably in the aftermath. He had been far gentler, he thought, far less demanding on that long-ago occasion. But Boadicea was not anything like Millicent, and he was heartily grateful for that, at least.

I like me. Who thought such nonsense, let alone spoke it to one's future husband while standing naked in a strange chamber without the benefit of marriage vows? She was so bloody ridiculous and yet so bloody captivating, and it was rending him apart from the inside out, rearranging everything he'd thought he had known about himself. He had gone three years without giving in to temptation. He had never wanted to take another wife. The notion of bedding another woman had filled him with nothing but cold dread. Yet, he just had, and he had relished every fucking moment of making her his. Could not wait to do it again.

And again.

He did not know what to say to her. They were two naked strangers who had just shared the most intimate act a man and woman could share, at a standoff. She confounded him. "Do you intend to walk back to the duchess's chamber in the nude?" he bit out.

She gave him a regal shrug, another smile playing at her lips. "If it pleases me, I will."

Damn her. She was goading him, and he knew it, but the thought of Boadicea strolling down the hall on full display to anyone who passed by made him feel positively vicious. "Your body is mine, for my eyes only."

"And is yours mine alone as well?" she asked.

Yes, utterly.

He stiffened. "I will not have this discussion with you now, when it is imperative that you return to your chamber, clothed, before what we have done here has even greater ramifications."

"When would you prefer to have it, Your Grace?" She tilted her head, her expression faintly mocking, as was her tone.

Bleeding hell, he could not think properly when she stood before him like a pagan sacrifice. Every part of him roared to take her in his arms, throw her on the bed, and fuck her until she spent so hard on his cock and his tongue that she forgot how to be impertinent.

"Cover yourself," he demanded, forcing a coolness into his voice that he did not feel. Indeed, he was a raging inferno, about to combust and do something even more foolish than bedding his betrothed in the midst of the morning beneath the noses of their family members and a belowstairs full of gossip-loving domestics.

"I will not be bellowed at, Spencer."

While he was gratified that she was calling him by his Christian name at long last, he was still staring at a naked goddess, doing his damnedest not to drag her back to the bed. Or fall on his knees before her and worship her with his eager mouth. He could still taste her, and it was better than the finest delicacy he had ever consumed.

She stared at him, pursing her lips. Her breasts rose and fell. Even the indentation of her navel bewitched him, and he longed to dip his tongue there, kiss a path over the slight curve of her belly to the juncture of her thighs.

Damn it all. "Please. Cover yourself."

Apparently, he had appeased her, for she bent and scooped up her dressing gown in one elegant motion, shrugging it on and belting it at the waist, putting an end to his unabashed ogling but not his arousal, which refused to abate. Stifling a curse, he found his breeches and slid them on, fastening them and hissing out a breath at the friction of the fabric over his sensitive cock.

"I meant what I said," she said, and now that she was ensconced in the robe, she looked less like a siren and more like the young, lovely innocent that she was. Or rather, that she had been prior to his unfettered lust. "I do not need you to like me to accept myself. But if we are bound together, you could try not to look upon me with such distaste any time you are not running your hands or mouth all over my body. You are marrying a woman who reads bawdy books, who is not afraid to say and do things that are inappropriate, who feels strongly about her beliefs, and who will not bend to any man's whim. Who will not bend to your whims, specifically."

She thought he looked upon her with distaste? He had to admit that his reaction to her had initially been both visceral and unkind, borne as much from the way she drew him to her as from her rebellious nature. He could hardly fault her for her poor opinion of him, as he'd earned it. But in truth, his opinion of *her* had slowly changed.

Now, if there was distaste, it was only for himself, for how little control he possessed over his reaction to her. Once again, he did not know what to say. She stared at him, defiant as ever, and he wished she had not done as he'd asked and donned her robe. He missed her skin, the curves of her waist and hips, those luscious breasts.

"I am sorry. If I look upon anyone with distaste, it is myself. Not you. Never you."

He felt as startled as Boadicea looked by his apology. For so many years, he had either been trapped in the untenable hell of his marriage to Millicent or paying the price for her death. It occurred to him now that he did not know how to conduct himself with a lady. With his future wife. With this vibrant, gorgeous force before him. But it was true that while he did not understand what she did to him, he had no wish to cause her pain or embarrassment.

A pink flush crept over her cheeks. "Thank you, Spencer. I can only imagine how much that cost you."

He smirked, which was unlike him, but he could not seem to maintain jurisdiction over any part of his anatomy, so his mouth may as well go rogue too. "You have no idea."

She smiled back at him, and it was an intimate smile. Soft and warm and secret. "I daresay I may have an inkling. And just so we are clear, I will marry you in haste because I do not wish to delay my enjoyment of the marital bed, and not because you ordered it."

Her enjoyment of the marital bed. He could not speak.

But he didn't need to, for she chose that moment to sweep from the chamber, head high, auburn curls rioting down her back. It took every bit of restraint he had not to go after her, catch her in his arms, and bring her back where she belonged.

Chapter Fifteen

WEDDINGS WERE MEANT TO BE JOYOUS, celebratory occasions, but the breakfast immediately following Bo's vows with Bainbridge in the chapel at Boswell Manor possessed the stilted air of a funeral. Silence reigned among the sparse guests, all close friends and family with the exception of the Duke and Duchess of Cartwright.

Naturally, the dowager duchess—who wore the pained expression of someone walking barefoot upon a bed of hot coals whenever she deigned to speak to Bo—had ignored her wishes and invited the duchess anyway. Just as the dowager had insisted upon orchids to adorn the chapel, when Bo had wanted orange blossoms and lilies. And just as Bo had selected the wedding breakfast menu only to discover upon reviewing the fifteen-course menu card before her that the dowager had once again superseded her.

Bo could not abide by fish and had made the grievous error of imparting that fact to her mother-in-law. Which was why the dowager had chosen it to be the keystone of every dish except aspics during the *entrées froides* portion of the menu and the *entremets*.

Astonishing that her mother-in-law had not finagled some way of landing kippers in the *meringues à la Chantilly*, but if the menu card was to be believed, Bo would need to placate her rumbling stomach with thoughts of sponge cake and chocolate cream while she drowned her sorrows in the wine glass a blessedly capable servant continued to refill.

She lifted her crystal goblet to her lips and took another fortifying sip. The wine did nothing to numb the clawing fear within her that she had just made the greatest mistake of her life, but it did fill her with a pleasant enough warmth. Yes, perhaps she ought to get soused. And then cast up her accounts on the dowager's gown, which she had kindly confided to Bo she had worn to Bainbridge's first wedding as well.

The notion of vomiting on her mother-in-law should not be so entertaining, but now that it had infiltrated her mind, she could not quite squelch the inappropriate laughter rising within her. Perhaps spurred on by her admittedly generous consumption of wine, a giggle bubbled forth, slipping past her lips, ruining the silence and the clink of cutlery on delicate china. All eyes turned to her, and she was acutely aware of the scrutiny of the reserved man at her side.

In the month since she had shared such scorching passion with him, he had been icy and polite, perfunctory in all his correspondence, withdrawn whenever their paths had crossed. They had not even had a moment alone since that day. Bo was certain it was by design, but the haste of their wedding and the distance between her family estate and Boswell Manor had not made matters easy either.

"What amuses you, Duchess?" he asked quietly, the timbre of his voice sending a tremor of something warm and delicious down her spine.

Duchess.

How strange to hear it said aloud, by him. To realize she was, in fact, married to the Duke of Bainbridge. It was not what she had wanted, not at all the fate she had once envisioned for herself, but it was her reality now. If only they could bypass the breakfast and be alone, for she longed to discover whether or not the fiery lovemaking had been a fluke.

She glanced at him from beneath her lashes, knowing she could not very well reveal to him before their assembled guests what had caused her to laugh. "Can a bride not be happy on her wedding day, Duke?" she asked instead, arching a brow and daring him to question her further.

Another glass of wine and she just may be inclined to share so that the entire assemblage could laugh as well. She raised her glass toward him in a mock toast, and downed half the contents. It was rude, and she did not care. Her corset was too bloody tight, her mother-in-law detested her, her new brother-in-law continued to send her lovelorn glances when he thought no one else watched, her husband still seemingly disapproved of her, and she was famished with nothing but thirteen courses of fish to eat.

At her own wedding breakfast. Or rather, at the breakfast for the wedding she had not wanted to the man she had not wished to wed. Bed, yes. Wed, decidedly not. She frowned fuzzily at her glass, thinking the last quaff had rather more of an effect upon her than she had anticipated.

Her husband leaned nearer, and his decadent scent washed over her. All the irritation she felt toward him dissipated in the beauty of that scent and the sight of his handsome face in such proximity to hers. If nothing else would come of this miserable match, at least that frowning mouth was now hers to kiss whenever she wished.

"My dear, perhaps you are *too happy*," he murmured into her ear.

Her eyes narrowed. Of course he would ruin her equanimity with a suggestion that she was ineriab—inedriab—inebriaterated? No, that did not sound right. Oh dear. Perhaps the dreadful man was correct after all. But her wine glass was once more full, so how could she have over imbribed? Er, over imbibed?

Yet another fish course was whisked away from her, untouched. She reached beneath the table to give his thigh a reassuring pat, but missed his thigh. Instead, she found his hard length straining against his trousers.

"Oh," she whispered to herself, snatching her hand away. Bainbridge was fully aroused, and the knowledge sent a pulse of forbidden, delicious warmth to the flesh between her thighs. Not a fluke, then. She knew the sensation for what it was now—hunger, desire, need.

"Yes," he muttered darkly, his gaze burning into hers. "*Oh*."

Heat suffused her cheeks. She looked away from him, meeting Cleo's concerned gaze. *I am fine*, she reassured her sister with a pointed look. Of course, Bo was anything but fine. She was likely soused, in addition to being terrified, dismayed, suspicious, and eager, simultaneously and not necessarily in that order.

She forced her gaze to move on. Thornton at Cleo's side was tucking into the next course, quite pleased. None of her sapskull brothers were in attendance, which was just as well for Bo, nor was her beloved sister Helen who was in America with her husband. Her sister Tia, ever the wild one despite being the Duchess of Devonshire, gave her a gamine grin. Her husband the duke offered a commiserating smile.

Then there were her parents—Father seemed quite pleased with the fish courses as well, and of course there was the matter of his final daughter having been safely married. Mother stared at her with a disconcerting intensity, and given that she had been the least impressed by the forced betrothal and wedding, it was hardly surprising. Bo reached for her glass, taking another hearty sip. The dowager duchess glared at her as if she were a bug that had dared to befoul her hem, and her bosom bow the Duchess of Cartwright was little better. Her husband, perhaps not entirely to his credit, reserved his glowers for the servant tarrying too long in refilling his wine.

How she wished her best friend Clara had returned from her extended honeymoon in Virginia and New York. The haste of Bo's nuptials had not allowed it. And then, Bo's gaze stopped on the last guest in attendance. Lord Harry. He was staring at her with equal parts frustration and…oh, dear. Something else that was wholly inappropriate when aimed toward the woman who had only just married his brother earlier that morning.

Bainbridge's words returned to her then. *He fancies himself in love with you.* At the time, she had thought it an overstatement. Unrealistic, but looking upon Lord Harry now, she could not deny that he seemed genuinely upset. Guilt pricked through the wine-soaked haze clouding her mind.

She sent him an apologetic smile, wishing for his sake that things had been different. That she had cared for him in the same way he had cared for her. How much simpler would life have been if she and Lord Harry had fallen hopelessly in love, and she sat with him at her side now rather than a cool, imposing stranger who desired her physically but could not abide by her otherwise?

"Regrets, Duchess?" Bainbridge's voice, *sotto voce*, penetrated her introspection once more.

She swallowed, turning her attention back to the man she had married. He watched her with an impassive expression, but his green eyes were flat and cold. His tone too had been deceptively smooth. The wine had addled her mind and she knew it, but she could still see that Spencer was livid. He hid it well beneath his icy façade, but there was no mistaking the underlying fury in his eyes, his tone, his clenched jaw.

"What of you, Duke?" she countered rather than responding.

His lip curled. "An endless ocean of them."

Of course she would be the biggest one. That he had been weak enough to want her, to touch her, to compromise her when he did not even like her—for a man who governed himself with such control, it must still smart. Just as his careless divulgence smarted.

His words should not have hurt her, but they found their way past her bravado, beyond her carefully built defenses, and hit her heart with the unerring precision of a honed dagger. His admission pained her. Made tears prick her eyes. For as much as she had not wanted any of this, neither did she wish to feel as though he would rather have married anyone else but her.

"How lovely to know," she said with false cheer, reaching for her glass and draining it yet again, only to be rewarded with the vigilant servant whose role it was to ensure she never went without wine. It occurred to her that perhaps this was the dowager's doing as well—yet another crafty attempt at sabotage—but she was too far gone to care.

The next course arrived, salmon this time. Bo didn't even bother pretending to put her fork in the sauce-smothered filet on her plate. Nothing could induce her to raise a bite of the stuff to her lips. Not even her growling stomach. She pressed a hand to her bodice discreetly as her stomach made its hunger known yet again. The dowager had made certain that no tray was sent to her this morning as she prepared, and so Bo had been existing on tea and wine and nerves and irritation ever since.

"You have not eaten a bite," her husband observed at her side, his voice low and meant for her ears alone yet ringing with an air of ducal authority.

She pinned a false smile to her lips, for she would not engage in this dialogue now, before their wedding guests. Even the least well-behaved lady in all England knew not to criticize her mother-in-law before guests on the day of her wedding.

"Of course I have," she lied. "Each course has been more delicious than the last."

"Go on, then." He quirked an imperious brow, waiting.

"I am parched." She found the wine goblet, drank some more, reasoning it could not possibly hurt.

"Eat the salmon, Your Grace," he ordered calmly, his eyes daring. Taunting.

He knew, the blighter. He had been watching her, and the realization filled her with unwanted warmth. If she must be his burden and part of his ocean of regrets, she hoped that a small part of him at least longed for her in the same way she did for him: inexplicable, undeniable, all-consuming hunger. For as she looked at him now, taking in his handsome face, strong jaw, the long nose that was almost too sharp, that beautiful mouth, those vibrant green eyes, and his head of dark, lustrous hair, his broad shoulders, strong chest, she could not deny just how much she desired him.

Good God, why should her rotten mind choose that moment to recall his head between her thighs, the divine pleasure of his tongue teasing her flesh, his cock hard and large and demanding, how perfect he had felt inside her? How much she wanted all that again? How she wished a mere snap of her fingers would take them back to where they had been a month ago, ready to consume each other?

But, no. She could not. They could not. Pretense always needed to be upheld, that vain little twit.

"I do not like fish," she hissed back at her husband, rather than place even the tiniest morsel of disgusting, scaled river creature in her mouth.

Bainbridge's expression changed then, understanding dawning, his gaze unerringly seeking out his mother. "Ah."

Before she could attempt to distract him, he hailed a servant. "Ask Chef Langtois if he might prepare a chicken or veal dish for Her Grace," he ordered quietly, though the entire table of guests seemed to be straining for their every word.

"That is not necessary," she protested, aware that their seating at the head of the large banquet style table made them the center of attention.

She did not think anyone could overhear them, but she did not wish to be watched with the dowager's undisguised censure or her mother's thinly veiled concern. Her parents had been absent for most of her life, forever caught up in their own whims, and now was not the time for that to change.

"It *is* necessary," he countered, his lips firm. "You cannot subsist on wine and air, princess."

Bo couldn't be certain if he was being his arrogant self or if she detected a note of concern in his deep voice. Perhaps he was concerned she would shame him before the assemblage if she continued to enjoy her magically reappearing wine. She stared at him for longer than necessary, partly because he was so dratted beautiful she couldn't look away and partly because the wine was rendering focusing on anything other than Bainbridge quite difficult.

"I dare not eat the food lest your mother attempts to poison me," she said at last, louder than she had intended, for Cleo sent her a warning look with raised brows, diverting her attention.

Beneath the table, her husband's hand wandered to her skirt, falling in heavy warning upon her thigh. She resisted the urge to scoot nearer to him so that his hand would hover between her legs instead. Bo had attended a premier finishing school, after all. She knew how to act with comportment and decorandum—decorative—oh, fiddle. What was the word she sought?

Decorum! She smiled brightly, her hand returning to the stem of her glass, bringing another gulp of wine down her gullet. That was the one.

Decorum.

"What of it?" Bainbridge muttered, his mouth so close to her ear that she could feel lips grazing her eager skin.

Had she said that aloud? Devil take it all, she had not meant to. "Your hand," she murmured instead of explaining.

"Mmm, yes, it is where it belongs." His tone was easy, low, meant for her ears only. Intimate. He paused before leaning even nearer, his moist breath making her shiver. "*Almost.*"

The breath fled her lungs. A fresh, familiar ache pulsed at the juncture of her thighs. She wanted his bare touch on her. In her. His fingers, his cock, his mouth, his tongue. Her cheeks burned at the wanton thought, the triggered memory of how he had pleasured her. Of how his tongue had worked over her, how it had felt. How he had felt.

Was it his voice or his wicked words or his nonchalant claiming of her that made her pulse with want and greedy desire? Naturally, he did not remove his hand, and she felt the weight of it, the heat of it, of him, through her elaborate tiers of skirts and petticoats. Felt it to the heart of her. She wanted more than ever to leave the interminable wedding breakfast they were being subjected to, to lead him away so that she could have him all to herself with no audience to interfere.

Chatter surrounded her, her siblings and their spouses making polite conversation. Her parents exchanging pleasantries with Lord Harry, the dowager, and the Duke and Duchess of Cartwright. Servants appeared with a new course, and a steaming dish—*les poulardes à la jardinière*—was laid before her. Chicken. Heavenly.

She tucked in, the world around her becoming less misty about the edges with each bite she consumed. Her ravenous stomach thanked her new husband for his perspicacity. And there—her ability to choose the correct, multi-syllabic word was surely an indication that she was venturing down the right path. And furthermore that Bainbridge—though she must begin thinking of him always as Spencer now—had been correct in his assessment. She had needed sustenance.

He had been observing, watching her, seeing what she required before she knew it herself. Casting a furtive glance about to be sure no one noticed, she reached beneath the table and closed her hand over his. He turned his palm up, lacing their fingers together, squeezing gently. Up until that moment, he had been cool, detached, aloof and reserved. Even their chaste kiss upon exchanging vows had left her chilled, despite the sparks that tingled through her whenever his mouth met hers.

Here, at last, in their silent bonding over his mother's despicable behavior, she felt as though they had made progress. She had hope that their marriage could be more than a forced, awkward joining that neither of them had wanted. For if Spencer did not care, he would never have noticed the plates she had left untouched or requested a substitute dish. Nor would he be holding her hand beneath the table as though that raw connection between them was as imperative as a lone rope suspending him over a cliff. But then, she had to admit, she held his hand in the same manner.

The remainders of the courses passed with ease, and at long last the breakfast was at an end. Bo, still somewhat giddy from her overconsumption of wine, hugged her sisters with a most unladylike show of enthusiasm.

She embraced Tia first. "My darling sister, I love you so."

"As I love you," Tia murmured into her ear, returning her hug wholeheartedly. "Dearest, that man is halfway in love with you, as he should be. Use it to your advantage. Make him beg. And above all, never forget how beautiful and wonderful you are. Oh yes, and if he dares to so much as make you cry, I will bludgeon him to death with the nearest blunt *objet d'art*."

Bo chuckled, knowing her sister and understanding that it was no idle threat she issued, respectable duchess or no. As for the other portion of her soliloquy—that she could not believe. The Duke of Bainbridge was many things, but halfway in love with Boadicea Harrington was not one of them.

She was grim. "Thank you, Tia. I fervently hope I shall never require your sisterly services."

Tia raised a brow. "As do I. But never forget the offer. Devonshire would beat him to a pulp without hesitation, you know."

Spencer was tall and strong and well-muscled—Bo knew this from experience—so she doubted that Tia's husband could beat him to a pulp, but she appreciated the sentiment. Odd though it was. Bo's family was nothing if not unconventional. "Thank you, sister."

Cleo was next, sniffling into Bo's elaborate updo of braids, coils, and orange blossoms. "You deserve every happiness, Bo. Are you happy?"

She didn't know the answer to that question, not yet. "I love you," she said instead, embracing her eldest sister with a heartfelt squeeze. "Thank you for managing my nonsense with grace."

It was true. She had rather placed a great strain upon Cleo and Thornton with her carelessness, and she knew it. They had borne it all, and here they were. She knew Cleo felt responsible for her having to marry Bainbridge, but she was also more than aware of the role she'd played herself. If she had not wound up in his private library, if she had not been reading a naughty book, if she had never kissed him, she would not be standing here now, dressed in ivory satin trimmed with silk roses and a train as long as the hall, the new Duchess of Bainbridge.

"I will poison his tea if he so much as makes a tear fall from your eye," Cleo whispered.

"Thank you, but I do not think resorting to murder will be necessary," she reassured her sister, wondering when her siblings had become so bloodthirsty.

Next, she exchanged stilted embraces with her parents. "I am relieved to see you wed, and a duchess no less," was all her mother said with a semi-affectionate pat to her back. Bo gratefully accepted genuine embraces from her brothers-in-law, whom she adored for their unparalleled devotion to her sisters. And then, Lord Harry stood before her.

She swallowed, the smile on her lips fading as she took in his grim countenance. "Lord Harry," she greeted in the same manner she had her other family. "I am honored to consider you another brother." Particularly since her wayward male siblings had elected not to attend.

It was not what he wanted to hear, and she knew it before his mouth twisted into a self-deprecating half smile. "Indeed. I am honored as well, *sister*."

Bo stared at him, stricken. She had suspected he harbored tender feelings for her, but she had not comprehended. He stood before her now with the expression of a man who had been sent to the gallows: accepting of his fate, utterly grim. Indeed, in the intervening time since she had last seen him, he seemed to have aged. He was no longer the man she had initially met, so free to trust and listen, eager to hear her voice. It hurt her heart to think that she was the cause of his pain.

"I am sorry," she managed.

"No more so than I." Lord Harry gazed at her, his scrutiny intense. "If he hurts you, he will answer to me. I cannot bear to see history repeat itself."

Bo's frown deepened at the statement, as much for the mentioning of her predecessor as for the alarming trend she was beginning to notice. Everyone who cared for her believed that Bainbridge would hurt her. They all supposed she needed their defense, their stalwart protection, and that she ought to heed their dire words of warning. But she was more than capable of looking after herself, just as she had always done. Just as she always would. Becoming the Duchess of Bainbridge did not render her any less capable of being her indefatigable self.

"He will not hurt me," she assured Lord Harry, careful to keep her voice as quiet as possible.

"Your concern for my wife is most appreciated, brother," Spencer said then, appearing from behind her to slide a possessive arm about her waist and haul her into his side. His tone suggested that Lord Harry's words were the antitheses of being appreciated. Indeed, his hard, cold voice suggested that he was furious once more.

His lean warmth melted into her, along with his scent, and as much as she hated the confrontation between the two brothers, she could not deny that she relished her husband's possessiveness toward her. At least it meant that he felt something for her beyond mere lust.

She did not wish to consider why she found such vindication in the notion. Why it mattered to her that Bainbridge should feel anything for her at all, even. Theirs was not, nor would it ever be, a love match. A frozen heaviness settled within her with the weight of a boulder, and she could not shake it.

"I care about her a great deal," Lord Harry said then, his gaze and his tone unyielding as he pinned Bainbridge with an intense glare. "You would do best to remember that, Duke."

"And she is my wife." Spencer's fingers tightened on her waist. "You would do best to remember *that*, brother."

"Be good to her," Lord Harry clipped, his jaw hardening. "We would not want her to end up like the last duchess, now would we?"

The air rushed from Bo's lungs at the vicious verbal blow Lord Harry had just dealt. Spencer went utterly still and stiff, and it was as if she absorbed his fury. She sensed that the brothers were near to coming to blows. Indeed, it seemed as if Lord Harry's mission was to incite Bainbridge to the first swing.

"Lord Harry," she rebuked, pressing what she hoped was a calming palm to her husband's lower back. He was all sinew and muscle and strength, hard as marble.

But her brother-in-law had not finished. He continued to lock Bainbridge in a stare. "Did you tell her what happened the last time you had a wife, brother? Your history is not promising, I am afraid."

"Bainbridge," she tried next. The situation had taken on the horror of a runaway carriage about to overturn. She felt like a bystander watching, helpless to stop it. Helpless to save those who would be wounded by the inevitable upending. "Lord Harry, cease this nonsense at once."

"Is the truth nonsense?" Lord Harry raised a brow, turning the full force of his gaze upon her once more. It was luminous, burning, sparking with anger. "Some would say he killed her, you know. *Millicent*. That was her name."

Spencer jerked forward, stepping into his brother's chest, nostrils flaring. "You. Go. Too. Far."

Bo's mind spun. Panic gripped her chest like a fist, squeezing. She did not want the brothers to come to blows, especially not over her. And she did not want to know the name of her husband's dead wife, for somehow it made her less a murky figure of the past and more real. The day had been a whirlwind—first her wedding, then the dowager's meddling followed by Bo's injudicious consumption of wine, and now an irate brother who would not stop until he made Bainbridge bleed. It was too much, more than she could bear.

"Stop," she whispered to them both, begging. "For my sake."

For the first time, she saw Harry as a man living in his brother's ducal shadows. A man still trying to find his way in the world, by being an MP, by making his voice heard. While none of that made his behavior acceptable, it at least rendered it understandable.

But Spencer's brother cocked his head, looking unapologetic. "That is why I have spoken up at last. For your sake, Bo."

"Enough," Spencer bit out. "Do not dare to ever again be so familiar with my wife. I alone am responsible for her. Not you."

He turned on his heel, giving his brother his back, and hauling Bo along with him all the way to the waiting carriage. As beginnings went, it was rather ignominious, and she could only hope as she settled on the squab alongside her husband that she could melt his ice forever. That she might have a chance at happiness with him, or at the least, contentedness. That marrying him had not been the biggest mistake of her life.

Chapter Sixteen

SPENCER HAD MADE MANY MISTAKES IN HIS LIFE.
Marrying Millicent.
Failing to save her from herself.
Failing to save himself in the wake of her death.
Compromising the lady his brother loved.
Nearly coming to blows with his brother on his own bloody wedding day over that same lady.
Choosing a quiet honeymoon at one of his northern estates rather than the long, indulgent trip abroad Boadicea undoubtedly deserved.
Being too icy and arrogant, too stubborn, too prickly, too temperamental. Christ, he was an endless list of wrongheadedness, lapses of judgment, and grievous errors.
Yes, any number of sins could be laid upon his shoulders, and he would accept the mantle. Wedding Lady Boadicea Harrington? That had been but one more of his mistakes. For he was not whole, nor would he ever be. And he would not jeopardize the precious sense of peace he had achieved before her—*without* her—not for any reason and not for anyone.

He couldn't forget the words of Dr. Clyde from the asylum where Millicent had spent much of her last year. *I have seen such puerperal mania cases before. Giving birth to a child can affect a woman's mind.* And he had vowed on that day that he would never again run the risk of casting himself headlong into the fires of hell by fathering another child.

He stopped in the act of pacing his chamber, an occupation that had riveted him for the last half hour at least as he allowed his wife time to get settled for the evening. The altercation with Harry had left him at sixes and sevens, rattling him down to his core, and he had been distant and quiet to Boadicea for the entirety of their journey from Boswell Manor.

He had performed a perfunctory introduction to the domestics, and when they had reconvened for dinner, it had been a formal, staid affair presided over by the butler and two footmen. Boadicea had been uncharacteristically reserved. The ghosts of his past, unearthed by Harry's vicious words, had returned to haunt him in full force, and he had not been able to shake them.

Spencer stared at the door separating his chamber from hers. Ensconced at Ridgely Castle, they were far enough removed from Boswell Manor and the heaviness they left there. Built in the fifteenth century and rebuilt by his father some twenty years ago, it was not as palatial as Boswell Manor, but that meant that it also was not as cavernous. They shared a dressing and bathing area, and their chambers, while still elegantly appointed and generous in size, were far smaller when compared to Boswell Manor's ostentation. But the park, settled in the woods and almost enchanted in its backdrop, had always been one of his favorites. He had never brought Millicent here during their marriage, and it seemed somehow fitting to begin his marriage with Boadicea within walls that were untainted by the past.

Even if he was.

A foolish part of Spencer wished he had more to offer her. She was not the self-centered flirt he had once imagined her to be, and he knew that now. It was not lost upon him how astute she had been during his conflict with Harry earlier when he had been yearning to plant a fist in his brother's jaw to stem the flow of unwanted revelations. He well understood why Harry would be jealous that he had Boadicea all to himself, but his bitter words had been almost unforgivable. Yet, through it all, his fierce wife had held fast, her palm pressed to his back to give him strength, never wavering from her championing of him.

He was humbled.

Gratified.

Hell, he didn't know what he was. What he did know was that he had finished two fingers of whisky, he had just married the most beautiful, desirable, vexing, stubborn minx in England, and she was even now only separated from him by wood and precious little distance.

Here, at least, was something he could freely give her: his body.

He could not wait another moment more. Need, primitive and all-consuming, pulsed through him. More than anything, he wanted to burst through her door, take her up in his arms, and carry her to the bed where he would lick her everywhere and then plant himself so deeply inside her that she would feel his possession forever.

And she was his now. His wife. He had married Boadicea Harrington, impetuous, reckless, stubborn, outspoken, ridiculously maddening Boadicea Harrington.

He stalked toward the door.

It swung open.

Wide, blue eyes met his. There she stood, glorious and wild, her auburn hair unbound and falling in a curtain to her waist. She wore a white silken dressing gown, her bare feet peeping from beneath the hem. She was bloody beautiful, even more than she had been earlier in her ivory gown with its elaborate skirts and cluster of satin roses.

He had never seen a fucking lovelier sight. He couldn't speak. Couldn't breathe. Everything else—the tension between them, the trials of the day, his interfering mother and angry brother, his past and all his fears—fell away. There was only her, and a fresh wave of need slid through him.

"I could not wait," she said, her voice husky, a hesitant smile on her lush lips.

Thank Christ. She had come to him. Of course she had. He should have expected nothing different from the bold, fearless woman he had married. She was the same woman who had stood before him nude without a crumb of shame, who had kissed him that day in his library. He found himself, as he savored the sight of her now, in awe of her tenacity.

He realized belatedly that he was gawping at her like a callow youth, as though she was the first beautiful woman he had ever seen. Whether it was the tender expression on her face or the hesitant way she lingered at the threshold—the only sign that her bravado had a hairline crack—he was pleased that she was his. Pleased that she had come to him. That she had wanted to. They had both been a ragged bundle of nerves for most of the day, and he had not been sure what to expect from her this evening.

"I am glad you did not," he admitted finally, his tone rough and raw with need and pent-up desire. It had been a month since he had last touched her with anything other than polite courtesy. A month since she had been naked beneath him, and he had relived the delirious joy of that day each night since, alone in his bed with only his bloody hand for solace.

At long last, his wait was over.

"You were dawdling." Her daring was firmly back in place as she walked toward him, and he could not be certain if it was her intention or if it was the natural way she glided across the floor, but the sway of her hips was going to be the death of him.

"I was being a gentleman." Drawn to her, he moved, helping to close the unwanted distance between them. Three strides was all it took. He inhaled deeply. *Jasmine.* His cock went painfully stiff. "I wished to give you ample time to ready yourself."

"I am ready," she said, a becoming flush tingeing her cheekbones.

He wondered if she would be wet if he pulled aside her dressing gown and pressed his fingers into the warm folds of her cunny. Would she be dripping? Lord God, he had to stop or he would not last the next ten minutes, let alone the night.

Instead of touching her there, he traced the backs of his fingers over her jaw, and her skin was every bit as soft and perfect as he remembered, like fresh whipped cream that he longed to devour.

"I have a gift for you. Two gifts, actually," he elaborated, wanting to give them to her before he lost his mind and himself inside her.

Her smile deepened, and his heart almost stopped. He swore she grew more beautiful by the minute. "I have a gift for you as well. I nearly forgot. Wait here whilst I fetch it."

Before he could protest, she spun away from him, hurrying back across the thick Axminster and disappearing into the duchess's chamber. Although he knew it was a temporary loss, that she would return momentarily, he felt it like a physical ache. She had filled the room, and both the space and he were emptier for her absence.

Bloody hell. What ailed him? Perhaps it was that he was sorely in need of relief. All the blood in his body had been diverted to his straining, erect cock. Yes, he decided. That was precisely what was making him as witless as a March hare.

He forced himself to retrieve the box containing her wrapped gifts, wondering at the wisdom of his second gift, which he had purchased on a whim and against his every sense of reason and fine judgment. But before he could think better of it, she had returned, clutching a small parcel, hips sashaying, mouth smiling, eyes gleaming.

Damn, she was lovely. He cleared his throat, feeling unaccountably nervous and more than just a bit silly, and thrusted the box toward her. "Here you are."

She accepted it with one hand and gave him the package she had retrieved. "And here you are, husband. Open yours first, if you please. I went to great lengths to find it, so I do hope you will not be disappointed."

He almost told her that he could never be disappointed by anything she saw fit to give him—particularly if it was herself—but he held his tongue and opened the box instead. His heart thumped in his chest as he spotted a gleam of silver in the glow of the lamps.

With a shaking hand, he picked the object from its nest of paper inside the box, holding it aloft for his inspection. A pocket watch, and not just any watch but a finely crafted one of silver, etched with a rearing stallion. An engraving on the reverse read *from your favorite horse thief*. His mouth went dry, and everything he could have said fled his mind in that instant.

"Presumptuous of me to assume I would be your favorite horse thief, I know." Her smile widened, and he became briefly mesmerized by the beauty mark alongside her mouth. "But I reasoned you likely do not know many, and the competition would not be fierce."

He stared at her, swallowing past the lump that had risen in his throat. Bloody hell. No one had ever given him a gift before, and as the silver watch in his palm warmed to his flesh, it seemed to burn straight into him. Something happened. Some sensation, foreign, unwanted, whipped through him. Something shifted inside him, and he felt it like a skeleton key fitting into a lock.

Click. Open.

The ability to experience happiness that he'd thought he had lost forever the day that Millicent had killed herself before him seemed within his reach. Perhaps it had never been gone, only hidden away, waiting for someone to look close enough to rescue it. To make him realize he still possessed the ability to *feel*.

"Why do you look upon me so strangely?" Boadicea's smile faltered, a bit of the riveting gleam fading from her gaze. "You do not like it, do you? Oh, bother, and here I had been thinking myself massively clever."

"Like it," he repeated, his lips moving slowly, as though he were relearning to speak. And in some ways, perhaps he was. He was relearning himself in the process. Relearning everything he had once believed. She was changing him. Melting him. *No. I will not let her. I cannot let her*. He cleared his throat, chasing away any maudlin sentiment before adding, "I love it."

And he did, in spite of himself.

"You do?" Her hopeful expression was adorable. He wanted to kiss her and gather her up in his arms and throw her on his bed all at the same time.

"I do." He allowed his eyes to roam appreciatively over her. "Thank you, Boadicea. It is an exceptionally fine piece, and I will think of you when I need the time."

And every second in between, but there was no need to say that bit aloud. He would not have his wife thinking he was obsessed with her. Or worse, in love with her. He most assuredly was not in love with her.

Was he?

Good Christ, no.

There was no bloody way. Love was an illusion. A chimera. It didn't exist.

Her expressive face lit up, having no inkling of his inner battle. "Oh, Spencer. That was a lovely thing to say. I hope you meant that you will think of me happily and not with vexation. Imagine if whenever you checked the time you thought of me stealing your horse or infiltrating your library. Poor, innocent watch, to suffer your ire so."

He grinned, thoroughly enjoying the much-needed levity between them. Enjoying himself for the first time that day, in fact, as they were finally allowed to be each other. Alone. "You are the most peculiar female I have ever met."

She arched a brow, her expression turning wry. "Why, husband, you do know how to charm a lady."

He winced. "I meant it as a compliment, though perhaps my gifts to you will help to ease the sting of my blunder. Will you open them now?"

"Of course." She turned her attention to the box, unwrapping and opening it, withdrawing a small box first and glancing up at him with question.

"Allow me." He took the larger parcel from her. "I shall hold this one until you open the first."

When she removed the lid of the box, a gasp tore from her. He knew what she looked upon—the Marlow sapphires set in an ornate collar he had chosen himself, along with a glittering assortment of diamonds. The price of the necklace had been astoundingly dear, but there was nowhere else the Bainbridge sapphires belonged other than Boadicea's throat, and he would pay the same sum thrice over if it meant she would wear them and stand at his side for the rest of their lives.

"Spencer," she said, her voice hushed with reverence. "This is a small fortune. You should never have—"

"It is the Marlow sapphires," he interrupted gently. "They belong to the Duchess of Bainbridge."

"Oh." She lowered her head, studying the glinting stones.

He understood her well enough to know that his explanation had not reassured her, and he also wished her to know that he wanted her to have them. That they belonged at her throat, that they were hers and she was his. That he had never given them to his first wife, for it had never seemed right, even before she had descended into madness. "You are the only duchess I have given them to, Boadicea. I had them placed in a new setting expressly for you. Do you like it?"

She looked back up at him, her expression unreadable. "You had this done for me?"

He couldn't resist trailing a finger over the curve of her cheek, running it down the bridge of her nose, across the captivating expanse of her smattering of freckles. "Of course, and rest assured that acquiring your second gift caused me a great deal more difficulty than this necklace did."

That had her curious, just as he had expected. "Do tell. What can it be?"

Since the gift in question was shaped like a book and her intelligence rivalled her looks, he was fairly certain she had an idea already. "Patience, princess. First, try on the necklace."

He guided her to the looking glass and placed everything upon the top of the mahogany chest of drawers upon which it sat before taking up the necklace. He stood behind her, both of them facing their reflections, and it was oddly disconcerting and arousing all at the same time. Their gazes met, an arrow of heat zinging straight to his loins. Unable to help himself, he stepped closer to her, until they were leg to leg, back to front, his cock nestling into the sweet curve of her bum.

"Lift your hair," he commanded, his voice hoarse. He had never wanted anyone or anything more than he wanted to be inside his wife at that moment. *His wife.* For the first time in years, that phrase no longer filled him with icy dread, but instead with fierce, profound longing.

Silently, she did as he asked, her gaze still fastened to his in the looking glass. Her scent filled him, making him ache. She made him more inebriated than the whisky he had consumed. She made him burn hotter and hungrier than an inferno.

Somehow, seeing the two of them together in the glass was arousing as hell. He watched as her breasts rose with her movement, her nipples pebbled and hungry, poking the delicate fabric of her dressing gown.

Swallowing, he reached around her to lay the necklace upon her throat. It glittered and gleamed, the sapphires a complement to her lustrous eyes. His fumbling fingers tried to fasten it at her nape and only succeeded on the seventh or eighth attempt. And there she stood, the reflection of his untamed duchess, her riotous auburn curls framing her lovely face and falling down her back, her lips parted as if in anticipation, her eyes burning into his, her breasts straining against her dressing gown, and a small fortune in sapphires and diamonds winking from her elegant throat. He wanted to fuck her while she wore nothing but the necklace.

Hell, he wanted to fuck her like this, standing up, watching their reflections, thrusting into her from behind, sinking his cock so deep and hard inside her that neither of them would ever be the same afterwards.

"Beautiful," he whispered, leaning into her, drawn like a child to the promise of sweets. He wanted to indulge. He wanted. Needed. Had to have. *Her*. "You are so bloody perfect. Those sapphires cannot compare to your eyes."

"The necklace is lovely," she murmured. "Thank you, Spencer."

He could not control his hands. They smoothed over her shoulders, following the gentle curvature that led from her neck and sloped down toward her arms. His fingers found her muscles, worked into the tense cords, and before he knew what he was about, he was massaging, using his thumbs and fingers to loosen her knots. So much stress trapped in her fine-boned shoulders. Was it all because of him? He hated to think it.

"Do not thank me for what is yours, princess," he said, pressing a kiss to her ear. My God, he could lose himself in her so effortlessly. For days. Months. The rest of his bloody life. She was intoxicating, and he knew exactly why his brother had been so furious that she had slipped from his grasp. Boadicea was a woman worth fighting for.

She smelled so good, and he was lost, grinding himself into the tempting swell of her bottom, touching her everywhere. His hands went lower. He watched, fascinated, aroused out of his mind, as they parted her dressing gown. Slowly. Reverently. Giving her the opportunity to arrest his movement, to stop him. But she did not, and the robe opened with ease.

He pushed it aside, down her arms, and it fell to the belt at her waist. His chest pressed into the smooth, delicious curve of her back and the soft web of her hair as he stared at the reflection of her full, peach-tipped breasts and her hard nipples and her open mouth. Her glazed eyes glittered in competition with the necklace, shimmering against her pale skin. She was bold and gorgeous and unafraid.

Dear God, he had to be inside her.

Spencer dipped his head, fastened his mouth on her throat, inhaled deeply of her scent. He kissed and nipped, raising his gaze to watch in the looking glass all the while. Saw his hands cupping her breasts. Felt the tight buds of her nipples in his fingers, watched himself roll them between his thumb and forefinger, saw her arch her back, felt her arse pressing into his cock. He canted his hips, thrusting against her cleft, witnessed the way her mouth fell open, how her pink tongue licked her sensual lower lip, watched her pupils grow large and round with need. Heard the moan escape her at the same time as he saw it fall from her beautiful lips.

His name was all she said.

"Spencer."

But it was the tone, the need, the combination of all his senses devoted to her, to the erotic picture of her porcelain and pink curves on display, his hands claiming her. He licked and bit his way to her shoulder. Here, he sank his teeth into her sloped flesh, not hard enough to cause her pain, but enough to let her know his intentions. The beast within him could not be controlled this night.

She did not seem to mind. Instead, he watched her fingers move nimbly over the belt at her waist, making short work of the knot. Her robe pooled around her feet on the floor, and the mirror was just long enough that he could see the fullness of her hips and the sweet beckoning flesh at their apex. Exhaling on a fresh wave of raw need, he dragged his lips back over her shoulder, up her throat, to her ear where he pressed a hot, open-mouthed kiss to the shell.

"I have wanted to fuck you all day," he whispered, because he knew what it would do to her. He knew her love of wicked words and deeds. Knew that while they might be mismatched in other senses, here, in the bedchamber, they were a perfect fit. Here, he could be as depraved as he wished, and she would beg him for more.

She reached behind her with her left arm, hand cupping his head, and turned to meet him, face to face, nose to nose. The startling blue of her eyes gave him a jolt as he was removed from the fantasy of the looking glass. He could see the exact shape of each of the freckles on her pert little nose, and he was entranced. He had never supposed that freckles could make his cock hard, but he stiffened even more, his hips twitching, his need to be inside her becoming more frantic by the moment.

"I have wanted the same thing," she whispered, undoing him with her sweet voice and her glorious confession and the way her lips grazed his as she spoke.

"Tell me," he prodded, wanting to hear her say the words. Wanting so much he almost slammed into her then and there without even touching her cunny to see if she was ready. But of course, he knew she was ready. The scent of her arousal, musky and delicious, lingered in the air. Her body was so bloody responsive to his, seemingly made for his, made for him, and were he not so ruined by what had come before her and were she not the antithesis of everything he had hoped to have in a duchess, he would have sworn she had indeed been fashioned by the Lord specifically for him, and he for her.

But none of that mattered, and his every coherent thought ceased to exist, the moment she said the words he had been yearning to hear from her lips.

"I want you to fuck me, Spencer."

Ah, hell. That undid him. The tip of his cock was already wet and he had not even yet been inside her. He was going to fuck her, but only after he worshipped her. He closed the distance between their lips, kissing her. It was fiery, passionate, a bit unhinged. Lips and teeth and tongue, messy and wild and everything he craved.

And then he broke away, slipped from her grasp, went down on his knees. He palmed both cheeks of her arse, thinking that even it was beautiful, perfectly shaped and pale and curved. He squeezed gently, then ran his hands with wonder down her thighs, circled his thumbs in the hollows behind her knees, trailed down her sleek calves and then lower still. He gripped one slender ankle in each hand and guided them apart until she was opened to him, her pink, glistening folds on full display.

"Jesus, princess, you are so damn beautiful." The words were torn from him. His hands traveled back up her long legs—so long, so riveting, so fucking lovely—and then, he leaned into her, found her with his tongue.

He licked her slit, up and down, found her dripping, so ready for him, heard her breathy exhalation. She tasted as sweet as he remembered, better than anything he had ever known, and he licked and licked into her, dipping inside her channel, burying his face deeper, breathing in her essence, making her the center of his world.

His left hand found her hip, gripping, and his right hand dipped between her legs from the front, finding her hungry clitoris and stroking, working it until she writhed against him, rocking back and forth between the demands of his mouth and his fingers. He could sense that she was close to finding her release, and he wanted that more than anything. He pointed his tongue, drove it home inside her, increased the pressure on her pearl. Faster, harder, more.

Her entire body tensed beneath his touch, and she was shaking, trembling violently, crying out as she spent all over his tongue. He lapped it up eagerly, wanting more, anything she could give him. She was so wet, her essence soaking his mouth, his face, his fingers.

Yes. God, yes.

He rose to his feet, tearing his robe away until there were no more barriers remaining between them. His conscience decided to reassert itself in that moment, reminding him that this was her second time, that he should be gentle and easy with her.

Taking a deep breath, he willed his raging lust to temper itself, and planted his hands on her waist. He dropped a kiss on her neck. "The bed or here?" he gritted.

"Here," came her ragged response. "Anywhere, everywhere. All I know is that I need you inside me."

Bloody hell.

Her reflection in the mirror was that of a goddess. Her hair was everywhere. Her eyes shone. She looked half drunk, worlds away from the hesitant creature who had murmured her vows to him earlier that day and the lady who had lingered at the threshold between their chambers. So bloody beautiful. So untamed. So much his.

"Hold on to the top of the dresser," he ordered, catching her ear in his teeth. He could still smell her, and it was intoxicating, as was her complete submission just now when he knew that she was anything but acquiescent. She was doing this for him, because of him, because of how he made her feel.

He reveled in it. Her hands went to the top of the dresser. His fingers dipped into her folds, stroking her slick seam before sinking inside her. Two fingers. She was hot, so hot, and tight. He slipped a third finger into her channel, and she gripped him, moaning. She was ready. More than ready. He stroked his cock, coating it in her wetness, and then tipped his hips, bringing him to her entrance. He licked the whorl of her ear, tongued the hollow behind it, feasting on the sensitive skin that he knew drove her to distraction.

"Ready, princess?" he asked, his every instinct screaming to take her but the deep-rooted sense of honor ingrained within him forcing him to wait. To allow her to maintain control.

She rolled her hips, rubbing her slick folds against him. Her curls cascaded down her back, over her face, partially obscuring her luscious breasts. "Yes."

Her sibilant surrender was his final undoing. He positioned himself, and in one deep thrust, he was inside her to the hilt. "How do you feel now, Boadicea?"

A sigh escaped her. "Full." She tilted her head back, locks of hair falling from her face, and met his gaze in the looking glass. "I want you so much that it hurts."

Jesus. Christ.

His control fled. His honor. His mind. His comprehension of anything that wasn't her disappeared, full stop. He was raging, needing, hungry, so damn hungry, and she felt better than anything had in all his thirty-three years. Better than anything he deserved. Just *better*.

He almost withdrew entirely only to drive inside her again. She tightened, moved against him, welcoming, urging. He was lost. Lost inside her. He thrust, faster and faster, slamming into her. He was mindless. Weightless. Relentless. Everything in him screamed, hungered, wanted, longed, took. Deeper. Harder. More. In and out, again and again, and she was slick and smooth, warm and tighter than a fist, and she was everything.

She was his.

His wife.

His…

Bloody hell, he could not even think. Could not do anything more than fuck her. Take her. Own her. Faster still, thrusting, possessing. In the glass, she looked as if she were intoxicated. Her face was flushed becomingly, head tipped back. He sucked her neck, found her racing pulse and licked furiously, hoping that he would make a mark. That he would find the proof of his lovemaking upon her delicate skin in the morning.

He looked down then, watching his cock slide in and out of her, seeing it rigid and glistening with her sweet arousal. He slowed for a moment, attempting to regain control, but he could not. He was dangerously close to coming, and as much as he loved being inside her, he would never lose himself so much that he would spend within her. He would not beget another child ever again, and it mattered not that she was his wife.

He thrust forward, his fingers finding her clitoris again, teasing in slow, perfect circles. Her flesh was so warm and slippery, so needy and inviting. He worked her, withdrew, sank deep inside her again, and then she was unraveling. She tightened, clenching on his cock, her body releasing a shower of delicious tremors yet again that he knew to be her climax.

Damn it, he almost came inside her. But his instinct worked in his favor, and he withdrew in haste, fisting his cock in his hand, spurting his seed all over the perfection of her lower back. He watched it fall, marking her as his. It was not enough. It would never be enough. But it was all he could offer her, because the part of himself that had once believed in love and hope had died a long time ago. This—the beast—was all that remained.

Chapter Seventeen

BO WOKE IN A STRANGE BED, in a strange chamber. And she wasn't alone.

The warmth from a hard male chest radiated into her back. An arm, strong and possessive, wrapped round her waist. A cock, stiff and erect, pressed against her bottom. As wakefulness sifted through her, she arched instinctively, seeking him, as if it were the most natural act in the world. As if she had done it countless mornings before.

She felt...at home. His scent enveloped her, pine and soap and something indefinably wonderful that was simply *Spencer*. While she had spent much of the previous day wondering if she had made a massive mistake in marrying the Duke of Bainbridge, his passion and intensity last night had gone a long way toward assuaging her doubts. Elsewhere, he may be icy and forbidding, but when he touched her, kissed her, took her, he burned, and she burned along with him.

The origin of their union was rather extraordinary, their courtship nonexistent and rushed, but the desire between them was not forced or feigned. It gave her hope that they could at least become friends, given time, though they may never love each other. That they were not doomed to an icy marriage of mutual loathing in which they sought passion in the beds of other lovers.

The mere thought of Spencer taking another woman as he had taken her last night—with such fierce possession—disturbed her. It occurred to her that she had never asked if he intended to remain true to their vows. For some reason, it had not been something she considered until this moment, when it all became quite clear to her in the early morning's glow.

He was hers now. Vexing, arrogant, stubborn Spencer Marlow belonged to her. He was her husband. The beautiful, maddening, insufferable Duke of Bainbridge. In so many ways, he remained unknown to her. And yet, every part of him, all that she knew and all that she had yet to learn, was in her possession. She would not share him.

"What is it?" he whispered into her ear then, his hot breath sending a shiver of awareness through her. "I can practically hear your mind whirring like a machine."

She had not known he was awake. Indeed, it surprised her that he had not disengaged himself but continued to hold her. After making love to her before the looking glass, he had taken her in his arms and carried her to his bed, where he had made love to her all over again. She had expected to return to her chamber, but he had kept her here with a simple command. *Stay*. And she had spent her first night sleeping in a bed with a man only to wake and find it the most natural and delightful thing.

How could he tell her thoughts were busy?

"It is nothing," she said, not wishing to dispel the enchantment of the moment with her wayward fears.

"It is something." He kissed her ear, the hollow beneath it, the side of her throat where she was sure her pulse pounded against his knowing lips. "As husband and wife, we must speak to each other with honesty."

He had a valid argument, but how was she to concentrate when his tongue flicked against her skin and desire, new and simmering and wondrous, shimmered through her? She swallowed as his hand glided to her breast, kneading the sensitive flesh. He rolled her nipple, tugging it, and an answering ache bloomed between her thighs. Lovemaking was still new to her, and she was sore in strange places after last night, but she wanted him again in spite of it.

"Was I too rough with you?" he asked when she did not respond, his voice hesitant.

Most definitely not. She wondered, not for the first time, what his marriage had been like with his former duchess, before shoving all thoughts of it from her mind. She did not wish to allow whatever had come before her to intrude upon their burgeoning marriage.

"I will not share you," she blurted.

He stilled. "Share me?"

Oh, drat. She had rather bollixed it up, hadn't she? She took a steadying breath, grateful she did not face him. "I asked you before if you had a mistress, and you told me that you did not. I wish to make certain that you will not seek one out now. I know it is the way of things for many husbands and wives, but it is not what I want. I hope it is not what you want either."

He was silent for a beat too long for her comfort, and then he kissed her shoulder. "I do not stray from vows, princess."

She closed her eyes, allowed herself to revel in the sheer bliss of his body against hers, his mouth upon her skin, his masterful hands at work bringing her to life. "Good."

"What of you?" he asked with deceptive calm.

Bo knew how much weight lay behind his question, for she recalled all too well his revelation that his wife had been unfaithful. She rolled over, facing him at last, meeting his seeking green gaze, and took his face in her hands. An unexpected burst of tenderness shot through her at how vulnerable he looked, how far removed he was from the supercilious Spencer Marlow she had come to know.

"I am yours," she said softly, "and yours alone."

The tension ebbed from his body. "Good," he said in an echo of her one-word response.

"Very good." She traced his lips with her fingers. How odd that in the span of a day, she was now free to touch him as she pleased without fear of recriminations. She could lie naked in bed with him, do whatever she wished, and she had no one to answer to. Propriety could go hang. Everyone else be damned. This man, this beautiful, complicated man, was hers at last. In every way. He had told her so. Just as she was his. "You were not rough with me, Spencer. You could not be. It is not in you."

His expression shifted, growing shuttered. "You do not know what lies within me, Boadicea. Perhaps it would shock you. Appall you, even."

There it was again, Bo was sure of it, the specter of his former wife. She wished she could undo all the wrongs, erase every hurt the woman had dealt him. With time, perhaps he would confide in her. Perhaps she could help him to heal. But not yet, not with their union being so new, all this territory between them uncharted.

She kissed him instead of answering or questioning him any further. Leaned into him, closed the distance, set her lips upon his. It was not the first time she had initiated a kiss, but its effect was nevertheless incendiary. He caught her to him as though he feared she might disappear unless he anchored her to his body, his mouth opening, their tongues tangling. The kiss was voracious. Consuming, needy, and rough.

His hands swept over her body, and he turned them as one, never breaking the kiss, so that she was on her back with him atop her. Her legs were spread open, his cock already nestled against her where she wanted him most. He reached between their bodies, fingers finding the bundle of flesh that was so responsive to his touch. What her bawdy books referred to as a gem.

As he worked her, it felt like a gem, bright, sparkling, bold. He already knew how to please her so well, understanding when to stroke her fast, when to touch her slow, when to increase his pressure. She was wet for him, so wet that she could feel the slick evidence of her desire. How she hungered. He made her mindless, weightless, so that all she could think and feel was him and what he did to her.

How he undid her.

She moved against him. Their mouths clung. Her breath caught, and she gripped the sinewy plane of his back, reveling in its smooth, hard strength. He pressed harder, faster, and she was close to the edge, about to unravel. Her nails sank into his skin. She sucked his tongue. And she was on fire in a way she had never imagined possible, all for him, because of him. He completed her.

He…

Oh.

She lost control, raked her nails down his back until she found his tight buttocks and gripped him, her climax spiraling through her, rushing upon her, taking her with the force of a locomotive. She spent, upon his wicked fingers, his tongue in her mouth, and she shook and tremored and savored every second of the release he gave her. But it wasn't enough. Would never be enough. She still wanted more. All of him.

Bo tore her mouth from his, arched against him, gave him the forbidden words that had so aroused him before. "Fuck me, Spencer."

With a primitive growl, he guided himself to her center and thrust, seating himself deep, complete, straight to the hilt. One thrust and she was filled with him. Stretched, hungry, more alive than she had ever felt. He kissed her again, deep and dark and devouring. His left hand sank into her hair, fisting in it, his right remaining on her folds, teasing her gem, making her so wild that she feared she would splinter into a thousand shards of herself at any second. He slammed into her, hard and rough. She gripped him to her, urged him onward, angled her hips to match his every thrust.

It was inevitable.

She was combustible.

He was going to drive her over the cliff.

And she could not stop it. Could not contain herself. Could not wait one minute more. His fingers, his mouth, his cock. He was so deep, so perfect, and he completed her in a way she had never fathomed. In a way she could not have known before this, before him. Her husband.

God, yes.

More.

She wasn't sure if she said it aloud or in her head. All she did know was that he increased his pace, sank so deep inside her it seemed he would forever remain there, and worked her sensitive flesh so that she could not fend off her climax for another heartbeat. She came apart, tightening on him, crying out, clutching him to her, wrapping her legs around his waist, drawing him deeper still. As deep as she possibly could.

And then he withdrew, slipped from her body as the blissful ripples of her pleasure still resonated through her, and held himself tightly in his fist, spilling his seed into the bed linens. For as much pleasure as he had given her, Bo watched him find his release somewhere other than inside her yet again, and something cold and hard lodged itself in her chest. Something unknown, mingling with emotions she found all too familiar: worry, fear.

He collapsed alongside her, breathing heavily, and she stared at the ceiling. He had brought her the sort of pleasure she had imagined was fiction, silly hyperbole in the forbidden books she devoured. He had shown her the height of ecstasy, had promised to be faithful to her, had stood before their families and God and taken her to wife. They had made love four times. Three times as husband and wife.

And yet, he had never spent his seed inside her. Not one time. Though most refined ladies of her age remained blissfully ignorant of the details of matters betwixt a husband and wife, Bo was not. She knew how children—how the heirs of a duchy—were created, and it was not by the duke spending his seed into the sheets.

The chamber was silent except for their mutual labored breathing. Bo allowed the enormity of her realization to settle within her. Turned it over in her mind. Waited a few more breaths until she could not contain it another minute more.

"You do not want children?" she asked into the false tranquility, staring at the ceiling.

"No," came his clipped response.

She felt his answer like a blow to her midsection, and she did not know why. She had never given thought to having children. Indeed, she had never imagined she would marry. Had not wanted to, would not have married anyone had she not felt it was the best thing for her beloved family. For her sister and Thornton. And to help improve the consequence of her Lady's Suffrage Society.

Why, then, did his revelation that he did not want to beget an heir—that he did not want to raise a brood of stubborn, dark-haired lads and spirited red-haired bluestockings—affect her so? It should not, she knew. She had not wished for this life with him. A lack of children would mean more time spent pursuing the causes she found most important. Indeed, she finally had her independence.

She was a married lady. A duchess. Free to enjoy the pleasures she had only read about. Free to pursue her dreams and goals. Free to be who and what she wanted. To make her life *hers*. It was everything she had always wanted, there for the taking.

Why, then, did she feel so hollow inside?

She rolled away from Spencer, to her side, and waited for sleep to claim her once again.

This time, it never did.

Spencer could not stop staring at his wife.

A buffet of rich breakfast foods scented the air. His full plate beckoned: eggs and bacon, *jambon de Bayonne*, muffins, sauces, jams, plump sausages. So much food he could consume it all and have no need to eat for the remainder of the day. Servants hovered, eager to please the duke and his duchess on the first morning of their honeymoon.

He wished they had gone to Paris.

He wished they had never left his chamber this morning.

More than anything, he wished he had rolled her over on her back after waking for the second time that morning, kissed away the pinch of worry knotting her brow. He should have taken her slowly and deeply, licking and kissing every bit of her glorious skin, fucked her until she forgot about whatever caused the shadows in her eyes, the firmness of her mouth.

But they had not gone to Paris, and she had slipped from his chamber in silence, thinking him still asleep, and he had watched her go without saying a word. But he had felt the change between them. She had withdrawn, ever so subtly. Now that she had finally joined him at the breakfast table, some of the brightness was gone from her gaze, and the brief smile she flashed him had lost its luster.

Of course, she was beautiful as ever, turned out in a gown of indigo silk with a nipped waist and a tulle underskirt, trimmed with lace and bows. The necklace was gone from her throat, and though he knew it was far too sumptuous to be appropriate for this time of day, he rather wished she had chosen to wear it anyway. He waited until she was served a plate before dismissing the servants so that they had some privacy.

He stared at her, willing her to look back at him, when the last footman had gone. But she kept her gaze trained upon her plate, her fork in hand, prodding her *ouefs en cocotte* without actually consuming a bite. It would seem that he needed to make the first move in this impasse.

He cleared his throat. "Good morning, wife."

Her eyes flew to his at last, delicate brows lifting as though she was surprised he had addressed her. "Good morning, husband."

Stubborn as ever, it would seem. He had hoped she might offer him something more. While neither love nor children would ever emerge from their union, now that he had unleashed the flood of his desires once more, he had no wish for a passionless marriage. They were tied to each other for the rest of their lives, and he had meant what he said about remaining true to his vows.

"How did you sleep?" he prodded, knowing what the question implied. They had not spared much time for slumber.

A becoming flush colored her cheeks. God, she was lovely. It required every bit of willpower he possessed to remain seated and not rise from his chair, close the distance between them, and lift her to the table where he could have the true feast he wanted for breakfast. The thought had him shifting in his chair, attempting to ease the discomfort caused by his tailored trousers.

"I slept well, thank you," she said with cool, quiet poise, her eyes dropping once more to her plate.

Devil take it, where had the passionate warrior queen gone? The woman who had set him on fire with her body and her unabashed desire? He did not know what to make of this. Did not understand the cause of her distance. Was she embarrassed, perhaps, by the raw passion they had shared? He did not think she could be, for she was the selfsame lady who had stood naked and fierce before him a month ago.

"Excellent." He kept his tone light, took a sip of his coffee, watching her still. He thought he could look upon her all day long, every day, for the rest of his life and never tire of seeing her. It wasn't her beauty alone that drew him to her—though to be sure, she possessed a rare vibrancy that was undeniably breathtaking—it was something else, something unique. Something that was simply Boadicea. He had not been able to resist her from the first moment he had been alone with her, and his reaction to her had only intensified with the intervening time and their marriage rather than lessening.

He would do well to hold it in check, lest it get out of hand. He could not allow her to think that he would ever be able to give her more than the slaking of their mutual desires.

"Tonight I do think it may be best if I sleep in my own chamber, however," she said calmly, using her knife to cut a bite of sausage on her plate.

Her words, so casual, shook him. The primitive part of him roared to life, and he said the first thing that rose to his already addled mind. "No."

She paused, her gaze flicking back to his. "I beg your pardon, husband?"

There was no way in hell that she wasn't sleeping in his bed. He was aware of the sleeping arrangements that most married couples had. His marriage to Millicent had been no different—they never spent the night in the same bed. In fact, he had never spent the night sleeping in the same bed as any woman before Boadicea. But the moment he had laid her on his bed, it had felt inherently right. He would not allow her to put this wedge between them on the first day of their marriage. He had enough wedges for the both of them.

"No, *wife*," he repeated. "You will sleep with me, where you belong."

She pursed her lips. "I am sure that is a most unusual arrangement, Bainbridge. It is ordinary, in fact, expected, for a husband and wife to maintain separate quarters."

Boadicea was determined, but he was equally so, and she would find that in a battle of intractability, he would always emerge the victor. "Do I snore?"

Her flush deepened. "No."

Damn it, he wanted her so much he ached with it, and he couldn't be certain if it was because of her obstinacy, because he wanted to prove to her that she was his, or because she was so bloody beautiful. Perhaps all three. But it didn't signify. All that did was that he wished to get what he wanted, and what he wanted was his wife in his bed. Beneath him. Astride him. Any way he could have her.

"Do you find fault with the bed?" he asked, relentless.

"Of course not." She sighed, looking quite vexed with him now. "It is fine."

"Were you too cold?"

"Bainbridge." Her tone and use of his title told him he had irked her.

"Too warm, perhaps?" he persisted.

Her full, kissable lips flattened into a grim line of irritation. "Bainbridge."

"I am using rationalizing and logic." He shrugged. "There must be a reason you do not wish to share my bed. I want to know what it is."

"You do not want children," she blurted.

Ah, perhaps he had finally found the root of the problem. "And what has that to do with sharing my bed?"

For truthfully, one had no bearing upon the other. He was definite in his decision. Nothing she could say or do would sway him. What he had lived through with his former wife had been sheer hell, and he could not run the risk of enduring it a second time. Harry was his heir, and while Spencer had never supposed he would marry again, circumstances had demanded that he do so. But neither circumstances nor his new duchess could force him to once more make himself vulnerable to madness and death.

"You should have told me," she said quietly, her eyes searching his, and he could not shake the feeling that she saw far more than he would have preferred. "Did you not think I had a right to know such a thing before we married?"

Her words gave him pause, for he had not considered the ramifications of his wishes. In the years following

Millicent's death, he had remained celibate, with no intention of marrying again. Then, Boadicea had appeared in his library with her vibrant beauty, her bawdy book, and her rampant boldness, and he had lost his head. He had ruined her, himself. Christ, he had ruined the both of them. It had all been so sudden and unexpected that he had not given thought to much aside from his desire for her and his duty to wed her.

"Our courtship was rather extraordinary," he reminded her, his voice wry. "I did not wish to marry again."

She stiffened. "Then why did you?"

"Because I had no choice." The words were torn from him, and he said them before he could think better of it.

Once they were spoken, there was no rescinding them.

It was true that he had married her because his hand had been forced—after being caught compromising her by his mother and the Duchess of Cartwright, what option had he left? But having married her, he could not deny that he was pleased by the physical connection they shared. More than pleased.

She had come from seemingly nowhere, appearing in his life and in his library, then in his arms, and now he could not fathom his life without her in it. He wanted her. Hell, who was he trying to fool? He *needed* her.

But he was not accustomed to emotions, having spent the better part of the last six years attempting to drown them out however he could so that he was able to survive. And so he did not tell Boadicea any of the things she likely would have wanted to hear.

He did not tell her that kissing her brought parts of him he had thought long dead back to life. He did not say that she could undo him with a mere look. He did not divulge that her scent made him weak, or that her curvy thighs and the sweet pink skin between them made him want to spend all day discovering her. He didn't share that she was the best, the most wondrous gift life had ever bestowed upon him. No, he said none of those things. He did not warm her with his soft words, with whispered seduction, with cajoling or kisses or seduction.

Because he could not.

Instead, he watched her.

If he had thought her pale before, he had been wrong. Every bit of color leached from her countenance. She went white as the fine china on the table, standing with such abrupt force that her chair toppled backwards to the carpet with a dull thud.

"I am no longer hungry, Your Grace," she hissed. "If you will excuse me?"

He leapt to his feet as well, stalking toward her, catching her when she would have retreated. His hands landed on her waist as if finding their natural home. This was not how he had envisioned their breakfast unfolding, and he did not like being the cause of her distress.

He studied her, noting that she refused to meet his eye. It was all he could do not to drag her against him, bury his face in the fiery luster of her hair. Drop to his knees and worship her the way she deserved. "Do not go." It was the closest he would come to begging.

She gripped his wrists, attempting to remove his touch, her lips compressed in the same frown she had been wearing ever since entering the room. "Release me."

"Boadicea, look at me," he demanded, ignoring her request. "I will not let you go until you do."

Her eyes snapped to his at last, glittering with anger and something else he could not define. "Here you are, Duke. Are you satisfied now? The wife you did not want is gazing upon your regal countenance."

Hell. He was perverse, and that was why her defiance made his cock twitch. It was the beast, the uncontrollable part of him that he had worked so hard to cage, breaking free. He slid one of his hands up the curve of her back, skimming over the laces of her corset, the silk covering them, feeling her heat. He knew how soft she was there, over her spine, between the blades of her shoulders, and he longed for the barriers to be gone. Hated the fabric and boning that kept his skin from hers.

His fingers trailed over her nape, sinking into her coiffure, gripping with a gentle tug designed to master rather than hurt. "I have always wanted you. From the moment I first saw you in my library wearing that red dress covered in roses, you were all that I could think of. The need to touch you, kiss you." His eyes fastened on hers, he lowered his head, pressing a kiss to the beauty mark that drove him mad. "To make you mine. That is all I have wanted." He kissed her cheek, her ear, nuzzled her hair and felt her shiver. "You."

And it was true. All of it. He had wanted her—wanted her still—with a ferocity that stripped him bare and left him raw and aching. He had not wanted a wife, no. But there was nothing and no one he had ever wanted more than Boadicea Harrington, and that was a bloody fact.

"You speak of desire," she said.

He kissed down her throat, finding her racing pulse that belied her calm tone. "Yes." Another kiss, a drag of his teeth. He wanted to mark her, to see the evidence of his mouth on her creamy neck. His need for her was almost vicious, pounding inside him, beating like a heart.

"I want your respect as well as your lust, Spencer." She caught his face in her hands then, and he allowed her to urge his head back so that they stared at each other once more. "We may not have wished it, but we are husband and wife now. Treat me as your equal. Do not make decisions for me."

She was a peculiar creature, the woman he had wed, and though she clearly did not think it, he had never met a woman he respected more. But that did not mean he would unbend from his position on children. There would be none.

"I will treat you as my equal in all matters," he said solemnly, "as you are. But I remain firm on one matter. There will be no issue from this union. I am sorry I did not make my wishes in this regard clear prior to our vows, but I will not waver."

For some reason, the notion of planting his seed in her filled him with a brief sense of awe. Worse, it made him more desperate to be inside her than he already was. But that was instinct. He would not be ruled by his base nature. The depths to which he had sunk at Millicent's side was ample reason to keep him from ever making such a grievous error again. He would sooner hold a pistol to his own head and pull the trigger.

The thought made him cold, sent ice through his veins, chased away the fire licking through him. He released Boadicea abruptly, stepping back, something seizing in his chest, like a band closing around him, a vise. His ears hummed.

Suddenly, he was back in his study on that long-ago day, Millicent's wild eyes and tear-stained face confronting him. She pointed the pistol at him, and he recalled looking down its dark barrel, thinking it would be the end of him. In that odd space of time, the eerie silence, the awful prescience of knowing he was about to die, he had taken in every detail, the sound of birds singing outside, the color of her gown, the ribbon trim on her hem, the way her brown hair had been greasy and flat, running down her back unbound.

She had once been beautiful, but the further she had slipped into madness, the more the disease had stolen her. Or perhaps that had been the asylum. He remembered thinking that it was the best place for her, that she would be healed and return to her former self, and they could live again. But instead she had emerged gaunt and bruised, talking to herself, preoccupied with angels and demons. His mother had warned him that she saw Millicent screaming into the rosebushes, raving about the devil and redemption, and he had not wanted to believe it. He had wanted, with a desperation born of his own futility, for his wife to be whole once more.

But then she stood before him, about to commit murder.

"Say it," she had demanded. "You killed our baby."

He had not been able to say the words, for they weren't the truth, and it hadn't mattered if it was the last thing she wanted to hear him say before sending him to oblivion. "No," he had said slowly. "No one killed our baby, Millicent. He was stillborn."

But she had raged, insisting that he confess. That he was the devil. Until finally, he had given in, thinking that he could somehow save himself, dissuade her from her path. He had gone closer, had told her what she wanted to hear.

And before he could reach her, take the gun from her hands, she had screamed, pressed the pistol to her own head, and pulled the trigger.

The report echoed in his brain, and now he was somewhere lost between the past and the present, a sheen of sweat over his skin, a sickness in his gut, and he could scarcely breathe.

Until Boadicea stood before him, dragging him from the depths of his mind with her calming touch on his shoulders. With her sweet scent drifting over him and a concerned frown turning down her lips.

"Spencer," she whispered, drawing him into her embrace. "I am here."

She was, and even though it had been a long time since he had suffered an episode like this before anyone else, he was somehow unashamed to have lost control before her. He clutched her to him, drawing a sense of peace and comfort from her, the tension seeping from him.

"I'm sorry," he murmured into the silken cloud of her hair. It was all he could say, and he wished he could elaborate, tell her he was sorry that he could not ever again be whole, that he could not be the man she undoubtedly deserved. That he could neither love her nor give her children as he ought. That she was left with the shell of a man, that part of him had died that day with Millicent, and he could never get it back.

But he said none of those things. Instead, he inhaled the fresh scents of jasmine and lily of the valley and tuberose, held it deep in his lungs as though it were a panacea. He held her to him as if she could resurrect him, as if he were yet capable of being salvaged.

Even if he was not. Even if nothing would ever again return him to the man he had once been. Not even the woman in his arms.

"I am here now, Spencer," she repeated. "And I am yours. Whatever came before me, I cannot change. What comes next is up to you."

She was wrong about that, but he didn't bother to correct her.

Chapter Eighteen

"YOU ARE AN ACCOMPLISHED RIDER, PRINCESS."

Bo cast her husband a sidelong glance, suppressing a smile. "Do not sound so surprised, Duke. I know I almost killed myself on Damask Rose, but there is nothing I love more than galloping across the land, feeling the wind in my face."

They trotted side by side on Arabian mounts, early afternoon sun gilding the lush Warwickshire landscape and lending it an almost ethereal air. Since breakfast, they had not strayed from each other's sides except to change for riding. While Bo knew there was much her husband had yet to reveal to her, she was willing to wait, to allow him to his own time, and she could not help but feel closer to him after seeing him seize up that morning.

She had witnessed him vulnerable and shaken, lost somewhere in the depths of his past, and he had allowed her to pull him through it. That he had accepted her embrace rather than pushing her away suggested there was hope yet for their marriage. If he did not wish for children, she would not force the matter. Not today. Not yet.

"You were reckless with Damask Rose," he agreed,

studying her in a way that made her feel as if he saw inside her. "Promise me that you will not ride with such disregard for your own safety ever again."

"What is this? Concern for my wellbeing?" she teased. "Have a care or I may begin to suspect you actually like me, Your Grace."

He grinned back at her, his emerald eyes rivaling the lush flora surrounding them. "I do like you."

For some reason, his simple statement sent a warm rush of pleasure straight through her. She looked away lest her expression gave away more than she wished for him to see. "I may like you as well."

"You may?" He laughed, and it was a beautiful laugh, masculine and rich. It did odd things to her insides. She wondered then how often he found amusement in anything. His life had not seemingly been filled with levity, and she longed to see more lightness in him, especially if she was the source. "I daresay I shall have to try harder to persuade you if you remain uncertain."

Her lips twitched. "I can think of ways you might try."

Another bark of laughter left him, and she turned toward it, unable to resist his magnetic pull. He was gloriously beautiful, laughing in the sunlight, strong and lean atop his mount. The man seated a horse with such effortless grace it made her sigh.

"Did you open your second gift?" he asked her then, surprising her with the change of subject.

She thought of the wrapped gift she had left in her chamber that morning. "No. I thought perhaps you would like to be there when I opened it."

He nodded, his gaze dipping to her mouth. "Capital idea, princess. I would like nothing better."

She wondered what the other gift could possibly be, though its shape was rather familiar. Some sort of book, she would guess, but she could not imagine what manner of book the Duke of Bainbridge would have purchased for her as a gift. An etiquette guide perhaps?

"I only got you one gift," she said then. "It is not fair that you had two for me."

"My gift was more than enough." He reached into his waistcoat and extracted it. "I have consulted the time on no less than three occasions already today, and each time I was reminded of my favorite horse thief."

She laughed, grateful for the abatement of the tension that had been growing between them. The sides of him that she had witnessed today—vulnerable and lighthearted—appealed to her. There was far more to the icy Duke of Disdain than she had once believed.

"Your taste in horseflesh is impeccable." This was yet another part of him that intrigued her. Her mount today, Majestic Iris, was sleek and beautiful, though a great deal better behaved than Damask Rose had been.

"Thank you." His tone was butter soft, setting off an answering flutter low in her belly. "Horses were not always a passion of mine, but in the last few years, I have found much solace in them. They are such noble creatures, so intelligent, capable of doing great harm and yet also incredibly gentle. The contradiction appeals to me, I suppose."

She noted his careful phrasing. Breeding horses had been his way of healing, she would imagine, thinking again of the trauma he had experienced. Her mind could not grapple with the horror he must have endured, watching his wife take her life before his eyes, the shock and pain of it. Her heart gave a pang in her breast as she recalled again how he had looked earlier at breakfast.

He had gone pale, his eyes glazed, and he had seemed like a man lost, adrift somewhere inside himself in a hell that only he could see. She had seen him suffer a similar fit before his mother, and she had to imagine it was not an uncommon occurrence. Bo wondered how much he had suffered on his own. His mother did not seem to possess a warm or maternal nature, and he and Lord Harry were not close. Who else did he have?

No one seemed the obvious answer.

But that time was at an end, for she had meant every word she had spoken to him. He had her now, and regardless of the manner in which their marriage had come to fruition, she was his. She would chase away the darkness with light, banish his ghosts. Whatever he required, she would be there if he would but let her.

She realized she had been quiet for too long, and that he was looking at her oddly now, as if he could sense the bent of her introspection. "Your stallion is impressive," she said, thinking of the muscled, rich brown horse back at Boswell Manor. "I should like to ride him some day."

"Pharaoh," he answered, giving her a pointed look. "I imported him from Aleppo. He is a wary beast, and you are never quite certain where you stand with him. One moment, he can be docile as a lamb, and the next he is a force of nature."

She raised a brow. "Why does that sound familiar?"

"Minx," he said without heat. "You cannot ride him without me. I alone can sense his moods. It seems to be a particular talent of mine. Perhaps the only one I possess."

"I do not know about that." She cast a sly look his way. "I can think of several others."

A wicked smile curved his sensual lips, and it sent a pulse between her thighs that was only heightened by the rhythmic plodding of her horse beneath her. "Oh? What would those be? Perhaps you would care to enlighten me."

Bo smiled right back at him. "You excel at arrogance, for one thing. For another, you are quite good at stealing books. You are also brilliant at insults."

"Allow me to argue that arrogance is a ducal obligation." He paused, cocking his head at her. "As for stealing books, I have only ever taken one book into my possession without having purchased it, and as that tome was decidedly contraband, I do not think it signifies. And I admit to having a difficult time recalling a single insult I have issued."

She pursed her lips. "You did call me a wanton tart masquerading as a lady."

Was it her imagination, or did a flush stain his high cheekbones?

He glanced away from her for a moment, clenching his jaw, before meeting her gaze once more. "I was an ass, and I am sorry. I…you are unlike any other lady in my acquaintance. I was not certain what to make of your, er, reading proclivities or your bold nature."

His awkward admission touched her, as much because she knew it was sincere as because it was so very Spencer. Now that she was beginning to learn the man beneath his façade, she could well imagine how she must have flummoxed him. She was not unaware of her own shortcomings. Her sisters referred to her as a rapscallion in skirts. She had never pretended to behave. Had never wished to be the meek and mild-mannered lady her parents had longed for her to become. Finishing school had not finished her, as she had no wish to change. She was herself, and she had a tendency to find trouble, and every part of her balked at rules and propriety. She could not reconstitute herself to make her more palatable for others. It was not in her nature.

"I accept your apology," she told him, something alarmingly warm and tender sinking through her. He was so handsome, the sun clinging to the hair peeking beneath his rakish hat, bathing him in a glow. His expression was so pained, so vulnerable once more, and she loved it.

She could love *him*.

Dear God.

The thought struck her, unwanted. Unneeded. Alarming. No, she did not love her husband of one day. It was all the lovemaking that was rendering her maudlin, ruining her mind. That and his undeniable masculine beauty. And his halting, heartfelt apology. Not to mention the way he had embraced her earlier, as if she were the life sustaining him, how he had buried his face in her hair as though he wanted to inhale her. And his laugh. How beautiful it was to see him smile, hear him give in. The heady knowledge that she could melt his ice. That she was already melting it, like a summer sun, even in this moment.

That he was hers.

Yes, it was all those things working at her feverish mind, tricking her into thinking nonsense. She did not love Spencer Marlow. No, she did not. She could not.

Loving him would be foolish. Dangerous. Stupid. Naïve.

Their marriage had been forced. He had not wished to wed her. She had not wished to wed him. He was damaged by whatever he had endured with his previous wife. That woman's demons still haunted him. And yet…

"You say you accept my apology, though you are glaring at me now as if we are at daggers drawn." His quizzical observation burst through her tortured musings.

Oh.

Oh no.

Oh damn it all.

This was happening whether she wished it to or not, and she most decidedly did not wish it to happen.

She stared at him, and her heart, her stupid, ludicrous heart, expanded in her chest. Warmth filled her from the inside, as though the sun had somehow managed to infiltrate her body. Her heart pounded, a strange exhilaration sluiced over her, and it was the most surreal moment of her life.

Bo sat atop her mare, completely motionless, being carried across a verdant field, staring at the man she had married, realizing that this was the sort of moment from which there was no return. Understanding that everything had changed. That what she least wanted was blossoming inside her, undeniable and demanding.

That she was falling in love with her husband.

"Let's ride," she blurted, desperate to end the moment. To fly in the wind, attempt to grind these unwanted emotions beneath her horse's hooves and send them splintering into the ether.

"We *are* riding." He looked at her oddly yet again.

She swallowed. What did a woman look like when she realized she was falling hopelessly in love with a man who did not love her in return? She felt suddenly as if he could see into her and read her feelings. Good God. "A race," she managed. "From here to the tree line in the distance. On the count of three, we go."

"Boadicea."

Even the way he said her name, her full name rather than the abbreviated version, sent a fresh frisson of feelings skittering through her. She attempted to compose herself, hoping that her expression was as bland as she struggled to make it. She stared at him, thinking *please do not notice I am a complete fool for you*. "Spencer. Are you afraid you will lose?"

His expression changed, and she knew her challenge had been accepted. "I do not lose, princess. To that end, I do think your proposed race should have a reward. What goes to the victor?"

In addition to harboring an aversion to rules, Bo also had a deep-seated competitive side. She was an excellent horsewoman, and she had no doubt that she could beat Spencer in any race, and that regardless of the victor, she would challenge him. "The loser must do whatever the winner wishes for the remainder of the day," she invented. "No questions asked."

His eyes gleamed. "Those stakes are acceptable. Who will count?"

"Me," she decided, feeling the need to race into the wind. Hoping it would dispel the ridiculous emotion lodging in her chest at that moment. "On the count of three. One, two, three."

And just like that, they galloped, soaring over the field. Their mounts were neck-and-neck, the well-trained horses eager to unleash some of their energy at last in much the same way that Bo was grateful she had finally been given the opportunity to revel in the speed and thrill of racing a horse.

Though she had taken a horrible spill from Damask Rose and this was the first time she was riding with any speed since that day, she was unafraid. She was, in a word, exhilarated.

She lowered her body over Majestic Iris's neck, spurring her on, gratified when she pulled into the lead. The tree line loomed. She was getting nearer to victory. To beating him. And any inconvenient thoughts of love had been thrust into the back of her mind. Winning was all she could think about. Winning and riding, riding faster, harder, spurring her mount. She was one with her horse. She was going to win.

And then, a movement in her peripheral vision. He was gaining on her. No. She could not let him win any more than she could admit she was falling in love with him. Oh, drat it all. There it was again already, forcing itself into her mind when she least wanted it.

Love.

He spurred his mount on, and their horses were once again even with each other, their powerful hooves hammering on the ground in tandem. The tree line was closer. His horse went faster, and she was staring at his back, staring at defeat, knowing that he had already won this race, but in addition to the race he had won far more from her.

She wasn't just falling.

Holding her breath, she attempted to spur her mount into a final burst of speed. But none was forthcoming, and Spencer galloped past the tree line with ease, a full horse length ahead of her.

She had lost. The race, her heart. She slowed Majestic Iris, allowed defeat to sink into her bones as she reined her in. Her husband turned his mount, trotting back to meet her, grinning with unrepentant triumph.

"Well done, princess. You almost won." He stopped alongside her, lightness dancing in his eyes, and a strange rush of giddiness fluttered through her at the sight. "I am afraid it was not meant to be, however. You are now mine to command for the remainder of the day."

If he only knew. She was his for the remainder of their lives. Her heart was his. She drank in the sight of him, staring for far longer than was necessary, loving the sight of him so carefree, a world away from the broken, disillusioned man he had been that morning.

"Do not look so terrified, wife." He winked. "I promise not to be too much of a tyrant."

Bo gawped some more. The Duke of Bainbridge had just winked at her. Why, if she had not witnessed it herself, she would not have believed a secondhand account. As it was, part of her was convinced he had gotten something in his eye.

"I find your victory dubious," she said at last, attempting to squelch the seemingly unstoppable surge of emotion roiling through her. "I believe you already knew you would win the race when you suggested it, that you were well aware that your mount would outmatch mine."

He did not defend himself, his gaze burning into hers. "Certain victory is the best kind."

"Spoken like a man who has never known defeat." She kept her tone flippant as she parried back, desperate for him not to suspect the turmoil raging behind her calm façade. He was so observant, those moss-green orbs always plumbing and seeking, and she was not prepared to reveal the depths of her feelings to him. Not now. Not yet. Perhaps not ever. Self-preservation and pride would not allow it.

"I am beginning to think I have won when it matters most." He nudged his mount back into a walk. "Come," he called over his shoulder. "Let us find a proper place to have a picnic, and I shall begin enjoying the spoils of my victory."

She urged Majestic Iris to follow, smiling as she admired Spencer's strong shoulders and lean waist from behind. Here, in the calm tranquility of the day, with nowhere to go, no one to see, and nothing but time and sunshine in their favor, it was easy to pretend they were a true husband and wife. That their marriage had not been forced or unwanted, and that not only did she love him, but he returned that love.

Relentlessly, she forced that fantasy from her mind, reminding herself that the truth was far bleaker, and that she could not forget she had married a man who was broken in ways she could not fathom. Broken beyond her ability to fix him, no matter how much she wished she could. That she had married a man who did not and never could return her love. Despite the warmth of the sun, a shiver worked through her, and she knew she would have to do everything she could to keep from falling any deeper for him than she already had. She must guard her heart at all costs.

Above the plod of their horses' hooves, she heard the happy trill of a ditty she could not name. Good heavens, the Duke of Bainbridge was whistling, of all things. She had not even known he had such frivolity in him.

Chapter Nineteen

"Another tart?" Spencer asked, holding a cocoa tart near Boadicea's tempting mouth.

He had already fed her one of the decadent confections straight from his hand, and when she had licked a crumb from the pad of his thumb, it had taken every bit of his restraint to keep from pressing her down upon the blanket he had spread over the grass, throwing up her skirts, and sinking deep within her. Which meant, of course, that he wanted to feed her another. And another, until he fed her his tongue and his cock simultaneously.

It was inevitable that he would take her here, in the bounty of late summer sun, in the midst of a field, nothing but the glorious sky above them and the sweet-scented earth beneath them. But first, he wanted to watch her consume another bite-sized bit of chocolate and meringue heaven. For Boadicea did not sample a dessert in a ladylike fashion—of course she didn't. Instead, she licked, moaned, and savored. She devoured.

And he wanted to devour her in turn.

"A tart for a tart?" she asked archly.

Bloody hell, she was not letting that one go, was she? It shamed him to think he had once been so dismissive of her, that he had believed her nothing more than a beautiful flirt with a wild streak. There was so much more to her, so many hidden depths he had only just begun to discover.

"You are not a tart, princess," he said firmly. "And since, as the victor, I am entitled to your complete cooperation for the remainder of the day, I both insist you cease referring to my idiocy and eat another tart."

A slow smile curved her lips, and he could not stymie the answering slide of heat in his veins. "I shall save referring to your idiocy for tomorrow."

A laugh tore from him. "How generous. Now, eat the bloody tart before it melts all over my fingers and I am a sticky mess."

"As you wish, husband, since I am at your mercy." She obliged then, opening her lips to nibble lightly at the shell of the pastry. His cock twitched as he watched, as much from her words as from her actions. How was the sight of a woman taking a bite of dessert so erotic? He had not imagined he would ever find it so.

Then again, he had not imagined, even days ago, when he had been facing his impending nuptials, any of the maelstrom of sensations buffeting him now. He had dreaded their union, hated the notion of another marriage when the first one had ruined him, had imagined Boadicea unsuitable for him in every sense other than base physical attraction. And yet…

He felt lighter than he had in… Hell, in as long as he could recall. How incredible that it was owed to the woman seated opposite him with such elegant perfection, her purple riding habit contrasting her pale skin, the jaunty hat she had worn earlier removed to allow her fiery curls to glint in the sun.

His chest filled. His heart thumped. Never had he shared such a simple, pleasurable afternoon with Millicent, even before her madness. He could not help but notice the disparity between the two women. It was an irony that perhaps only he appreciated that neither one of his marriages had been his wish but fostered instead by varying forms of duty.

With Millicent, it had been that their families—her lineage older and more prestigious than the Marlow line—wished to align. The match had been well-received by all. His father had pressed, and Spencer had consented, and he had been young and so bloody naïve when he had welcomed his young and green bride to Boswell Manor. Spencer had been twenty-five, Millicent scarcely twenty. Within five years, both his father and Millicent had already been consigned to the grave.

"You are frowning," Boadicea observed, trailing her fingertips in a whisper of a touch over his brows.

He swallowed, realizing that he had frozen, still holding out the remainder of the tart. He offered it to her for another bite, watching as her white teeth sank into the meringue center, her tongue licking a bit of chocolate from her lower lip. She missed a trace in the corner of her mouth, and without hesitation, he used his thumb to wipe it away, bringing it back to his waiting tongue.

Sweet. So bloody sweet. But he wanted more.

"Spencer," she whispered, her hands cupping his jaw. Her eyes sparkled with a depth of emotion that stole his breath. That told him she felt the pull between them every bit as strongly as he did.

To hell with the tart. He tossed the remainder of it over his shoulder, and where it landed he did not give a damn. His hands went to her waist, hauling her to him so that she straddled his lap, skirts pooling around them. Her soft thighs and the irresistible heat from her sweet cunny branded him through his riding breeches.

Fuck, she was wet for him, soaking into the layers of fabric separating them. How grateful he was for the split in her drawers, for the heat and seduction of her. For her beautiful mouth, her floral scent, her curves, her husky voice saying his name, for her body moving over his.

"Kiss me," he ordered, his palms seeking more of her, gliding over the small of her back, finding her shoulders. Luncheon had been pleasant, but this was what he hungered for most: her. His wife. Boadicea. The only woman capable of making him burn with outrage and hunger all at once.

"Boadicea," he urged when she still denied him. She stroked his jaw instead of aligning her lips to his, caressing him with a wonder that touched him in a way he had no longer imagined possible. "Please."

"Spencer." She removed his hat, laying it on the blanket at his side, her fingers plunging into his hair. He forgot about wanting her mouth on his, forgot about desiring her surrender.

Instead, he took her in as if it were the first time he was seeing her: oval face, delicate brows, locks swept into a Grecian braid. Freckles on the bridge of her nose. High cheekbones. The most kissable mouth he had ever seen. The beauty mark that drove him to distraction. By God, she was more gorgeous than he had even comprehended before, and her beauty burned from within. She glowed. She was so much more than he had expected, more than he had ever dared imagine.

And she was his. How was it possible?

Hope burst open inside him, like a rose going into full bloom. Hope that he could one day resurrect the pieces of himself he had lost. That he could be the man Boadicea deserved. That his fits would cease, that he would never again wake trembling from the maws of a demonic nightmare, that he could be…her husband. A man she could love.

The enormity of his thoughts shook him. Could he ever be that man? He was afraid to look inside himself, to find the answer, to wonder whether or not, in spite of all he had endured, a part of him still believed love could exist after all. The enormity of it all threatened to cleave him in two.

So instead, he turned to what he did know: the need that sparked between them with an unquenchable flame. Desire, pleasure, was what he knew without doubt he could give her. Was all he could ever promise.

One of his hands sank into her hair, the other cupped the side of her face, and he looked at her, mesmerized. Not just by her beauty, which was undeniable, but by her. "Have you any idea how gorgeous you are?" he rasped, watching his fingers trail over her jaw, his thumb caress her cheekbone. She was warm, alive, more exquisite and responsive than he deserved.

More of everything than he deserved.

"So lovely." He lowered his lips to her throat. Here, she tasted as sweet as she smelled. He trailed his mouth over the tense cord, nibbled the side of her neck where her pulse hammered furiously. He kissed below her ear. And then he found the secret spot that was so responsive to his touch, that silken hollow that smelled like lily of the valley and longed for his tongue. He licked.

She moaned his name. "Spencer."

Dear God, all he needed was his name on her lips, and he was about to spend. This wouldn't do. He shifted beneath her, easing the pressure of her warm, wet flesh over his straining cockstand. He bit her earlobe, ran his tongue over it to quell the sting. She clutched him tighter, and an answering need burned within him.

"You still have not kissed me," he said into her ear.

"Mmm." Her voice, low and husky, sparked a fresh onslaught of hunger inside him. "You ought to know I do not do well with acceding to the wills of others."

He smiled, his lips grazing the delicate whorl before him. When she shivered, he pressed his advantage, blowing lightly over it and catching the top curvature of cartilage between his teeth. "What if it is your will as well?"

She rubbed her cheek against his, much like a cat, as though she wished to brand her imprint upon his skin, or perhaps vice versa. "My will is at war. Part of me wants to kiss you, but part of me wants to deny you."

"Deny me and deny yourself, minx." He moved her once more, settled her back over his burgeoning rod, canted his hips into hers.

She arched against him and scooted her rounded bum nearer, so that his entire length pressed her seam. "Tell me something, Spencer, and I will kiss you as you wish."

Her teasing heightened his arousal. Ever since he had first laid eyes upon her, she had driven him to distraction. And rather than feeling sated after their heated bouts of lovemaking, he only craved her more. Everything she did, everything she said, every movement, every breath, amplified a hundredfold in him. Her eyes, her scent, her lips. That beauty mark. Good God.

But still, he had won their race. He would not forget, regardless of how warm and wet her pussy was through the slit of her drawers.

He raised his head and gazed down at her, absorbing the sight of her, flushed and lovely, her hair glinting in the late summer sunlight. Her irises, at the center of those forget-me-not orbs, were dark and large, betraying her arousal every bit as much as her body did wherever they came into contact.

"The race, princess," he said. "I won, and it was agreed that the loser must do whatever the victor wishes for the remainder of the day. I distinctly recall you saying you found the stakes acceptable."

She blinked. "Your victory is suspect. You were already assured of it when you set the terms of the race."

He raised a brow, enjoying their banter and the glorious brightness of the day. He couldn't recall ever feeling so unfettered. "Never say you are a poor loser, Duchess."

Her eyes narrowed. "I am no such thing, Duke. I will gladly meet your terms on one condition."

Clever of her, but he was having none of it. He shook his head slowly. "No conditions. Our terms were clear."

"Your knowledge that you had the faster mount was not." She pouted.

Here was a side of his wife he had yet to learn. She did not lose well. He found it rather endearing. "Darling, I can assure you that our mounts were evenly matched. I employed no deceptions. I daresay your heart was not in it. Victory was almost yours, but in the end, I raced past you."

"Yes," she said, her voice solemn, her gaze slipping to his mouth. "You did."

"A kiss is all I require." He grinned. "At the moment."

She pressed a quick, chaste kiss to his lips, so hurried in her movements that he couldn't even respond. "There you are, debt settled."

He raised a brow. "Not that sort of kiss."

She raised one in return. "You did not specify. Next time, do take care to elaborate on your wishes, husband." She rocked against him then, clutching his shoulders, and he lost his bloody breath at the impact of her grinding on his painfully erect cock.

Bloody. Hell.

He gritted his jaw, attempting to control the commanding hunger coursing through him and doing everything in his power to tamp down the vicious need to tear open his trousers, free his cock, and guide her down upon it. To sheathe himself inside her, where he belonged. The need to be inside her nearly undid him.

He clenched his teeth. "Kiss me."

She rocked again. "Answer me."

A battle of wills. She did not play fair, and he shouldn't be surprised, really. He had known from the start that Boadicea Harrington was a wily thing, a termagant, a rebel, every bit of her in her namesake's mold. She was sent to conquer. Bold, beautiful, unrelenting.

His.

He kissed her throat, sank his hand into the hair at her nape. He felt her inhalation against his lips, her pounding pulse. "What is your question, darling?" he asked into her silken skin.

The landscape seemed to pulse with vitality all around them, glinting with bright possibility. A kaleidoscope of rays and green leaves surrounded them, summer's revival on full display, the redolent scent of hay and grass and flower, the whisper of a breeze in the trees. The sun was warm, golden, beating upon his back. Her skin was warmer still, scented with her sweet perfume. Their bodies were intertwined, her skirts billowing about them on the blanket, her thighs bracketing his.

He stilled, waiting, heart beating in competition with hers. What did she want to know? What did she want to hear? He hoped it had nothing to do with the past, for he could not—would not—allow it to intrude upon them now. Nothing could shatter this fantasy in which he pretended he was an ordinary man, that madness and death had never scarred him. That he was a husband hopelessly in his wife's thrall, newly wed and free to lose himself in her.

How he wished all that was true.

But it wasn't.

It was fantasy bound to be dismantled.

For the moment, however, he could convince himself. He could forget everything, everyone, every black moment of his past, just by her responsive curves merging with his hard planes. Just with her earnest gaze on his. Just with her, so that it seemed that they were the only two people in all the world.

"Your question," he asked again, for she had seemed to come undone, her body thrusting against his, riding him, bringing him to the edge of reason.

"The book." Her eyes were bright, insistent. "Tell me what you read."

Hell. Thoughts of the book did not bode well for his longevity. He had not been wrong with his initial estimation of it, not entirely. Yes, it was bawdy. Yes, it was also forbidden. The obscenity laws barred literature of its sort from being printed. But the devil of it was, that the more he had read, the more he had wanted to read. He had not been able to put the thing down. Each page he turned, he could not help but think of Boadicea eagerly scanning the page, reading the same wanton words as he.

And he had wondered, God how he had wondered. Had the stories aroused her? Shocked her? Had she read the letter from Lady Lovelorn to her friend Lady Pearl about their adventures in finishing school? The mere thought of Boadicea reading such licentious words made him go hard as a marble bust.

He held her gaze, unwavering. "All of it."

Her mouth fell open in a perfectly formed 'o' of surprise before she gathered herself and schooled her features back into a semblance of order. "All of it?"

He continued his regard. "*All* of it."

Her lips pursed. "The birching?"

"The birching," he confirmed.

"Lady Lovelorn's letters?" she asked next, sliding her warm, wet cove across him again.

His cheekbones felt red as any virgin's at the mere mentioning of those wicked epistles, and he was decidedly not a bloody virgin. He cleared his throat. "The letters, the groom and Lady Letitia, the French governess who had a fondness for His Lordship's Priapus. I read the whole bloody thing. I read it because you had read it, and I wanted to see and know what you had seen and read."

He was aware that he was being crude, but she had pushed him and surely she knew better than anyone how to accept vulgarities. After all, the book he had read was hers before he had taken possession of it. The words he read, the situations he referred to, the unhindered nature of the language, it was all to be expected by Lady Boadicea Harrington.

Strike that, for she was no longer Boadicea Harrington, was she? No indeed, she was Boadicea Bainbridge, his duchess. She was his.

She stayed her torturous moving over him, her eyes going wide. "Oh. I had not yet finished the volume in question, because it was taken from me. Therefore, you are, I daresay, ahead of me in your reading."

"You still have not kissed me," he pointed out, rolling his hips beneath her. "You can read the remainder of it when I return it to you. *If* I return it to you."

She arched back, rubbing her soft folds over him. "Do you wish me to kiss you, Your Grace? I confess, I have forgotten in our lengthy dialogue. Remind me, won't you? You are the winner, and I am at your mercy. What would you have me do?"

Saucy wench.

One more twitch of her hips against his, and he almost lost himself, lost sight of what he was about and what he was meant to do. She teased him with such practiced ease, and if he had not known he had taken her maidenhead, he would swear she was a polished flirt.

But she was not a practiced flirt. She was his wife. His outrageous, rebellious, beautiful, daring, fearless duchess. "Give me your mouth," he told her. "And your pretty little pussy. That is what I want. Take control. Show me what you want, what you desire."

He did not need to urge her twice. Her mouth crashed over his, open and wanting. It was a messy kiss, hungry and needy, sudden and demanding. He clamped his arms around her, drawing her nearer, opening to her onslaught. When her tongue slipped inside his mouth, he sucked.

The delicious anticipation that had made each interaction so heady and delicious vanished. They became one, mouths fusing, tongues thrusting, bodies moving. He undid her bodice. She opened his waistcoat and shirt. Her breasts, perfect handfuls topped with hungry nipples that poked into his palms, sprang free. She found the fastening of his trousers. Thank Christ he wasn't wearing smalls this morning. When her hand closed over his shaft, he nearly came all over her dainty fingers.

His touch traveled beneath her voluminous riding habit, between them, finding the center of her without err. She was pure, molten heat. Smooth and wet. Warm and soft. Everything he wanted. He stroked down her slit, then back up again, found her clitoris engorged and eager. As he played with her, she jerked into him, moaning.

"Yes." The single word was a hiss, torn from her.

He agreed wholeheartedly. His fingers continued to work the eager flesh between her thighs. Wet, so wet. He could not wait a moment more. He gripped his cock, positioned himself at her entrance, and guided her downward.

He impaled, hot and hard, straight to her core. Her tight channel sucked him deep. He lost his breath. Nothing had ever felt so bloody good, so bloody right. If he never did another thing worthwhile in his life, at least he could remember this moment, when he was ballocks deep inside the most beautiful, maddening, intelligent, and determined woman he had ever met.

The wife he had not wanted.

The wife he could not fathom his life without.

The wife he wanted so much that he ached with it.

Good God, he was losing himself, losing himself in her, and it was as physical as it was metaphorical. She clenched on him, drawing him deeper, a sound of satisfaction rolling from her lips and straight into his mouth. He kissed away the sound, swallowed it down, made it his. He surged forward, one hand splayed on the blanket behind him for leverage, sinking his cock as deep as he could. Her perfect cunny tightened over him, milking him, drawing him into oblivion.

They rocked together, a blend of breath and lips and tongue, his cock buried inside her to the hilt, her luscious body riding his, taking and withdrawing, taking and withdrawing again. His other hand found her waist, gripping, guiding, urging her to find her own pace. To fuck him as hard and as fast as she liked.

It didn't take much urging for her to settle into her rhythm. Watching her ride him was so arousing that he was about to come inside her, without preamble.

This would not do.

He pulled out and held her above him, his hand gripping her waist. "Touch yourself."

Her eyes were smoky with desire, lips swollen and red and glistening from their frantic kisses. Without a word, she slipped her hand between her thighs, and though her abundant skirts pooling around them obscured the erotic sight of her pleasuring herself, the knowledge was enough. A soft moan fell from her opened mouth, her head tipping back so that he could admire her throat's creamy elegance. He longed to feast on her there, but he would not lose control. Not now, with her hand moving quicker, her breath expelling in short bursts.

Dew dripped from her, bathing his waiting cock. She was a bloody goddess. His goddess. His forever, and he could never get enough of her. He watched, waiting until she was on the brink of ecstasy before he guided her back down. Her slit, slick and hot, beckoned, and he notched his cock to her entrance. In one swift thrust, he was seated deep at home.

"Oh, Spencer." She tightened around him, clutching his engorged rod like a fist.

"Don't stop," he ordered tightly, barely holding himself in check. "Don't ever stop."

On another moan, she worked her clitoris, hand moving faster beneath her skirts. And then, her pussy clenched and trembled. She rode him to oblivion, taking her pleasure, slamming up and down, up and down.

Gritting his teeth, he allowed her the full rapture of her spend. When the last tremor worked through her, he withdrew, fisting his cock, coming all over her inner thigh. Boadicea collapsed against him, panting, and his breaths were every bit as ragged as he held her to him, embracing her, burying his face in her hair.

He wished he had come inside her.

The fervent thought, arriving out of nowhere, took him by utter surprise and frightened the hell out of him. He could never be so reckless, could never take such a foolish chance. He would have to steel himself, learn to control these wayward impulses coursing through him. Or he would have to keep his distance from her. It was as simple as that.

Why then, did the realization leave him feeling empty and cold, even with her wrapped in his arms and the sun blazing high above? Why did it make his heart feel as if it had seized in his chest? Why did it make his head a confused jumble of past fears and present worries?

"Unless I am mistaken," his wife murmured into his neck then, "that is what the book referred to as riding a St. George."

She was right, though it was a phrase he had heard well before ever coming upon it in her bawdy book. A startled laugh tore from him, and just like that, the anxiety clouding his judgment dispelled, and it was once again the two of them, Spencer and Boadicea, holding each other in the glorious late-summer sun. The ghosts of the past—for the moment—were buried firmly where they belonged once more.

He kissed the place where her jaw began, just below her ear, smiling against her skin. "Good God, I think your wickedness is rubbing off on me."

"I certainly hope it is," came her throaty response, "for there is nothing I would like more than to ride a St. George with you again."

Chapter Twenty

BO'S HEART FLUTTERED AT THE SOFT KNOCK at the door adjoining her chamber to Spencer's. After riding back to Ridgely Castle, they had shared a bath in the massive tub, alternating between washing each other and kissing until she had once again ridden him with the warm, fragrant water lapping at their skins. From the bath, they had gone straight to Spencer's bed, where their intention to nap had proven impossible once Spencer's wicked mouth had begun an inquisition into her body that ended between her thighs. He had feasted on her like she was the finest sweet, and when she had climaxed, he'd turned her over and taken her from behind while his fingers played over her pussy.

Dinner had been a proper affair, quite interminable, with Bo counting the minutes until she could once again be alone with her husband. As he walked through the door now, his sculpted lips quirking into an intimate smile that was just for her, a fresh tingling began in her core, her nipples going hard. She pressed her thighs together in an attempt to stave off the ridiculous need that overcame her whenever she was in his presence, but it only made the ache worse.

While he had been all refined elegance at dinner, this was how she preferred him, nude beneath his black dressing gown, his bare feet and strong calves visible to her admiring gaze. The ache turned into a steady pulse as she met him halfway across the chamber. Already, she was slick and ready for him, and he had not even touched her yet.

He took her in his arms, his seductive pine scent settling over her senses. "You are so bloody lovely."

Her heart thudded in her chest as she looked up at him, flattening her palms on his chest. *How I love this man*, she thought, before chasing the sentiment away. It was too much for him, she knew, and far too soon. Besides, she was not ready to make herself so vulnerable, to allow him the chance to break her heart. The darkness remained within him, simmering beneath the surface, his past a mystery she had yet to unravel.

Slowly, she reminded herself. *Proceed slowly and with caution.*

"I could say the same to you," she said, taking in the perfect masculine symmetry of his face. He was all hard angles, from his high cheekbones to the sharp swath of his nose and the wide plane of his jaw. Only his lips were full and supple. He was so beautiful, so beloved. She never could have imagined, upon their initial introduction, just what he would come to mean to her.

That he would be hers.

That she would be so irrevocably his.

He flashed a wry grin. "I am not lovely, princess."

"You are to me, Duke." She rose on her toes and pressed a kiss to his lips, taking his grin and molding it to her mouth.

He groaned, his arms tightening around her, before lifting his head. His emerald eyes sparked with that fierce brand of intensity she had come to expect from him. "Ridiculous woman," he said without heat. "As much as I would like nothing better than to take you straight to bed and make love to you all night long, there is something we must do first."

"Oh?" Her heart still beat a rapid pizzicato within her breast. Ever since that morning, she had been awash in exquisite sensation. Everything felt more vivid, seemed more vital, more meaningful than it had before. How was it possible that one man could completely alter her world?

"Do not look so disappointed, minx," he teased, and he was grinning anew.

He seemed lighter, younger, his relaxed expression lending him an air of boyish charm that she had never seen him exude. Just a month ago, she would not have recognized the man gazing down at her with what her foolish heart construed as adoration.

Adoration. She wished.

Calm down, heart, lest ye be smashed to bits.

"What must we do?" she asked before her madly whirling mind could think up any more nonsense.

"You must open the rest of your gift." He took her mouth in another kiss, this one longer and more thorough than the first they had shared, before abruptly breaking away and setting her from him when the kiss threatened to burn into a roaring inferno. "Damn it, I cannot resist your sweet lips."

She gave him a smile of her own. At least they were of the same mind on that account, for she could not resist his either. "I am glad for it, husband."

Husband.

Yes, he was that, and she could not suppress the gratification the knowledge filled her with. It still felt so new and strange to her, and yet, contentment was a river that had flooded its banks, running straight through her, washing away all that had come before. She had not wanted to marry, had not wanted to tie herself to him forever, but now it seemed impossible for her to imagine any other outcome. She did not want one.

He was all she wanted.

But the trouble was that perhaps she was not all he wanted.

As she turned to retrieve the gift, she gave herself a stern warning that she needed to guard her heart. He remained closed off from her, his past a barrier that may well prove insurmountable. It was possible that he would never return her feelings, that he was too damaged by what had come before her.

The prospect sent a pang through her heart even as she took up the prettily wrapped bundle. She forced herself to forget about the heaviness invading her and spun back to face him, the gift held aloft like an offering on an altar. It felt like a book.

"Allow me to guess," she said, strolling back toward him with care, enjoying the way his eyes fastened to her hips. If she swayed them a bit more than natural as a result of his perusal, it couldn't be helped. "You bought me *The Lady's Guide to Comportment*."

He shook his head. "No."

She pretended to think. "*The Hoyden's Manual to Reform*?"

His lips twisted. "No again, princess."

Bo stopped before him, holding the gift between them, and fell into his emerald eyes. "*How to Please One's Husband, and Other Gems of Knowledge?*"

"You are incorrect." He raised a dark, imperious brow. "However, I'm beginning to think I should have purchased *How to Gracefully Accept a Gift, by a Husband Whose Wife Drives Him to Distraction*."

She laughed, and something in her heart shifted into place. She felt, in that moment, that she was where she was meant to be, that he was meant for her, and she for him. That somehow, fate had thrown them together when they had least wanted or expected it, but the universe held a larger plan for them both. A path they were meant to travel as one. And she knew an intense burst of gratitude.

Who would have thought that the Duke of Disdain knew how to make a joke?

"Very well, I shall take pity on you." She tossed a grin up at him as she untied the ribbon and opened the paper to reveal the book within. It was handsome, red Morocco leather, a gilt title stamped to the face that read *The Jewel*. Her mind spun as she took it in, certain she knew what awaited her within the pages and yet certain it could not be so.

"It is a new journal with a small run," he said, his low voice crushed velvet to her senses, smooth and seductive. "It features hand-colored woodcut illustrations that I thought you may find…illuminating. Your other book had no such embellishment."

She stared at the book in her hands, then her husband. He watched her with an expectant expression, and an unmistakable trace of scarlet coloring his high cheekbones. He looked, in fact, equal parts eager and ashamed, as though he could not believe he had purchased such a gift and yet he could not wait for her to crack its spine.

"You bought me a bawdy book," she said, awed.

His color deepened. "Smut, yes. I do not know what I was thinking. I ought to burn the thing in the grate along with its predecessor."

She clutched the book to her bosom like the treasure it was—for not only did it contain the forbidden, but *he* had bought it for her. Spencer Marlow, the icy Duke of Bainbridge, who had once looked down his nose at her, decrying such literature as filth. It was rarer than all the diamonds and gold in the world. And also, it touched a new place in her heart, unlocked another door she had not known existed to be opened.

"Oh, Spencer." She could not keep the tenderness from her voice. She knew what this had cost him, knew how he clung to his frigid control. And she dared to hope it was proof, leather-bound and gilt-edged on her palm, that he cared. Or that he might, one day.

"You had best forfeit it now." He extended a hand. "I will do away with it. The gift was improper and not the sort of thing one ought to buy one's wife. The illustration of the lord gamahuching the governess is positively filth."

Oh. None of the other books she'd read had illustrations. Now she was desperate to know what *The Jewel* contained. And had he just so blithely spoken such a wicked word aloud? It defied logic. Ordinarily, he only uttered obscenities when he was overcome by passion and let down his guard. Who was this man, and what had he done with the Duke of Disdain?

She held his stare, unflinching. "What page is it on?"

"Bloody hell," he growled.

"Well, you cannot say such a thing and then expect me not to look." She would not apologize for her nature. She was who she was. "Surely you must know that by now."

"Forty-three," he clipped.

Bo could not contain her smile. "You had it memorized, you scoundrel."

"I may have gazed upon it a time or two in the achingly long month between when I made love to you and our wedding day," he admitted, and he looked even more discomfited by the revelation.

Adorably so. How she loved him, for all his hard angles and his ice and the way he could inexplicably melt and surprise her. For buying her this book. For marrying her. For making love to her in the outdoors with the sun shining around them. For saying "gamahuching." For flipping through the bawdy book on his own and surrendering to his curiosity. For relinquishing his tight grip on control long enough to allow her to see a different, heretofore unimagined, side of him.

For all those reasons and so many more, more than she could even name or count. Her love became a waterfall, bursting and rushing inside her. Unstoppable.

She opened the book, flipped to page forty-three, and stared at the depiction of a nude man atop an equally naked female. But it was not the scene she had expected from his description. Oh no indeed. In the woodcut, the woman lay supine upon a bed, with the man prone atop her, but facing opposite ends. The woman had the tip of his large cock tucked in her mouth, while the man's bent head feasted upon her pussy. It seemed at once impossible and shockingly perfect.

"Oh my." She swallowed as she stared at the picture, desire sliding through her and landing between her legs as a slow, insistent pulse. "Why is she still wearing stockings?"

"Some men find such a thing arousing," he said thickly.

Did they? She had not known it.

Bo glanced up, fixing him with her gaze. "Do you?"

He swallowed, his eyes on her mouth, then traveling lower, to her breasts, and lower still, encompassing her entire body with one long, devouring stare. She felt it as if it were a stroke of his hand or a lick of his tongue.

"Yes."

Dear heavens. She snapped the book closed. "Spencer?"

His breathing was becoming more labored now, an indication of how aroused he was, and they were not even touching. "Yes, sweetheart?"

She placed the book atop a nearby table. "Tonight, I want to do what is in the picture, and tomorrow, I will leave my stockings on for you."

"Holy God." He continued consuming her with his glittering gaze. "How did I ever get so bloody fortunate?"

"You stole my book," she reminded him. "And then I kissed you."

"Tell me about your Lady's Suffrage Society."

Spencer's question startled Bo out of her reveries concerning the sheen of water clinging to his delectable chest. They were once again sharing the impossibly large bathtub, facing each other, and despite the fact that she had seen him shirtless too many times to count already in their short marriage, she could not stop admiring him. He was so masculine and strong, and the light dusting of dark hair on his pectorals fascinated her.

Oh dear. This was a slippery vein of thought to be entertaining. She was meant to be paying attention to what he had said.

She blinked. *Ah, yes.* The Lady's Suffrage Society. "It is a group for like-minded ladies who are concerned by our lack of representation and wish to affect change."

Beneath the water, his hand traced her ankle, sparking hunger within her that had nothing to do with her desire to reform England and everything to do with the man touching her.

"How many members have you?" he asked intently.

A queer flutter took up residence within her then, and it wasn't mere arousal but something else. Spencer's interest in the Lady's Suffrage Society was genuine. Most gentlemen in her acquaintance were condescending whenever she spoke about her beliefs. They smiled indulgently as one would upon a younger sister who had asked for sweets.

"We haven't many yet. My friend Clara, the Countess of Ravenscroft, arrived at the notion, but she recently married and is only just due to return from her honeymoon in America. At the moment, our number is about two dozen or so, including my sisters. We will need to begin with funding first, so that we can print pamphlets and attract more members." She paused, realizing as she spoke just how much had altered in the time since she and Clara had first conceived of their plan. "I hope you will not object to my continued involvement."

She held her breath as she awaited his response, for she was prepared to wage a bloody battle against him if she must. But Bo hoped that would not be the case, and that her husband would have an enlightened enough mind to appreciate that a woman should have the opportunity to be a man's equal in every sense of word, law, and deed.

His leisurely caress continued, sliding over her calf. "Naturally, I will not stand in your way. God help the man who would try to thwart you from your course. But more than that, I think it a worthy cause. This will not be a war easily won, mind you, but there is no logical reason why a woman should be denied the right to have her voice heard. Lord knows most females are far more intelligent than their male counterparts anyway."

Relief swept through her, and she smiled as his fingers trailed to her kneecap, running slow circles over it. "Thank you, Spencer. The Lady's Suffrage Society means a great deal to me."

"Just as you mean a great deal to me." His gaze burned into hers. "In truth, I am impressed by your devotion. I admire your mind as much as I admire your stubborn nature."

Had he just said she was important to him? And that he admired her? Hope was a fragile bud in her breast, threatening to burst open. *Calm thyself, heart.* "I do believe I must have misheard you, Duke, for there is no way you just told me that you admire my stubborn nature."

He swept back down her calf. "I must be ailing."

"Feverish," she decided, swallowing when he rubbed her instep with his thumb. "Or perhaps you are an impostor. What have you done with the real duke? The one who glowered at me in his private library that first day?"

His sensual lips quirked in the briefest ghost of a smile. "He stole a hellion's smutty book, and she kissed him in an ill-conceived plot to win it back."

Her heart beat faster. The way he looked at her melted her faster than Wenham Lake ice beneath a blazing summer sun. She felt flushed and buoyant, weightless in the water, her every care washed away in the steady lick of the warm bath.

"And then?" she dared ask, before adding a post script for good measure. "Though I must object to your characterization of the plot as 'ill-conceived.' It seemed quite inspired at the time."

"Ill-conceived is what it was, for she did not regain her book. Instead, she was compromised. And then he married her." He gripped her ankle and tugged, pulling her to him effortlessly.

She floated toward him, straddling his powerful thighs, and wrapped her arms around his neck. "And then?" she pressed again, bringing their lips to within an inch of touching.

And then she fell in love with him.

Her heart tripped, the breath leaving her in a rush. No, she could not say that. No matter how true it was. No matter how much she longed to. He was so near, so beloved, and how she wished she might have the bravery to confess her feelings. But in this matter, she was a coward, and she held her tongue and watched him instead.

He leaned forward, aligning their mouths for a quick, hard kiss before disengaging. "And then she attempted to seduce him in the bath, but he resisted."

She raised a brow, reaching beneath the hot bath water to find his shaft. He was hard and full, ready for her. "Are you certain he resisted?" Feeling wicked, she stroked him, the silken sensation of the water between them heightening her awareness.

"Quite," he gritted, "regardless of how tempting the hellion's touch, he wished to worship her slowly and lingeringly."

Oh. My.

She licked her lips. "How?"

"With his hands and his lips." He kissed her again, catching the pout of her lower lip in his teeth before soothing the sting with a lick. "And his tongue." He kissed her jaw, working his way down her throat. "Not to mention his cock."

She could not suppress the sigh that left her lips. What wicked things he did to her. Who would have thought that the icy Duke of Disdain would marry the least behaved lady in all the *ton*, and that beneath his frigid façade smoldered such unrestrained passion? He awed her. The pain he had suffered, the horrors he had endured, she could not fathom. But here he was, raging with desire, gloriously alive. She vowed then that she would do her best to give him however much time he needed to reconcile his past with their future, that she would not press or push him. When he was ready, he would tell her, and she would be waiting for him, arms and heart wide open.

Bo tightened her grip on his erect cock. "What if the hellion did not wish to be worshipped? What if she wanted to worship the duke instead?" she whispered. It was the closest she dared come to revealing her feelings for him.

He shook his head, catching her wrist beneath the water, gently removing her hand. "The duke insists."

"The hellion was never particularly adept at complying with the orders of others." She slid the hand he had dislodged from his staff up the taut plane of his abdomen, enjoying the ripple of muscle, the way he tensed beneath her touch. She watched the water dripping down the wall of his chest, and could not resist lowering her lips to catch a droplet before flicking her tongue over his nipple.

The breath hissed from him. "Damn it, Boadicea, you don't know what you do to me."

If she did as little as a fraction of what he did to her, she would be well pleased. As it was, she relished him this way, needy and aroused. His cock a steely protrusion against her thigh. All for her, because of her. She loved how much he wanted her.

"Mmm." She worked her way up his chest, to his neck, licking the slight protrusion of his Adam's apple. "You taste and smell so good," she whispered against his wet skin. "Everywhere. It is my turn, Spencer."

"Your turn?" he rasped, his hands sliding wetly up her back, beneath the curtain of her hair.

"My turn," she repeated, kissing his ear, running her tongue over the whorl, rewarded by the tremor she felt run through him. Here, he was every bit as responsive as she, every bit as affected. "To worship you. With my mouth, and my tongue." She licked again, kissed his clenched jaw, loving the abrasion of his stubble on her lips. "Let me, Spencer.

Let me love you."

He stiffened, and she stilled in the same instant. She had not meant to say it, but she had lost jurisdiction over herself, caught up in the moment and the desire. For a beat, she turned her options over in her mind, wondering what she ought to do. Fear won, and she rained kisses all the way across his jaw, to the corner of his sensual lips. Passion was a language he understood.

She cupped his beloved face, gazed into his eyes. "Let me make you come."

"Bloody hell." The epithet sounded torn from him. His fingers tangled in the wet locks of her nape, and he slammed his mouth into hers. The kiss was open-mouthed, hungry. Almost savage in its insistence.

She kissed him back with everything she had, unleashing all the desire, all the pent-up need, every last drop of the love welling inside her. If she could not tell him with words, she would tell him with her body, with her actions. Bo moaned into his mouth, letting him know how badly she wanted him, unashamed of his effect on her.

On a growl, he rose from the water, scooping her into his arms as he went. She gasped, hands flying to his shoulders for purchase. "Spencer!" She could not help but protest, conscious of the fact that he could so easily slip. Though he had lifted her into his arms on previous occasions, she knew that her tall frame was by no means light as a feather. "Put me down."

"No." With a masterful illustration of his exquisitely honed strength, he stepped from the tub, still holding her tight, in one fluid motion.

"Spencer," she tried again, when he began striding from the bathroom to his chamber.

"Hush," he chastised, his tone gentle. "The duke insists."

They were both soaked, and though the castle was drafty in the cooler evening air in spite of its renovations, she was not at all cold. No indeed, she was positively aflame. She clung to him as he carried her all the way to his bed and laid her upon it with such tender care that her heart ached.

As he joined her, she admired the rugged beauty of his body. He slid between her legs, their wet skin connecting in perfect, delicious friction. But when he would have once more taken charge of their lovemaking, she was determined to thwart him. Some far recess of her mind recalled the manner in which he clung to control, and she wanted to upend him. Perhaps if there was a way to break him free of his past, it was this, the only dynamic between them that was easy and without conflict.

While he did not love her, he did desire her every bit as much as she desired him. In this, they were equals. And she longed, how she longed, to break him free of the cage he had built around himself. Maybe this was the way.

She braced the heels of her palms flat against both his shoulders and pushed, not stopping until he relented and submitted to her dominance. He allowed her to roll him on his back. She straddled him, her wet, hungry flesh upon his stomach, and leaned over him until their noses touched.

"The duchess insists more," she challenged.

And then, without waiting for another word from him, she lowered her mouth to his neck. Here he smelled so divine, of the soap from their bath, and all man. All wonderful. She kissed the cords down to his hard clavicle and then lower, across his pectoral, over each slab of his abdomen, to the soft trail of hair that led lower still.

Mmm.

Her hands trailed after her mouth, and she breathed him in, deep and full, her palms framing his hips. She caressed, moved down, to where his cock strained, full and proud, jutting toward her, dark and engorged, a drop of seed weeping from the slit on his crown.

When they had enacted the woodcut from her bawdy book a few nights ago, he had not spent in her mouth. Instead, he had pulled away, sinking inside her for a few deep thrusts before slipping from her body and delivering his seed into the sheets once more. This time, she was not going to allow him to withdraw.

"Boadicea."

She paused, glancing back up the sculpted planes of his body to meet his gaze. "Spencer, hold your tongue. Let me worship you." She kissed the patch of skin beneath his navel.

"Fuck."

She smiled, dipped her head. "Yes." Then her fingers circled his shaft, and her mouth closed over him. His hips jerked, and she took as much of his length as she could, sucking and stroking with her tongue. His moan spurred her on, sending moisture between her thighs, a deep pulse of want.

"Sweeting, stop. I don't want to…"

She ignored him, continuing her assault, gratified when his words trailed off. She wanted him to lose his mind, to lose his thought, to lose every instinct that told him he must restrain himself. If she could not have him spend inside her womb, then she would at least have this.

His fingers tangled in her hair once more, but instead of dislodging her, he held her fast, guiding her, showing her what he liked. How much suction, how fast. She found her rhythm, relaxed her throat, and welcomed him deeper still, moaning her pleasure in time to the sweet sounds of his surrender.

"I cannot," he groaned.

But he could. And he would.

Bo sucked greedily, wanting as much of him as she could have. Wanting all of him. Everything. Anything he would give. One hand palmed his bum, the other cupped the base of his shaft, her lips and tongue and throat moving over him, up and down, up and down.

A guttural sound tore from him, his hips jerking upward, and then the molten spurt of his seed hit the back of her throat. She swallowed all of it, all of him, and it was not enough, but it would have to do.

For now.

When she was satisfied that he was spent, she rose to her haunches, pleased to see the relaxed lines of his handsome face, the glazed pleasure in his vivid eyes. "And then?" she could not resist asking.

"And then he knew he had somehow found the only duchess in the world who could ever suit him," he said softly.

It was not a declaration of love, but it was enough.

Chapter Twenty-One

SPENCER HAD A PROBLEM.

A large and unexpected and most definitely unwanted problem.

He spurred his mount into a gallop, feeling the wind and early morning mists in his face, hoping it would rattle something loose inside him and send the problem flying into the atmosphere. But the problem remained lodged in his chest, stubborn, refusing to go away.

The problem was a sensation, a physical ache. But it was also something far more imprecise, the stirrings of something terrifying. Something he did not believe in. Something he would not feel.

He had woken that morning, his wife nuzzled against his chest, her auburn hair unfurled across him in silken curls. And he had felt it then, gazing down at her slumber-softened face, the pink lips he loved to kiss, the ethereal dusting of freckles on her nose, the beauty mark he could see in his sleep. It had struck him, in one swift and breathtaking rush.

Something was shifting, changing inside him. It was a change he did not need. And so he had disengaged from her, taking care not to disturb her sleep, dressed for riding, and left without her. That in itself had felt almost like a betrayal, for he had not ridden without her since that first day. She was an accomplished horsewoman, and her enthusiasm for his Arabians pleased him.

But he had gone anyway, hoping that the separation would do his addled mind some good. It was the sixth day of their honeymoon. Tomorrow would be the last, and they would return to Boswell Manor, his mother, his brother, his endless string of duties, and the onerous weight of the past he had managed to shake during their idyll. Every minute of the last week had been spent wrapped up in each other, and he was loath for their time together to come to an end. When they weren't riding, they were making love. It came as no surprise that Boadicea was an eager, passionate, and bold lover. She was everything he had never dared to want.

She scared the hell out of him. The feelings she roused within him frightened him witless as well. He pounded across the park, his horse's flying hooves taking him farther and farther from the sleeping wife he had left behind. But not the problem. The problem remained, burrowed too deep to remove, inescapable and all-consuming. The problem was a part of him now, and he must deal with it somehow. It would not be ignored or excised. It would not be avoided or silenced.

It was there, beating beneath the surface of every waking moment.

It was there, beating like a bloody heart.

Because it was a heart. It was *his* heart. And it was feeling things it had no right to feel. Everything was changing. He had changed.

He was falling in love with his wife.

There, he had allowed himself to think it, to entertain the hideous word in his mind for the first time in relation to Boadicea. *Love.* He had not believed it possible, not for him, at least. He had thought the past had inured him to any such superfluous complication.

But the problem, the damnable emotion swelling in his chest, was insistent. It burned, growing each time he kissed her, each time she looked at him with such open affection, each time he sank inside her body and lost himself until they became one.

It was like a wound that must be cauterized, and he had to stem the bleeding to prevent further loss. He leaned low over his horse's neck, urging her on, needing the speed and the thrill, the wide-open distraction. The mere thought of loving Boadicea made his mouth go dry and his hands tremble as they gripped the reins.

Yes, loving her was a big, bloody problem. Because as it was, the strength of emotion surging within him whenever she walked into a chamber nearly knocked him on his arse. What he felt for her was a different world from the way he had felt for Millicent.

Their marriage had been arranged by their families, an alliance rather than a love match. But he had nevertheless grown to care for his former wife, and even when the madness had taken her and she had betrayed their vows, even as she'd trained the pistol upon him with every intent to commit murder, he had not stopped caring. He knew that the person she was before, the innocent, mild-mannered lady he had wed, would never have done what she did.

No, that came later, after the grief of their only son's death.

He rode harder, forcing himself to recall the sight of his infant in his arms, pale and still and perfectly formed. Born without taking a single breath. He could still remember every detail of the death mask, though he had buried it alongside Millicent. He made himself feel, once again, the bitter agony of losing his flesh and blood, of the babe that never lived, of the abject despair of watching his wife's lucidity slip away.

Darkness roared through him, and he embraced it, allowing it to infect him like the disease it was. He stared into the horizon and saw Millicent's flat, dead eyes. Heard again her voice, tinged with unhinged desperation.

Say it. You killed our baby.

The pistol, rising before him. His own mortality staring him in the face.

You are the devil, Bainbridge. You murdered my son, and now I must murder you.

And then his own voice, feigning a calm he did not feel.

I did it, Millicent. It is my fault, all of this. Please, give me the pistol.

The final fury of her scream rang through his brain, mingling with the pounding of his mount's hooves into the earth. He held his breath now as he had in that moment, certain his life was over. And then the pistol had gone off, its bullet tearing through her temple with such eerie precision.

Blood, so much of it.

He lifted his head to the skies and let loose a bellow of his own as he galloped across the land, and it echoed through the valley and ricocheted off the surrounding trees. No matter how much time passed, no matter where he went, he would never be able to erase the past or the reach of its skeletal hand. Where once it had tortured him, now it spurred him on, reminding him that while a part of him had survived Millicent's madness and death, he could not risk opening himself to such devastation again. For as strong as his feelings for Boadicea were, he would never endure a second time.

I have seen such puerperal mania cases before. Giving birth to a child can affect a woman's mind.

He could not watch the light leave her blue eyes. Could not watch her seep away from him. No, indeed. He could not afford to allow his love for her to grow any more than it already had. Because inevitably would follow her desire to have children, and his to please her.

Distance was what he needed. Physical as well as emotional. Whatever had happened between them here at Ridgely Castle, this was all that they could ever have. He would do whatever it took to ensure that it did not develop into something more.

It was for the best that they return to Boswell Manor on the morrow. He would fall back into his familiar, dutiful role, and Boadicea could busy herself with her Lady's Suffrage Society. Distance and distraction was all he needed.

That and to regain the control he had somehow lost.

Those were his only options for self-preservation, and the realization was a stone sinking in his gut as he galloped away from his future and his past all at once.

Bo returned to Boswell Manor to the greeting of the domestics, sans the pained face of her mother-in-law and the bitter quietness of her brother-in-law, who were thankfully nowhere to be found upon their arrival. A week had passed since she had left, somewhat in shock and quite nervous to be the new Duchess of Bainbridge. In the intervening time, so short and yet so transforming that it might have been a lifetime instead, much had altered.

She had fallen in love with her husband. Headlong, deeply, and unabashedly. Stupidly, foolishly, and perhaps even wrongly. The latter because, for as much as had changed for her and as much as she had thought Spencer had changed as well, during the last twenty-four hours, she had witnessed his slow reversal. Before her eyes, he had withdrawn.

As she stepped back into the familiar entryway of what was to be her new home, the portraits of the illustrious members of the Marlow line confronted her, some of whom bore a marked familial resemblance to her handsome husband. She cast him a sidelong glance, wishing she could read his thoughts. The trip back to Boswell Manor was eerily similar to the trip from it a week before, and it was almost as if they had gone back in time, all the advancements and connections—all the pleasure and joy and tenderness—of the last week, had been nothing more than a daydream.

When she had woken yesterday morning to find him gone, the bed smelling of his pine and musk, his side rumpled and yet empty, she had known an initial spear of concern. She'd lingered in bed, waiting, hoping he would return and make love to her. When he had not, she'd reluctantly risen, dressed, and descended for breakfast. Still, no sign of him.

Finally, he had returned from what she learned had been a lengthy ride—the first he had taken without her since their honeymoon's onset—moody and quiet. At dinner, he had not spoken unless she required it of him. The entire affair had been staid and forced, before an audience of servants. Bo had grown tired of asking him questions and they had finished the final courses in stilted silence, she drinking too much wine and he frowning with an alarming frequency.

She had not been able to escape the thought that the specter of Marlow Manor had already leached into their happiness, sucking it dry. She wondered now, as she walked by his side through the dimly lit, cavernous hall with its monuments to the past, whether it was going back to the place where Spencer had experienced so much upheaval and despair that altered him, or whether it was something else.

And she did not know which would be worse.

He stopped at the foot of the grand staircase with its intricate carvings and gothic ornamentation, and caught her hand in his, bringing it to his lips for a chaste kiss. He met her gaze for a moment before fixing his stare upon something behind her, as though she were not interesting or important enough to hold him. "I imagine you would like to rest and refresh yourself following our journey, Duchess, while I have many obligations awaiting me."

His tone was formal. Cold as marble. Detached as he had been ever since his ride.

She looked up at him, studying him, noting the flush on his cheekbones, the stiff manner in which he held himself. Something was amiss with her husband. Where was the man who had shown her the surprising depths of his passion, who had awakened her body in a way she had never known possible, who had laughed with her, bathed with her, tasted every inch of her body? Where was the man beneath the Duke of Disdain?

"Obligations?" she forced herself to ask, cursing the emotions rising within her that affected a slight tremble in the lone word.

"Correspondence. Estate matters." His gaze darted back to her, the ghost of a smile flitting about his lips. "Nothing to concern yourself with, my dear. Shall I see you at dinner?"

Dinner was hours away. She could not hide the dismay roiling through her. Why did he insist upon creating this chasm between them? She did not like it any more than she liked the condescension in his tone when he said *nothing to concern yourself with*, as though his obligations were far too complicated for her feeble female mind to comprehend.

"I do not want to take dinner," she announced, feeling mulish. If he wished to impose a distance and coolness between them, he could suffer dinner with his harridan of a mother and his beastly brother on his own. "Perhaps I shall see you tomorrow at breakfast. Though, perhaps not, as I too have important obligations to attend to. Lady Ravenscroft is returned from her honeymoon now, and we are eager to get to work."

His expression remained smooth, unperturbed. "Of course, my dear. Whatever you require. Indeed, perhaps you ought to spend some time with her ladyship so that the two of you can organize yourselves. Will the earl and countess be in residence in the country, or will they return to London?"

She blinked, not liking the polite manner in which he spoke to her one whit. Why, it was almost as if they were strangers. As if he had never gifted her a bawdy book or acted out some of its wicked illustrations with her. "She writes that they are to be in residence in London for some time, since Ravenscroft's country seat is undergoing extensive renovations."

"Hmm." His tone as well as his air were distracted. "Perhaps you would be well served to spend some time with her. I do not object to you joining her there. I will have the townhouse readied and refreshed for your use."

For her use. Meaning he would not accompany her. They had been married for a week, and he was suggesting she go to London without him. But of course he would not travel to London, would he? He had not been to town in years. He was as well-known as a recluse as he was an ice block.

How had she been foolish enough to hope that he could change?

Bo reeled. "How…kind of you."

He flashed her a tight smile. "I know how important your Lady's Suffrage Society is to you. Perhaps it would do us both some good to refocus and spend some time apart."

To refocus.
Spend some time apart.

How could he be so cool and detached, so polite and reserved, as though they were strangers? As though the last glorious week had never happened? The urge to lash out at him, to force him from whatever had descended upon him, was strong within her.

She could not resist tilting her head, considering him in a mocking fashion. "By refocus, do you mean forget we are husband and wife?"

He clenched his jaw, a scowl darkening his features. "Of course not. We are linked, inextricably."

Why did he make it sound as if it were a sentence? Why did he insist upon undoing all the advancements they had made together? They had ridden, laughed, made love, bathed, had shared every intimacy, reached the heights of pleasure. And yet he dared to stand before her now, shrugging her off as though she were an irritating spinster aunt who had outstayed her welcome rather than the woman he had made blistering love to.

"Are we?" she asked, considering him. "If you have tired of me after a mere sennight, I do wonder at the longevity of our union."

"The servants are about," he clipped.

"Yes," she agreed, unmoved. "But not your mother or your brother. Little wonder the dowager did now await me with a sharpened dagger. Perhaps she will wait until I am asleep and attempt to extinguish me with a pillow."

"Jesus, Boadicea." He caught her elbow, hauling her into a nearby parlor and slamming the door behind them.

Naturally, this parlor—a study in shades of vivid orange—was as ghastly as every other chamber his mother's questionable taste in decorating had blighted. The dark oil landscapes on the wall contrasted in bilious fashion against the bright paisley wallpaper.

Lip curling, irritation surging, she spun on her heel to face him. "Perhaps you are right to object. Poison, I should think, would be more of a weapon of choice for Her Grace. Would she deliver a fatal dose all at once, do you suppose, or would she make me suffer slowly over the course of many days, going mad from it?"

Spencer's eyes darkened, his fists clenching at his sides, sensual lips tautened into a long, mirthless line. He was livid. "Do you dare to suggest that *my mother* was responsible for my former duchess's madness and death?"

Ah, there it was. The ghost that would not leave.

Millicent, and how she resented that woman now, for all that she could help and even for all that she could not—madness, death, every bit of it. She resented her for having known Spencer before he had been touched by the ugliness of life. She resented her for having come first.

It was small, and it was futile, but there it was. She was a weak and imperfect creature, jealous of a dead woman. She loved her husband with a vehemence that almost obliterated her, and he had taken that love as his due and promptly returned to being the Duke of Disdain.

"I would never suggest such a thing," she said honestly, "for I was not thinking of your dead wife, Spencer. Though apparently you were."

Perhaps it was horrid of her to make such a cutting comment, but she had lost her ability to blunt her tongue with her emotions running rampant. His sudden reversal had shocked her. That, coupled with his refusal to fully confide in her about his past, suggested he had no wish to heal. Indeed, his every action and word in the last day bespoke a man who was firmly lodged in the grief and desolation of his past. A man caught up so deeply in what had come before that he had lost sight of what was to come.

It broke her heart.

"Of course I think of her. She was the mother of my child," he bit out.

Boadicea absorbed those two sentences as if they were a blow. They may as well have been, for they possessed every bit as much force. They hurt even more. His former duchess had born his child, a right he now withheld from her each time he spent his seed into the bedclothes.

He had had a child. A child who was obviously no longer living. How had she not known? Why had he never told her? It made so much, horrible sense. All the pieces of him that she had come to know seemed to fit together at last, and the picture it presented was awful. He had suffered even more than she had realized.

She raised a hand to her mouth, stifling whatever would have burst forth. A sob? A gasp. She didn't know. What she did know was that he did not wish to have another child, and that his dead wife and his dead child haunted his thoughts. How could there ever be room for her, for a life together, when he was so mired in old tragedies that they consumed him?

The vow she had made to herself not many days before to give him as much time as he needed to heal was moot. She realized the gravity of her situation now, and it was dreadful and bitter.

"Your child," she managed to repeat.

"My son," he elaborated. "Stillborn. He is buried alongside his mother."

Tears stung her eyes. He had lost a son. The full, gut-wrenching impact of his revelation descended upon her. Dear God, he had lost a child and his wife, both in traumatic fashion. And she had not known. He had never said a word. *How* had she not known?

Her muddled mind sifted through the events of the last week, his refusal to get her with child. His adamant vow that he needed no heir. He was still mourning the babe he had never gotten the chance to know. She gazed at him, stricken.

"I am so sorry for your loss," she said, meaning every word of it. "Why did you not tell me?"

"It doesn't signify." His tone was aloof.

But she could sense the emotion he hid so well. He was not a stranger to her any longer, though perhaps his need to gird his heart convinced him that he ought to be. "Of course it does." She went to him, taking his hands in hers, squeezing them in reassurance. "I want you to share everything with me."

He withdrew from her touch, his expression harder than ever, lips firmed into a grim frown. "Did it never occur to you that there are certain things I have no wish to share with you, Boadicea? But of course it would not to a girl like you, who is without boundaries and has never known a modicum of pain in her sheltered life."

She flinched, the combination of his rejection of her touch and his dismissive response making her feel as if he had slapped her. "A *girl* like me?"

"You are twenty years old to my thirty-three," he said coolly. "Forgive me if that distance seems apparent when you pry where you are not wanted."

A humiliating sting of tears burned in her eyes at his deliberate cruelty. "I'm beginning to think I have never been wanted, aside from my body. Tell me, is that all I am to you, Spencer? A naïve girl to warm your bed, one who is not worthy to access your mind and heart?"

"I do not have a heart," he growled, stalking away from her and plowing a hand through his hair before pivoting to face her once more. "Do you not see? You are expecting things from me that I cannot give. Emotions that I do not have the capacity to feel. Everything I once had, the man I once was, part of it died with my son, and the rest of it died the day Millicent took her life before me. This is no bloody fairy tale, Boadicea. What do you want from me, damn you?"

"I want you to be honest with me." Her hands trembled, and she thrust them into the folds of her traveling skirt to hide her distress. "Will this marriage ever be more than sharing a bed?"

He stared at her, his gaze as inscrutable as his expression, every bit as obdurate. "What am I meant to say, Boadicea?"

That you might love me back one day.
That you return even a fraction of the feelings I possess for you.
That you will not break me.

A sick sensation fluttered through her, and she said none of those things. None of what she longed to utter. "You are meant to say the truth. I thought the last week brought us closer together. And yet, before we even returned to Boswell Manor, you withdrew from me. Since yesterday, you have kept me at a distance. Now, we return here and you cannot wait to be free of me, to send me away. Why, Spencer? What changed?"

"Nothing changed, and that is the bloody problem." He strode toward her, anger flashing through his eyes, tightening his jaw. "I cannot escape who and what I am. I have not made a secret of my expectations for this union. Ours is not a love match. We married to blunt the scandal we created."

He stopped just short of touching her, so near that she could smell his woodsy scent. So familiar and yet so stark and strange. The need to step forward and throw her arms around his waist rose within her, but she remained still. His ice had returned. Indeed, perhaps it had never left, and she had been a fool to think she could ever melt it. His words of two days before returned to her then, taunting.

And then he knew he had somehow found the only duchess in the world who could ever suit him.

She swallowed hard against a sudden rise of misery. "Of course, I am aware of the actions that necessitated our marriage. How could I forget?"

His nostrils flared, as though he was having a difficult time marshaling his emotions into order. Or mayhap that was her wish. "We have mutual desire and respect, and that is more than many husbands and wives share."

The desire was there, as ever. There was no denying that he had shown her a deeper part of herself, that he had introduced her to not only the pleasures she'd read about but to her body and its responses. With him, she could be fearless and bold.

But there remained another side to him, dark and foreign and hard, like uncharted land. A side he kept to himself. It was as if he were a garden she could only admire from the other side of a fence. And she wanted in. She wanted to pick the lock, break through to him. If she had thought that pleasure and the easiness they'd found during their honeymoon would be enough to see her through their life together, she could easily see now that it would not be so. If he remained unyielding, she did not think she could bear it.

She took a deep, steadying breath. "How dare you pretend to respect me when you just told me I'm naught but a girl who has led a sheltered life? When you won't be honest with me, when you won't share any part of yourself with me beyond your body?"

"I respect every bloody thing about you," he growled, catching her arms and hauling her into his chest. "Never doubt that. But I cannot give you more than I have already done. I wish I could be the man who would love you and give you half a dozen pretty flame-haired girls, but I cannot."

"You mean to say that you *will* not." She pushed free of his grasp with little effort but a heavy heart. "The choice is yours, Spencer. You can let the past dictate your future, or you can free yourself."

With that, she turned away and left him standing in the parlor, watching her go. She could not stay a moment more, or she would risk breaking down before him. Holding her head high, she fled to the inauspicious confines of the duchess's chamber.

In the center of the gaudy room, her legs gave out and she sank to the rug, feeling like an interloper in this cavernous home, far away from everyone who loved her.

And then he broke her heart.

Chapter Twenty-Two

THE SOUP COURSE WAS LAID BEFORE BO'S NOSE the next evening at dinner. She did not even need to make a discreet sniff of the air to know that what swam in her bowl was not anything she wished to eat. No amount of sherry could mask the distinct, unwanted scent of haddock and oysters.

Apparently, the headache that had kept Spencer's mother abed for most of the previous and present days combined had not impeded her ability to oversee tonight's dinner.

Bo clutched her spoon and met the triumphant gaze of her mother-in-law across the finely set table. How had she forgotten to consult with Chef Langtois regarding the menu? In the whirlwind idyll of her honeymoon followed by the manner in which her marriage had seemed to fall apart upon their return to Boswell Manor, she had overlooked the dowager's evil plot to poison her by *poisson*.

Between that, Lord Harry's harsh mien, and Spencer's frigid politeness followed by his glaring absence altogether, including a lack of appearance at first breakfast, then luncheon, and now dinner, her ignominious homecoming was complete. But then again, if she required any more proof that this sprawling edifice, adorned in garish color and reminders of the impeccable Marlow lineage, was not her home, she would be as mad as the duchess who had preceded her.

"What a splendid welcome home," she drawled to the table at large—all two occupants besides herself—but to the dowager in particular. "I must confess, I had quite missed it here."

"Indeed, you are fortunate to now find your shelter here at Boswell Manor," the dowager duchess said with a false smile. "King George IV was a guest here, as you should know."

Her mother-in-law spoke as if Bo was a stray hound who had been grudgingly allowed into the kitchens for some scraps. She feigned a smile in return. "Was the king an admirer of fish in all its forms as well?"

The dowager's lips tightened. Her small barb had found its mark. "Tell us, Daughter dearest, how did you find Ridgeley Castle? Perhaps, since it is smaller and far more eccentric than Boswell Manor, it was better suited to you than a grand structure such as this."

She wished that Spencer had not withdrawn. She had received only a vicarious notification earlier, passed from him, to his valet, to her lady's maid, to her, that he had pressing matters to attend to with his broodmares. Some nonsense about an upcoming sale and a horse that had gone lame. Bo had been careful not to allow her disappointment and hurt to show upon hearing the news.

Why had she imagined her entreaty yesterday would have made a difference to him? Clearly, it had meant nothing. He had not come to her chamber last night, and she was not even of enough import for him to see her once during the course of the day, let alone defend her against his domineering mother as he had on their wedding day.

She pinned the dowager with a cutting gaze now. "I found Ridgeley Castle charming, thank you. The air was quite restorative. There were none of the *snipe*, for instance, that I find so prevalent here at Boswell Manor."

Her opponent lost a bit of her vigor at that, but she quickly redoubled her efforts. "Indeed? How comforting to know that you enjoyed your stay there. Bainbridge's last honeymoon was so much more prolonged. I confess I was surprised that you both had kept to your schedule and returned within such an abbreviated span of time, but given the forced nature of your union, I suppose it is only to be expected."

Bo could not quite conceal the intake of breath caused by the mentioning of Spencer's former wife and the suggestion that he had honeymooned with the woman for far longer than the fleeting week she had enjoyed with him.

But she held herself still, using every ounce of her admittedly stubborn will for her expression to remain serene. "Indeed? How lovely that extended time must have been for them."

It was all she could manage to say, and of course she did not mean a word. Gone was her wit, her ability to parry the dowager's rapier insults. One mentioning of Spencer's dead wife—Millicent, as Harry had once so helpfully supplied—and she was reduced to a trembling, weakened mess.

Through it all, Lord Harry remained silent, a troubled witness to his brother's inability to relinquish the past and his mother's shrewish nature. She drew her spoon to her lips without tasting and pretended to take a sip before lowering it carefully down.

"Yes, quite." The dowager's smile did not reach her eyes, and Bo noticed that they were not warm and green like Spencer's but instead a cool, faded blue. "Bainbridge was rather out of his head then, however. Like a green lad, he was, hopelessly in love."

Bo's veins turned to ice. How fitting it was that she should feel as cold on the inside as her husband was on the outside.

"Mother," Harry intervened at last in a brazen attempt to change the subject. "Bo has begun an estimable cause in the Lady's Suffrage Society. Have you told her about it yet, Bo?"

Bo stared at her brother-in-law, wondering if he was attempting to help or hurt matters. It did not escape her that he referred to her familiarly, which not even Spencer allowed himself to do. She still wondered why. Maybe some day she would ask. Maybe by that time, it would no longer matter. As fiery as their passion was, they had drifted apart, and she was powerless to stop their slide.

"Lady's Suffrage?" The dowager's lip curled. "I am sure you might find better methods of utilizing your time, now that you are the Duchess of Bainbridge. There are expectations to uphold. I realize it may be a novel concept for you, but having become a part of the Marlow family, you must learn to adapt."

Bo stared at her mother-in-law. "There is no better use of my time than the Lady's Suffrage Society, Your Grace. It is my greatest hope to help in giving a voice to the voiceless, to my fellow sisters who have not been granted the right to choose how they are governed."

The servants whisked away their bowls, Bo's untouched, and the next course arrived. Steaming tureens of *filet de sole à la Gasconne* were laid upon the table. More fish. Bo was not surprised in the least. Her stomach growled, feeling the effects of depravation.

"What nonsense," the dowager pronounced. "I can only imagine all the world would go to the dogs if inconstant women were given the vote. Even our queen cannot countenance such a travesty."

Bo could not hold her tongue, for egregious opinions such as the dowager's were the sort that had kept women from their rights for far too long. "The only travesty is that women are still being denied their most basic right to this day."

The dowager stared at her, not bothering to conceal her disgust. "What is it that they say? From the pan to the flame? It seems we have traded one lunatic duchess for another."

"That is enough, Mother," Lord Harry broke in at last, his tone forbidding. "It is hard of you indeed to insult the duchess in such fashion."

"Oh." His mother blinked. "I did not mean to insult Millicent. May God rest her soul."

Silence descended upon the table. A wave of nausea stirred to life in her gut, prompted as much by the redolent aroma of fish as by the duchess's pointed revelations about Spencer's prolonged honeymoon and endless adoration for his former wife. Not to mention the matter of the dowager's open aversion to Bo.

Coming back to Boswell Manor had shifted everything out of place. Being here before had not felt so out of place. Now, fulfilling the role of duchess, and with Spencer clinging to the past, she was hopelessly mired in an untenable position. To hear the dowager wax on, it sounded as if Spencer had shared the love match with his former wife that he pointedly declared he did not have with Bo.

He must have loved his wife deeply. What he had said to her long ago returned, mocking her, twisting her heart. *Do you know what it's like to watch someone you care for lose their mind, Lady Boadicea?* And she had been the mother of his son, while Bo was the wife he would entertain with bed sport like any doxy. She stared at the sole on her plate, unwilling to eat it, feeling more hopeless than she had upon returning, when she had curled into a ball on the floor of the duchess's apartments and cried into her skirts.

"Mother," Lord Harry bit out again, splintering the awkward silence. "I was not referring to Millicent, as you undoubtedly know, but to Bo."

"Oh dear." The dowager's expression resembled nothing so much as a feline who had just enjoyed a feast. It was rather fitting, given her boundless hunger for scaled, water-dwelling creatures. "Forgive me, will you not, Lady Boadicea? I'm afraid that the newness and suddenness of your marriage to Bainbridge combined has addled my wits."

"Yours are not the only wits that have been addled, judging from Bainbridge's absence." Bitterness laced Harry's voice as he met Bo's gaze across the splendidly turned out table. "Tell me, where is my sainted brother yet again this evening?"

His question was pointed. Probing. He sensed that something was amiss, and she could not muster the ability to care about contriving a convincing denial. "Attending to his stables. He sends his regrets."

Harry's brow spiked up. "His stables? I daresay I thought that was the duty of the head groomsman. Has my brother taken to shoveling shit?"

The dowager gasped. "Lord Harry Marlow, I beg you to abstain from such uncouth language at the dinner table."

Bo smiled in spite of her best intentions regarding him. While she had counted him a friend, his treatment of Spencer following their wedding had been cruel and unjust. She had not forgotten, even if her husband had seemed to forget he had a wife the moment his soles had connected with the cobbled drive of Boswell House.

"Forgive me, Mother," Harry said without a hint of contrition, "but I shouldn't think one vulgar word outweighs the sins of an entire dinner marked by your insults directed at Bo."

"Lady Boadicea is your brother's wife," the dowager informed him coolly, "a fact which you seem to forget given your penchant for referring to her in such a familiar fashion."

"She is my sister now." He stared his mother down, over the tureen still teeming with leftover sole. "Just as she is your daughter. This is her home, Mother."

Twin splotches of color mottled the dowager's cheekbones, and here at least, Bo could admit that Spencer resembled his mother. Those high, angular blades were one and the same.

"Yes," the dowager said, her tone infused with false cheer, turning back to Bo with yet another manufactured smile. "It is your home now. Welcome back, Daughter. If you do not care for the sole, perhaps you will find the next course more to your liking."

Harry met Bo's gaze, a glint of understanding passing between them. Gratitude trickled through her that she would have at least one ally within these imposing walls. The servants were called back in with another course, and when the *Saumon au Vin Blanc* arrived with its accompanying boat of shrimp sauce, the decision that had been reverberating through her mind finally was made.

She was leaving in the morning for London, and Spencer and his townhouse could go rot. Earlier, she had sifted through her correspondence and had been heartened to see a lengthy note awaiting from her dear friend. Clara had demanded more information upon return from her honeymoon—apparently, she had garnered all the information she required from her stepmama, who also happened to be Cleo's sister-in-law. And Clara was desperate for news. She wrote that she hoped she would see Bo soon, and that she and her husband were in residence at their townhome. The Duke and Duchess of Bainbridge would always be welcome.

Bo intended to take her friend up on that offer.

Sans the Duke of Bainbridge, of course. She would give him the space he required, and perhaps, in so doing, she would find a way to muddle through the emotions clouding her judgment. Maybe she would find a way to stop loving him.

Spencer woke before dawn in a strange bed.

He jolted awake, trapped in that odd purgatory between sleep and wakefulness, his mind sluggish, dredging up the nightmares that had claimed his slumber. A fine sheen of sweat coated his skin, locks of his hair plastered to his forehead. This time, the nightmare had been different.

This time, he had been alone in his study, the pistol in his hand. A voice, sinuous and cloying, had woven its way into his consciousness. *You are the devil. It is all your fault. End this.* And he had taken the pistol, held it to his temple, finger poised on the trigger. He had been about to obey the voice, to send himself into oblivion where he belonged, but something else had stayed him.

A presence. A scent.

Jasmine. Boadicea.

But it had been a nightmare, all of it, and now he was here, lying supine alone in a bed, coverlet pooled round his waist, chill morning air restoring his lucidity to him. As he shook the memories of the horrible dream from his brain, he scanned his surroundings. In the semi-darkness of pre-dawn glow through the window dressings, he thought for a moment that he was back at Ridgeley Castle. That he could roll over and nuzzle his face into the silken cloud of his wife's hair, and that his hands would find the heavy weights of her breasts filling them, the erotic points of her hungry nipples stubbing into his palms.

But this was not Ridgeley Castle, and the cavernous reaches of the chamber told him that. He was at Boswell Manor, and he had spent the majority of the day before alternately busying himself with an upcoming sale of some of his horses and avoiding the one woman he longed for most.

He stared into the ceiling, finding the familiar molding and vaulting, the plasterwork shaped in the coat of arms, the ornamental roses and leaves, the details he had looked upon so many times that they had all but ceased to exist. How odd that a bed he had slept in for so many years should feel strange after only a week. That he should wake here, in his home, and feel bereft.

But he did, and he did not like to think of the reason for any of those troubling matters. Because he knew the reason. The reason was too tall for a fashionable lady, with a mass of auburn curls, snapping blue eyes, the lushest lips he'd ever claimed. The reason smelled of jasmine and lily of the valley and had a marked tendency to trespass. She enjoyed reading bawdy books and liked acting them out even better. The reason was bold and desirable and brave and unflinching and the most beautiful, seductive woman he had ever bloody well seen.

And he was terrified. So terrified that his mouth went dry even now, as he lay on his back and stared into the ceiling he had seen without truly seeing five thousand times before. How was it possible that he just realized, for the first time, that the plasterwork contained acanthus leaves and acorns? And how was it that everything he saw anew seemed to somehow be caused by her?

Distancing himself from her had driven him yesterday. The necessity had been beneath his skin, an itch, a desperation that he couldn't shake. Part self-preservation, the old demons returning to claim him. Because he had longed to go to her every moment he had been away. His inner beast had yearned for her, setting him aflame, and she was all he could think about, all he wanted, his confounded need for her consuming him.

But he could not weaken now. He would not, any more than he already had during their honeymoon. Spencer should never have allowed his defenses to fall so easily. He should never have allowed her to wedge herself so firmly within his heart that he could not remove her no matter how hard he tried.

He had been cool and aloof.

He had kept her at arm's length, not kissing or touching or otherwise making love to her.

He had remained absent all day, leaving her to face dinner with his mother and brother on her own. Yes, he was a coward. An abject and pathetic piece of lowly pig shite. When he had found his chamber last night, there had been no light beneath her door, and he had forced himself to maintain his distance, for it was the only way he could keep himself from falling in love with her any more than he already had.

Expelling a rush of air, he stared at the plaster some more, and Christ if he wasn't still seeing new patterns and decorations as a subtle sound reached his ears. Movement. Footsteps. Doors closing. Shuffling. Muted voices. The music of it all rained together to create a cohesive sound that he recognized from his youth, from every time his parents had planned a journey and left he and Harry behind.

The sounds could only mean one thing.

His wife was leaving.

He swallowed, gazing into the intricate arched ceiling overhead as if it could answer his queries. Pain and loss slammed into him. He could not let her go. He had to go to her, to fall on his knees, apologize for his mercurial mood.

But what good would that do? Explanations would not make him whole. Revealing the ugliness of his inner scars to her would not free him. He would still be the man whose wife had killed herself before him. He would still be wracked by nightmares. He would still be unable to love her, to have children with her, to enjoy a true marriage with her the way she deserved.

No.

He could admit a truth to himself in this quiet moment with no one else about: he loved his wife. He loved Boadicea, the woman who was equal parts interloper, siren, and spitfire. He loved her so bloody much that his heart was a physical ache in his chest.

He loved her so much that he would let her go.

She deserved more than he could give her.

She deserved everything.

And he was not what she deserved. He was less. He was a broken man, too damaged by death and betrayal to ever be worthy of her love.

The sounds of her leaving continued to linger in the air, all muted. Servants knew better than anyone to have a care for those around them. They were quiet in their packing. Had he not already been awake, he would never have realized that his wife was leaving him.

He should not feel the knife of loss in his gut now. Instead, he should feel relieved, for this was what he had wanted, what he required: time and space between them. Control. His ability to withstand the way she attacked his every defense. Perhaps distance would hinder the effect she had upon him, or at least grant him the strength he required to continue to keep her from scaling the walls he had so carefully built around himself.

The door adjoining their chambers slid open in a hushed rush of sound over carpet. He closed his eyes and lay still, feigning sleep. Footfalls approached, soft and hesitant. Denied his vision, he became acutely aware of every sense, and he had no doubt of his visitor's identity. Her silken skirts swished. The scent of jasmine trickled over him, just as it had in his nightmare. The hair on his nape prickled and he knew she stood near and silent, watching him.

A touch, featherlight, smoothed through his hair. He almost jolted from the contact. From the tenderness. It took every bit of his willpower to keep his breathing steady and even, not to turn his face into her palm and kiss it, to dart his tongue over the lines intersecting its smooth perfection. Not to haul her into the bed atop him and beg her to stay before taking her so hard and fast and deep that they lost themselves.

But he remained there, pretending he was lost to the bliss of unconsciousness, too much of a bloody coward to trust himself.

"Goodbye, Spencer," she whispered.

He steeled himself against the stab of pain tunneling through him. He felt the loss of her touch, heard her quiet footsteps retreating once more. As she walked away, he told himself letting her go was the right decision—the *only* decision—he could make.

Chapter Twenty-Three

Bo arrived in London a tired and bedraggled mess, not because her journey from Oxfordshire had been arduous or even long. The train ride from Oxford lasted not an hour and a half, but she had spent the duration of her trip alternately crying and glowering at the countryside.

A discreet look into the small mirror she kept in her reticule as the hired coach she had procured delivered her to the Earl of Ravenscroft's townhome confirmed her sorry state. She bore red-rimmed eyes, tear-stained cheeks, and a pink nose. Clara would take one look at her and *know*.

But wasn't that why she had decided to accept her friend's invitation? For support and distraction? For a respite from the daily reminder that her husband did not and would never love her, while she loved him more with each passing moment? Yes, for those reasons and more. Helplessness, for one. Companionship, for another. She could have gone to any of her sisters, of course, but she missed Clara. They had been thick as thieves during their finishing school days and best of friends ever since.

In some ways, she wished she could return to those simpler times, when she'd had no concern more pressing than how she could get even with the odious Miss Caroline Stanley.

Bo sighed, weariness sinking into her bones. She had left for the station terribly early, eager to leave the stultifying atmosphere of Boswell Manor behind. Leaving Spencer, however, had not been an easy decision or one made lightly. She had done it because her heart could not bear his icy withdrawal. She should not have gone to see him before departing.

Watching his beautiful face in restful repose had torn her apart. Touching him had been even more foolish, for she had wanted, with everything in her, to cast her pride aside, strip away her traveling gown, and slide into bed beside him. In the place she had come to feel she belonged. She had lingered there, willing him to wake and tell her not to leave. But he had not moved, and her pride had won, and she had gone.

The carriage slowed to a stop.

She had reached her destination. Part of her wondered about Spencer back at Boswell Manor. He would have risen by now and discovered her gone. Would he care, or would he be relieved? Would he miss her at all?

Bo swallowed lest she embarrass herself by bursting into tears on her way to the door and forced all thoughts of Spencer from her mind. Her heart was his, but her brain, at least, remained hers, if unruly. She descended from the conveyance, gripping her reticule, and took a moment to compose herself.

A grim, silver-haired butler answered the door. She presented him her card, feeling somehow that he had passed judgment upon her and found her lacking, even though she was now a duchess. Perhaps it was the puffy eyes and the strawberry-hued nose?

She awaited her fate while he checked to see if Lady Ravenscroft was at home.

"Bo!"

Her friend rushed to her in a whirl of navy satin skirts. Her golden hair was braided and pinned at her crown, a fringe of bangs adorning her forehead. She was as strikingly lovely as ever, but there was more to Clara's appearance than normal. Bo's gaze narrowed as she studied her. There was something she could not quite define, beyond the fact that she radiated sated happiness. She almost…glowed.

Bo was denied further contemplation when her friend reached her and threw her arms about her in an unabashed embrace. Clara had been born and raised in Virginia, though she had come to England at fifteen, and she still possessed a vitality and warmth coupled with a sweet drawl that were not always appreciated amongst the *ton*.

Bo loved her for being who she was, not to mention for daring to help hide a frog in the knickers of Miss Caroline Stanley during finishing school. The squeals of horror alone had been worth the effort, in Bo's opinion. She hugged her friend and fellow finishing school hellion tightly. It had been so long since they had last seen each other. Too long.

"My dear friend, you look positively wonderful," Bo said as she stepped back. "Life as the Countess of Ravenscroft is happy, I trust?"

Clara's smile lit up her eyes. "More than happy. Our honeymoon was wonderful, Bo. I wish you could have seen Virginia—the lush green grass and the honeysuckle blossoms. My God, I can still smell them. And then New York, such a bustling, thriving metropolis! Why, I cannot believe you have never been to visit your sister and her husband there. I have Julian's word that he will take me back to America at least once a year. I find that I do miss it after all." She linked her arm's through Bo's. "Come, you mustn't stand on ceremony. Will you stay, or is this a mere call?"

"I…" Bo faltered, uncertain of how to explain. Uncertain if she wanted to explain. "I shall stay, if you will still have me."

"Of course!" Clara tugged at her arm. "Osgood will see to your trunks. Ravenscroft and I were just having breakfast with his sisters. Have you eaten?"

"I do not wish to interrupt," Bo protested, feeling awkward to have interrupted their family breakfast. "I shall go have a lie down while you finish, and then we can visit. I want to hear all about your honeymoon."

Her friend paused in the act of all but dragging her down the hall, giving her an assessing look. "But that is just it, isn't it? You are married, Bo. To the Duke of Bainbridge, no less! What happened, and why isn't he accompanying you? Darling, are you upset? You look as if you've been weeping."

"He…we…it is complicated," she managed, not saying more when Clara's husband, the handsome and rakish Earl of Ravenscroft appeared before them.

With his dark hair, blue eyes, and arresting looks, he was the ideal foil for Clara's light, spritely beauty. The frown marring his expression vanished when he saw the two of them, a smile replacing it.

"Ah," he drawled. "The troublesome friend returns."

Bo flushed. It was true that she had earned his opinion of her the hard way, namely through encouraging Clara to offer herself to him in marriage in return for a share of her dowry and her return to Virginia. At the time, it had been what Clara wanted most, and her protective father had been thwarting her at every turn. Ravenscroft had been notoriously pockets to let and in need of funds—it had seemed the perfect plan. But once Clara had married the earl, everything had changed.

She had fallen in love.

And Bo knew now how powerful and all-consuming that emotion was. How much it altered the landscape of one's life. Fortunately for her friend, the man she'd married returned her love. Bo was not so lucky.

"She is not troublesome," Clara chastised her husband, breaking through Bo's saturnine thoughts.

Ravenscroft raised a brow, but humor danced in his eyes. "Need I remind you of the first night we met, my love?"

Clara flushed, her eyes glued to her husband. "How can I forget it?"

Bo cleared her throat, the open adoration bouncing back and forth between husband and wife making her uncomfortable. Not to mention envious. "I am troublesome," she admitted.

"And I am grateful." Ravenscroft shared another private glance with Clara before turning back to Bo with a wink. "Your advice, while abominable, turned out quite wonderfully in the end, Duchess."

Duchess.

Bo almost looked behind her to see who he addressed. Of course, it was she. She was the Duchess of Bainbridge, Spencer's wife. But their marriage almost seemed as if it had been a dream, and that she had awoken, alone and cold and empty for knowing all she now missed.

"Thank you," she forced herself to say, painfully aware of both Clara's and her husband's searching gazes upon her.

"Bainbridge did not accompany you?" Ravenscroft asked.

"No." She feigned a smile. "He is busy readying his Arabians for a sale, but he sends his regards."

It was a lie, and Bo knew that Clara and the earl were aware of her subterfuge in the name of pride. Oh, perhaps there was a sale, but Spencer had never deigned to mention it to her until it became his excuse for acting as if she had ceased to exist the moment they returned to Boswell Manor.

"Breakfast," Clara suggested brightly. "Join us. No lie down for you, not when you've just arrived, Bo. Come along and be entertained by the whirlwinds that are Julian's sisters."

"Patience-trying minxes," the earl muttered good-naturedly, "the lot of them."

Bo allowed Clara to drag her into the breakfast room.

She was gone.

Spencer should feel the sweet breath of relief wafting through him, refreshing his mind and body both. He should certainly not feel as if someone had punched him in the gut. As if the best part of himself had been unceremoniously amputated.

Six days had passed since the morning she had crept into his chamber at dawn, run her fingers through his hair, and bade him farewell.

Spencer knew because he could account for each bloody day like a black mark on his soul. Oh, he carried on. He discussed the upcoming sale with his head groomsman. But as the auctioneer, Tattersall's was well-prepared. The day of the sale would arrive, and a small selection of the impeccable horseflesh he had curated would be sold. Lords and American business tycoons alike were clamoring for the chance to own one of his Arabians. He had no doubt that the prices they fetched would be good.

And he didn't give a bloody goddamn about any of it.

He was not a man often given to blasphemy, but if there was anything that made him feel like committing such a sin, it was the glaring absence of the fiery, bold, fiercely wonderful woman he had married. His duchess. Boadicea. The gentle-hearted hellion with a love of wicked books who had matched wits with him, who had presented herself to him without shame, who had brought him to his knees with the force of her passion.

The woman he had pushed away so that the pain he'd suffered in the past would never again be inflicted upon him. She had gotten too close. He had let her. And now she was in his heart. Distance did not change the way he felt. The passing days only made him more certain.

He loved her.

It was morning, and a gentle mist fell from the sky, and his general mood matched that of the day: gray, unseasonably cold, dismal. He walked past the chapel where he had married both of his wives and where he had attended far too many funerals. Beyond, the gravestones stood from the grassy earth in stark relief. Some of them were weathered, the engraved stones and hewn marble worn by centuries. The Marlows had spent many generations within Boswell Manor's manicured park. They had loved here, lived here, died here.

He stopped before the grave that he sought this morning. Millicent's, and just alongside hers, their son's. As he had done many times over the years, he knelt, staring at the reminder of his former life, cold stone and smoothly planed angles. Names and dates. Nothing to suggest that they had once been something more than entries in the chapel register.

A hand fell on his shoulder. He started, looking down to find it large and masculine, forcing the brief hope that flared to life inside him that it was Bo's to sputter and die. He rose to his full height, turning to see Harry in the mists, a pained expression pinching his once carefree face.

It hurt Spencer to think he was the source of his brother's jadedness, that he alone had ruined all the people who cared for him: Millicent, Harry, his mother, and Boadicea most recently. But that was supposing she felt something for him beyond lust, which he could not be sure that she did. Especially not now that he had succeeded in sending her away.

Perhaps she did not care at all, for she had left him and gone silent. No intention of returning, no word. He had learned that she had not even gone to his London home, nor had she made use of his carriage. She had gone to the station in Oxford, and from there, she had vanished. For all he knew, she was halfway across the globe at this moment, leaving him behind for good.

The notion made him want to plow his fist into the nearest inanimate object.

"You look like hell," Harry observed unkindly.

"What are you doing here?" He had not wanted anyone else to see him here at his lowest, humbly bending his knee before the grave of the woman who had almost killed him and the son who had never had the chance to live.

"Looking for you." His brother's tone was grim. "I knew you would be here, trapped in the past, the last place you ought to be."

He stiffened, straightening his spine. He had an inch on Harry, and he always would. He also had age, if not wisdom. "I am mourning what I have lost," he bit out.

"Are you?" Skepticism tinged Harry's voice. "I could have sworn you were wallowing in self-pity, mourning what you could have had with Bo. What you're too bloody stubborn and stupid to fight for."

Bo. The shortened form of her name ate at his gut like acid. He disliked the reminder that his brother had shared something with her first. Regardless of her insistence that their friendship had been platonic on her side, it made him gnash his teeth.

He stalked forward, primitive possession and rage soaring through him. "You will not speak of my wife with such familiarity," he gritted. "Do you understand? Never again, damn you."

But Harry held his gaze and did not flinch or take one step in retreat. "Bo."

Spencer lunged forward, an animalistic roar emerging from his throat, and grabbed two fistfuls of his brother's coat. "Say it one more time, and I will not be responsible for what I do."

"Is it my saying her name that displeases you, or is it the reminder that she exists?" Harry raised a brow, his expression smug. "I daresay you've been doing your best to forget the fact that you have a wife over the last week. She *left you*, and you go about as if it is business as usual.

Dithering over your bloody horse sale. Poring over crop analyses. Looking down your pompous nose at anyone who crosses your path."

Spencer went cold. His brother's accusation taunted him, repeating itself over and over in his mind. *She left you.* What in the hell? "She did not leave me. She went to visit her friend, Lady Ravenscroft."

Hadn't she? It was what he had assumed, even if he could not be certain of her whereabouts.

"Oh? Did she mention when she planned on returning?" his brother asked.

Fuck. She had not even told him she was leaving, let alone where she was going or when she would return. If ever. His mouth went dry, and he felt as if the wind had been knocked out of him. Icy tendrils of fear unfurled, closing over his heart and constricting.

He refused to believe that she had left him. That she had no wish for their union to continue. If she left him, it would tear him apart piece by bloody piece. It would be a hundredfold worse than what he had endured before, because he loved Boadicea. He loved her more than he had ever believed possible.

"I can surmise from your bilious expression that she did not deign to provide you with an idea of when she might come back to Boswell Manor." Harry clapped his palms upon Spencer's shoulders. "And I cannot blame her. From the moment you returned from your honeymoon, you hid yourself in the stables. Mother planned a full menu of fish in all its various forms, knowing Bo hates the stuff. The next morning, she was gone at dawn. I'm not a gambler, but if I had to make a wager, I would bet against you, brother."

Bloody, bloody hell.

He absorbed Harry's diatribe, and he had to admit it did not paint a pretty picture. He couldn't even argue the facts, for his brother had provided an accurate summary. Spencer had returned from spending the best damn week of his life—full stop—and had been so consumed with fear that he'd closed himself off. Telling himself it was for the best, he had retreated, returning to his comfort of the last three years, his stable.

In effect, he had abandoned her.

He should have known his mother would not have warmed to Boadicea's presence at Boswell Manor after a mere week. He should have been present at dinner, noting his wife's distaste for the courses presented her. He should have demanded something better. He should have required his mother to treat her with the respect she was due.

And most of all, *he* should have treated her with the respect she was due. He was her husband, after all. He was the man who loved her. But maybe he had been too caught up in his own selfish fears to realize that what he needed most was also what terrified him the most.

"Have you nothing to say for yourself?" Harry gave him a shake. "Why did you insist on marrying her if you do not love her? She deserves to be loved, Spencer. If you cannot love her—"

"I do love her," he interrupted, the confession torn from him. "Of course I love her. What man could not fall in love with her? She is bold and beautiful, witty and wonderful. She is fearless and determined. I stand in awe of her. She is my better in every bloody fashion I can fathom. I do not deserve her."

"Of course you don't deserve her, you miserable horse's arse." Harry's mouth tightened into a thin, forbidding line. "You need to earn her. Bo is not like anyone else. She is a law unto herself. Cease looking at me as if you wish to poison my tea. I have accepted your marriage. You are my brother, and I love you enough to wish you happy. I am sick to death of watching you eke out an existence, cold and aloof, trapped in the misery of the misfortune that befell you in the past."

He didn't wish to poison Harry's tea. But he did want to make certain that his brother never again entertained a single, lascivious thought regarding her. That privilege was solely his.

If she would still have him.

If she had not left him.

If he had not mucked up his marriage so badly after a fortnight that Boadicea would never wish to see or speak to him again. Not that he would blame her. His harridan of a mother had smothered her in fish, and he had been too cowardly to even appear at dinner so that Boadicea had a champion on her side.

They had spent their honeymoon making love, losing themselves in each other, forgetting about anything and everything other than Spencer and Boadicea, husband and wife. Only for him to return and promptly revert to what was safe: distance, chill, not allowing anyone past his sky-high battlements. He had closed her out. What choice had she other than acceptance?

"I love her so bloody much I ache with it. She is all I can think about, all I want, everything I need." Once he uttered it aloud, he felt as if a great weight had been lifted from his chest.

"Then go to her," Harry advised quietly. "Tell her. She needs to know. You both deserve to be happy."

Spencer stared at his younger brother, thinking it odd indeed that he should be receiving advice from him. Love and marital advice, when Harry had yet to be married and Spencer had entered the institution twice. Once out of obligation and once out of necessity.

But it had not been mere necessity, had it? He could never qualify what he had shared with Boadicea using such a bloodless word. Though he had compromised her and it had sparked the wheels of their marriage into motion, in truth, he had begun falling in love with her that first day. She had been so stubborn, demanding the return of her book. Defiant at every turn. And how she had kissed him…

The memory of that kiss alone still set him aflame.

Still, it was not enough. He could not be enough. He could win her back to his side now, but to what end? He did not dare to hope.

"I cannot give her what she wants," he revealed to Harry. He felt as if he had stripped part of himself away, holding it up for his brother's inspection. He felt ill. "After what happened with Millicent…she went mad because she lost our child, Harry. Something happened to her mind, and she was never the same. She killed herself in front of me. She almost shot me instead, but some odd quirk in her unhinged mind decided to turn the pistol against her own temple at the last moment."

His brother gripped his shoulders. "Jesus Christ, Spencer. Why did you not tell me before now?"

"I never told anyone." It was the truth. The aftermath of Millicent's death had been a whirlwind of shock, guilt, and grief. Initially, he had not told anyone the extent of her actions that day in an effort to protect her. As time had passed, he had attempted to move forward. Revealing what she had done had seemed to serve no purpose. She was dead. He was not. He alone would bear the scars of her actions.

But now, for the first time, he realized that he wasn't the only one bearing the scars if he perpetuated them upon those he loved.

"You should have bloody well told me," Harry said. "I would have wanted to know. I *do* want to know. Spencer, you are my brother. We may not always get on as well as we ought, but I am here for you. *Let* me be here for you."

At long last, the burden of the past sprung forth, freeing him.

"Her intent was to kill me." He said the words with calm detachment, and it was strange indeed to think he could now recount the events of that day in such an aloof manner. But he knew he needed to press onward. Some instinct deep within told him that he must make peace with the past if he ever hoped to have a future.

"Spencer." Harry hauled him into a hug.

He returned his brother's unexpected embrace. "Harry."

They thumped each other on the back before stepping apart and clearing their throats. Their moment of connection had been achingly real, but it nevertheless left them feeling awkward as hell.

"Do you think Boadicea left me?" he asked then, because desperation had begun to tear him apart.

"I don't know," Harry said. "You need to find her. Tell her how you feel. And Spencer, whatever your fears are from the past, you cannot apply them to the future. No two situations are alike. Life is strange and wild and unpredictable. It takes us where we least want it and where we least expect it. Live your life for tomorrow rather than for yesterday."

"Damn." He frowned at his younger brother. "When the hell did you become so wise?"

Harry raised a brow. "I am not wise. I see what is before me, and I wish the people I care for to be happy."

Spencer knew there was one way for him to be happy. It involved taking a great risk, the sort that left him with a frozen tongue and a fearful heart.

He had to find his wife, and when he did, he would do away with any traces of the past. Moving forward scared the wits out of him, but even he could see that it was the best option for him. The *sole* option.

He clasped his brother to him in another sudden hug. "Thank you, little brother. I do believe that this was the talk I needed."

"Any time," Harry said. "One day, I hope you can return the favor."

He patted his brother's back. "One day, you will find the woman who drives you to distraction. The one woman you cannot live without. Never settle for another."

Harry nodded. "All you need to do now is find Bo."

Yes, that was exactly what he needed to do. As expediently as possible.

Chapter Twenty-Four

"I CALL TO ORDER TO THE FIRST OFFICIAL MEETING of the Lady's Suffrage Society," Bo announced, though she really did not need to be so formal since the only members present for the inaugural gathering were herself, Clara, and Ravenscroft's sisters Lady Alexandra and Lady Josephine.

They were seated in a spacious salon in Clara and Ravenscroft's townhome, tea and cakes aplenty on hand, papers and pens at the ready. The three other women's expressions suggested an eagerness that Bo wished she could replicate. In truth, she had been feeling apathetic toward everything of late, and she knew the reason why.

But being heartsick was not an excuse. Nor was it a state in which she preferred to dwell. There was work to do this evening. It was their intent to draft up some ideas for the sorts of campaigns they might employ to attract additional members, funds, and support, all of which the Lady's Suffrage Society currently suffered a dearth of.

Bo and Clara had thrown themselves into their little society over the last week, and the earl's sisters—spirited ladies prone to landing themselves in trouble and girls after

Bo's own heart—had been happy to join in the effort. Bo was heartily grateful for the much-needed distraction.

Living beneath the same roof as a husband and wife who were as besotted with each other as Ravenscroft and Clara were posed something of a dilemma for someone nursing a broken heart. She was beyond happy for her friend—the way the earl looked upon Clara when he thought no one else watched made Bo long for Spencer to gaze at her the same way.

Or at all.

Hush, foolish heart. We have been down that road, and it only led back to London and loneliness.

"What shall we discuss first?" Clara's tone was laden with relish and she was lovely as ever in that bright, inimitable fashion only she possessed.

The Countess of Ravenscroft was glowing again today, and just yesterday, she had shared the reason with Bo: she was *enceinte*. There was nary a hint of a burgeoning bump beneath her snug bodice, but Clara's sparkling eyes and the way her hand occasionally strayed to her abdomen had given her away before her revelation.

Once again, Bo was thrilled for Clara in the most heartfelt and bittersweet manner. She would never have a child of her own, and the realization, even as she sat amongst her friends attempting to lead a meeting for the most important cause in her life, struck her with enough force to make her jolt.

"Bo?" Clara asked, frowning. "You're quite pale. Are you well?"

No, she was not well. Nor did she ever hope to be again. Some part of her had hoped that Spencer might at least write her. She was well aware that he had not been to London in years, and that she had no hope of him daring to venture there. But a word, a sentence—drat it all, a blob of ink on a scrap of paper—would have been enough to give her hope. Their week at Ridgeley Castle had changed her forever. If she had nothing else, she had those stolen, fleeting moments of bliss.

"Indeed, you do look as if you had bad kippers at breakfast," Lady Alexandra helpfully elaborated.

"Bo?" Clara prodded.

She stretched her lips into a smile. "Of course. Forgive me. I was lost for a moment in my thoughts. I can assure you that I did not consume kippers bad or otherwise, Lady Alexandra. I do not partake of fish." She gave a shiver at the last, thinking once more of the dreadful procession of odiferous dishes her mother-in-law had foisted upon her.

"A wise lady indeed." Lady Alexandra nodded with approval. "Did you know that salmon are born in freshwater, live most of their lives in saltwater, and then only return to freshwater to spawn? Disgusting creatures. I shan't eat anything that cannot make up its mind."

Bo stared at Ravenscroft's sister. With her fiery hair and tall, willowy form, she already stood out as something of an oddity. Her forthright tongue and odd tendency to spew scientific minutiae did not help matters. For all that, she was strikingly attractive, if not in a traditional sense. Her peculiarity rather endeared her to Bo.

"I had no idea that salmon switched between waters, shillyshallying, Lady Alexandra," she admitted.

"This is the sort of thing I caution you against saying in mixed company, Lex," Clara said to her sister-in-law, taking on a motherly tone. "While it is good to be possessed of a vibrant and well-versed intellect, you simply cannot speak about spawning in regards to any creature. It is not done."

Alexandra raised her brows. "Fortunately, we are not in mixed company, sister dear."

Clara sighed. "Alexandra's comeout is to be this spring, and up until recently, she has been spending far too much time under the questionable auspices of her elderly Aunt Lydia."

"Alexandra is still in the room," the subject of the conversation drawled. "You cannot speak about her as if she is not present."

"Oh do stubble it, Lex," Lady Josephine grumbled. "You know you ought to get out of the habit of saying such outrageous things. Clara is only trying to help you land a proper match."

"I do not want a proper match," Alexandra grumbled. "I do not want a match at all."

"A wise lady indeed," Bo said before she could think better of it.

Three sets of eyes swung to her.

Clara spoke first, frowning with sympathy. "Oh, Bo. Are you certain I cannot hire a thug to rough him up?"

She would have laughed had she not been certain that her friend was partly serious. Americans were a frightfully bloodthirsty lot, and Clara was no exception when it came to defending those she loved. Bo had shared everything with her, from the inauspicious beginning of her courtship with Spencer, to her marriage and honeymoon, to losing her heart, and then the aftermath. She knew everything, and she had been endlessly supportive and kind. A true friend to the last.

"Is that the sort of thing one ought to say in mixed company?" Lady Alexandra queried before Bo could respond, sounding arch.

Clara glared at her sister-in-law. "We are not in mixed company at present."

A smug smile flitted about Lady Alexandra's lips. "Precisely."

Bo did not envy her friend the task of launching such a minx into society. She would be trouble, and coming from someone who had spent her entire life steeped in it, that was a serious assessment.

"Oh, do let's talk about the Lady's Suffrage Society," Lady Josephine said then.

Bo knew a spear of guilt that she had been so caught up in her own selfish thoughts. How could she have lost sight of what was most important?

She cleared her throat. "Yes, of course. Our first orders of business are simple. We are in need of members and funds. As you know, granting women the right to vote has not been looked upon with favor by many members of the peerage. When the queen herself is against it, our work is more than cut out for us. We must also find a means of driving up our coffers. If we have funds, we can publish articles and pamphlets for broad distribution."

"Donations would do nicely," Clara chimed in. "Julian and I have already pledged five thousand pounds, which will go a long way toward getting our cause underway."

Of course Ravenscroft would have supported his wife, the mother of his child, the woman he loved. Bo felt a fresh stab of pain commingled with envy at what she was missing with Spencer.

The door to the salon swung open. Bo turned to find the source of the interruption and froze. Surely her eyes deceived her. Surely she was delusional.

That was the only explanation as to why Spencer Marlow, Duke of Bainbridge, stood on the threshold. Her eyes feasted on him, not daring to look away lest he disappear. He seemed somehow taller, broader, more handsome after a week away from him. His dark hair, green eyes, and sensual mouth complemented his rigid jaw to perfection. The jacket, trousers, and waistcoat he wore were tailored to display all of his quiet, muscled strength.

His emerald gaze found and scorched her. "Forgive me for the interruption, ladies, but I wish to offer a donation to your cause. Twenty thousand pounds, to be spent however the Society wishes."

The harried-looking butler Osgood appeared behind him then, frowning as if he had just stepped into a pile of horse dung. "My pardon, Lady Ravenscroft. I asked His Grace to wait, and he refused."

"Think nothing of it, Osgood." Hesitant optimism tinged Clara's Virginia drawl. "His Grace is long overdue."

"Yes," Spencer agreed, his tone grim, his eyes never leaving Bo. "I am."

The butler bowed and took his leave. Bo scarcely noticed his departure, too fixed upon the tall, beautiful man she loved.

The stark reality of it resonated down her spine.

Spencer was here.

He was in London.

The man who had not travelled to the city *in years* had come here on his own. He had appeared in the salon, beautiful and forbidding. He was still harsh angles and planes, still dark and austere and severe. But there was something different about him as he stood bathed in golden morning light, something indefinable. The way he looked at her now…it made her heart pound.

And she knew then and there, instinct telling her body what her mind would not yet believe: he was hers. He had come here for her, despite his fear, in spite of everything that kept him too afraid to move forward. He had not just met her halfway. He had made the entirety of the journey.

All for her.

"Spencer," someone said, and she supposed it must have been her, for everyone looked at her expectantly when she did not even recall saying a blessed thing. She took a deep breath, found her voice again. "Spencer, you are in London."

A half grin shattered the asceticism of his somber visage. "Oh? Is that where I am? I had not realized."

She stood, the papers in her lap upon which she had jotted copious notes in preparation for this meeting flying everywhere. She did not care. Could not care. The only person she saw—the only person she wanted to see—was her husband. With no more than half a dozen purposeful strides, she crossed the room and stood before him.

"Do not dare joke," she warned. "Not now. Not like this."

His lips firmed into a solemn frown once more. "I do not joke. Indeed, I have it on the best authority that I am ordinarily frigid and humorless. Insufferably arrogant as well. Also a nodcock."

He was using her words against her, and it was unravelling her as if she were a ball of yarn. She stared at him, hating him for raising her hopes, loving him for coming to her, for offering to donate to their cause in such an unimaginably generous fashion. For being Spencer Marlow, equal parts ice and fire. She could not stop staring. Or smiling. Or loving him.

Just loving him. Always loving him.

Her heart thumped wildly in her chest. She stared up at him, inhaling deeply of his beloved woodsy scent. "Why are you here, Spencer?"

"Is it not obvious, princess?" His voice was low and intimate, pitched for her ears only, velvet seduction to her senses. "I am here for you. Come home with me to Bainbridge House, Boadicea. Please."

It was all she needed to hear.

It was all she had ever wanted to hear.

She turned back to their startled audience. "Ladies, I fear I must adjourn this meeting for now."

"Yes." Clara gave her a look rife with meaning. "Go with your husband, Bo."

She nodded, feeling halfway as if she were in a trance as she turned to leave with Spencer.

"Oh, and Bo?" Clara called after her.

She stopped, looked back. "Yes?"

"If the outcome is anything less than ideal, you cannot keep me from doing what we discussed earlier." Clara's tone was pointed, her expression unflinching.

Oh dear heavens. The Countess of Ravenscroft was a veritable outlaw. She met her friend's gaze. "I would not expect anything less."

And then she took her husband's extended arm, feeling unaccountably awkward and nervous, allowing him to escort her from the salon. His big, warm body burned into hers. Shock still reverberated through her as they left Ravenscroft's townhome, exiting past the watchful eye of the much-aggrieved Osgood.

She could not seem to find her tongue, so it was just as well that Spencer informed the butler that they would send word regarding what was to be done with her belongings. She left with nothing but the dress she wore, and she didn't care. It was only when she was ensconced in the carriage, seated opposite her husband, that the enormity of it all finally hit her.

She could not look away from him. "You came for me."

His emerald gaze was intent upon hers, inscrutable. "Yes."

"To London."

"Yes."

She shook her head. "When was the last time you were in London?"

A muscle in his jaw ticked. "Not since before Millicent's death."

The admission cost him, she could tell. Relinquishing the tight rein on his control in such astonishing fashion could not have been easy. Indeed, she suspected nothing about this was easy for him, which meant that he must care a great deal for her.

Hope, that stupid and persistent creature, bubbled up within her once more. It had been years since he had been in London, and yet here he was, handsome and elegant as ever, seated opposite her in a gently swaying carriage that smelled of oiled Moroccan leather. He had come for her, and surely that had to mean something. She loved him so much that being in his presence once more was enough to soften her toward him. But still, she could not deny that he had explaining to do.

If he would deign to, that was.

"What has changed, Spencer?" she pressed.

"Did you leave me?" he asked instead of answering her question, leaning forward, elbows on his knees, peering at her face as though he could read all the knowledge he required there. "Please tell me that you do not wish a divorce. I cannot—losing you would be more than I can bear, Boadicea."

Oh.

"Of course not." She paused, gathering her tumultuous thoughts. "I left because there was not room enough for me and all your ghosts both. I cannot be the sort of wife who does not want to own your whole heart. It isn't in me."

"You *do* own my heart." His husky baritone sent a frisson through her. "It is all yours. Only yours. If you will have it, that is."

You have my heart.

Had she heard him correctly?

"Spencer." His name escaped her lips as a plea. She did not care. To hell with her pride. She was begging him to say the words she needed to hear most. The words she had been convinced he would never give her.

"Boadicea, I love you." He paused, his gaze plumbing the depths of hers. "I fell in love with you the moment you dared to kiss me in my library. I love your daring and your fearlessness. I love your incorrigible love of smutty books. I love that you make me laugh, that you ride better than anyone else I know, that you are bold and feisty and intelligent as hell. I love the freckles on your nose, the beauty mark next to your lips. I love your fiery hair and the way you smell so fucking good that I want to lick you everywhere like a candy. I love it when you say wicked words and when you wait for me in bed wearing nothing but stockings."

"Spencer," she whispered, wanting to tell him the same.

But he shook his head, intent upon his mission. "Let me finish. I love you so bloody much that it is a physical ache within me. This last week without you was hell on earth. It made me realize that I cannot live without you, that I've allowed my fears to rule me for far too long. It made me realize that I need to fight for you, to be a better, stronger man for you. To be the man you deserve. It will take time, Boadicea, and I cannot promise I will ever be worthy of you. But if you grant me this chance, I swear that I will do my utmost to never let you down."

She didn't think twice. In a blink, she moved across the carriage, lifting her skirts, straddling his lap. She caught his beloved face in her hands, gazing down at him with all the love bursting inside her. "Oh Spencer, I love you too. I love you with everything in me, more than I ever imagined possible." She kissed his nose, unable to help herself. "I love you exactly as you are. You are all I want, all I have ever wanted without even knowing it. I loved you the moment you stole my book to read for yourself." She grinned at the last, removing his hat to tunnel her fingers through his soft, dark hair.

His lips quirked into a smile, his hands sliding up her back in a hot brand she felt through her dress and undergarments. "I had no intention of reading it when I took it from you, minx."

"Of course not." She kissed his cheek, his chin, the patch of skin on his throat where he smelled of shaving soap and delicious man. Bo inhaled. "Tell me this is real. Tell me this is not a dream and I won't wake up alone and without you."

"It's not a dream, love." His fingers tangled in the hair at her nape. "I'm so sorry I tried to keep you at a distance. When I fell in love with you, I allowed the past and my fears to get the better of me. I was not honest with you about Millicent."

She stilled, her lips pressed over the pounding of his pulse. "I know you loved her, Spencer. I am so sorry for the losses you suffered."

"I didn't love her." His voice rumbled beneath her mouth. "I cared for her—ours was a match desired by our families rather than a love match. When the babe was born stillborn, something inside her altered, and she was never the same. And I—I feared that it was having the babe that caused her madness. The doctor at the asylum said he had seen other similar cases of puerperal mania. When she died, I vowed I would never again take such a risk, that I would never father another child."

Her heart ached for him, and at last she fully understood. "Oh, my love." She caressed his cheek, a fresh surge of tenderness rushing through her. "I do not need children to make me happy. You are all I require."

He shook his head, gazing at her with such open adoration that her heart gave an answering pang. "There is something else, love. The day that Millicent killed herself, it was her intent to kill me. All the signs had been there. She had been raving, talking to herself, but I wanted to hope so badly that her time in the asylum had made her well."

He stopped, seeming to gather himself.

Shock warred with horror within her. How much he had endured, more than she had ever imagined. "Dear God, Spencer. You do not need to say anything else. I understand, my love."

"I want to tell you," he insisted. "I would have there be no more secrets between us. No more impediments or obstacles. Millicent found me in my study. She had a pistol that belonged to my father, and she had it trained upon me. She was going to kill me. I will never understand why she did not, why she took her own life instead. But she did, and I was spared. The trauma of that day…it remained with me.

"I was like a traveler in a carriage with no destination, watching everything pass by me and too damn afraid to live again. And then you swept into my life, with your red dress and your beauty and your bawdy book and glorious impudence. You are such a force, Boadicea. You changed everything for me, and I did not know how to cope with it. It took me some time to understand that you were exactly what I needed—what I *need*—that you make me whole again, that you make me feel again, that you make me so bloody happy. All I want to do is spend the rest of my life attempting to make you as happy as you make me. All I want to do is love you. If you'll let me."

The carriage stopped.

Bo scarcely noticed. Tears were streaming down her cheeks by the time he had finished speaking. Tears of sadness for what he had gone through, tears of deep and abiding happiness, of gratitude and love.

Above all, love.

"Of course I will let you, my love." She kissed him at last, and it was wild and messy and filled with passion and emotion, wet with her tears. A frenzied gnashing of tongues and teeth.

A rap on the carriage door startled them both, and they broke off the kiss, staring at each other with what she was sure were matching smiles of dazed joy.

"We are here," he said, helping her to disentangle herself from him and move back to the opposite squab.

"We are home," she returned, and no word had ever felt more right aside from one.

Love.

It had been years since Spencer had stepped inside Bainbridge House, and so it seemed fitting that when he did once more, it was with his beautiful wife in his arms. Heart swelling with love, he stalked past a row of gawping domestics who had been assembled for the customary introduction to their new mistress. He had sent word ahead to expect him, and his butler and housekeeper had done their diligence.

But introductions could bloody well wait.

"Your Grace," intoned his butler, sounding uncharacteristically flummoxed.

"Not now, Leland," he called, not even pausing in his stride. "The Duchess and I have an urgent matter to attend to."

"Spencer," Boadicea protested, her tone scandalized. "Put me down at once. You cannot carry me past the servants like a ruffian."

He continued on, undeterred, finding the staircase.

"I do believe that I just did." Fancy that. He had shocked his wife, who up until that moment, he would have sworn was not even shockable. He grinned, happiness rising within him like an ascension balloon. "I will not be impeded, my love. Introductions can be performed tomorrow. Or next year. I don't give a damn. All I want is you."

As he growled the last sentence into her ear, desire surged, joining the happiness and the love. Nothing was getting in the way of him making love to his wife, properly and thoroughly the way he should have done from the onset. He was ready. Confessing everything to her in the carriage had left him feeling lighter than he had in years.

And, for the first time, not just hopeful but confident. Confident that he had found the one woman who was meant for him, that every risk he took in opening his heart to her was more than worth it, that loving her was the best thing he would ever do.

Up the stairs he carried her, leaving the astonished servants behind them. Exhilaration pulsed through his veins. He wasn't even winded. Love was like a sun burning in his chest, and he felt invincible and strong, as if he could carry her up and down St. James's all day long. As if he could fight a hundred battles. As if he could overcome anything as long as she was by his side.

"I want you too," she murmured, and then her mouth was on his neck, feasting on his skin, and he felt the hot lick of her tongue. "I have missed you so."

Two more strides, and he had found his chamber door. If he didn't have her alone and naked soon, he was going to explode. With a bit of juggling, he opened the door and stepped inside with her, kicking it closed behind them. The bed was turned down, the room aired in preparation of his return.

It was all so right. As right as the woman in his arms. He lowered her to her feet, and then his lips were on hers, open and seeking. Demanding and taking and giving. She licked into his mouth, her hands scrambling to remove his jacket. He found the fastening of her bodice and tore when it would not cooperate.

The sound of rending fabric filled the silence. He didn't care if he ruined her silk. He would buy her a hundred dresses to replace this one. She tasted sweet like honeyed tea, and he was drunk on her. He never wanted to stop kissing her. His waistcoat was gone, and then his shirt. Her dress fell to the carpet. He undid the knot of her corset strings, slid the hooks from their moorings. He gripped the embroidered décolletage of her chemise in both hands and tore it from her body. Her fingers opened the placket of his trousers.

Dragging his lips from hers, he toed off his boots and shrugged his trousers and his smalls to the floor. He removed his stockings, her drawers. Bo stood before him, all creamy curves and brilliant beauty, wearing nothing but her lacy black stockings. His mouth went dry, a combination of love and need slamming him in the chest.

"My God, princess, you are the most beautiful bloody woman I have ever seen." He hauled her to him, claiming her mouth in a slow, possessive kiss before breaking away. "Get on the bed, love."

She reached for his hand, twining her fingers through his, and pulled him across the chamber, her forget-me-not eyes never leaving his. "I love you so much, Spencer."

They fell upon the bed together. He worshipped her as he had dreamed of doing this last week they'd spent apart. With his tongue, with his mouth, with his hands. He sucked her pretty peach nipples until she moaned. He licked the silken skin behind her ear until she bucked. His fingers dipped inside the warm, slick folds at the heart of her, finding her clitoris and working it until he dragged his mouth down her luscious skin and replaced his fingers with his tongue.

He didn't stop until the strength of her release raged through her body and she trembled beneath him, the sweet nectar of her spend flowing over his lips and tongue. And then he rose, settled himself between her thighs, met her gaze, his rigid cock probing her slick cove.

"I'm going to spend inside you," he gritted. "Nothing else will do."

"Spencer," she whispered. "You don't have to. I can wait. I will wait."

"No." He took her left hand in his, aligned their palms. "It will not wait. Not ever again. You are all I want. You are everything."

"As are you, darling man." With her free hand, she cupped his face, and he pressed a kiss to it. "I'm ready."

"So am I, my love."

He notched himself to her channel, canted his hips, and slid home in one thrust. They discovered their rhythm together, raining hungry kisses on each other, moving as one. When she found her second release and her pussy clamped on his cock, he followed right behind, burying deep to empty himself inside her.

Good. Sweet. God.

This woman. She had rescued him from himself.

Breathless, boneless, mindless, he rolled to his side, taking her with him, not about to miss the heady sensation of her bare flesh on his.

"And then?" she asked, her voice breathless.

He smiled, kissed her delectable mouth. "And then he realized he could never be happier than he was in this moment, with the woman he loved in his arms."

Epilogue

Bo was late getting back to Bainbridge House.

She had not meant to linger for so long following her speech, but the rapidly expanding membership of the Lady's Suffrage Society meant that the hall she and Clara had booked for today's meeting had been filled to capacity, with ladies spilling out into the vestibules and streets. They would need to find a larger venue. Their little group had swelled to include not just ladies of the *ton*, but working women among its ranks as well. Bo was hopeful that together, they could affect change.

But as she made her way to the nursery, the rush that filled her emerged from a different origin than her pride at the hard work she and Clara had put into their cause. Rather, it was a rush of love and awe, the twin emotions that washed over her whenever she thought of her husband and her daughter, her two most precious loves.

When she slipped into the cheerful confines of the nursery with its pale pink and ivory striped wallpaper and dainty child-sized furniture, her eyes instantly went to the most magnificent sight in the world. The tall, beautiful man seated on a rocking chair across the chamber, holding a blanketed bundle in his arms, met her gaze and smiled.

How she loved her husband and daughter. Her heart filled, a deep sense of contentment unfurling within her.

"Your mama has finally returned from her speech, little princess," Spencer murmured. "She is determined that you will have the right to vote when you are old enough."

Bo reached his side and trailed a hand over her sleeping daughter's soft, rosy cheek, before pressing a kiss to her silky auburn hair. "I am sorry that it took me so long this evening," she said, careful to keep her voice hushed lest she wake Elizabeth.

"How did it go?" he asked.

She leaned in to kiss him next, a quick press of her lips to his that sent the languorous slide of heat straight through her. "My speech was quite well-received. I do think we may be able to drum up enough support to get another resolution before the House of Commons."

"Wonderful, my love." His green eyes glowed into hers, shining with love. "I am so proud of you."

"Thank you." She kissed him again, unable to help herself. "Mmm. You smell so wonderful. I missed you terribly."

"You were gone for all of three hours, darling." Amusement laced his voice.

"Three hours too many," she said, caressing the slash of his cheekbone, loving the abrasion of his whiskers on her skin. "How did I get so fortunate to have the best husband in all England and the sweetest, most beautiful daughter?"

"You trespassed in my library to read a bawdy book one day." His grin deepened. "And the rest is history."

Her heart ached looking at Spencer cradling Elizabeth with such loving protection in his arms. Bo was so happy, so ridiculously, wonderfully happy. Their love had grown over the last year and a half, and they were closer than ever. Spencer's ice was long melted, and in its place burned a steady, magnificent warmth. Even his dragon of a mother had softened, ceasing all attempts at drowning Bo in fish.

It was almost too good to be true, this life she lived.

She could not seem to stop smiling or drinking in the sight of her husband. "Thank heavens for bawdy books."

"Thank heavens for you, my love." He caught her hand and raised it to his lips for a worshipful kiss. "You saved me, and you have given me the most precious gifts a man could ever ask for: our daughter and your heart."

She stared at him, love bursting in her heart, and the news she had been waiting to impart would not be contained a moment more. "There will be one more gift to add to that list soon."

His gaze sharpened. "Surely not another pocket watch from my favorite horse thief?"

Bo shook her head. "No. This is the sort of gift that takes many months to arrive."

"Another babe?" he asked, hope lacing his voice.

"Yes." She studied him, pressing a hand to her abdomen where the new life they had created already grew. "Are you happy, Spencer?"

"My God." He rose to his feet, taking care to bounce Elizabeth in a soothing motion lest she wake, and then hauled her to his side with one arm. "I am happy beyond words." He kissed the crown of her head.

She slid her arm around his lean waist, cuddling nearer to him as his pine scent enveloped her. "As am I, my love. I could not ask for more." She paused and for old time's sake, she could not resist asking him one more question. "And then?"

He smiled down into her eyes. "And then they put their daughter down to sleep for the night, and they went to their chamber and spent the rest of the evening making love."

Bo raised a brow. "That sounds like the sort of story I would like to read."

Dear Reader,

Thank you so much for reading *Darling Duke*! I hope you enjoyed the latest installment in the Heart's Temptation series. From the moment Bo and Spencer first met in his library, I knew these two were going to lead each other on a merry chase on their way to happily ever after, and they didn't disappoint.

If you'd like to keep up to date with my latest releases, sign up for my email list at www.scarsco.com/contact_scarlett.

As always, please consider leaving an honest review of *Darling Duke*. All reviews are greatly appreciated!

If you'd like a preview of the new stand-alone historical romance in the Wicked Husbands Series, *Her Deceptive Duke,* do read on.

Until next time,

Scarlett

Her Deceptive Duke

Wicked Husbands Book 4

Georgiana, Duchess of Leeds, hasn't seen her husband since he left her on their wedding day for an extended hunting expedition and never returned. But she isn't the sort to wait around pining for an arrogant oaf who can't bother to recall he has a wife, no matter how sinfully handsome he may be.

She finds all the fulfillment she requires in caring for the stray cats and dogs of London's streets. Until, that is, the duke returns, and she uncovers the truth about where he's been…

Kit, Duke of Leeds, never wanted to be duke. He was content with his life as one of Her Majesty's most dedicated spies until his brother's unexpected demise left him forced to marry an American heiress to save the family estate from ruin. The day he married her, he left for a secret assignment in America, with no intention of returning.

Seriously wounded and his cover ruined, Kit's forced back to London where he finds a townhouse brimming with creatures and a wife who can't bear the sight of him.

With husband and wife beneath the same roof at last, their marriage of convenience sparks into a passion that's as undeniable as it is unexpected. But is desire enough to bring two wary hearts together? And once Kit's wounds are healed, will Georgiana's love be enough to make him stay?

Chapter One

London, June 1881

SIX MONTHS AFTER HE'D LEFT LONDON, brimming with the thrill of a new mission, Kit Hargrove, the Duke of Leeds, returned in ignominy. He didn't return to legions of admirers or effusive headlines in *The Times* or the gratitude of Her Majesty. He didn't return a hero; quite the opposite, as his arrival on England's shores had been shrouded in secrecy. And he certainly didn't return to the loving arms of his abandoned wife, who likely never gave a damn if she ever saw him again.

He returned alone, save for the company of the servants he'd employed for the dubious task of assisting him on his journey. He returned, uncertain if he would ever be able to regain the proper use of his left leg again. Unable to walk himself to the front door of his palatial London townhome without assistance.

He returned and knocked on the bloody door of his own home as if he were a visitor.

And a behemoth bearing an ominous glare and an ugly scar on his cheek opened the portal. "Her Grace is not at home," he announced grimly, and then slammed the portal closed.

Devil take it.

Kit gritted his teeth. He was weak, he was weary, and he was currently at the last place he wished to be, undertaking the most demeaning task his mind could fathom. He leaned on his cane, exhaling as a fresh onslaught of pain speared him. Of all days that he could be denied entry to *his own home*, this was not the goddamn day he would've chosen.

He rapped on the door again.

The rude, mountain of a man masquerading as a butler reappeared, scowling. "Told you. Her Grace isn't at home. Sod off."

Kit was prepared this time. He caught the door's slam with his opened palm, even though it nearly cost him his balance and what remained of his pride. He steadied himself and glared at the bastard barring him entrance.

"Do you know who I am?" he demanded.

"Do I care?" the insolent bastard returned. "No."

"You'll care when I sack you," he growled. "I'm the Duke of Leeds. Your employer. Now grant me entrance at once."

The mountain's eyes narrowed. "We aren't expecting the duke. He's abroad."

"Behold. He has returned," Kit deadpanned.

The blighter remained unconvinced. "How do I know you're who you say you are?"

"Shall I summon the bloody queen?"

"Ludlow," came a lilting alto voice with an accent that wasn't quite proper. "I need your assistance with Lady Philomena Whiskers. I think she's about to give birth to a litter of kittens."

Surely that sweet voice didn't belong to *her*. And she was talking to the varmint who blocked the doorway to his home as if he were a lord.

From behind the mountain, Kit caught the swirl of navy silk, a glimpse of chestnut braid, a smooth brow, one wide, green eye. Oh, bloody hell. It was her, alright. He may not recognize her voice, but he would never forget those eyes. Green and gold with flecks of cinnamon, and fringed with decadent lashes.

"Your Grace?" came her hesitant voice.

It would seem that she, on the other hand, didn't quite recognize him.

How lowering.

"Madam," he bit out. "I've traveled an ocean. I'm injured and tired and severely lacking in the sort of patience and understanding one would require in a circumstance such as this."

"Do step aside, Ludlow," she ordered the mountain.

The mountain complied with great reluctance and another scowl. And there she stood in his place. She was lovelier than he remembered. Her hair was plaited in a basket weave and worn high atop her head. Her gown was navy silk with bottle-green underskirts, lace and ribbon adorning a bodice that couldn't help but draw attention to her narrow waist and generous bosom. Even in his weakened state, he felt an unexpected, odd flare of awareness as he took her in.

"Your Grace," she said at last, her too-wide pink lips pressed into a severe frown. "You look ill."

Well, hell. He'd been standing about, thinking how remarkably fine she looked while she'd been taking in his gaunt frame, pale skin, and cane. He was a wreck and he knew it. He leaned heavily on the cane now. "I've been injured. Will you grant me entrance, or am I to stand in the street like a bloody tradesman?"

She blinked, color blooming in her cheeks. "Did you suffer a *hunting* injury, Your Grace?"

Clever minx. He gave her his haughtiest stare. "Yes."

His wife took a step back, allowing the door to open fully. "Come in, then. I suppose I cannot deny you entrance."

With the aid of his servants, he stepped over the

threshold. But the effort of walking to the door, combined with the length of time he'd been forced to wait at the door and the crippling pain searing him had made him even weaker. He swayed, losing his balance, humiliation stinging him simultaneously.

How had he ended up here, in this moment, standing before the wife he'd never wanted like a bloody invalid, a strange butler presiding over his disgrace?

Her gaze raked the length of him, going wider still. "Oh dear heavens. His Grace is bleeding. Ludlow, have my chambers prepared for him, if you please."

He glanced down to see that his wound had indeed begun to weep once more, soaking through his trousers. Damn it. "Prepare *my* chambers," he commanded the insolent mountain, gainsaying her.

"I'm afraid that won't be possible," his duchess said without a hint of remorse.

What the bloody hell?

"There's no longer a bed in your chamber," she explained. "It's the main dog chamber now. Even if there were still a bed, I doubt you'd wish to convalesce there."

"The dog chamber," he repeated, wondering if he'd lost his mind along with the blood that had seeped from his body.

"Yes. It will have to be my chamber, I'm afraid, or nothing at all." She turned to give the butler a look that was far too intimate for his liking. "There's no helping it. You'll have to move Lady Philomena Whiskers somewhere else for the birthing."

Dogs and cats and a mountain of a butler who was too familiar with his wife. And he no longer had a bed. Of course, this was precisely the homecoming he should have expected.

Her Deceptive Duke is available now.

About the Author

Award-winning author Scarlett Scott writes contemporary and historical romance with heat, heart, and happily ever afters. Since publishing her first book in 2010, she has become a wife, mother to adorable identical twins and one TV-loving dog, and a killer karaoke singer. Well, maybe not the last part, but that's what she'd like to think.

A self-professed literary junkie and nerd, she loves reading anything but especially romance novels, poetry, and Middle English verse. When she's not reading, writing, wrangling toddlers, or camping, you can catch up with her on her website www.scarsco.com. Hearing from readers never fails to make her day.

Scarlett's complete book list and information about upcoming releases can be found on her website.

Follow Scarlett on social media:

www.twitter.com/scarscoromance
www.pinterest.com/scarlettscott
www.facebook.com/AuthorScarlettScott

Other Books by Scarlett Scott

HISTORICAL ROMANCE

Heart's Temptation
A Mad Passion (Book One)
Rebel Love (Book Two)
Reckless Need (Book Three)
Sweet Scandal (Book Four)
Restless Rake (Book Five)
Darling Duke (Book Six)

Wicked Husbands
Her Errant Earl (Book One)
Her Lovestruck Lord (Book Two)
Her Reformed Rake (Book Three)
Her Deceptive Duke (Book Four)

CONTEMPORARY ROMANCE

Love's Second Chance
Reprieve (Book One)
Perfect Persuasion (Book Two)
Win My Love (Book Three)

Coastal Heat
Loved Up (Book One)

Printed in Dunstable, United Kingdom